Praise for *The Pelican Bride*

"Rich in historical detail. . . . A fascinating and little-explored historical setting peopled with strongly defined characters and no lack of romance makes an intriguing start for White's new series."

—*CBA Retailers + Resources*

"White's carefully researched story, set in what would become Mobile, Alabama, is filled with duplicity, danger, political intrigue, and adventure."

—*Booklist*, starred review

"With a fast-paced plot full of dynamic characters inspired by the real settlers of the Gulf Coast, . . . White has fashioned a richly layered and engrossing tale."

—Historical Novel Society

"Fresh as a gulf breeze, *The Pelican Bride* is the perfect pairing of history and romance. Finely tuned characters and a setting second to none make this a remarkable, memorable story. Beth White's foray into colonial Louisiana is historical romance of the highest quality."

—Laura Frantz, author of *The Mistress of Tall Acre*

"Not your usual setting, not your usual historical romance— *The Pelican Bride* breaks new ground in the historical genre. Choosing to write a story set in the French colony that became Mobile, Alabama, draws the reader into a new and exciting period. A winning beginning to a new historical series."

—Lyn Cote, author of The Wilderness Brides series

Praise for *The Creole Princess*

"The second entry in White's Southern historical series (after *The Pelican Bride*) combines a lushly portrayed, exotic setting with an in-depth portrait of the complex mix of cultures, races, and divided loyalties that defined Gulf Coast residents in the eighteenth century. With its focus on a little known aspect of the American Revolution, this novel will also provide plenty to discuss for history book clubs."

—*Library Journal*

"Lyse and Rafael have an instant rapport that will keep readers interested. White skillfully includes thoughtful questions and concerns about Christian approval of slavery, along with difficulties presented when politics threaten to tear families apart, without turning a charming story into a history lesson."

—*RT Book Reviews*, 4 stars

THE
Magnolia Duchess

Books by Beth White

GULF COAST CHRONICLES

The Pelican Bride
The Creole Princess
The Magnolia Duchess

GULF COAST CHRONICLES • BOOK 3

THE
Magnolia Duchess

A NOVEL

BETH WHITE

R
Revell
a division of Baker Publishing Group
Grand Rapids, Michigan

Published by Revell
a division of Baker Publishing Group
PO Box 6287, Grand Rapids, MI 49516-6287
www.revellbooks.com

Printed in the United States of America

Library of Congress Cataloging-in-Publication Data
Names: White, Beth, 1957– author.
Title: The magnolia duchess : a novel / Beth White.
Description: Grand Rapids, MI : Revell, a division of Baker Publishing Group,
    [2016] | Series: Gulf Coast chronicles ; book 3
Identifiers: LCCN 2015045024 | ISBN 9780800721992 (softcover)
Subjects: LCSH: Man-woman relationships—Fiction. | United States—History—
    War of 1812—Fiction. | Mobile (Ala.)—History—Fiction. | GSAFD: Christian
    fiction. | Love stories. | Historical fiction. g
Classification: LCC PS3623.H5723 M34 2016 | DDC 813/.6—dc23
LC record available at http://lccn.loc.gov/2015045024

Scripture used in this book, whether quoted or paraphrased by the characters, is taken from the King James Version of the Bible.

The author is represented by MacGregor Literary, Inc.

16 17 18 19 20 21 22   7 6 5 4 3 2 1

To Donna Sularin,
my Betsy-Tacy friend
who wrote stories with me before I knew I could,
and who shared her bountiful library
of Nancy Drew and Trixie Belden books.
My love and admiration know no bounds.

1

She could set fire to the letter in her pocket and it would still be true.

Smearing away tears with the heel of her hand, Fiona slid down from her buckskin mare, Bonnie, and landed barefoot in the sand. She led the horse to the water's edge and splashed along beside her, knee-deep in waves chugging straight up from the Gulf of Mexico. At home, on the bay side of the isthmus, the beach was quieter and gentler, but here on the gulf side the wind tore at her hair and the salt mist stung her eyes. Perfect.

Her brother was on a British prison ship lurking off the coast of North Carolina.

The words from that terrible piece of paper floated like sun-spots in front of her eyes. Her twin, the other half of herself, wasn't coming home this time. Sullivan had been at sea since he'd turned fourteen, and in six years had worked his way up to lieutenant in the new American maritime service. His letters

9

had been full of adventure and optimism, and twice he'd managed a few weeks' leave between assignments.

But this . . . this was so final.

She knew what the British did to prisoners of war. Grandpére Antoine's stories of Revolutionary War days, when he'd been held in the guardhouse at Fort Charlotte, were burned in her brain. Short rations, rancid water, little sleep. Beatings.

She shuddered. Their older brother Léon said a prisoner exchange might be arranged. But who would do that for an insignificant young lieutenant from the backwaters of West Florida?

There had to be a way. Every day since Sullivan left home, she'd prayed for his safety, and God had protected him so far.

There *must* be a way.

She threw her arms around Bonnie's damp neck, pressed her face into the warm hide, and let the tears come. *Please, God, don't take my brother.*

Bonnie blew out a breath and stood patiently, while the waves rolled in, rocking Fiona, wetting her dress from the knees down. Eyes closed, she let her thoughts drift to long-gone, lazy summer days when she and Sullivan had wandered Navy Cove beach, crab buckets banging against their legs and never a care in the world. Then came the year she went to England with Aunt Lyse and Uncle Rafa, leaving Sullivan behind. By the time she returned, he'd become a sea-crazy young man, determined to travel the world on anybody's ship that would take him.

With a sigh, she looked up at the steely sky. What was done couldn't be undone, even by prayer.

The wind picked up, a gust that nearly knocked her off her feet, so she took up the reins once more. Grabbing Bonnie's mane, she hiked up her sodden skirts and swung astride the horse's bare back. Her impulsive ride to the beach was going to make her late getting supper together. Yesterday's storm had put the men behind at the shipyard. They'd be working until dark tonight and would come home hungry as bears.

She'd ridden a ways down the beach, lost in thought, when Bonnie suddenly shied and stopped. Absently Fiona kicked her in the ribs. Bonnie shook her head and refused to move.

"What's the matter, girl?" Fiona leaned to the side. Bonnie had almost stepped on a pile of seaweed all but covered with wet sand.

Wait, not seaweed. Material. Clothing. A body. A roll of surf washed up, stirred the folds of cloth, but the body did not move. Dead?

Oh, please not dead.

She slid down, throwing the reins to keep Bonnie in check. The body was facedown and hatless. A young man, judging by the thick, wet dark hair. Kneeling, she flipped him over just as another wave crashed in, sousing her. Coughing, shivering, she struggled to her feet and grabbed the man's arms to drag him farther up onto the beach. He was tall and muscular, unbelievably heavy, inert as a sack of potatoes, and the tide was rolling in fast, but she managed to get him out of the reach of the waves. Bonnie wandered after her, snuffling in irritation.

"I know," she panted. "This wasn't in my plan either." Léon was going to grumble about supper being late.

She let go of the young man's arms and dropped to her knees, then put her ear to the wet wool covering his chest, praying for a rise and fall of breath. Maybe . . . maybe there was a faint thud under her cheek.

Tugging and shoving, she got him turned over, facedown again, and pressed the heels of her hands against his back. Push, push, push, wait. He didn't move. She tried again.

He seemed to be dead.

She sat there with her hands flat against the broad back. What would her brothers have done? She'd heard them talk about breathing into the mouths of men pulled from the sea. Should she try that?

All but blinded by tears, she hauled the poor man onto his back and pushed his hair back from his face to look at him.

She stifled a scream. "Charlie!" Grabbing his face in shaking hands, she tried to make sense of what made no sense. Charlie Kincaid would be across an ocean, in England, not washed up on a beach in West Florida. "Charlie, Charlie, don't be dead! Father in heaven, don't let him be dead!"

Not knowing what else to do, she put her mouth to his and breathed, willing him to come to life. Again she blew air into his lungs. When nothing happened, she sat up panting, searching the familiar but man-grown face. The same, but not the same, as the boy she had known nine years ago. His face had lengthened with slashing angles of brow, cheekbone, and jaw, and he'd grown into the commanding nose. But there were the same ridiculously long, dark eyelashes and a mouth made for smiling and teasing a bookish, horse-crazy little girl.

"Wake up, Charlie," she muttered, "or I'm going to tell your grandfather you're ditching your lessons again."

She bent to seal his lips with hers again, but his chest lurched under her hands. He gave a strangled cough, and water bubbled from his mouth. Relieved, terrified, Fiona scrambled to shove at his shoulder and back until she had him half turned. He continued to cough, weakly at first, then with hoarse, agonized gasps. Fiona pounded his back with all her strength, helping him rid his lungs of the suffocating seawater. "Don't die, don't die, don't die."

Finally she heard him whisper something.

She paused to bend close to his lips. "What?"

"Sto . . ." He wheezed.

"What?"

"I said st . . . stop hitting me," he choked out. "Headache."

Abruptly she straightened. "You're alive! Oh, thank God, you're alive!"

Charlie winced. "Yes, but would you mind . . . lowering the volume?" He opened his eyes, those familiar, piercing cerulean eyes that she saw in her dreams.

Well, one was blue, and the other had that odd hazel-brown splotch. Perfect, Charlie was not. "It's so good to see you."

"Er . . . you too." He coughed. "Do I know you?"

"You don't remember me?"

He stared at her, his face sunburnt, sand-encrusted, and bearing a deep, bloody gash over his left eyebrow. But of course he was Charlie. She didn't know anybody else who had those oddly colored eyes. No wonder he didn't recognize her, though, for nine years had made a significant difference in her appearance.

As if following her thoughts, Charlie's gaze traveled downward from her face, and one eyebrow rose with that droll quirk she'd loved so much. "I think I'd remember you if we'd met before."

Suddenly aware that she all but sat on him, Fiona jumped to her feet. "Oh, you! You haven't changed one bit—except it used to be Maddy you were drooling over."

"Maddy who? If there's another one as pretty as you, I've landed in heaven." He got an elbow underneath him and levered himself to a semi-sitting position. "What's your name?"

She stared at him in chagrin. "You really don't remember?"

"Right now I barely know my own name." He looked around irritably. "If I haven't broken down the pearly gates, where are we? Did I fall off my horse?"

Fiona looked around and found Bonnie ambling closer,

probably looking for food. "This is *my* horse, Bonnie. You seem to have washed in from the Gulf. There was a storm last night." She paused. She'd heard of people losing their memory after a head wound. "You had to have been on a ship." But where was it? Frustrated, she scanned the empty horizon. There wasn't a hunk of wood or other detritus anywhere to indicate the type of vessel he'd arrived on. She shifted her gaze to the east, where an Indian trail ran toward Perdido Pass and on to Pensacola. Could he have come overland and then gotten injured and washed into the Gulf during the storm?

Clearly no more enlightened than she, Charlie shut his eyes and lay back as if too exhausted to even look at her any longer.

Now what was she going to do? She wasn't strong enough to lift him onto the horse, and she couldn't drag him back home to Navy Cove by herself.

"I could go get Léon," she said doubtfully.

"So there's a Maddy and a Léon, and a horse named Bonnie. I'll just call you Duchess."

She whirled to look at him, and found one eye open—the solid blue one—and his lips curled in a smile. "Then you *do* remember me!" As the only girl in a family full of boys, she'd been called "Duchess" since she was just a little thing.

"I don't think so." The smile faded. "That isn't really your name, is it?"

"Of course not. But I told you about it the night we blew up the—never mind." Drowning in memory and anxiety and confusion, she dragged in a breath. "I'm Fiona Lanier. My cousin Maddy and my aunt and uncle all stayed at your grandfather's estate the summer I was eleven years old."

"If I hadn't gotten brained and nearly drowned, I'm sure I would remember you," Charlie said gently. "But don't you think we ought to get off the beach? Because, and I hate to mention it, I think the tide is going to carry us back out to sea before very long."

"Oh!" With a start Fiona realized he was right. The surf had crawled inland until the waves had almost reached Charlie's feet.

He was on his elbow again, clearly intending to stand up.

She shrieked. "No! You'll faint!"

But he rolled to his knees. "I'll be fine," he managed, panting. "Do you have a saddle for that horse?"

"Of course I do, but it's at home. I just came out for a quick ride on the beach." Suddenly she remembered the letter. How could she have forgotten Sullivan? She wrung her hands. Now she had an injured British aristocrat to care for, and Léon was going to be mad as a wet hen.

"All right, well, bareback it'll be then." Charlie was on his feet, swaying like a man coming off a five-day bender. He lurched at Bonnie, who quite understandably pranced away from him. Charlie landed on his rear and began to curse in Spanish.

Laughing in spite of their predicament, Fiona grabbed Bonnie's reins. "Shhh, it's okay, girl. He looks like a lunatic, but he can't hurt you."

Charlie snarled and began again in French.

She let him run down, then said, "I'm sorry she hurt your feelings, but she doesn't like to be mounted from the right." She reached down a hand. "If you can stand again, I'll give you a leg up."

"She didn't hurt my *feelings*, it's my *bum* that aches." But he laughed and grasped her wrist, coming to his feet with surprising agility. She let him regain his balance with a hand on her shoulder. He was so tall that the top of her head barely reached his lips. She looked up at him, trying to find the boy she'd known in this mysterious stranger.

He stared back at her, his expression just as muddled as she felt. "I *do* know you, somehow," he muttered. "I just can't remember . . . You said my name is Charlie, and that's right. You mentioned my grandfather. Where is he? Did he bring me here?"

"No, he's—" Did he know he was English? Did he know there was a war between their two countries? "I don't know how you got here. This is Mobile Point, the isthmus that separates Mobile Bay from the Gulf of Mexico. I live about two miles across on the bay side, at Navy Cove."

Charlie squeezed her shoulder in friendly fashion. "All right, then, duchess of Navy Cove, if you'd be so kind as to cup your hands, I'll endeavor to boost myself onto your trusty steed. Then I'll swing you up, and we'll away." He grimaced. "We'd do it the other way 'round, except I fear I'm not exactly in fine fettle at the moment."

The deed was accomplished with more comedic effect than grace, but in a few moments Fiona grasped Charlie's extended hand and let him pull her up behind him onto Bonnie's back. She put her arms around his waist and took the reins, clicking her tongue to give Bonnie leave to walk.

She had ridden astride behind her brothers all her life, but this . . . clutching Charlie-the-stranger round the waist just to stay on, her shins bare and feet dangling, was another kettle of fish entirely. Not only was it awkward and uncomfortable, but she had enough sense to know that it was highly improper. Mama would not have approved. Maddy would definitely not approve. Léon would likely challenge Charlie to pistols at dawn.

None of them must ever know. She and Charlie would enter the barn from the back, put the horse away, and hope nobody saw them. She could pretend Charlie had walked all the way from New Orleans. Or something.

There had to be some way to explain his presence, his injury, his obvious Englishness.

Oh, dear Lord, what was she going to do?

⌒⌒

By the time they rode the scant mile across the sandy, jungle-like spit of land, Charlie felt as if an army of Goths had marched around in his head, leaving death, decay, and destruction in its wake. No wonder he couldn't remember this beautiful girl named Fiona, much less her cousin Maddy or her brother Léon. She had rattled on about her family behind his shoulder, as if silence terrified her.

When they at last reached the edge of the woods, where three more horses grazed in a grassy field outside a large, well-kept barn, Fiona clutched Charlie's coat. "Stop! I don't want my brother to see you."

"Why?"

"Because . . . because he doesn't like the British."

"Why not?"

"It's a long story."

"Are we in a hurry?" He hoped not. In spite of the headache, he was rather enjoying the feel of her slim form pressed against his back.

"I'm supposed to fix supper for everybody, and . . ." She paused as if searching for another excuse, then released a gusty sigh. "My brother Sullivan says if you have to lie, you'd best stick as close to the truth as possible. I'll tell them you washed up on the beach, and you don't remember who you are."

"Sullivan? Another brother? Will he also object if he finds out I'm British?"

"I'm sure he would if he saw you, but he's on a prison ship off the coast of Carolina."

He turned to look at her. The words had been spoken stiffly, without inflection, but there was no mistaking the tremble of her lips. Suddenly the pain in his head roared, and nausea overtook him. "Miss Fiona, I . . . I fear I'm about to cast up my accounts. Perhaps you'd better look the other way." He leaned over the horse's neck.

"Oh, Charlie, I'm sorry!" She slid to the ground. "Here, get down before you fall. I'll hold your head."

"No—"

But she was already pulling him toward her, and he had no choice but to awkwardly slip-slide down from the horse. He managed to stagger off behind a tree, where he knelt and proceeded to be violently sick. The world turned green, then blue, then dark purple. His shoulder hit the tree hard as everything went black.

He woke sometime later in a shadowed room with a streak of dying sunlight slipping under the curtain over the single window. The aroma of food, perhaps roasted chicken, turned his stomach, and he rolled over, covering his mouth and nose.

"Charlie! Be still! You'll start your head bleeding again." Fiona's voice came from the open doorway. He heard her hurried steps approaching.

He gained control of the gagging sensation. "Somebody just . . . shoot me."

"That's not funny. You're lucky to be alive." She sounded aggrieved, justifiably, he supposed. He would be an inconvenient houseguest.

He rolled onto his back and touched the thick bandage holding his forehead together. It hurt like blazes. "Where are we?"

"My bedroom. It's next to the kitchen, where I can keep an eye on you."

"Your brother allowed this?" He squinted upward at Fiona.

"It was his idea." Swathed in a big white apron, she flitted about, tucking the coverlet over him and adjusting the curtain. "He's really a very kind man, Charlie. He wouldn't throw you out in this condition—in fact, he and Oliver carried you in."

"Oliver?"

"My cousin."

"How many cousins do you have? Never mind." He could only take in so much information at a time. Strange that he could carry on a conversation, understand basic concepts like cousins and brothers and aprons, yet couldn't remember what he'd done yesterday. Fiona had called him by name. Somehow she knew him, yet she wanted to hide his identity from the rest of her family. "Sit down so I can see you," he said abruptly.

Her hands went to fists at her hips. "You are not my lord, and I am certainly not your servant."

"That's not what I meant." But had there been a note of imperiousness in his voice? He sighed. "Miss Fiona, you must forgive any bad habits from—from my past. I am of course grateful for your rescue. I owe you my life, I'm certain. I merely want to look at your face when we talk. Please?"

The fists relaxed. She went to the kitchen, returned with a ladder-back chair, and set it down close to the bed. Seating herself, she turned a pair of big blue eyes upon him, along with a faint smile.

He felt better immediately and caught her hand to bring it to his lips. "Thank you. Now, please, where are we?"

"I told you—"

"Yes, yes, your bedroom, but what country? What city?"

"Charlie, this is America. Navy Cove isn't really a city. It's just a little community near the fort—Fort Bowyer. The closest city is Mobile, but that's half a day's sail up the bay."

Thinking made his head hurt, but he gave it his best effort.

Try as he might, however, he had no recollection of traveling toward a city called Mobile. "What year?"

She stared at him. "1814. What is the last thing you remember?"

He hesitated. "I was sent down from Eton." Everything after that was a jagged blur.

Her eyes widened. "You don't remember meeting me and my family?"

"No. But if you tell me I did, I'll have to believe you."

"This is insane."

"I'm not insane. I just don't—"

"I didn't mean—"

They stared at one another for a long moment. Fiona bit her lip.

Charlie closed his eyes. "My head hurts."

He felt a small callused hand laid gently upon his brow. "I'm sorry," Fiona said. "I think you'd better rest, so I'll leave you alone. But first, do you want something to eat?"

Charlie's stomach rumbled. He laughed. "I don't know how one can be sick and hungry at the same time. But something smells good."

"Dumplings. I'll fix you a plate." Her thumb gently brushed his eyelid. "There's a doctor in Mobile. I could send for him."

Alarmed, he looked up at her. "No, you're right. The fewer people who see me the better. A good night's sleep will put me right as rain."

"I hope so." Fiona withdrew her hand and rose. "I'll bring you something to eat."

He watched her disappear into the kitchen again. Not daring to sit up, he carefully turned his head to look around. The dying light revealed a small room, barely larger than a closet, with walls made of some rough plaster-like material and a high-beamed ceiling. He ran his hand along the wall to his left. It felt like seashells embedded in the plaster. Strange.

It seemed the Laniers were not wealthy people.

So how would a young lady living in an American coastal village cross paths with the son of a British earl? He picked through their conversation on the beach. She claimed to have visited his grandfather's estate with her aunt, uncle, and cousin ... Maddy? Yes, that was the name. He had no memory of such a meeting, but neither could he deny it.

One thing he knew for certain. Concentration on anything beyond his physical body was cursed painful. He must lie very still and allow his head to heal—and hope the protective brothers and other assorted relatives of his attending angel did not decide to put a period to his existence for reasons beyond his control.

2

Charlie's sudden arrival had yanked aside the curtain of time, flung open the window, and all but blinded Fiona.

She stood in her bedroom doorway with the bowl of steaming dumplings. He was sound asleep again. It didn't seem like a good idea to awaken him, but she'd been hoping to question him further before Léon and Oliver and Uncle Luc-Antoine returned from bedding down the horses. Normally, she and Uncle took care of that job, but because of Charlie, she'd been left in the house.

She stood there for a moment, drinking in his sleeping face. For years, every thought of the Kincaid family—indeed any memory of that trip to England with Uncle Rafa and Aunt Lyse—had been like ripping a scab away from a painful wound. So she had stuffed it all, good and bad, into an attic place in her mind. She'd hoped to one day be able to safely bring the memories out and turn them over, perhaps even learn to enjoy them.

If she closed her eyes, she could still see Charlie seated at his grandfather's desk, poring over a book of maps, chin in one hand and idly twirling a sextant with the other. He'd looked up at her with those blue-splotched eyes, and with one lopsided grin stolen her heart right away. And he'd promptly taken to calling her "duchess" as Uncle Rafa did, delighting in making her blush at the attention.

She'd remained in a perpetual state of warmth for the entire month they remained at Riverton Farm in Essex. And now he was here in her own room, making her feel warm and uncomfortable again. While Sullivan languished in prison.

This was not what she'd prayed for at all.

Blinking away the tears blurring her eyes, she returned to the kitchen, poured the dumplings back into the pot, and went out to the pump to wash the bowl.

She was walking back to the house, shaking out the last drops of water, when she heard the sound of voices carrying from the direction of the shipyard. She squinted into the gloaming. The few neighbors scattered around the Cove would all be at their evening meal or otherwise occupied in family pursuits.

Uncle Luc-Antoine came to the open doorway of the barn. "Who is that, Fiona?"

"I don't know." The voices grew louder, and now she could distinguish one male, deep and strong, and the other that of a young female. The girl spoke English, but her accent was both odd and familiar.

Fiona glanced at the house, where Charlie slept. This seemed to be a day for reacquaintances.

Uncle Luc-Antoine joined her on the porch. "You're not expecting anybody else?"

"I didn't expect *anybody* today."

He gave her a skeptical look. "A young man with a gash in his noggin just happens to wash up on the beach? A strapping young man who makes you blush like a rose in bloom?"

Her cheeks warmed. She didn't like to lie to her uncle, but something made her hold her tongue. "You wouldn't have had me leave him to die?"

"Hmph. Something fishy in this fish tale of yours." But Uncle's dark eyes twinkled. "Come, let's see who our new visitor is." He limped down the steps and met Léon and Oliver on the path leading toward the water.

"That sounds like Nardo," Léon said. He glanced over his shoulder at Fiona, eyes narrowed. "You know he was coming?"

"No!" One washed-up relic on the beach and she was suddenly suspect for everything. Fiona pushed between her brother and uncle, hurrying down the path toward Nardo Smith and his companion. "Nardo! Welcome! What are you doing here?"

"Miss Fiona!" Nardo's deep voice boomed like cannon fire. A massively built black man in his early thirties, he was a metalworker after the trade of his blacksmith father, but he specialized in the chains and hasps and other accoutrements of the shipbuilding industry. "I've brought you a surprise!"

Fiona strained to see the young woman with Nardo. She didn't at all resemble Nardo's tall, buxom wife. "How nice. But I—"

"Fiona? It's me—Sehoy."

"Sehoy!" Fiona ran to fling her arms around her fifteen-year-old distant cousin. "Oh oh oh—you came!"

Sehoy laughed and returned the embrace. "Yes, I came—thanks to Mr. Smith here, for bringing me from Mobile. I'd forgotten how long a trip it is down the bay."

"But you're trembling!" Fiona released Sehoy and grasped her hands. "What is wrong? And where are your parents?"

But before Sehoy could do more than draw breath to answer, Luc-Antoine and Léon closed in, with Oliver lurking shyly in the background. Giving way to noisy greetings, Fiona looked up into Nardo's dark face. "Do you know what brought Sehoy down here? Is something wrong?"

He shook his head. "Miss Fiona, you better let her tell the story." His voice was gentle but firm. "Ain't my place."

Worried and impatient, she watched her brother turn with an arm about Sehoy, directing Oliver to pick up the small trunk Nardo had carried from the pier. Léon was smiling, but Fiona knew he would be calculating the expense of another mouth to feed. Uncle Luc-Antoine had already begun to tease Sehoy about the broken hearts left behind in Indian territory.

As the others talked, Fiona took the opportunity to study her cousin's clear-skinned oval face and almond-shaped brown eyes. The glossy black hair was caught in a braid down her back and tied with a green ribbon to match her simple dress. Indeed, Sehoy had grown into her name, which meant "beautiful" in the Creek language.

The last time the Indian branch of the family had visited Mobile—perhaps a half-dozen years ago—political turmoil had already begun to simmer between native peoples and American settlers. Since then, people didn't travel much, at least not like when Uncle Rafa's diplomatic assignments had taken the family to exotic places like New York and St. Louis and England. And when Mama and Papa had sailed the world on business.

Sehoy, blushing at Uncle's nonsense, caught Fiona's gaze. "I'm sorry to burst in on you all with no warning, but I have no place else to go."

"You're always welcome, dear one." Fiona hooked her arm through Sehoy's. "Come, let's go in the house. I'll give you a cup of tea, and we'll sit down for a nice catch-up visit. Are you hungry?"

"No. But tea would be nice. Makes me think of Aunt Daisy."

"Mama loved a cup of tea, didn't she?" Fiona smiled and led

the way to the house arm in arm with Sehoy, leaving the men to follow with the trunk. "Papa and his chicory, so Creole in every way, and Mama so proper and British."

Sehoy bit her lip. "I know you miss them."

"It's been over two years and I still . . ." Fiona swallowed. "And now Sullivan's gone."

"What?" Sehoy clutched her arm. "Sullivan's dead?"

"No—at least they say he's alive and well. The Brits took him prisoner. They're holding him on a ship off the Carolina coast. We got a letter from the admiralty just this morning."

"Oh, Fiona! But thank God he's alive." Sehoy blinked back tears. "This awful war. It's all I can do to hold on to my sanity. Andrew Jackson—how I despise him!" She spat the words as if they choked her.

Fiona vaguely knew who Andrew Jackson was—a militiaman from Tennessee, perhaps a general? News was slow to travel all the way to the Gulf. How had Jackson crossed paths with Sehoy? She opened the screen door and held it for Sehoy to pass inside. "Come, my dear, sit down and rest. Mama's little rocker you liked so much is right here."

While Sehoy settled in the cane-bottom rocking chair and the men set the trunk in the corner, Fiona assembled the tea things. In a short while they all sat in a cozy circle, with the windows and doors open to a lethargic evening breeze.

Uncle Luc-Antoine lit his pipe. "All right now, tell us what brought you all this way by yourself, little girl."

"I didn't travel alone. A man named Desi Palomo came with me, as far as Mobile. He had been serving as General Jackson's interpreter, and they sent him down with messages—"

"Desi's here?" Fiona smiled in delight. Maddy's foster brother had always been one of her favorites.

"I'm sure he'll come to see us at some point." Uncle waved a hand. "I'm interested in what that wild man Andrew Jackson has been up to."

"It's not a nice story." Sehoy's teacup rattled as she set it in its saucer. Her voice was tight. "I know you remember when Tecumseh came down to rally the Creek against all the squatters coming into our territory along the new federal mail road through Georgia and Alabama. The US government had promised no more settlers would stay, but they just kept taking land, taking or killing our horses and cattle, tearing down our homes . . ."

Léon nodded. "We'd heard about the controversy. The Burnt Corn affair was in the papers. The Indians were moving arms in from Florida—and the US Army stopped it?"

Sehoy's mouth flattened. "Yes. Shot every one of them without a trial. So about this time last year, Red Eagle and the other chiefs decided enough was enough, and they gathered the men and rode to attack Fort Mims. It was—harsh, I admit it. But there was no going back. And what General Jackson did in response was—" Sehoy shuddered. "The things I saw . . ."

Fiona bit her lip. "Oh, honey."

"They had us trapped at Horseshoe Bend—you know, where the Tallapoosa River takes that crazy sideways turn? It's holy ground, and we thought we'd be safe there. But we were surrounded and the soldiers were about to attack, so that night Red Eagle managed to get most of the women and children out, across the river and into the woods. I was in one of the first canoes across, and I've never been so . . . Oh, Fiona, the sounds and the darkness, and the snakes!" Sehoy bent over her teacup. "Mama and I stayed close to the edge of the woods right at the river, and I could hear the soldiers whooping as they made it across the water and charged. Our men were so brave, but they didn't have a chance." Sehoy pressed her hands over her ears as if to block the sounds in her head.

Fiona grabbed her in a fierce hug. Horrified, she sought Uncle Luc-Antoine's eyes.

He shook his head. "How long ago was this?"

"Late March." Sehoy dragged in a painful breath as she pulled away from Fiona. "Those of us who made it out wandered around in the woods all summer, trying to find food, afraid to show our faces. The general had set up camp at Fort Toulouse—which he had the gall to rename Fort Jackson after himself! Finally, one day a couple of white soldiers came through the forest, yelling for us to come out and go with them, that they wouldn't hurt us. They said Red Eagle had survived the massacre. He'd apparently realized there was no going back, and the Americans weren't going away, so he surrendered to Jackson and asked him to take care of the Creek women and children still starving in the woods."

"And Jackson did that?" Fiona exchanged incredulous glances with her brother.

Sehoy nodded. "I still don't understand it. Red Eagle signed a treaty giving the federal government all our territory—twenty-three million acres—and we were to move on west of the Mississippi, out into Oklahoma Territory."

"Where are your parents?" Oliver so seldom spoke that his quiet voice drew everyone's attention. His bony, freckled face was set, tragic. He had never known his own mother, who died giving him birth, but Fiona's mama had helped Luc-Antoine raise the boy, and her death at sea with Papa had been as devastating to Oliver as to Fiona or her siblings.

"Papa was killed at Horseshoe Bend. Mama got so weak from hunger that she didn't make it. I didn't want to go to Oklahoma, and I—I didn't know where else to go but here." She paused, sending an anxious glance at Léon, then Fiona. "That is, if you'll have me. I know it's a lot to ask—"

"Of course you'll stay." Fiona looked at Léon, daring him to object.

Her brother nodded without hesitation. "Fiona will be glad to have another woman in the house, won't you, Fi?"

"Yes, there's only . . ." Fiona glanced at her open bedroom door. "We've got our guest in my room—"

"Who will be moved into the storeroom." Luc-Antoine jabbed his pipe in the direction of the kitchen. "Not proper for him to be in your room anyway."

"A guest?" Sehoy blinked. "I didn't know—"

"It's been a topsy-turvy day." Fiona sighed. "We go for months with nothing to interrupt the monotony, then all of a sudden . . ." She opened her hands and laughed. "The roof all but falls in."

"But who is it?"

And that was the question that Fiona must decide how to answer. Lying wasn't in her nature, but she had to protect Charlie, at least until he was on his feet once more. "He says his name is Charlie Kincaid. I found him on the beach this afternoon, unconscious from a head injury, all but drowned, and he doesn't remember much more than his name."

Sehoy's big brown eyes widened. "My goodness. How can that be?"

"I don't know." Fiona shrugged. "He keeps falling asleep before I can get anything out of him. Which reminds me, I'd best check on him again. If you'll excuse me?" She rose, avoiding the menfolks' eyes and setting her teacup on the tray, and ducked into the room where Charlie lay asleep.

But his mismatched eyes were open, watching the doorway, and when she stopped just inside, his mouth curved in a smile. "Hello, Fiona," he said softly, his voice burred with sleep. "I was dreaming about mermaids, and there you are. Perhaps you'd like to dance?"

AUGUST 14, 1814
MOBILE, WEST FLORIDA TERRITORY

"Mommy, I want a yellow lure with a red feather. Uncle Rémy says the fishes thinks the feather is another itty-bitty fishy-wishy, and they tries to bite it and gets hung up on the hook. 'Cause then I can cook you dinner. Can I?"

"Yes, darling, you can have a red one—if Mr. Counselman has made one, that is." Maddy smiled down at her little son, whose spiraling dark curls, dimples, and big brown eyes gave him a deceptively cherubic appearance, even with his nankeens ripped at both knees and a large smear of mud beneath his nose. She didn't like to think how the mud had got there.

Madeleine Gaillain Gonzalez Burch was the daughter of a diplomat and the wife of a soldier. Half Spanish, half Creole, and one hundred percent American, she was also the grand-daughter of a slave and blessed to have been educated at one of the finest female finishing schools in the nation's capitol.

A study in contradictions, she thought, hurrying to keep up with four-year-old Elijah as he skipped along the bumpy brick streets of downtown Mobile toward the Royal Street market. Elijah was determined to spend the *real* given him by Uncle Rémy Lanier as soon as possible.

Uncle was good to the boy, and Maddy was grateful. But her life bore little resemblance to the dreams she'd once spun to entertain her younger cousin Fiona during the year she'd danced her way across Europe—before she'd met Stephen and before war with England recommenced. Mama had warned her that marrying a career soldier would mean long separa-tions, but she'd been so in love—mostly, she now had to admit, with Stephen's dashing uniform and roguish grin—that she had cajoled Papa into giving them his blessing. And then she'd merrily followed the drum, reveling in playing house in tents and barracks all over the western territories.

Until, that is, she found herself with child. Perpetual morning sickness turned adventure into misery, and tending to a colicky infant made her long for her mother's godly wisdom. And worrying about Stephen brought her father's crazy jokes to mind at the oddest moments.

Ironically, she'd go back to those anxious days in a heartbeat—the days before she knew the truth about her husband.

Determined not to eddy into the abyss these sorts of thoughts generally produced, Maddy took Elijah's hand and pulled him away from the puddle he showed every intention of jumping straight into. "This way, 'Lijah," she said firmly. "Unless you want to go home for a nap."

"No!" was the predictable wail.

"All right then. Come along." She marched him past the enticing mud.

Uncle Rémy had entrusted her to retrieve the mail packet for Lanier Shipping. She wanted to complete the errand and still have time to look through any new dress materials available in the Emporium. She had been building a reputation as a skilled dress designer and needlewoman, and at a party last evening, socialite Anna de Marigny had requested an appointment for a fitting. It was an unbelievable opportunity, and Maddy could hardly wait to get started on the project. Madame de Marigny cut a wide swath of influence along the Gulf Coast, from her home in New Orleans all the way to Pensacola.

But first a fishing lure.

She and Elijah entered the open-air market and found themselves amongst a colorful crowd of businessmen, housewives, slaves, and sailors on leave. After ten minutes or so of patient dodging, muttering "Excuse me, please," and yanking Elijah out of harm's way, she reached the center of the market, where C. C. Counselman's fishing lure stall had been drawing enthusiastic custom since the early days of the Spanish occupation of the city. Along with his beautiful and famous angling accoutrements, Counselman always kept a large iron pot of stew bubbling on the stove at the back of the stall. Maddy wasn't sure which provided the greater draw.

Elijah slapped his coin onto the counter. "Mr. Counselman, I told you I'ma earn enough for a lure next time I come, and look! I gots a whole *real*!" He paused and wrinkled his short nose. "Is that enough?"

The elderly merchant put down his work and leaned over to peer at the coin as if he'd never seen one before. He adjusted his glasses and squinted. "Hm. I believe it might be. With a little left over for a lemon drop, if Monsieur Delucey hasn't run out by now."

"Mama! I can have a lemon drop too!" Elijah flung his arms around Maddy's legs. "Thank you!"

Maddy laughed and met Counselman's twinkling brown eyes. "You'd best remember to thank Uncle Rémy. And perhaps remove the mice from his traps again next week."

While Elijah and Mr. Counselman poked through his colorful display upon the workbench and discussed the various merits of painted wood, feathers, beads, and bits of silk, Maddy's attention wandered to a cluster of gentlemen holding a heated political discussion just a few feet away. Well, at least two were gentlemen, judging by the exquisite tailoring of their coats and the fine leather boots. Not many men in this backwater city could afford to dress with such expensive care.

Her curious gaze must have lingered a tad too long, for the younger of the two gentlemen, the handsome one with a mop of thick black hair, glanced around and caught her staring. Blushing, she turned back to the lure negotiations.

"Maddy? Madeleine Burch? I didn't know you were back in Mobile!" The young man excused himself from his companions. Face lit with a smile, he approached Maddy, took her hand, and kissed it. "How are you?"

"I'm well." She stared up at Desi Palomo, trying to find her old friend in this tall, dark-eyed stranger. Of course it was him, but he looked so . . . authoritative, so confident. He even used to stammer a bit, before he went to college. "I think the last time I saw you was at my wedding."

He tipped his head in that familiar way of his when he was teasing her. "Yes, you married that bumpkin soldier and left your papa wishing he'd taken you anyplace but Washington that summer. Where is your so-fortunate husband?"

Maddy swallowed, groping for a way to get past the awkwardness of speaking aloud Stephen's death.

"Mama!" She felt a tug on her skirt and looked down to find Elijah scowling at her in high dudgeon. "You said I'm not to talk nonsense, but *you* did! No fair!"

She blinked, realizing Desi had addressed her in Italian, and she'd unthinkingly answered in the same language. They'd learned it together as a way to pass the time when he'd traveled with her family from New York to Mobile for a visit. It had become a private joke, their means of secret communication.

She withdrew her hand from Desi's warm grasp and ruffled her son's hair. Switching to English, she said, "Elijah, please be polite to Mr. Palomo. Desi, this is my son, Elijah. His papa was killed in action at Crysler's Farm last November."

Desi's smile collapsed. "Oh, Maddy. I can't tell you how sorry I am." He offered a hand to Elijah. "I'm very pleased to meet you, sir, and please accept my condolences. You must be a very brave young man to take such good care of your mama."

Elijah shook hands with comical gravity. "I don't want no c'ndolens, but I am brave, cuz my papa gave me a sword and I'm gonna get a fish for our dinner. Would you like to have supper with us?"

"Indeed I would, if I can complete my business with these gentlemen in time. But perhaps your mama has other plans?" Desi gave Maddy an inquiring look.

"Of course not—I mean, certainly you are welcome, but you don't have to—"

"I would like it above all things." Desi smiled. "Perhaps you could give me the direction of your home. The city has changed a good deal since last time I was here."

She wanted to ask him where he'd been all these years, why he was here now, and above all, what had put those little creases of experience at the corners of his eyes. But he was coming to dinner, and all that would come out later. Excitement warmed her cheeks. She hadn't entertained male company in a very long time. "You remember Uncle Rémy's house on Conti Street? Elijah and I are in the little white cottage next to it."

"Ah. Yes, I remember. And at what time should I present myself?"

"We eat early because of Elijah's bedtime. Would six-thirty be too soon?"

"That would be perfect. I'll be there." He bowed, winked at Elijah, and returned to the other men.

They had all kept glancing at Maddy as she conversed with Desi. She recognized none of them, but that wasn't unusual. To keep herself and Elijah fed, she spent a lot of time at home sewing, and outside of family and church-related activities, the soiree last night had been the first party she'd attended since her widowhood.

But now that she had a guest for dinner, she'd best think about what to feed him. Oh, and Uncle Rémy's family must be invited as well. Desi had been a great favorite of Aunt Giselle.

She took Elijah by the shoulders and firmly turned him toward Mr. Counselman, waiting with an indulgent smile for his young customer to return to business. "Make up your mind, Elijah, if you want to have time to go fishing. We have lots to do before our company arrives this evening."

Elijah poked at the lures laid out upon the table and chose one with alternating yellow and blue wooden beads and the obligatory red-dyed feather. "This one. I bet I could catch a shark with it!"

Maddy shuddered. "I certainly hope not!"

"Don't worry, Miss Maddy," Counselman said with a smile. "Every self-respecting shark in the Gulf of Mexico will be swimming to Cuba when they hear Master Elijah's about to drop his line in the water."

～

Navy Cove

As bedrooms went, the storeroom could have been worse. Charlie gingerly sat up, one hand to his aching head, and propped his back against the soft, unpainted wooden wall of the storeroom. The hot, moist climate permeated every surface, and he found himself dragging air into his lungs with conscious effort. At the same time, there was something familiar and comforting about the humidity. He had no memories that would connect a lad from the craggy tors of Scotland to this tropical coast, and his brain hurt from trying to force them to resurface.

Perhaps if he concentrated on getting himself physically back to normal, his mind would correct itself.

Last night he had managed to endure the process of being moved to a pallet of blankets in the storeroom without groaning aloud. Fiona's menfolk were a generally stoic, uncommunicative lot who clearly regarded Charlie with suspicion, but they tried not to jostle him too hard. The older one—Fiona and Léon's uncle, father to the youth they called Oliver—had remained after the others left, squatting on his haunches and puffing on his pipe. He'd asked all manner of questions Charlie was unable to answer, all the while studying his face with a disconcerting glint of amusement in his dark eyes. Then with a cryptic "Never mind, laddy, she'll make sure you know what you need to know," Luc-Antoine rose and left Charlie to drift off into an uneasy sleep.

He'd awakened early, managed to stagger outside to relieve himself, and returned to his pallet for another long sleep. Once he thought he heard Fiona's voice, felt her gentle hand upon his brow, but perhaps he'd been dreaming the mermaid dream again. Such an odd thing, that he couldn't remember recent details of his real life, but that dream felt as familiar as the shape of his hands. He knew it originated in a story his nurse had told him as a child, but the fish-girl in his dreams was always the same, her iridescent tail spangled with shades of blue and gray and green the same color as her eyes, her long, sunlit hair floating in waves about her face. She seemed to have been dressed above the waist in a childish white long-sleeved nightgown, buttoned up to the neck—which made absolutely no sense. And was, frankly, a bit disappointing.

He was just about to lever himself further upright when the door opened a crack.

"Charlie? I thought I heard you. Do you need anything?" Fiona's voice.

"Just someone to talk to. I think I'm going mad."

She stuck her head past the edge of the door. "Is it all right if I come in?"

Her hair was braided and wrapped in a neat coronet about her head, and he noticed for the first time a charming sprinkle of freckles across her nose. She looked tidy and normal and distinctly un-mermaidlike.

He pulled himself together. "Of course. I'm sorry to be such a slug-a-bed. I imagine you need something—"

"Oh, no, I was just worried that you might . . ." She blushed as she came into the room, leaving the door open. "That is, do you want me to get Oliver to help you . . . ?"

"Oh!" He laughed. "No, I took care of that myself earlier."

She grinned. "Well, good. Then maybe you're hungry. I kept some grits and biscuits hot for you, and I can poach an egg."

"I've no idea what grits are, but the other sounds splendid."

"Oh, you have to try the grits. They're useful when one is ill."

"I am certainly ill. So I shall bow to your wisdom." He thought of Luc-Antoine's prediction as Fiona ducked back into the kitchen and began to bang pots and pans. She had already begun to let him know what he needed to know.

He smiled and settled back into a half doze.

Sometime later Fiona returned bearing a tray loaded with the promised eggs and biscuits, steaming alongside a pile of yellowish cereal and a rasher of bacon, and a cup of coffee. With a smile she settled the tray on his lap.

He poked at the cereal with the fork Fiona had thoughtfully wrapped in a napkin. "It looks a little like mush."

"It's made from corn—hominy, to be precise." She sat on the floor beside his pallet, arranging her skirts about her legs for modesty. "You won't see it in England."

Probably he had eaten worse things, he thought, shoveling a forkful into his mouth and chasing it with a swig of coffee. "Not bad," he conceded. "I thank you." There was enough butter and salt to make it quite tasty, and he discovered he was ravenous. He ate while Fiona sat looking at her hands linked loosely in her lap. Her silence made him uncomfortable. "Perhaps you could tell me more about the time when we met. I swear to you I can't remember it."

The big sea-colored eyes lifted to his face, their expression troubled. "I couldn't sleep last night for thinking about it. And wondering how you got here. Perhaps you're a sailor. That's all you talked about that summer."

"Couldn't be. My father wouldn't have it."

"Your father the earl. Is he still alive? Is it possible you're the Earl of Scarborough now?"

"Fiona, I don't know. I have two older brothers, so even if the pater is dead, I'm third in line. Little chance I'm anything but the black sheep youngest of the Kincaid brothers. More likely I'm a pirate got washed overboard from the *Jolly Roger*."

Fiona laughed. "Now that's a story. The British don't make good pirates. Too starchy."

"Do I look starchy to you?"

She tilted her head and surveyed him, head to bare feet. "With the bandage and whiskers, you do look a bit . . . scruffy."

"I just imagine I do." He rubbed his bristly face. "I don't suppose you could scare up razor and soap, could you? Oh, and a mirror?"

She jumped to her feet. "I'll be right back."

By the time she returned, Charlie had finished his breakfast and set the plate aside. The headache had abated somewhat, and he thought if he could just shave and put on some clean clothes, he might even feel human again.

Fiona dumped the shaving accoutrements, along with a clean towel and a pile of garments, on the floor. "I raided my brother's

old trunk and found some things I thought you might be able
to wear. There's water in the pitcher over on the table. I'll be
in the kitchen. Call if you need anything else." Picking up the
tray, she backed toward the door.

"Wait! Fiona, you never told me about our meeting. You said
you came to Riverton Farm with your relatives . . ."

She paused, biting her lip. "I was just a little girl then, not
quite eleven years old. I was raised here on the Point with three
brothers, and I'd become rather a hoyden." She grimaced. "My
mama convinced my papa I needed to see more of the world,
spend some time with my older cousin Maddy. Her father, Uncle
Rafa, is a diplomat, and the family wanted to take me with them
to Europe that summer—it was 1805, I think . . ."

"That was right after I got sent down." He tried to think past
the row with his father over that fiasco, but came up against a
blank wall. "I imagine Grandfa was going to try to talk sense
into me."

"Uncle Rafa admired your grandfather very much, even
though they had been on opposite sides in the wars. Admiral
Lord St. Clair had saved Uncle's life at the siege of Gibraltar."

"Huh. Then your uncle is a Spaniard?"

"He was. After the War for Independence, he served as as-
sistant envoy with the Spanish ambassador to New York. In
fact, Maddy was born there. But President Washington wanted
Uncle Rafa on his foreign policy staff—that's another long story
I won't go into now—so Uncle swore the oath of allegiance to
the United States. When the Capitol Building was finished, he
and Aunt Lyse and Maddy moved to Washington."

Charlie scratched his head. "Then your Aunt Lyse is American?
Is she your father's sister? Or your mother's?"

Fiona laughed. "I warned you it's complicated. My father,
Aunt Lyse, Uncle Luc-Antoine, and three other siblings all grew

up in Mobile. They were French-Creole, but somehow the family managed to hang on to their property under the British and Spanish occupations. The Spanish governor awarded this chunk of land here at Navy Cove to my papa and Luc-Antoine for service during the invasions of Mobile and Pensacola. They were allowed to keep it when West Florida finally came under US control, on condition that they agreed to maintain the shipyard that serves Fort Bowyer."

"Your parents . . . where are they now?"

She lost a little of her rosy color but said steadily, "They were killed at sea over two years ago, on a merchant ship attacked by a British sloop-of-war. Charlie—you mustn't tell anyone here that you're British. I'm not sure they'd let you live long enough to be remanded to the authorities in Mobile."

3

Sehoy stared up at the giant hulk of a half-completed ship taking up nearly two hundred feet of the Navy Cove beach. Armed with hammers and wearing aprons that bulged with pegs and nails, some twenty to thirty half-dressed carpenters crawled about the vessel, clinging to her curved hull like a colony of worker ants. Having grown up in the interior of the Mississippi Territory, Sehoy knew little about oceangoing ships—barely enough to understand that the bottom was called the *keel*, *port* was on the left, and *starboard* on the right—but even to her untrained eye this one was a thing of beauty. Her cousin Léon, the designer and engineer of the family business, clearly possessed an extraordinary talent for the art and science of shipbuilding.

"Hey! Sehoy! Up here!"

Shading her eyes against the fierce sun, she spotted a lanky figure teetering upon the topmost row of planking, ten feet above the ground. "Oliver? Good gracious, be careful!" She picked up her skirts and hurried toward him.

He laughed, but lowered his arms and sat down with his long

legs hanging over the edge of the hull. "What are you doing here? Where's Fiona?"

In the shade of the ship, Sehoy craned her neck to look up at Oliver. "She's making breakfast for the man in the storeroom. Or possibly lunch. I'm not sure what time it is." She shrugged. "I needed to get out of the house."

"I can tell you right now it's lunchtime." He squinted up at the sun, directly overhead. "I was just about to ask Léon if we could stop and eat. Want to join me? I brought an extra sandwich."

"I suppose I could eat." Nonplussed, she watched him jump to his feet and nimbly pick his way to the back of the ship, where Léon crouched in deep conversation with a couple of other men. When Oliver spoke to him, Léon nodded absently and went back to his discussion.

While she waited for Oliver to scramble down a ladder to the ground and slip on the shirt that had been tied about his waist, she wondered at the general sense of energy that permeated the place. According to Nardo Smith, the shipyard had been commissioned last summer. With a mess hall and barracks for the carpenters, plus a small office building and the ship frame itself, it was turning Navy Cove into quite a center of modern industry. Nothing was as she remembered from the visit with her family during Mardi Gras season a few years ago.

She'd never forget the laughter and games and stories of the Lanier children—bossy Léon, adventurous Judah, and the twins Fiona and Sullivan, two sides of a bright coin. A plethora of cousins had been at the party too, including Oliver—closest to her in age but whom she barely remembered because of his tongue-tied shyness. Instead she had developed a painful case of unrequited love for sea-mad Sullivan.

Oliver swung toward her now, the crooked Lanier smile upon

his freckled, sunburnt face, auburn-streaked hair bound back in an untidy queue, and the wrinkled shirt hanging loose at his hips. The admiration in his gray eyes was gratifying.

Sullivan was a prisoner of war. She must not cease praying for him until he was released.

She resisted the urge to smile back at Oliver with immodest eagerness. "Are you sure I won't be in the way? I just wanted to see the ship and walk on the beach a bit."

"You're welcome to come anytime." Oliver halted in front of her, extending a large hand scarred with multiple scrapes and cuts.

Common civility demanded that she place her hand in his and allow him to carry it to his lips. Oliver might be bashful, but he clearly possessed the address for which the Lanier men had become famous.

Do not blush, she ordered herself.

To cover her confusion, she turned to watch a pelican dive for a fish. "I hardly know where I belong anymore."

"You belong here with us, you know that." Oliver moved to stand beside her, towering over her by several inches. How tall he had grown in four years!

"I probably should have gone to Oklahoma with my people." She held out her hands, bronze-colored hands with short, broken nails and unladylike scars across the knuckles from dressing game and cooking and handling grasses the Creek women wove into baskets.

"Sehoy." Oliver grabbed one of her hands and held it this time. "*We* are your people. Our great-grandmothers were sisters." When she looked up at him, he smiled. "Well, I'm not sure about the generations, but the Laniers come from the Koasati just like you do. No more talk about Oklahoma. Let's find a place in the shade to eat our sandwiches. I'm starved!"

Swinging hands, they walked together toward a small wood-framed building that stood a short distance from the beach. Its long, narrow windows stood open to the sea breeze, and from inside it Sehoy could hear a rumble of male voices and the metallic clank of dishes. But instead of heading for the open doorway, Oliver led her around the side of the building, where a couple of pine benches squatted against the wall.

"Is it all right if we eat outside?" He brushed sand off one of the benches and gestured for her to sit. "The men's language is . . . a bit rough for a lady."

Pleased at his courtesy, she sat down, arranging her skirts. "This is lovely." The building provided a shallow bank of shade, and she had an unobstructed view of the glittering surface of the bay.

"Good. I'll be right back." Oliver disappeared into the mess hall and returned a few minutes later with a pair of thick ham sandwiches.

With a smile of thanks, Sehoy took the one he offered her. "I should have brought food with me. Didn't realize the time."

Oliver sat down beside her. "Is it all right if I return thanks?"

"Of course."

Oliver's voice was quiet but sincere. "Thank you, Father, for this gift of food. And thank you for a pretty girl to talk to while I eat."

Involuntarily she giggled and looked at Oliver. He opened one twinkling gray eye, and she burst out laughing. He seemed to have overcome a good deal of his initial bashfulness. "Doesn't Fiona ever bring you boys lunch?" she asked, nibbling at her sandwich.

"Fiona?" He snorted. "She's training horses all day long. And anyway, she's my first cousin, might as well be my sister. That's no fun." He settled back against the wall and addressed his own food with enthusiasm.

"Hm. I suppose." She relaxed, enjoying his quiet company and the beautiful surroundings. "What kind of boat is this you're building? Who is it for?"

Oliver nearly choked on his laughter. "Don't let Uncle Luc-Antoine hear you calling it a boat! This, mademoiselle, is a ship—a brigantine to be precise. The United States Navy commissioned her to help boot the Brits off our land and out of our waters."

"I didn't know the United States had a navy."

"Of course we have a navy." Oliver sounded mildly annoyed. "What do you think Sullivan has been doing all these years?"

"I suppose I thought he'd sailed on one of the family's merchant ships." She didn't want to think about Sullivan being held prisoner, far from his home and family. She looked at Oliver, who favored Sullivan, except for the reddish hair. Sullivan had always had a wild mane of dark blond curls. "This family is ocean crazy. Didn't you want to go to sea too?"

"Of course I like the water. But I'd rather be home with the folks. I'm training to be a bar pilot like Papa."

"What does a bar pilot do?"

"We escort ships through the channel and up to Mobile, keep them from grounding out on the sandbars in the bay. But I'm finding I like carpentry just as much." Oliver gestured toward the ship under construction. "It's hard work, but the pay is good. I'm saving for a ship of my own."

Sehoy nodded, though the concept of enjoying one's work was a bit of a foreign idea. The men of her family were hunters, trappers, and traders, nomadic and restless. The women followed them, cared for them, and raised their children. The families were close and loyal, but unsentimental. She couldn't remember a time when her father had more than patted her head in approval.

She glanced up at Oliver. "I understand why you wouldn't want to leave such a beautiful home."

He laughed. "Well, when the breeze dies down and the bugs drive you mad, you might change your mind. How long did it take you to get here from Horseshoe Bend?"

"A couple of days." It had been a long, hard trip overland with the interpreter Desi Palomo, who had, upon discovering her connection to the Laniers, offered to travel with her as far as Mobile. She hadn't wanted the American's help, though Mama's dying wish was that she accept. Palomo was a charming man, and his gift for language was apparent—he addressed her in fluent Muskogee, the tongue of her people—but she had treated him to a dignified silence except when absolutely necessary. She was glad when they parted ways at the ferry, he to cross the bay and report to the commander at Fort Charlotte, Sehoy to continue the journey in Nardo Smith's pirogue along the eastern shore to Mobile Point. "Do you know Desi Palomo?"

"Sure, he grew up with Uncle Rafa and Aunt Lyse's family. They practically adopted him. 'Course, he's been gone to the northeast for . . . I don't know, a long time. So he's come back?"

"Yes. Apparently he's been attached to General Jackson's staff as an interpreter, and they sent him ahead to Mobile to prepare for the general's arrival."

Oliver whistled. "Really? The general is coming here?"

"Mr. Palomo wouldn't say much, but I gather they think the British are planning to attack New Orleans and take control of the Mississippi—"

"—with Mobile as the jumping-off point." Oliver jumped to his feet. "I have to tell Papa and Léon."

"But—"

"I'm glad you came, Sehoy, and you're welcome anytime, but I've got to get back to work now. Here, you can have the rest of my sandwich." He thrust the half-eaten sandwich at her and tore off across the sand toward the construction site.

Sehoy stared after him, mouth ajar. Men were such *volatile* creatures. One minute flirting, the next set to grab a gun and fire at some real or imagined enemy. Perhaps after all she'd go back to the house and see what Fiona was up to.

⌒

She knew she shouldn't hover. She'd brought Charlie what he needed to shave and dress. He was a grown man, and if he needed her, he would call.

But as she and the bay stallion she planned to sell as a cavalry mount worked on disciplines critical for hand-to-hand conflict, Fiona kept an ear open for Charlie's voice. He was very quiet. What if he'd fainted again and cracked open his head? What if he bled to death while she was out here with Tully?

Carefully using knees and reins to coax Tully into a fore-leg half-pirouette called "On the Forehand About," she heard only the omnipresent sounds of the water, seagulls squabbling over food, and in the distance, the shipbuilders shouting to one another over hammers banging and metal clanging at the forge—the usual comforting sounds of a day at Navy Cove.

Perhaps she should go inside to check on Charlie. But if she did, the rhythm of Tully's lesson would be broken and she would have to work twice as hard next time to straighten him out.

She kept working, riddled with guilt over Charlie, as well as the uncomfortable thought that she seemed to have somehow offended poor Sehoy, who had inexplicably wandered off alone this morning after breakfast. Until yesterday, the daily routine of cooking and cleaning for her three menfolk plus the horses had been fairly simple, but now there were two guests depending on her. Unbidden, she wished her mother were here to advise her.

Mama seemed to have had a bent for caretaking ingrained in the very fiber of her being, and she'd tried to teach Fiona how to develop and exercise it.

But, no, Fiona must turn herself into the veriest tomboy, tramping about after her brothers, trading her skirts for breeches at the least excuse. She looked down at herself ruefully. As usual when working the horses, she wore a pair of tall riding boots over Sullivan's outgrown, cast-off tan breeches—because after all, one couldn't train a cavalry horse in skirts.

No wonder Mama had despaired of her only daughter ever becoming a lady. No wonder she'd asked Aunt Lyse to take charge of Fiona's education, effectively sending her into exile.

And here she was, drifting back into the same old habits. Some days she forgot to change back into her dress, even when the horses' training was done for the day. The men of her family seemed not to mind, but now . . .

Now there was Charlie Kincaid in her home, and what would he think to find a young lady dressed with so little regard for propriety? Even Sehoy would expect better of her.

Like it or not, she was going to have to change her ways.

She sighed and patted Tully's neck. "Come on, let's get you settled with a nice handful of hay. Your work's done for the day, sir." Clicking her tongue against her teeth, she neck reined the bay toward the barn.

And found Charlie sitting on a box in the shade beside its open door. Judging by his relaxed posture and amused expression, he had been watching her for some time.

She reined Tully in with uncharacteristic awkwardness. "What are you doing out of bed?" She slid down from the saddle and pulled the horse with her toward her crack-brained patient.

He grinned, apparently not intimidated by her scowl. "That's a prime bit of blood you have there. I'd buy him off you in a heartbeat if I had the blunt."

"No you wouldn't. He's earmarked for the cavalry." Pushing Tully's head away when he blew in her ear, she grudgingly added, "You look better." Sullivan's clothes fit Charlie remarkably well, and his still-damp hair turned out to be a dark umber with streaks of sienna.

"I'm certain I smell better too." He levered himself to his feet, wincing. "Apologies if I've overstepped my bounds by coming out to watch the show, but I thought a little fresh air might help put me on the mend."

She stared at him, trying to decide if he was being sarcastic. His expression was bland, unreadable. Finally she huffed and led Tully into the barn without another word, then set about currying the horse. When she'd finished, she gave him a handful of hay and let him out to pasture.

Coming back to the barn, slapping dust from her hands and the seat of her breeches, she found Charlie leaning over a stall door, smiling at a pair of newborn goat twins lying in the hay with their mother. They snuggled together, nudging their mama's belly in competition for a favorite teat.

She propped her arms on the top of the door beside him. "Aren't they the cutest things? Born just yesterday afternoon and already rivals."

"It's a male trait, I suppose. I never could stand for my brothers to best me at anything. And once I got to Eton . . ." He shook his head. "That was the source of my trouble there."

"Do you remember why you got sent down?"

When they were younger, he'd ignored her questions about his disciplinary action, but apparently he'd gotten over the embarrassment, for he laughed. "Bat guano."

"What?"

"I was a Scottish lad at Eton, expected to have neither native intelligence nor culture. One of the masters saw promise however, and promoted me over some older boys into the scientific society."

"You must have been proud."

"Say, rather, terrified." He shuddered. "My house captain found out one of my papers had been sent up for good and made my life miserable."

"Sent up for good?"

He reddened. "It's a form of recognition for outstanding work, which the heads store in the College Archives. I didn't like being known as a brain. I wanted to be on the rowing team."

"Hm." She studied him. Precocious, competitive, self-effacing. And a good storyteller. "What does that have to do with bat guano?"

"Oh, that." He grinned. "The paper that was recognized was about the chemical efficacy of excrement as a fertilizer. Percy, the house captain I mentioned, said it was hooey. He took to calling me 'MacGuano' and making me empty and clean the chamber pots every morning while the others ate breakfast."

"That's horrible!"

"It's what boys do." Charlie shrugged. "But I got back at old Percy by spelling his name with the substance of choice on the house lawn. Headmaster investigated, I was the obvious culprit, and they made me clean it up. But as spring came on, the fertilizer did its work. I was sent down, but Percy was immortalized on the lawn all summer."

Fiona giggled. "No wonder your father was so outdone with you!"

"I know." Charlie laughed with her. "If Grandfa hadn't intervened and sent for me to come and rusticate at the Farms, I don't know what Da might have done to me. He wanted so much for me to be a gentleman and had me pegged for the church."

"And Mama wanted me to be a grand lady."

"It seems we were both a disappointment to our progenitors." He glanced toward the pasture, where Tully grazed with the other horses. "How did you learn so much about horses?"

"I studied. My family are all boat and fishing people, especially my papa. And Uncle Rafa was in the Spanish navy until he transferred to the diplomatic corps. But my mother was a schoolteacher, and she made me and my brothers read until our eyes bled!" Fiona smiled. "The boys hated it, but I didn't mind at all. I found I could go anywhere, be anybody, in the pages of a story or a biography or even a science book."

"You learned about horses from books?" He sounded faintly incredulous.

"Yes, haven't you read William Cavendish, Duke of Newcastle's work? Or Antoine de Pluvinel or François Robichon? Besides owning the largest library in Mobile, Great-grandpa Chaz kept several horses, and he gave me my first pony."

"My grandfather is quite my hero as well."

Fiona tipped her head. "Admiral Lord St. Clair, you mean?"

"Yes, I barely knew my father's father. He's also a military man—army—and a Member of Parliament. At least, I suppose he is yet. Who knows what has happened in the last years that I can't remember?"

She sensed his frustration. "Surely your memory will come back."

"The human brain is a mystery, even to medical men."

"I am going to pray for you every day and ask God to heal it."

"I'm not sure God cares about my brain."

The cynical curl of his lip stung Fiona's heart. "Charlie, God cares about every part of you." She laid her hand upon his forearm. The muscles there were tight from his clenched fist. "The Bible says even the hairs of your head are numbered."

He laughed. "See? I'd make a terrible clergyman. The church made a narrow escape when I went to sea."

She clutched his wrist. "You just remembered something! You *did* go to sea? Didn't you?"

He stared at her, confused. "No, I . . . everything is still gray and muddled, but I must be a seaman. Else how would I have gotten here from England?"

"Well, I suppose you could have come over as a passenger. But British ships aren't allowed into port here. So . . . had you run away and boarded a Dutch or Spanish ship, perhaps? Maybe you'd sailed to Pensacola or New Orleans before the storm took the ship off-course and you got thrown overboard."

"Maybe. But guessing does little good until I remember more details. And trying to remember only makes my head ache." Charlie sighed. "I don't want to keep you from your responsibilities, Fiona, in fact I wish you'd give me something to do. You've been nothing but kind to me, and I don't want to be a burden on your family." He glanced toward the house. "Speaking of which, who is that girl? Is she your sister?"

Fiona squinted against the glare of sunlight coming through the barn door and made out Sehoy's figure approaching from the beach. "No, Sehoy is a distant cousin from the Indian branch of our family. She arrived last night, after you fell asleep." She went to the doorway and waved. "Sehoy! Come here! I want you to meet Char—Mr. Kincaid."

"I've been down to the shipyard to see what they're working on," Sehoy said when she got close enough. "Oliver shared a sandwich with me." She gave Charlie her shy smile. "How do you do, Mr. Kincaid?"

"Much better, now that I've gotten up and around a bit."

Charlie's manners were evidently deeply ingrained, for he bowed over Sehoy's hand. "Your family has kindly provided shelter to this shipwrecked stranger, and I hope my presence will not inconvenience you."

"Oh no, of course not!" Sehoy gave Fiona a flustered look. "I am something of a refugee myself."

"I understand you've come from some distance. Where is your home, if I may be so bold?"

"I am of the Upper Creek, whose villages cluster mainly along the Tallapoosa River." Sehoy's expression darkened. "Though I am not certain many will remain after General Jackson drives my people out."

Charlie looked intrigued, but Fiona was reluctant to allow Sehoy to dwell in bitterness, however justified it might be. She gave Charlie a warning look and slipped her arm through Sehoy's. "You said you've already eaten, but perhaps you'll join me and Charlie with a cup of tea while we tuck into some of the dumplings from last night."

"Dumplings and tea," Sehoy sighed. "Yes, that will make everything quite all right." But she allowed Fiona to draw her toward the house.

❧

MOBILE

Following her parents about the globe on diplomatic missions, Maddy had dined with governors, generals, prime ministers, and heads of state, but she couldn't think when she'd laughed more or had a more interesting conversation during the course of a meal.

Truth be told, she couldn't remember the last time she'd allowed herself to relax and truly enjoy herself—not since Stephen left for Canada anyway.

She met Desi's twinkling dark eyes with a pang of guilt. Stephen had gone to war and died in service to his country. What was wrong with a woman who was glad her husband was dead?

"What's the matter?" Desi laid his big, warm hand on hers, his thumb tracing the edge of her wedding band.

She looked away. That was the problem, having a conversation with a man who'd known one since childhood. He could apparently still read her every mood.

"Not a thing." She smiled and pushed back her chair, sliding her hand out from under Desi's. "I'm going to fetch dessert. Who wants blackberry pie?"

"Me, me!" Elijah, who had been all but asleep in his plate, roused at the mention of sweets. "A big piece, Mama!"

"I'll help you." Aunt Giselle rose and followed Maddy into the kitchen. She was a small, pretty blonde woman, comfortably rounded after bearing Maddy's three cousins, Israel, Diron, and Ruthie.

The two women set about loading the pie, dessert plates, clean silverware, and serving knife onto a large, ornate silver tray that Maddy had inherited from her Spanish grandmother. The tray had rarely been used, as she so seldom entertained. Desi's return surely justified a celebration—

"Desi has grown into quite a fine-looking gentleman, has he not?"

Nearly dropping the wine bottle in her hands, Maddy whirled to face Giselle. "What? Oh! Yes, he—he's—" She put the bottle on the tray, then busied herself taking down from the cupboard the long-stemmed crystal flutes Mama had give her upon her marriage. "It's very good to see him again."

"He is clearly pleased to see you again as well." Giselle's tone was dry.

"Aunt Giselle, Desi might as well be my brother. Of course we're glad to see each other."

"Madeleine, Desi has not perceived you as a sister since he was out of short coats. You are a young and beautiful woman, and there is nothing wrong in enjoying the attention of an attractive gentleman."

Maddy turned, mouth open. "What do you mean? He has not—Are you saying he saw me as a—that he had feelings for me when—Oh dear. I had no idea . . ."

"Yes, I'm sorry to say that as a silly young miss you were unfortunately quite absorbed with yourself." Giselle propped the tray against her stomach and tsked. "Had your papa not sent Desi off to William and Mary at that exact moment in time, the poor boy would probably have offered for you and found himself ignominiously rejected."

Maddy put her hands to her warm cheeks. From the dining room she could hear Desi's laughter rolling under Elijah's high-pitched chatter. "I wish you hadn't told me. How am I to go back in there and face him now?"

Giselle rolled her eyes. "The same way you did ten minutes ago. What is the matter with you, child? You are a polished hostess with a world of breeding in your heritage and training. There is no reason to be so overset unless . . ." Her aunt peered at her sharply. "Unless you return those particular feelings."

"Don't be ridiculous, I only ran into him this afternoon." Maddy bit her lip. "It's just that he brings back such memories of our family—my family, I mean—and it makes me homesick for Mama and Papa." It had nothing to do with the delicious thrill of intercepting the caressing look in a pair of wicked black eyes. Of course not.

She snatched up the wine flutes and rushed past her chuckling auntie. Desi looked up with a smile when she entered the dining room, and they stared at one another for a long moment. She suddenly understood the image of scales falling from one's eyes. Desi's expression was tender, full of humor, and not in the least brotherly.

Oh, dear.

As she and Giselle served warm, sugary slices of crusty pastry, dripping with juicy blackberries, she scrambled to regain her composure, somehow carrying on light banter with her guests. As Giselle had said, Maddy had as a young Washington debutante effortlessly fielded the admiring advances of gentlemen of the diplomatic corps as well as those in governmental circles. But years of following the drum as a soldier's wife and the responsibilities of motherhood had forced her to put away that glamorous polish. Some days she felt like an entirely different person than that giddy young girl.

Which was as it should be. But with Desi here in her home—absent the protective presence of her father and the safety of her identity as Stephen Burch's wife—her equilibrium vanished. She sank into her place beside a juice-and-sugar-festooned Elijah and stared at her pie, bereft of appetite.

"Mama, if you don't want your pie, I'll eat it for you."

She looked at her little son, grateful for the attention he demanded. "And you would surely pop if you did." She picked up her fork. "Thank you, but I shall deal with it on my own. If you're finished, perhaps you and Ruthie and the boys would like to go to your room to shoot marbles."

"Israel! Diron! I don't gots to have a bath!" Elijah hopped down from his chair and shoved it with more enthusiasm than grace against the table. "Mama said!"

The Lanier boys, aged thirteen and eleven respectively, along with ten-year-old Ruthie, good-naturedly followed little Elijah out of the dining room. Soon they could be heard from the other side of the cottage, whooping and chattering over their game.

Desi pushed away his empty dessert plate and eyed Maddy over his wine glass. "I take it normal bedtime has been suspended for the evening. How was the fishing expedition this afternoon? I didn't notice fish on the menu tonight."

"Uncle Rémy took him, you'll have to ask him." Maddy smiled at her handsome, bewhiskered uncle, still savoring the last bite of his pie. "I was grateful for the break so that I could cook dinner and finish a sewing project that needed to be completed before tomorrow."

Rémy licked the back of his fork and put it down on his plate. "I'm always happy for an excuse to baptize a worm," he said, chuckling. "My older brothers were taking me fishing when I was smaller than Elijah. Never get tired of it."

"Don Rafael often took me as a boy as well," Desi said. "Maddy would go with us, but refused to touch the worms. She always took a book and read while we fished."

"Which is why my Latin and Greek are quite as good as yours." She wrinkled her nose at him.

"Languages are your strength," he said with a good-natured shrug. "You should have been allowed to go to college as well."

Giselle clicked her tongue. "A woman has no need of languages to run a household, and would be utterly out of place in an institution filled with rowdy young men." She folded her napkin and laid it upon the table as if daring anyone to contradict her.

Eyes twinkling, Uncle Rémy cleared his throat. "Desi, you must tell us more about your assignment here. Rafael wrote to say you'd been sent to New Orleans to serve as aide to Governor Claiborne."

"Yes, I enjoyed my stint in the capitol on Jefferson's staff, but because of my familiarity with the Louisiana and Florida Territories it was felt that I'd be more useful there." Desi's tone was casual.

So casual that Maddy's curiosity rose. He had demonstrated that he hadn't forgotten clues to her inmost feelings, and it appeared she remained sensitive to his secrets as well. Covertly she studied him as the conversation turned to politics—the dismally unpopular Embargo Act, power struggles between Federalists and Democratic-Republicans, the Indian wars in central Alabama, and locally, Governor Claiborne's struggle to control his recalcitrant Spanish and Creole citizens.

As a very young man, Desi had been a people-pleaser, intelligent and quick to make a joke. He possessed a rare ability to listen, to elicit stories and information from others, and the wit to remember it—qualities most likely learned at her own father's knee. But now . . .

Now there was some layer of danger beneath the urbanity, something flexible and sharply honed, like the blade of a fine sword. He was no less charming, to be sure. His smile came easily, he leaned toward one as if inviting confidence, and that glint in his deep brown eyes made one feel as if she were the only person in the room. But she knew. Instinctively she *knew* he listened for something specific and would file it away for his own purposes.

He wasn't going to admit what he was really doing in Mobile. Maybe his mission was innocent, even heroic. But whatever it was, he was up to something interesting. Something that served to wake Maddy up, as if from a long sleep.

And she was going to find out what it was.

4

The small oilskin bag hidden under his shirt was on Charlie's mind as he scattered seed for Fiona's chickens and watched them run after it, flapping and squawking. He enjoyed these homely little duties that had made him feel useful over the last couple of days. Lying abed with nothing to do but nurse an aching head and worry over the parchment code secreted in that bag had all but driven him mad. Ironically, the brainless nature of light physical labor freed his mind to think creatively.

After checking to make sure Fiona was out of sight, he leaned against the outer wall of the chicken coop. With a quick tug at the thin leather string tied about his neck and attached to the bag, he removed the paper and unrolled it. Only a couple of paragraphs written in his own crabbed hand, the encrypted message stared back at him as if daring him to pick its knots apart. He closed his eyes, letting the letters parade before his mind. Repeated patterns? Would that help? Frequent letters? There had to be a key.

He didn't remember writing it. Wherever he'd been, whatever he'd been doing before washing up on the beach, he was involved in something clandestine. Until he knew what that was, he mustn't allow anyone else to see this paper.

"Charlie! Where are you?" Fiona's voice came from somewhere close.

He tucked the message back inside its pouch and shoved it inside his shirt. "Here I am. Saw one of your chicks scoot back here, so I—" Rounding the corner of the coop, he came face-to-face with Fiona. "Oh. Did you miss me so soon?" He smiled at her and stepped closer. Even in men's breeches and boots, she really was pretty, and he'd quickly figured out he could rattle her with certain insinuating looks.

She retreated a step, a rosy flush spreading under that golden dusting of freckles. "I just wondered if you'd like to go riding with me and Sehoy. If you feel up to it, that is. I've finished my chores, and Tully needs exercise."

He touched the bandage tied about his head. The wound was still sore to the touch, but no longer ached incessantly. "That's the best suggestion I've heard all day. Let me put this bucket away."

In the barn they found Sehoy kneeling in the extra stall, playing with the baby goats. She looked around, laughing as one of the kids hopped onto her lap and licked her chin. "I see you found him," she said. "How are you feeling, Mr. Kincaid?"

"Please don't stand on ceremony," he said with a smile. "I'm just Charlie. And I'm feeling better every day. Still can't remember a deuced thing, but the old noggin is healing nicely."

"That's good." Sehoy pushed the little goat away and rose, dusting her knees. Self-consciously she looked down at her dress, which he suspected was a hand-me-down from Fiona, as it was half a foot too long and drooped at the neckline. "I'm not

the most experienced rider, so I hope I won't keep you from enjoying your ride."

He laughed. "I was just about to say, I hope you ladies will take it easy on me, since I'm not quite up to snuff."

"We're just going down to the beach." Fiona lifted a saddle and blanket off a nearby stall door and led the way outside. Three horses—Bonnie, Tully, and a small buckskin gelding called Dusty—waited just inside the corral, their lead ropes tied to the top rail. "Charlie, can you saddle Tully? I'll take care of Dusty for Sehoy, and I'll ride Bonnie."

Charlie patted the stallion's glossy withers and grabbed its halter. "Of course. Let's see if saddling a horse comes back to me."

To his relief, it did, and within a few minutes the three of them had mounted and were trotting the horses down the sandy, shell-strewn path through the woods toward the beach, Fiona in the lead. Charlie, bringing up the rear behind Sehoy, found the discomfort created by the jouncing motion far outweighed by the sheer exhilaration of the breeze in his face and the welcome stretch of his muscles. As they got closer to the water, they slowed to a walk, and he could hear the gentle lap of the waves against the sand. Gradually the trees thinned to brambles and shrubs, and he could see the water glinting like diamonds in the morning sun. As they broke free of the trees, a mild gust of warm, salty air swept his hair back from his face. Tully danced sideways, forcing Charlie to instinctively knee and rein him in the desired direction.

Pleased that horsemanship seemed to come naturally, he kicked the stallion with his heels and caught up to the girls, who rode abreast. "He's a splendid mount, Fiona," he said, leaning up to pat the horse's neck. "Some officer will be a lucky fellow."

She smiled. "I'm glad you think so. Bonnie's his dam, and he was sired by my stud, Washington—Léon usually rides him."

Charlie nodded, watching the Indian girl manage her horse. Sehoy wasn't as graceful a rider as Fiona, but she kept up well enough. Her thick black hair hung down her back in a braid tied with a blue ribbon to match the overlarge dress, and her expression remained cool, almost stoical. He didn't know much more about the girl than Fiona had told him the day after she arrived—that she was a refugee from some sort of massacre perpetrated by American militia in Indian territory. He guessed her to be fifteen or sixteen years old, possibly old enough to be looking about for a husband. Women got left alone, orphaned or widowed, every day. He wondered if she planned to stay here with the Laniers indefinitely.

He addressed her. "Do you mind telling me how your families are related? I confess to some curiosity."

Sehoy glanced at him, lips pursed. "It goes back several generations. My father's father was an Irish trader who lived with the Creek, but my mother's grandmother was sister to Fiona's great-great-grandmother."

"Irish?" Charlie looked in vain for any hint of European ancestry in the exotic features.

Sehoy's expression lightened. "Aye, laddy, I'm a Ferguson. One quarter, at least."

He shook his head. "I don't mean to be . . . that is, I suppose intermarriage does occur."

Fiona and Sehoy exchanged amused glances. "Indeed it does," Fiona said. "My ancestors are French, Indian, Spanish, and African. You can't get more mixed than that. You Brits, with your bloodlines—"

"He's British?" Sehoy stared at him.

Fiona's eyes were wide with dismay. "I mean—"

"Honestly, Sehoy, I'm not sure where I came from. I was born in Scotland and spent my boyhood there, but that doesn't

account for the last ten or so years, which I can't remember."
Charlie shrugged. "Please, forgive my rude comment and put
it down to brain injury. My mother would be appalled at my
manners. Now if you ladies will excuse us, Tully and I would
like to go for a run." With a loud *whoop*, he loosened the reins,
leaned forward, and pushed his heels into the horse's flanks.

As Tully leaped forward over the sand, Charlie reveled in
the motion, the wind in his face, the throb of excitement in his
chest. He'd always thrived on danger.

And he *was* British, he knew it in his bones, no matter what
he'd told Sehoy. From conversation amongst Fiona's family, he
gathered that England and American were at war. Mobile and
her environs sat in the middle of contested territory—Louisiana
and West Florida having in succession belonged to France, England, Spain, and the new United States of America. Spain still
claimed Florida to the east, but had ceded the giant western
Louisiana Territory to France, who then clandestinely sold it
to America before Spain could object or officially determine its
boundaries. There was concern that England wanted her finger
back in the Southern territorial pie, and had started gathering
forces toward that end.

Charlie could feel the pouch underneath his shirt bouncing
against his chest as Tully pounded along the water's edge. He
was British by birth, and he was some sort of spy, that much
was clear. But what if, as he had implied to Sehoy, there was a
possibility his recent loyalties had swerved from King George?
He dare not make a move until he knew for sure what that message said. And until he could remember to whom he'd intended
to deliver it.

In the meantime, he would listen, absorb, and learn as much
from his American hosts as he could.

He tugged on the reins, slowing the horse to a canter, a trot, and then a stop. Breathing hard, he turned and waited for Fiona and Sehoy to reach him. Two pretty young women on a sunny beach in paradise. How hard could it be?

~~

AUGUST 20, 1814

Watching Charlie grow stronger every day and aware of her menfolk's impatience with his continuing denial of any memory of his identity, Fiona struggled to maintain neutrality. Because she had expected never to see him again, as she grew into maidenhood the golden boyish figure from her trip to England had turned into wistful, romantic daydreams of a knight come to sweep her off her feet.

Confronted now with the reality of a charming but slightly damaged hero who willingly mucked stalls and fed her chickens, but still suffered bouts of dizziness and often forgot to wash his own dishes and pick his clothes up off the floor, she hardly knew what to think. He was a man, no more or less perfect than Uncle Luc-Antoine and her brothers. He would talk to Uncle for hours about obscure scientific references he remembered reading (though he couldn't remember where or when he'd read them), he picked Léon's brain about shipbuilding design, and he seemed fascinated by her experiments in improving the care and breeding of her horses. He also wanted to know everything that Sehoy, who by now had grown considerably warmer to Charlie, would tell him about the culture and beliefs of native Americans.

In short, he made himself useful, he went out of his way to blend into Lanier family life, and he remained an utter mystery.

Which perhaps explained how she came to be standing in the doorway of the kitchen storeroom, now Charlie's bedroom, on

a bright Saturday morning when everyone else had gone fishing. Charlie had nothing that hadn't been given him, of course, but he had somehow made the little room where he slept a reflection of himself. The bed, a simple pallet Fiona had made from an old quilt stuffed with pine straw, was rigidly squared away against the wall, with a woolen blanket folded at its foot, and at the head a down pillow fluffed and smoothed without a crease. The trunk full of Sullivan's clothes sat by the door, closed and latched with a piece of wire. The wire had been added since she loaned him the trunk.

Fiona hesitated, then crouched in front of the trunk to examine the knot in the wire. It went against everything in her moral code to breach Charlie's privacy. He was a guest in her home. She had given him the trunk, at least temporarily. She had no right to pry, no real reason to suspect him of any nefarious purpose. His grandfather had saved Uncle Rafa's life; therefore, their families were friends.

On the other hand, he was a citizen of England, with whom her country was at war. He could be lying to her, to them all, about what he did and did not remember.

She could look inside the trunk, just to make sure he hadn't hidden something dangerous there, put everything back exactly as it had been, and no one would be the wiser.

After all, the Bible was full of holy spies. Joseph. Caleb and Joshua. The men who went to see Rahab the harlot, and perhaps Rahab herself. She fingered the wire. Was that kind of spying different from what she was about to do?

Uncle Rafa had been an agent during the War for Independence. So had her mother and father and Aunt Lyse. Fiona had heard their stories of danger, excitement, and romance. But they had all been under direct orders from a military superior, the Spanish Governor General Gálvez, to be precise. Nobody had told Fiona to come in Charlie's room and break into a locked trunk.

This is my brother's trunk. I gave it to him.

She twisted the wire, unlooped it, threaded it backward, until it hung loose in the upper half of the latch. She hoped she could put it back the way it had been. Fingers shaking, she lifted the lid of the trunk and breathed in the man-smell of Sullivan's clothes combined with something uniquely Charlie.

The trunk was only half full. On one side lay the shirt and breeches Charlie had worn when she found him—laundered, mended, and folded. The other side contained a pair of plain dark stockings and a couple of white linen neckcloths on top of an extra shirt. Running her hand against the back of the trunk, she found a fine lace-edged handkerchief that she herself had embroidered for Sullivan's sixteenth birthday. Holding it to her face, she struggled against tears.

God, protect my brother.

Sniffing, she replaced the handkerchief and sat back. There was nothing of interest in the trunk, so she might as well close it up and—

"Fiona! Where are you?"

The lid of the trunk fell with a bang as her hand jerked in guilt. It was a woman's voice, but not Sehoy's, who wasn't here anyway—she'd gone fishing with the men.

Fiona fumbled with Charlie's improvised latch, desperate to get it back in its original configuration. "I'm in here—I'll be there in a moment! Who's there?"

"It's me, Maddy, and—and someone I brought with me. Where are you, Fi?" Maddy's voice now came from the kitchen, and Fiona could hear two sets of footsteps approaching the storeroom.

Why hadn't she thought to at least shut the door?

"I'm just getting something out of the storeroom! You can wait for me in the—" she looked around to find her cousin standing in the doorway with a tall, dark-haired, familiar-looking gentlemen peering over her shoulder "—parlor. Hullo, Desi. I haven't seen you in ages." She got up to hug Maddy. "Or you!" Shyly she offered her hand to Desi, who kissed it elegantly. He'd always had the nicest manners, even as a boy.

"It's been a long time," Desi said. "Maybe since Maddy's wedding?"

"Yes, my last week in Washington before Mama insisted I come home with the family." Fiona smiled at her cousin, who was as beautiful today as she'd been as an eighteen-year-old bride, though in a quieter way. "Sullivan was begging to go to sea, Papa missed his little duchess, and Mama said if I hadn't turned into a lady by then, I was hopeless!" They all laughed, and Fiona peered over Maddy's shoulder. "Where's little Elijah?"

"I left him with Rémy and Giselle's brood. Desi has been in town for a few days and asked about you, so I thought it would be a good day to visit. Are you busy?" Maddy glanced at the trunk with its dangling wire.

If the men came back from their fishing trip before Maddy and Desi left, the fat would be in the fire. Maddy would recognize Charlie.

"No! No, of course not, I was just putting some things away." Fiona took Maddy's hand and tugged her into the kitchen, and Desi followed. "Would you like coffee?"

"That would be lovely." Maddy seated herself at the big kitchen table, and Desi sat beside her. "I'm surprised you're not out with the horses on such a pretty day. Are the men all at the shipyard?"

"No, they closed it for the morning, and everybody went fishing." Fiona moved about the kitchen, filling the coffeepot with water and setting it on the stove to boil. She dumped a handful of coffee beans into the grinder. "Maddy, did you know that Sehoy Ferguson has come to stay with us for a while?"

"Yes, Desi told me he escorted her down to Mobile."

Fiona poured the fragrant ground beans into the boiling water. "Poor thing had quite a traumatic experience. I don't know how one ever gets over something like that. It's hard enough when—" She swallowed against a suddenly constricted throat.

"Oh, Fiona, I know. We've all had losses, and it's never easy." Maddy got up to pull Fiona into her arms. "First Uncle Simon and Aunt Daisy, then Sullivan's capture. My Stephen. And of course Desi lost his parents when he wasn't much older than Elijah."

Returning her cousin's embrace, Fiona closed her eyes. She sometimes forgot Desi wasn't actually Maddy's brother. Uncle Rafa and Aunt Lyse had taken the boy in when his mother and father—a fellow Spanish naval officer—had died in a fever epidemic.

After a quiet moment, Fiona sighed and pulled away, dabbing her eyes with the heels of her hands. "I'm sorry, I don't often get so weepy." She gave her cousin a wobbly smile. "It's really good to have another woman to cry with!"

"Oh, well, if I am *de trop*, I'll find something to do in the barn," Desi said on a teasing note.

"Don't be ridiculous. Besides, it's wonderful to converse with a man who can talk about something other than sailing and fishing." Fiona served coffee to her guests, then sat down at the end of the table with her own cup. "So tell me what brings you back to Mobile. You said you'd been at Horseshoe Bend."

"Yes. Interpreters were needed in the aftermath of the battle. General Jackson has taken command of the southern theater of war, and his plan is to remove the Indians west. The conflict with American settlers won't end until they're gone."

"But surely—"

"Fiona, it was inevitable. If we don't remove and resettle them, they will only continue to attack American forts and settlements. No one will be able to travel safely, including innocent traders and farmers and their families. The Indians don't understand property ownership, it's not in their culture." Desi looked away. "They are merciless in war, they have no code of honor in battle. I saw that with my own eyes."

Fiona thought of Sehoy's grief and bitterness. "I hate it. It's not fair."

Desi leaned forward and touched her hand. "I'm not a soldier, and it does no good to argue. It has happened. My job is to help negotiate peace between the nations. I understand why your little Sehoy doesn't like to forgive, but if she can bring herself to do so, she'll be happier in the long run. You might try to help her," he added gently.

"I'll try." Fiona forced a smile.

"Good girl." Desi patted her hand and picked up his coffee cup. "But you asked why I'm in Mobile. I was hoping I'd be able to speak with Léon and your uncle Rémy. They need to be aware that General Jackson is coming this way, to establish his command at Fort Charlotte. He also plans to garrison and refurbish Fort Bowyer here on the Point."

"What? I thought that rickety old fort was permanently abandoned last summer."

Maddy shook her head. "There's evidence the British are planning to attack Mobile and establish a base from which to take New Orleans. They're already gathering like jackals in Jamaica."

"They're coming here first?" Terror took hold of Fiona's

stomach like one of those feral dogs. "When? How long do we have to get ready?"

"No way to know," Desi said. "Sometime in September, maybe? But Jackson will arrive within the week, and you all will need to move into the fort. Or better yet, come with us back to Mobile. You'd be much safer there."

Fiona clenched her cup so hard she thought it might break. "This is my home! The boys need me, and I'm not leaving my horses. I can shoot a gun as well as any of them."

Maddy shook her head. "Of course you can, but don't be a goose, Fi. You won't be any good to anyone dead or—or—"

Fiona stood up, shaking. "I'll move into the fort if Uncle insists. But no British redcoat is going to force me out of Navy Cove." She wondered what Charlie would do when he found out soldiers from his country were prepared to invade her home. Would he keep quiet, sheltering with the Laniers inside Fort Bowyer, or would he slip away to join the British? She had to talk to him first, to let him know without being blindsided by the news.

The complications of the last few days had just become infinitely more twisted.

"Maddy, I have to tell you something," she said slowly. "And you're not going to like it."

The sun was beginning its pink-smeared descent into the western gulf as Charlie, lugging a net full of redfish, trudged up the beach path behind Léon and Oliver. Sehoy and Luc-Antoine brought up the rear, each with a couple of fishing poles and assorted tackle.

"Can't wait to see what Fiona's going to do with that." Oliver nodded over his shoulder at Charlie's reeking burden. "She's gotten to be a pretty decent cook." He laughed. "Though she like to have killed us all while she was learning."

"Now, boy, you be kind about your cousin," Luc-Antoine admonished. "She puts up with a lot, our duchess."

"I'll help her with the cleaning," Charlie said mildly. "Nobody should have to do that job alone."

Léon grunted. "Too bad we couldn't keep everything we caught. I'll take some of it to the Cove and see if I can sell it or trade for hardware. Nardo's always got something useful, and he's always hungry."

Within a few minutes the fishing crew reached the house and split up, Charlie to look for Fiona, and the others to take care of various errands before cleaning up for supper.

"Fiona!" Charlie shouted, depositing the fish in an iron pot in the yard. "Where are you? We brought in a big catch, and I need—"

"In here!" he heard her call from the barn. "I'm currying one of the mares."

He followed the sound of her voice and found her in a fading patch of light, crouched beside the palomino Spanish mustang Fiona planned to breed with Tully before he was sold. "She's a well-mannered little thing," he said, admiring the horse's Roman nose and fine, narrow muzzle.

"She is indeed. Did you have a good time on the water?"

"Yes, but I may be a bit burnt. My nose itches."

She peered around the mare and laughed. "More than a bit. You're going to peel."

"The story of my life." He grimaced, running his hands along the horse's pale gold flank. "What did you do today?"

He almost thought she wasn't going to answer. Finally she said, "I had more unexpected company."

"Really? Who?"

"My cousin Maddy." Fiona got to her feet, led the horse to the barn door, and released her. The mare trotted toward the pasture where the other horses grazed.

"Maddy?" Was that a name he was supposed to recognize? Fiona stepped back into the barn but stayed in the shadows near the stalls. "Yes, you know, you met her whole family with me in England. I told you about her, that first day I found you on the beach. You don't remember that?"

"I remember riding home behind you and then waking up with a crashing hangover." He hesitated, then walked over to lean against the stall door beside her. "Would she remember me, do you think?"

"I'm not sure. You've changed a good deal since then, and Maddy was preoccupied with being the belle of the neighborhood. The reason you and I got acquainted was because you were rusticating, and I was considered a child. I was bored one evening, discovered the library, and found you there looking up some awful chemical concoction or other . . . We went to the kitchen to try it out and nearly blew up the larder." Her laughter was infectious.

"I imagine the cook was anxious to get rid of us."

"I thought she was going to explode herself and create an even more colorful mess."

He peered at her. "Huh?"

"She was a redhead with cheeks like tomatoes."

He laughed. "Ah. But likely your cousin wouldn't recognize me after all these years, right?"

"I almost told her about you anyway."

He froze. "Why would you do that? You insisted that I tell no one I'm English."

"Charlie, I—I like you, and I don't wish you any harm. But having you here is getting more and more dangerous every day.

72

Maddy brought a family friend named Desi Palomo with her. Desi is a civilian interpreter for General Andrew Jackson."

"And?"

"And he came to prepare in advance of the general making Mobile his headquarters. Charlie, they're going to garrison both Fort Charlotte in Mobile and Fort Bowyer right here on the Point. There will be militia and regular soldiers swarming all over the area. If it's discovered I've been hiding a British citizen in plain sight, I'll be suspected of treason!"

He hadn't let himself consider that inconvenient possibility. He scratched his itchy nose. "I don't want to bring trouble on your family. You've all been kind to me, even Léon. My headaches are less frequent, so perhaps I should move along, possibly head for Pensacola. I could hunker down there with the Spanish until my memory comes back."

"I hate to say this, but you've got to consider the possibility that it won't." Fiona's voice was strained, and he could feel the tension in her shoulder against his. "Charlie, you could always go home. The people there love you. There might even be a doctor who could help."

"Are you trying to get rid of me?" He'd tried for humor, but feared he might have merely sounded pathetic. "I mean—just because I can't remember why I left home doesn't mean there wasn't a good reason for it. What if I'm wanted for some crime in England, and I walk right into trouble?"

"Now you're being silly. You can't change your basic nature, and you know you're a good person."

"Bat guano notwithstanding, I'd like to think so." He was quiet for a moment. "Fiona, do you want me to leave?"

"Do you want to leave?"

She'd turned the question back on him, and honesty was hard. He'd never been one to beg for help if he could avoid it. He also didn't like admitting how attached he'd gotten to Fiona and her merry band of fisherman-shipbuilders. To be perfectly frank with himself, he was mainly attached to Fiona—her bright, innocent way of looking at the world, her wholesome beauty, her infectious laughter, her ability to see past the way he hid his feelings behind teasing.

He dipped his head. "No, I do not want to leave. I don't know if I ever had friends before, but I know that I have at least one now."

She stilled. "Yes, you do."

The air vibrated between them. He would have kissed her, in fact his throat ached with the wanting. But what if there was already a woman in his life? He would not take advantage of Fiona's affections when he could be already committed to someone else. "Thank you," he forced himself to say lightly. "I'll stay—for now. But you'll tell me when I must go, yes?"

"Yes, of course."

Did she sound disappointed that she hadn't been kissed? His heart whistled a little tune as he stepped back. "Good. Now let's clean and fry a couple of those fish for supper. And you can teach me how to make hushpuppies." He took her hand and pulled her out of the barn, laughing.

5

Leaning on the rail of her front porch, Maddy watched the band and flag bearers pass by but still kept an eagle eye on Elijah, who seemed determined to launch himself headfirst into the shrubbery below in his excitement over the spectacle.

In the years since the Spanish invaded and conquered the Gulf Coast near the end of the American War for Independence, Mobile had dwindled to little more than a sleepy backwater of desultory commerce. In May of 1812, the city had been quietly annexed into the Mississippi Territory, though Spanish military authorities did not evacuate until nearly a year later, when American Major General James Wilkinson arrived to boot them out. Wilkinson established his command at Fort Charlotte, bringing along his young aide, Lieutenant Colonel Stephen Burch—whose wife and little son happily returned to the city of her mother's birth. When the general (and by extension Stephen) was abruptly summoned to the Canadian theater of war, Maddy remained in the bosom of her family while her husband performed his duty in the Frozen North.

Now the onslaught of Andrew Jackson's army, a good portion of them Tennessee militia, brought Mobile's citizens out to observe the soldiers parading toward their temporary encampment at the western outskirts of the city.

Maddy's heart twisted as the blue-uniformed soldiers passed by, followed by the uneven ranks of buckskin-clad militia. Stephen had used to ride at the front of these parades in the company of his fellow officers. General Wilkinson had been a crafty sort of leader, adept at currying the favor of important men despite rumors of his machinations with the Spanish, and later with the traitor Aaron Burr. Twice Wilkinson had been court-martialed but acquitted on lack of evidence. Because there had been something . . . well, slimy about the man, Maddy had wondered if some of the accusations of Wilkinson's traitorous dealings could have been true. But Stephen would never speak ill of his superior officer and cautioned her to hold her tongue as well.

Still, she couldn't help blaming Wilkinson for Stephen's death. The general had lost his command for his ineptitude in battle and then exiled himself to Mexico—and good riddance.

Thoughts drifting, she jumped at the sound of a shrill whistle from across the street.

"Maddy! Over here!"

She spotted a carriage just beyond the dwindling parade, its driver waving his hat.

"Desi!" She waved back. Since the day he'd escorted her down the bay to visit the Laniers, she'd seen little of him. As Jackson's agent to the Indians and a skilled translator, he had been busy with preparations for the general's arrival in Mobile.

As the last of the soldiers passed by, Desi set the carriage in motion, crossed the street, and pulled up in Uncle Rémy's carriageway. He jumped down from the open chaise and tied it to a hitching post, smiling as he crossed the yard and ducked under a low-hanging limb of the old oak tree. "I was hoping I'd see you while I'm in town this afternoon."

"Mr. Uncle Desi!" Elijah bolted toward Desi and grabbed him by the hand to tow him toward the porch. "Did you know I made a fort? You can play with me in it!"

Desi grinned down at him. "Can I? I'd like nothing better, once your mama gives me leave. We don't want to hurt her feelings."

"She won't mind. She said boys need to play outside a lot."

Desi's lips quirked. "Truer words were never spoken."

Maddy came to the steps, hands on hips. "Elijah, we must first offer our guest refreshment. You may show Uncle Desi the fort later, if he has time."

"Can we have lemonade? With lots of sugar?"

"Yes, and a tea cake, if you will play in the yard while Mama and Uncle Desi visit here on the porch."

As Elijah launched into a wild dance of joy, Maddy smiled at Desi, then whisked into the kitchen. When she returned with the promised lemonade and cakes on a tray, she found Desi and Elijah seated on the top step, heads close together as they studied a tiny lizard cupped in Desi's big hand. She stopped in the doorway, tears welling on a wave of emotion. Though she tried not to dwell on her own loss, how often had she brought to the Lord her little son's need for a strong man's example to follow? And here was the dearest friend of her childhood, come back into her life at a time when she perhaps needed him most.

The depth of her joy in his coming was almost frightening. He wouldn't stay forever. There was a war going on, and he was committed to duties that would take him far from here. What if she and Elijah got so attached to Desi that his leaving would create even more pain?

What if, what if?

Giving herself a little shake, she stepped out onto the porch. "Here we are! Just one tea cake," she admonished as Elijah scrambled to his feet. "Dinner will be ready before too long."

The three of them munched on cakes and discussed lemonade and forts, Desi and Maddy on the swing and Elijah seated cross-legged below them on the floor. With predictable speed, Elijah finished his treat and went to look for the lizard, which had had the good sense to escape through a crack between the boards of the step.

Desi leaned back and draped his arm across the top of the swing behind Maddy's shoulders. He'd removed his coat in deference to the heat, and she was acutely aware of the bulk of his shoulder muscles, the pleasant scent of his clothes. Odd that a man she'd known all her life could create this sudden uncomfortable flutter under her ribs.

"How are you managing without Stephen, Maddy? I hope you won't think me impertinent to ask."

He still seemed to have an uncanny ability to read her thoughts. Aware of his brown eyes warm on her face, she looked down at her hands pleating her skirt. "You're . . . family, Desi, you can ask anything you wish. Of course I miss Stephen, but we're getting along fine. Uncle Rémy helps me keep things running when I have a problem with the house, and Aunt Giselle takes Elijah off my hands when I need to focus on sewing projects." She looked up and smiled at his obvious concern. "And I have plenty of dress orders to keep us afloat. My work is in high demand."

"That I can imagine." His gaze wandered from her face to take in details of her dress, all the way down to her kid slippers peeking from under the flounced hem. "You are a beautiful woman, Maddy." His lips curved. "The dress is nice too."

Something contemplative in his eyes made her stammer, "I—I

hope you'll stop to see us often. That is—I'm sure you're busy with your duties for the general. How long does he think it will be before the British arrive on our doorstep, so to speak?"

He looked amused, but let her turn the subject. "As I told Fiona the other day, even the general can't say for sure, and he's got spies everywhere. We've begun reconstruction of the two forts in hopes that we'll be ready in time."

Maddy nodded. "Desi, I've been thinking about that conversation with Fiona the other day. What do you suppose she was about to tell me, when she changed her mind and asked if we could find out what happened to the rest of Sehoy's family? Fiona is generally an open book, but there was something very odd in her manner that day."

"I thought the same thing. She kept looking out the window." Desi shook his head. "You know her better than I, though. Do you suppose she's developed an affair with one of the men on the construction crew at the shipyard?"

"Fiona?" Maddy laughed. "The only male she is in love with is of the equine species."

"You might be surprised," Desi said lightly, setting the swing in motion. "Like the British, the tender passions are often quite unpredictable."

⌣

SEPTEMBER 1, 1814
NAVY COVE

Sehoy didn't think she'd seen anything so beautiful as the long, straight white oak timbers the carpenters laid along the hull of the USS *Declaration*. Two weeks ago she wouldn't have known white oak from yellow pine, but during her stay with the Lanier family, she'd grown conversant with a myriad of shipbuilding terms that had at first seemed as foreign as the babel of languages spoken by the laborers.

This morning she'd risen early to help Fiona prepare breakfast for the men, then the two of them mucked stalls, tended the garden, and began the process of canning vegetables too plenteous to be eaten. Chores completed, Sehoy left Fiona to her horses and went into the house to tuck her drawing supplies into the beaded satchel her mother had woven for her last birthday. Munching on a slice of sugar-cured ham sandwiched in a leftover biscuit, she left her shoes in the house and walked barefoot down to the beach.

She sat in the sand now, in the shallow shade of the parasol Fiona had loaned her, trying to capture with her charcoals the energy, detail, and sheer size of the ship construction process. She picked out Léon, standing atop a scaffold near the stern, shouting instructions to a crew who were making their precarious way up a ramp with timbers balanced across their brawny brown shoulders. Oliver, tall and lanky, his head covered pirate-fashion in a red kerchief, was one of the youngest. Sehoy stuck her pencil behind her ear and sat forward, squinting against the sun until he reached the top.

Despite the men's cheerful nonchalance about working at such dizzying heights, accidents happened, and wishing wouldn't prevent them. The world was not safe.

When Oliver safely reached the top, she flipped the pages of her drawing book backward to study the portrait of him she'd sketched yesterday evening as the family sat on the porch after the evening meal, watching the sun go down and listening to Uncle Luc-Antoine tell stories. Oliver was the quiet one, rarely contributing to the conversation but quick to notice if one's teacup became empty or if the mosquitoes became too much of a nuisance.

She'd drawn him in three-quarter profile as he sat on the top step, leaning back against the porch rail, his eyes following a pair of osprey in flight above the barn. He had such a nice profile, his brow and nose cleanly limned under the mop of auburn hair, his mouth and chin firm for a boy of his age. For all his gentle nature, he'd been given responsibility early on, he understood hard physical labor, and the intelligence in his expression came as a result of the sharpening influence of his father and older cousins.

The Laniers were a remarkable family, loyal and industrious in providing for one another and their community, but welcoming to strangers—as evidenced by their taking in Charlie Kincaid and Sehoy herself. Her attachment to them all had grown deeper daily, and the horror of the massacre was beginning to fade, just a bit. The sounds of the battle still jumped into her brain at unexpected moments, in the crack of thunder or with the falling of timbers, and she sometimes wept in secret with the longing for her mother and father. But it happened less often every day.

Staying busy helped. Finding beautiful things to draw helped.

In an odd way, even Fiona's reading of the Bible out loud every morning during breakfast helped. Sehoy hadn't grown up with much spiritual training, but she found that the old-fashioned words in the big leather-bound book nestled into a previously unmarked place in her mind and heart. Comfort. Reassurance. Structure. The Man, Jesus, who taught and healed and set an example of sacrificial love.

Her finger traced the strong line of Oliver's brow on the page of her sketch pad. He clearly worshiped Jesus and loved the Book. Perhaps its words were true.

Charlie stood at the highest point of the half-constructed ship's upper deck, looking out to sea. Across Mobile Point the Gulf of Mexico glittered in the sun, all but taunting him to come over and play. The building of the ship had for a few days scratched the itch of inactivity forced by his injury, but now that he felt stronger, now that he could run and swim and work for hours at a time without triggering one of the crashing migraines, a somehow familiar restlessness had begun to plague him. Something about the vast stretch of water, just out of reach, sang a siren song.

Should he leave? Should he take himself far away, leaving Fiona to her family? Every day he stayed he became more entangled with them all. Even the standoffish Sehoy had begun to soften toward him, and Léon had stopped looking daggers at him.

Which was one reason he accepted the backbreaking labor assigned to him with equanimity. The harder he worked, the more the Lanier men relaxed around him, the less guarded their conversation. He was learning that Léon carried a deal of anger toward his rascally middle brother Judah, who had abandoned the family fold in favor of illegal pirating activities, and Léon worried with unspoken depth about the youngest, Sullivan. With war raging in Europe as well as the Americas, nations wrangled over territories and international commerce, and Charlie's countrymen had taken to conscripting American sailors for service aboard His Majesty's undermanned naval vessels. Charlie could understand the frustration and anger of merchants who wanted the freedom to deliver their goods to market.

He couldn't settle on his place in this gnarly problem, but gut level, he knew running away wouldn't help.

So stay he would.

Turning his back on the Gulf to descend the scaffolding and fetch another load of timbers, he encountered Luc-Antoine Lanier, the ever-present pipe clenched between his teeth, swinging onto the decking with the lithe motion of a much younger man.

"Boy, you gonna fall overboard if you don't pay attention." Luc-Antoine removed the pipe and gestured in the direction of the Gulf. "Any British sails out there?"

"No, sir."

Luc-Antoine pulled a small brass spyglass from his back pocket and tossed it to Charlie. "Here, take a look with this."

Charlie extended the tubing and put it to his left eye. The panorama of ocean under sky jumped into focus as he adjusted the lens, and a raw exhilaration nearly burst his chest open. In his bones he knew he was born to this, perching on platforms at breath-stealing heights, scanning the skyline for sails in the distance.

At the moment there was nothing there. "Just sunshine, water, and air," he said, collapsing the glass and handing it back to Luc-Antoine. "What will you do when they come?"

"You mean what will *we* do?" Luc-Antoine gave him a sardonic look. "You're one of us now. Aren't you?"

"Of course," Charlie said quickly. "I meant you specifically. Are you going to join the defense? Move into the fort?"

"When I was a boy, I survived for weeks outside Mobile with my pére and a black slave, living off what we could catch in the river and the woods—this while the Spanish and English were shooting at each other over our heads. I'm going to defend my home come what may, and no British flag—or cannon, for that matter—is gonna make me turn tail and run."

"I wouldn't have thought you would, sir, I just meant—" What had he meant? Digging in deeper wouldn't help anything.

"What was it like in those days? This part of the coast was British-held, wasn't it? And the Spanish had their eye on it?"

Luc-Antoine nodded. "We French folk got caught in the middle, and picking a side wasn't easy. My uncle had been executed by the Spanish for stirring up a rebellion, but my grandfather chose to remain neutral and managed to hold on to the family property. When the Continentals declared independence, Spain secretly supported them with arms and ammunition and gold. My sister Lyse married a Spaniard—who turned my father and my brother Simon as well—and sealed that alliance for us." Luc-Antoine grinned. "We've had a carousel of nations circling through here, and you can see why." He gestured toward the rolling expanse of the gulf to the south, and the beautiful calm bay to the north. "The port's small, but you can't find better fishing or a milder general climate. And we've all the timber you need for shipbuilding."

Charlie found it hard to believe the British had simply given it up and slunk away. "What happened to make the Spaniards cede?"

With a skeptical look, as if wondering how Charlie could possibly be ignorant of such recent history, Luc-Antoine shrugged. "Jefferson worked an under-the-table deal with Napoleon, whose brother was on the Spanish throne at the time. Once he was in office, Madison sent the army here to garrison the fort in Mobile, but they've been gone since June. Speaking of under-the-table deals, I see the way you look at my niece." He seemed determined to jolt Charlie into revealing some prevarication. "You'd best not get any ideas in that direction until we know you better. And if I find out you've dishonored her in any way, you'll be a dead man." The tone was matter-of-fact.

Charlie understood he had been duly warned—and for Fiona's sake, he appreciated the older man's protectiveness. But if Luc-Antoine thought Charlie was going to back away just on his say-so, he was fair and far off. "I wouldn't have it any other way, sir."

Luc-Antoine nodded. "You're a smart boy, I reckon." Suddenly he lifted the spyglass to his eye and trained it on the western end of the isthmus. "Look there. Small boats coming in at Fort Bowyer. But the uniforms aren't British." He handed the glass to Charlie again.

"No, they're not," Charlie said slowly. "Looks like the Americans are back."

⟋⟍

SEPTEMBER 12, 1814
FORT BOWYER, MOBILE POINT

Fiona had grown up on her mother and father's stories of the Revolutionary War—some frightening, some thrilling, some downright funny. Uncle Rafa's proposal of marriage to Aunt Lyse to keep her from being arrested as a traitor to the British crown, and their ongoing argument about whether it had been a "real" betrothal was a favorite. She also loved her father's romantic tale of sneaking into Fort Charlotte to rescue his beloved Daisy from her room in officers' quarters, right out from under *her* British father's nose.

But this business of being swept from one's home into the crude shelter of a roughly constructed fort bore little of romance and much of inconvenience and sheer terror.

Truth be told, a large part of her concern was for her horses. The first bombs had exploded this evening at sunset, while the family sat outside on the porch listening to Uncle Luc-Antoine play his guitar. The younger men jumped to their feet, while poor Sehoy shrieked, hands clapped over her ears and eyes squeezed shut. Fiona grabbed Sehoy close, trying to comfort her, while above the racket she could hear the horses screaming in fear.

"What is it, do you think?" Fiona asked Léon, who had jumped down from the porch and stood in listening position, scanning the southern skyline.

Mouth grim, her brother glanced at her. "We're under attack, so we'd best ride for the fort as fast as we can. Oliver, go to the barn and saddle horses for the girls. The rest of us will gather guns and ammunition and follow. Fiona, you've got time to pack only essentials before you go."

Essentials? Fiona hurried to obey, hampered by Sehoy, who was all but catatonic with fear. By the time the two of them ducked into the barn, each carrying a small trunk filled with personal items, the sun had gone down and explosions lit the night sky along the shoreline.

Oliver had already saddled Bonnie for her and Dusty for Sehoy, and the other men were getting ready to ride by lamplight. Léon would take Washington, and the other three men had each chosen a mount from the remaining herd. When Fiona demanded to know what would become of the rest of the horses, Léon gave her an incredulous look.

"They can fend for themselves. There's plenty of grass and water."

"But—but—the guns! They'll be so frightened!"

"We'll come back to check on them as soon as it's safe."

"But the goats and chickens—"

"Fiona!" Léon's formidable brows snapped together. "Get on that horse and ride for the fort. I'm not arguing with you—"

Charlie stepped between them. "I'll stay long enough to settle the animals. Léon's right. The British will start landing before long, and you girls mustn't be here. Some of the soldiers won't be gentlemen—do you understand what I mean?"

She met his eyes, saw genuine concern and fear for her there. And something else that broke through, as her brother's shouts would never have done. She caught her breath on a little hiccup. "Yes, of course. I don't mean to be a baby."

"Good girl." He cupped her face in his palm, brushing her cheek with his thumb. "I'll come to you as quickly as I can. And you're not a baby at all—in fact you're one of the bravest people I've ever met." He bent to give her a boost into the saddle.

"I don't know how you'd know that," she said with a trembling smile. "You don't even remember all the people you've ever met."

Charlie grinned up at her, seemingly oblivious to Léon glowering behind his back. "And for that unkind remark, you owe me a kiss and a sincere apology—which I shall collect at a more opportune time." He handed her the reins and stepped back, allowing Luc-Antoine to lead the small caravan of horses out of the barn at a trot.

Now, as the night wore on, she huddled with Sehoy in a brick bunker in the center of the fort, listening to the American cannons firing shot after shot out toward the four warships spread across the entrance to the bay. And the British fired back. If they hit Fort Bowyer's powder magazine, it would explode, and the fort would fall to the enemy. Periodically a small shot would whiz overhead, find a target, and a soldier would cry out.

Fiona had never known such all-encompassing terror. How many had been wounded or killed? Had her brother, her uncle, her cousin been hit? Dear God, Charlie? How could he bear to remain here while his countrymen shot at him? Did he think of them that way?

"Fiona, are you praying?"

She'd barely heard Sehoy's frightened whisper. In the darkness she lifted her head from her knees. "Yes. There's nothing else we can do. And it's the best thing we can do." It wasn't exactly a lie, though fear had dampened her spirit.

"Will you teach me how?"

"Oh, Sehoy." Fiona took her cousin's hand, found it cold and trembling. "I just talk to God like any other friend—except I know he already knows my thoughts. He knows how afraid we are, and he will give us courage."

"But I don't know God like you do. I feel there's some spirit bigger than me, but that frightens me too."

"That's why God sent Jesus, so we would have a friend who knows how we feel. He faced pain and loneliness and fear and death, and yet promised not to leave us comfortless. I'm not afraid to die because he's right here with us."

"Does . . . Oliver know Jesus like that?"

"I'm sure he does." Oliver, after all, was a very spiritual, tenderhearted boy. Uncle Luc had taught him well.

"I can know Jesus too? I want to." Sehoy's voice was eager.

"Yes, just tell him so. The Bible says if we come to him like a little child, he'll make us new."

Sehoy pressed her forehead against her knees as Fiona had done earlier. She spoke hesitantly, clutching Fiona's hand. "It's me, God, Sehoy. Nobody important, but . . . Fiona says it's all right to talk to you. I want to know you, and I want you to know me. Mostly I want you to make me brave and keep the bombs away from Oliver. And the other men. Please please please keep them all safe and make the British go away. Oh . . ."

Then she was sobbing, and Fiona had to finish the ragged little prayer as she wrapped her arms around Sehoy. God was listening, of course.

Of course he was. And Charlie *would* be safe. And Léon and Luc-Antoine and Oliver and the soldiers.

At some point, Charlie realized as he shoveled powder into a cannon, he was going to stand before his father and his grandfather, both British naval officers, and give an account of the day he stood inside an American fort and helped sling cannonballs at four of His Britannic Majesty's warships.

But until that day came, he saw no way out of the quandary in which he found himself. He must do everything in his power to protect a young woman he had come to care for deeply and in a remarkably short amount of time. And Fiona's relatives, who mattered to her more than life, must be guarded as well.

He glanced to his left, where Oliver stood transfixed as a mortar screamed toward them. He bodily snatched the boy to the ground just in the nick of time. "Keep your head down, you idiot!" he shouted over the explosion that rocked the ground beneath them.

"Like you did?" Oliver sat up, pushing Charlie off him, his young face so pale the freckles stood out like gold dust.

Another grenade went off above them, setting the sky aflame. Knocked backward by the concussion, Charlie lay gasping for air, head throbbing like a bass drum, vision coming and going. Shards of pain sent him in and out of consciousness.

Thunder rolled—or was it cannon fire?—and bombs zigzagged overhead. Wait, no, it was only lightning. At any moment he would be swamped by the waves that crashed against the ship, rocking it all but sideways, then slamming it back into an ocean trough. He was a strong swimmer, never afraid of the water, but the fury of this storm was demonic, the wind howling against the sails, breaking the masts into timber as if they were matchsticks. Nobody could survive this—even Charlie Kincaid, who everybody said possessed the nine lives of a cat.

Something dragged him under, blackness took him.

He came to, pinned under a barrel. He struggled to free himself, shouted for help. "Easton, we're going down. Tell the captain—" Tell the captain what? No one knew his real identity. "If you make it to Pensacola, tell the admiral—"

He went under again.

And came back clutching the oilskin pouch against his bare chest. "Don't let anyone take this," he choked out to nobody in particular. Death was coming again. He'd seen it before, in all its terrifying blankness, but he'd always come back. Grandfa said nobody in heaven was ready for Charlie and laughed before caning him.

But perhaps the time had arrived after all. He'd always expected to drown. Or die in a sword fight above decks. Not expire from this crushing, sickening explosion of pain in his head.

He rolled sideways and was sick and, to his astonishment, felt a gentle hand on his forehead.

How had his mama gotten aboard? "No, it's not safe," he mumbled, dropping onto his back again. "You can't be here. Go home and tell Grandfa I'm sorry."

"I will," she whispered close to his ear, wiping his face with a damp cloth. "But the battle is over. They've drawn back and you're safe. We all are."

"Drawn back?" There had been a battle after all, which explained the shouts and explosions. But why could he not see? He strained to look, twisting his head. "Oh, God, not my sight."

"Shhh. Close your eyes and rest, Charlie, I'm sure it will come back. You only fainted, after you tackled poor Oliver. But thank God you did, because he's alive." She began to cry, the tears dropping onto his face.

"Who is Oliver?" he asked before losing consciousness again.

6

Fiona sat back, one hand still on Charlie's forehead, the other smearing away the tears that kept falling. He would waken again. Of course he would. He was simply out of his head with pain, and his body had taken the natural course, sending him into unconsciousness.

But at any moment, her brother or one of the other men would return, and if Charlie started raving about meeting admirals in Pensacola again, the fat would be truly in the fire. The oil lamp by the door flickered as she stared at the oilskin bag Charlie held against his chest. There was something dangerous inside it, something he didn't want anyone to see. Perhaps she could get a look at it before he came to.

She looked around. An eerie quiet prevailed over the fort, broken intermittently by the soldiers calling to one another as they recovered from the battle. The stench of sulfur set Fiona's stomach roiling. Outside the bunker, she could hear Sehoy tending to the flesh wound in Oliver's calf, the two of them murmuring quietly.

While the battle raged, she and Sehoy had clung together for what seemed like hours, praying as the bombs whizzed overhead. Then that massive explosion out on the water had set Sehoy to screaming as if the world had come to an end—which, to her mind, it probably had. Fiona simply held her friend, not knowing what to expect, until the door of the bunker suddenly slammed open.

"Fiona!" Backlit by the torches along the ramparts, smoke and ash floated behind Léon's blackened face as he peered in. "Come here quickly, I need you to—Sehoy, stop it! It's over. They're backing off."

Sehoy's screams wrenched off. "Wh—what?"

"I said they're gone. We hit a powder store on one of the British ships, and it went up in flames. They've backed off to lick their wounds—hopefully for good."

Something in her brother's face brought Fiona to her feet, dread twisting her insides. "What is it, Léon? What else happened?"

"We need a nurse. The surgeon is busy with a couple of severe wounds, and—never mind, just come with me."

She looked at Sehoy. "Are you coming?"

Visibly collecting herself, Sehoy rose, and they both followed Léon to the barracks that had been designated as the infirmary.

Fiona had grown up with three brothers, and the sights and sounds of bloody injury generally didn't faze her. But she'd never seen the aftermath of battle. This . . . this was brutal. The surgeon was busy binding up the amputated arm of a young soldier, who had passed out cold on the surgical table. She didn't want to see it, but neither could she turn away.

Then Léon put his arm around her shoulders and pulled her on, through the infirmary toward an interior door. He opened the door and pushed her inside a smaller room, where a dark-haired young man lay writhing in apparent agony upon an army blanket.

Charlie. She dropped to her knees beside the pallet.

"Take care of him, Fi. He saved Oliver's life." Léon ducked out of the room.

Fiona quickly examined Charlie to ascertain the location and depth of his injuries. A trickle of blood dripped from his left ear. Other than that, she saw nothing that could have caused such wretched discomfort.

For over an hour now, she'd anxiously tended him, bathing his head as he'd flung about, eyes closed, gripped by some horrid nightmare. At first he was incoherent, apparently battling the elements in some terrific storm, but gradually his words became all too clear—until he fainted.

What admiral was he supposed to meet? Had he been on his way to Pensacola when the storm that cast him ashore at Navy Cove stole his memory? Or had he been lying to her about that the whole time? Perhaps he had been spying on her and her family, and then on the soldiers in Fort Bowyer.

But Léon said Charlie had saved Oliver's life. Would he do that if he were a spy?

She had to know what was in that bag. Curling her fingers around his, she pried them away and moved his hand to rest on his chest. He lay relaxed, those heavy dark lashes fanned above his cheekbones, lips parted on shallow breaths.

Tugging at the drawstring, she watched to make sure his eyes stayed closed. When the mouth of the bag came open, she poked her fingers inside and withdrew a small scrap of parchment. Unrolling it, she scanned it.

Nonsense, a mishmash of letters separated into incomprehensible words—a coded message. She spent a minute trying to memorize it, but gave up frustrated. Now what? She had no materials with which to copy it down. If he were awake and lucid, she would confront him. But would he tell her the truth?

There was so much about him that she admired—the refusal to accept weakness in himself, the humor, the sheer masculine confidence. She tried to imagine what her father would have thought of him. Papa had been so protective, worse even than Léon. He would probably have tossed Charlie back into the ocean, broken head or no.

She smoothed Charlie's hair, touched the jagged, still-raw scar above his eyebrow. Familiar yet alien. He tugged her heart in ways she barely understood.

Without warning, his eyes opened, narrowed and dangerous, and he clamped her wrist in one hand, wrapping the other arm about her waist. Before she could blink, he rolled, and she was pinned beneath him.

"Charlie, no! It's me, Fiona!" Her heart thumped hard under his chest, and his face was so close she could see the striations in his mismatched eyes. His face was pale, so pale that the scar stood out like blood on a white sheet. "Charlie, look at me— don't you know me?"

He stared at her for several heartbeats, body rigid, a muscle in his jaw jumping. Then his mouth softened, the wild look in his eyes fading to confusion. "Fiona?" He released her wrist to touch her face. "What happened? Why are you . . ."

She knew she should push him away. Words would not form in her brain, let alone leave her mouth, and as his eyes went smoky with longing, she realized he thought she'd come to his room. And he was going to kiss her and she was going to let him, because she wanted it too. Sure enough his lips brushed hers softly, and she kissed him back even though she didn't really know how. Of course he was a good teacher, Charlie did everything well, and by the time her delinquent morals began to clamor for attention, her lips were bruised and her insides were melting, and things were beginning to get out of hand.

What had her brother been *thinking*, leaving her alone in here with him? Even knocked more than halfway into the next world and bleeding from the ear, Charlie Kincaid was a dangerous man.

She shoved at his chest and wrenched her mouth from his. "Charlie, stop it! I mean it! Léon could come back any minute!"

He grunted and kissed her under the ear. "I knew you'd be good at this."

And that made her want to laugh. "I assure you it's beginner's luck. Would you please get *off* me? I can't breathe."

He put a fraction of an inch between them. "Better?"

"Not much. *Move!*" She got a hand free and whopped the side of his head.

He yelped and rolled to his back. "That hurts!"

She sat up, yanking her skirt out from under his hip. "If you weren't already sufficiently injured, I'd grab somebody's rifle and put another crack in your skull."

"Now that's just plain mean."

"And you're a wretch, taking advantage of me like that."

"Clearly you can take care of yourself. My ears are still ringing." He put a hand to his head. "What happened to Oliver? I think I got him out of the way in time."

"You did. Canister shot caught him, but just a flesh wound. He'll not lose the leg."

"*Leg*, Fiona?" He smirked at her. "I didn't think ladies used that word."

She sighed and put her head in her hands. "I never claimed to be a real lady. As I have just demonstrated. You will please forget that disgraceful episode."

"I never make stupid promises. In fact, I plan to go to sleep thinking about it every night henceforth." He sat up carefully, but his grin was cocky. "And I wager you will remember it as well."

"I'll remember a lot more than that." She opened her hand to show him the roll of parchment. "I want you to tell me what this is and what it means. No more games, Charlie. What are you doing here?"

⌒

September 13, 1814
Mobile

Maddy had begun her day like any other, rising early to feed the chickens, sending Elijah to collect the eggs and take a few next door to the Laniers. Once the household chores were done, she and Elijah had sat down to lunch. By midafternoon, she couldn't help wondering what had happened to Desi, who had developed the daily habit of dropping by for a short visit between errands for General Jackson. Not that Desi was required to inform her of his every move. Still, slightly uneasy, she sent Elijah to play with his older cousins and walked toward the waterfront for news. If anyone would know what was going on, it would be Brigitte Guillory, who helped her husband Armand run the old tavern and inn called Burelle's.

Royal Street was aswarm with foot and carriage traffic this afternoon, an unusually long streak of dry, temperate weather bringing shoppers and merchants out in droves. Maddy hurried along the uneven sidewalk, past the old Spanish hospital and the schoolhouse where Aunt Daisy used to teach, to fetch up in front of the inn's deep front porch. Fortunately, Brigitte herself came outside just then, carrying a tray of drinks, and began to serve a group of gentlemen gathered around the table closest to the door.

Maddy hurried up the steps. "Brigitte! Could I talk to you for a moment, please?"

"Maddy! Good day to you, dearie!" Brigitte lowered the

empty tray and caught Maddy in a brief hug. "Have you heard from your mama recently? I do wish she and Rafael would come for a visit again."

"I had a letter from her a few weeks ago, after they made a trip to New York. I doubt they'll make it down here before next year . . . With so much harassment from the British and their Indian allies, it's not safe to travel."

"My stars, that's true." Brigitte pulled a towel off her shoulder to flick dust off the swing hung at one end of the porch. "Here, sit down and tell me what brings you to town. I need a break from all these men and their tobacco spitting and coffee spilling."

Maddy sat, smoothing her skirts. "Unusual number of people in town today," she said, trying not to sound as anxious as she felt. "I can't help wondering what is brewing."

"Trouble, I'm afraid." Brigitte's face creased with worry. "Last night the general sailed down to inspect progress at Fort Bowyer. On the way, he met a boat coming up from the Point, bringing a message that the fort had just come under siege by four British warships. A party of Indians and marines had landed for an attack."

Maddy felt as if she'd been punched in the stomach. In all likelihood, Desi had gone with the general. She closed her eyes. She could not go through this again. And what about her cousins and Uncle Luc-Antoine, down at Navy Cove? They would be in peril as well.

Brigitte gripped Maddy's clenched hands. "Now, the general is no fool. He turned right around and returned to Mobile. He and his staff pulled together a company of infantry and sent them to reinforce the poor fellows down at Fort Bowyer."

Maddy forced her eyes open. A soldier's widow knew how to face bad news. "There's something else, isn't there? What are you not telling me?"

Brigitte looked away. "Well . . . the relief force came back this morning, saying there was a great explosion just before dawn. The fort is in trouble. In fact, it's almost certainly lost. People say the British may attack Mobile next."

～

FORT BOWYER

Fiona spent the entire day after the battle helping to dress wounds. As she and Sehoy followed the surgeon from soldier to soldier in the little infirmary, the conversation with Charlie kept rolling about in her head like marbles on a crooked table.

She held up a young infantryman's head to take a sip of water from the ladle in her hand, all the while trying to convince herself Charlie had been telling the truth. He claimed he didn't know what the cipher meant. If he'd written it, he'd done so during one of the blanks in his memory. Yes, he admitted he was a British sailor, probably an officer, judging by the hallucinations he'd experienced during the battle last night. But he was in no shape to leave Mobile Point now, had no way to do so, even should he so desire.

Closing her eyes, she pictured his face when she'd confronted him with the coded message. Bland inquiry. He'd plucked it from her fingers, scanned it, handed it back to her with a smile, as if it were a shopping list. *What? What does that have to do with me?*

Angrily she'd snatched the pouch lying against his chest and stuffed the parchment into it. *You carried this around all this time and never wondered why?*

Of course he wondered why, but trying to force memory was useless. He would remember when he remembered and not a moment sooner.

Did you tell your brother or your uncle about the cipher? he'd wanted to know without a trace of anxiety.

She hadn't, of course, but that didn't mean she wouldn't. She needed someone with a wiser head than her own to tell her what to do. Just because Charlie kissed like an angel didn't mean he wasn't a snake in her bosom. And if that imagery gave her the shivers, it was only what she deserved.

"Thank you, miss," the young soldier whispered as she gently lowered his head and returned the ladle to the bucket.

She smiled at him and rose. "Rest, now. The doctor will check on you in a bit." She located Sehoy, kneeling beside another soldier, feeding him a thin seafood soup. "Will you be all right by yourself if I stretch my legs for a bit?"

Sehoy smiled. "Of course. I'll join you when Private Jepson is finished with his supper."

Fiona went to the infirmary doorway and looked about for Léon. The soldiers had cleared away the debris, leaving scorched ruts in the sandy ground and blackened walls to testify to the fierceness of the battle. The odor of sulfur still lingered, probably on her own clothes, which were soiled from her nursing duties. She longed for a bath, but that wasn't going to happen until she could return home.

Squaring her shoulders, she crossed the shallow drill ground between the infirmary and the main gate and approached the sentry on guard.

The soldier straightened and grinned. "Evening, miss."

"Hello. Have you seen my brother, Léon Lanier?" she asked him. "Tall civilian with black hair and a pair of frightening eyebrows?"

The guard laughed. "Yes, miss, he's in conference with Major Lawrence. I wouldn't interrupt if I were you, though. The major—oh, here they come."

Fiona turned to see her brother, accompanied by an equally tall, rugged-faced officer in the sober blue uniform of the

American Second Infantry. The major's hat was set in the center of his head, his boots shining, the neckcloth precisely folded. Next to him, her brother stalked like some kind of pirate king in open-necked shirt and sun-faded breeches, a kerchief tied loosely about his throat. Léon had grown to look so much like their father that it made her throat ache.

The major reached her first, took her hand and kissed it. "Miss Lanier, you are a credit to your illustrious family. Thank you for your service as a nurse to our boys last night—and all day today, I understand. Please, you must rest now. I would like to offer refreshment and the use of my quarters to you and your cousin—Miss Ferguson, I believe?"

She blushed and dipped a curtsey. "Yes, sir, but we do not expect special treatment. We're grateful for the protection of the fort during the attack. I just wondered if I could have a word with my brother."

Léon shook his head. "Sorry, little sister, no time for that now. The major needs someone to take a report of the battle to General Jackson, and I've offered to go. His men need to stand guard in case the British decide to return." Léon's eyebrows gathered in his habitual don't-cross-me way. "And you're not to leave the fort under any circumstances, not even to check on the horses. Uncle Luc-Antoine has agreed to do that."

"But, Léon—"

He cut her off with a raised hand. "Fiona, the British left over a hundred fifty marines and Indians dead on the beaches. It's not a sight for female eyes." His eyes softened on her face. "I know this is hard on you, but be a good girl and stay safe so that I won't have to worry about you. Promise me."

Fiona sighed. "Of course I promise—I'm not an idiot. But when you get back, I need to talk to you about something important."

"Hold onto it, then, you won't burst I'm sure." Léon grinned and kissed her cheek. "Any message you want passed to Maddy while I'm in Mobile? I'll drop by to see her and Uncle Rémy's family while I'm in town."

"Just tell her I'm safe and I'm praying for them all."

When Léon had left, conferring with Major Lawrence about details of the report, Fiona drifted back toward the infirmary. She could tell Sehoy what she'd discovered about Charlie, but that would do no good and might only further complicate the situation. Perhaps she should ask Uncle Luc-Antoine what she should do. He clearly liked Charlie and had always been a steadying influence in the family.

But he had good reason to despise the British. And what if he decided to visit that long-standing antipathy on Charlie—especially if he thought Charlie had been lying to them all?

She had best think about it and pray about it before committing an action that couldn't be undone. God help her.

September 15, 1814
Mobile

With her cousin Léon quartered in her sewing room, which occasionally doubled as a guest room, Maddy awoke feeling more refreshed than she had in a long time. Elijah had shoved his knees into her hip during the night. She sat up and pushed them away, patted his deceptively angelic cheek, and slid out of bed on the other side. She might claim to enjoy her independence, but there was something about the presence of a big strong man in the house that allayed the niggling anxieties she rarely allowed to surface.

With any luck, Elijah would sleep for another hour and give

her a chance to prepare breakfast without a loquacious and accident-prone little person underfoot. Hurriedly she dressed, then brushed and put up her hair. Peeking at Elijah to make sure he was still snoring softly, she slipped into the kitchen, closing the door behind her.

Léon was already at the table, reading a news sheet and sipping a cup of coffee. He looked up when she came in, his serious expression lightening to a smile. "Good morning, Maddy-Mo," he said, using the family's childhood name for her. "I hope you don't mind that I made my own coffee. I might've been a bit growly by now without it. I've been up since daylight."

"Growly, Léon? You?" She laughed and reached into the cupboard for another cup. "I'm glad you made yourself at home. Now I don't have to wait so long for it to drip."

Sipping her coffee, she went about the business of scrambling eggs and making biscuit dough, and soon had the tantalizing smell of bacon sizzling in the frying pan wafting through the kitchen. "You came in after I went to bed," she said over her shoulder. "I presume the general was happy to hear the fort still stands and the British are gone with their tails between their legs."

"Oh, indeed. If I were a drinking man, every man in the regiment would've bought me a round." He thumped the paper. "Good news is all too rare and welcome these days."

"I don't suppose you saw Desi Palomo."

"As a matter of fact, I did. He asked about you too. What's going on between the two of you?"

"Nothing," she said quickly. Too quickly.

Léon let out a low whistle. "Oh. That."

Distracted, she burnt her finger on the skillet. "Ow! Look what you made me do!" She popped the finger in her mouth and glared at her cousin.

"Don't be a goose. It's about time you settled down with somebody who can keep Elijah from becoming a brat. Desi's a good man, he'll do the job."

"Elijah isn't a brat!"

"Much longer without an occasional tanning and he would be."

"Ooh—you mind your own business, Léon Lanier!"

He burst into one of his rare and infectious belly laughs. "Fine. Maybe I should warn Palomo off, then. I'm sure there are lots of belles in New Orleans would be glad if he came back."

"Léon—"

"All right, all right. I'll stop teasing. You're about to burn my bacon, and we can't have that."

She turned her attention back to breakfast. "Since you seem to be so interested in people's romantic connections, perhaps you need a little help with your own. Madame de Marigny's daughter is a pretty little thing—"

"Who would be horrified at the idea of attaching herself to a scruffy bar pilot from Navy Cove." He got up from the table and took the fork out of her hand. "You do the eggs, I'll watch the bacon. All this jabber is making me hungry."

A short time later, as Maddy was setting the table while Léon took the biscuits out of the oven, Elijah came out of the bedroom, rubbing his eyes. "Uncle Léon, will you take me fishing?"

"And good morning to you too, sir," Maddy said, wagging a finger. "Wash your hands and come sit down to breakfast." She glanced at Léon. "I'm sorry, he's obsessed."

"I'm not hungry!" Elijah's bottom lip went out.

"See what I mean?" Léon picked Elijah up and turned him upside down to give him an affectionate swat on his bottom. "Don't talk back to your mama, boy. Go wash your hands."

Giggling, Elijah landed on his feet and ran back to the bedroom.

Maddy sighed as she poured another cup of coffee. Perhaps Léon was right—Elijah needed a man's strong hand to keep his willful temperament from getting out of control. But she couldn't get married to the first one who asked, could she? And what if the right man simply wasn't available?

But Léon said Desi had asked about her last night. Surely he wouldn't do that if he weren't just a little bit interested in—

A knock on the door interrupted her mooning, and she jumped, blushing as if someone had posted her thoughts in the newspaper. "I'll get that," she said, jerking at the ties of her apron as she hurried to the front door and opened it. "Judah!" She flung herself at Léon and Fiona's middle brother. "Oh, what a nice surprise! Come in, come in!"

Chuckling, Judah returned her embrace. "I heard my big brother was here, taking advantage of Aunt Lyse's biscuit recipe. I hope he left me some!"

"You'd better hurry, if that's what you're after." Laughing, Maddy took Judah's hand and tugged him into the kitchen. "Léon, look who's here! Doesn't he look like a big old bear?"

The Lanier men were all tall and rangy, but Judah had inherited his father's thick, curly black hair, broad shoulders, and arrogant nose, as well as the deep-set dark eyes. He had ever been the prankster of the three brothers. When he'd first sailed off to New Orleans as second in command of a merchant ship suspected of doing double duty in the free trade, the family kept expecting him to return and claim it was all a huge practical joke. But today was the first time in over six years that he'd been back to Mobile.

He took over the room, as he'd always done, grabbing a biscuit and devouring half of it, even as he bear-hugged Léon. "You're a sight for sore eyes, old man." Judah turned as little Elijah, wide-eyed with curiosity, ran back into the room. "And who is this fine young man? You wouldn't happen to be the famous Elijah Burch, master of the high seas, would you?" Judah swooped the boy up into his arms.

"I am, I am!" Elijah clapped his hands. "Mama, I'm famous!"

Judah laughed. "In that case, I left a box of treasures on the front porch, for you and your cousins to go through—as soon as you finish your breakfast, that is," he amended, catching Maddy's eye.

"Treasure? Let me down!"

As Elijah attacked his eggs and biscuit, Judah flung himself into an empty chair. "Close call getting into port at all. The Spaniards and the Brits are doing their best to board any ship that even smells American."

"Where did you sail from?"

"New Orleans." Judah smiled his thanks when Maddy set a cup of coffee at his elbow. "Interesting goings-on there."

Elijah bounced out of his chair. "Mama, can I go see what's in the treasure box? I'm done."

Maddy nodded. "But first take your plate to the sink." After Elijah had pelted outside, slamming the front door behind him, she leaned in toward Judah. "Rumor says you've been seen with Laffite."

"Laffite is a gentleman of broad commercial interests, Maddy. Daresay we've been in the same port at the same time upon occasion."

Léon made a rude noise. "We all know what you've been up to, Judah, and if the cut of your tailoring is any indication, you've been raking in the ready while you're at it."

"That's a backhanded compliment if I ever heard one," Judah said with a grin. "But you needn't look so disapproving. Even if I were one of the gentleman pirates of Barataria, they have letters of marque that give them the right to seize arms and supplies going to the enemy." He shrugged. "But my own trade is entirely legitimate—transporting goods between Grand Terre and the New Orleans markets."

Maddy couldn't resist tweaking the straight-arrow Léon. "And don't forget your own papa once took twenty-four thousand pesos in gold from my father's ship—at least, until Papa made him give it back."

"That's the story they tell." Léon rolled his eyes. "But who knows how much embellishment has been added with every telling? Uncle Rafa and his *parábolas*."

"Speaking of family parables," Maddy said to Judah, "did you hear that Léon and Uncle Luc and Oliver helped fend off the British down at Fort Bowyer?"

Judah's black eyes lit. "I understand the little duchess is quite the heroine as well."

"Fiona's grown up in your absence." Léon scowled. "Not so little anymore, and devilish independent, if you ask me. I left her and Sehoy nursing an infirmary full of wounded soldiers."

"Sehoy? The Indian girl who used to correspond with Fiona?"

Léon nodded. "Her family was caught in the Horseshoe Bend affair, and she came here to take refuge. She's grown into quite a pretty thing now—our Oliver seems quite taken with her."

"Oliver's just a baby!"

Maddy laughed. "Judah, you've been gone a long time. We've a new generation of babies—and the children you knew are making their own lives."

"Reckon so." Judah shook his head, his expression sobering. "As it happens, all our lives are getting more complicated by the minute. The British might have been temporarily repelled from Mobile, but don't think they've given up. Their plan is bold, and just as arrogant as every move they've made so far in this never-ending war. They sent agents to meet with Laffite. They want his help in attacking New Orleans."

～

Fort Bowyer

Trying not to retch at the pain exploding in his head, Charlie dragged himself into a sitting position against the infirmary wall, where someone had moved him after Fiona left. He supposed the blast that broke his eardrum and jogged his memory loose had also scrambled his common sense. As an officer of His Majesty's naval command, this apparent inability to seize a gun and shoot as many Americans as he could before they arrested him might be considered by some to be high treason, punishable by hanging.

On the other hand, he was also apparently a spy, under orders to observe and report whatever intelligence might be useful to Whitehall.

Gaining control over his convulsing stomach, he shut his eyes against the image of Fiona's face as she'd questioned him. The cipher. She'd seen it, and he wouldn't be surprised if she'd also decoded it, though she claimed not to have. She was far from stupid, and what was he going to do about her?

He was going to leave. He was going to get himself and his cipher out of the fort, make his way back to British command—presumably gathering now in Pensacola, if the chatter among the American soldiers could be believed—give his report, and resume his uniformed duties.

And pray to God that he never received another order to act as a spy.

And if the thought of leaving Fiona Lanier sent him into a pit of desolation, it was only what he deserved.

7

With the coast clear of British war ships, Fiona and the rest of the family moved back home to Navy Cove. The weather remained hot as blue blazes but, she was thankful to notice, wasn't as humid as when they'd evacuated for the fort. The horses had managed not to starve to death during their period of self-foraging. Fiona settled back into her routine of caring for them and her "minions," as Charlie insisted on calling the Lanier menfolk and himself, who all went back to the shipyard to work with hardly a hitch in their gait.

Oliver's wounded leg left him on kitchen duty for several days, and Charlie was prone to dizzy spells that frightened Fiona more than she liked to admit. But she kept her mouth shut for fear of drawing Uncle's attention, contenting herself with watching to make sure Charlie—and the others, of course—drank plenty of water and covered their heads in the scorching sun.

On the Saturday after the Fort Bowyer battle, Léon came back from Mobile with Judah in tow. When she saw him jogging up from the beach behind Léon, hat in hand and face lit by his grand white smile, she let out a scream of joy and threw herself at him. He picked her up, whirled her around in a couple of wild circles, then stood looking around at the yard and barn while she chided him vehemently on the length of his absence.

Eventually he got bored and interrupted with a laughing "Yes, yes, Duchess, I know you missed me, but that's enough. I have to leave again in the morning, and I don't have time to waste on nonsense. Where's Uncle Luc?"

"In the barn." She put her hands on her hips. "You are not going to leave again so soon!"

"Yes. I am. I've a message to deliver, and I've already delayed longer than I should."

"What kind of message? To who?"

"None of your business, missy." Judah bent to kiss her forehead and headed for the barn.

"Léon, what's this all about? What was he doing in Mobile before he came home, and where is he going?"

Léon shrugged. "I don't know why you can't know. It's not as if you've anybody to tell. Judah is in league with that scoundrel Jean Laffite. Laffite claims the British sent representatives to ask for the Baratarians' help in navigating the swamps up into the city of New Orleans, in exchange for a few hundred thousand pounds and pardon for all their pirating crimes."

"They wouldn't dare!"

"The Brits are arrogant dogs, and of course they'd dare." Léon gave a short laugh. "The incredible part is that Laffite would have us believe he's an American patriot. He sent Judah to tell General Jackson that he held the British off for a few weeks while he 'thought about the proposition,' giving Laffite time to offer his services to the Americans instead—assuming they'd be willing to pardon him and his cohorts as well."

Fiona stared open-mouthed. "And did General Jackson fall for that nonsense?"

"Apparently not. He sent Judah back with a flea in his ear." Léon frowned. "Well, at least Jackson seems to have taken the warning about the British invasion seriously. He's preparing to march troops to Pensacola and boot them out."

The implications of everything she had just learned exploded in Fiona's brain all at once. One, her brother was a free trader, letters of marque or no, a willing compatriot of renowned pirate Jean Laffite. Their mother, God rest her soul, would be rolling in her grave (though Papa, she suspected, might be slightly proud).

Two, the British might have been beaten back from Mobile, but clearly they were in cahoots with the Spanish and probably the Red Stick Indians—or what was left of them, anyway. From Pensacola they could easily sail across the Gulf of Mexico and get to New Orleans from the south or even march overland and approach from the northeast. They were the greatest naval power in the world, and even Andrew Jackson was going to have a hard time fending off, let alone defeating, such a well-trained and fully armed armada.

And third, perhaps most horrifying of all, she had harbored a spy of that enemy nation in her home. She had allowed him unfettered access to her brother's shipbuilding enterprise. What if Charlie had been sent here for that very purpose? If the British attacked and conquered New Orleans, it could be laid at her door.

Léon snapped his fingers under her nose. "What is it, Fi? Judah is certainly straddling the law, but it's not as if we didn't know he'd taken off into some suspect ventures."

She swallowed. "Léon, do you remember when I wanted to talk to you about something before you left for Mobile? I was going to tell you about Charlie. I just hope it isn't too late now."

"Charlie? If he has dishonored you, I will—"

"No! At least—No, of course not! But I should have told you—Léon, I know him. I've known him for a long time."

"What do you mean? He's a complete stranger. He doesn't even know who he is." Leon's voice dropped to a growl. "At least, he said he doesn't. Has he been lying the whole time?"

"No, not about that anyway. Obviously he had a head injury, and I'm certain he didn't know me at first. But I recognized him almost right off. He's the youngest son of the Earl of Scarborough. Maddy and I met him when Uncle Rafa and Aunt Lyse took us to England all those years ago."

"And you didn't think it important to tell us this, Fiona? Have you lost your mind?" Leon's face clouded with anger.

Fiona stepped back, fighting tears. "I'm sorry—"

"You're sorry? You stupid little twit! He's the enemy! What if he's been spying, sending information to Pensacola? What if he'd decided to murder us all in our beds?"

"Charlie wouldn't do that. He's my friend—his grandfather and Uncle Rafa are friends, for that matter, which is how we come to be connected." When Léon turned away, hands clenched as if in the effort to keep them off her throat, Fiona grabbed his arm. "Listen, I've watched him. He hasn't sent messages to anybody, and for heaven's sake, he saved Oliver's life during the battle!"

Léon whirled to glare at her. "Are you in love with him? Is that why you've protected him?"

"No, I—I don't know—but I couldn't leave him on the beach to die—"

"Come here, Fiona." Grim-faced, Léon hauled Fiona toward the barn. "You're going to tell Uncle Luc-Antoine what you've done. We'll make a decision about what to do next, and you'll be lucky if you don't get sent to prison. I hope you've said goodbye to your lover, because he's certain to be hanged as a spy."

"He's not my—" Oh, what was the use? Fiona felt as if she were drowning in guilt as she stumbled along behind her brother. She was glad Léon knew her secret, because she couldn't have contained it one moment longer. She jerked her arm out of his grasp. "Léon, there's more."

He halted, eyes closed. "What now?" he said between his teeth. "Are you with child?"

She drew back her hand and slapped him hard. "How dare you, Léon Lanier? How dare you insult me as if I were some trollop? I'm your little sister, raised the same as you to follow God and treat others the way I want to be treated—which includes our enemy, as you insist on calling Charlie. There's nothing dirty in my relationship with him, and he's never been anything but kind and grateful and chivalrous to us all. He's worked like a slave on that stupid ship of yours, without, as far as I know, being offered a penny in return." Knees trembling, she stalked toward the barn.

Léon caught her after three steps. "I'm sorry, Fiona."

She ignored him.

He grabbed her arm. "I said I'm sorry! I went too far. I'm just so—so angry!"

"Well, so am I."

They stared at one another. Léon looked away first. "Come on," he sighed. "Let's find Uncle and get this over with."

They followed the sound of voices and found Judah and Uncle Luc-Antoine in the blacksmith shop under a tin awning on the other side of the barn. Uncle had made most of the iron implements in the Lanier household, including wheels, locks, and hinges, and of course, horseshoes. Judah pumped the bellows while Uncle pounded with fierce precision on the blade of a knife. Fiona stood back until the blade was soused in a bucket of water, setting off a giant, sizzling cloud of boiling steam.

While Judah returned the bellows to its hook, Uncle wiped down the blade on his apron.

Smiling around his pipe stem, Uncle Luc laid the blade on Judah's gloved palm. "Hone this and carve a nice haft for it, and you'll have yourself a beautiful weapon, son."

Judah tested the blade with his thumb. "It's already pretty sharp, sir. Beautiful work, as always." He squinted at Léon. "You still doing any carving?"

"No time for that anymore, not since you left."

Judah sighed. "We're not going there again, are we?"

"Just stating a fact." Léon glanced at Fiona. "But it's good you're home, because we've got a situation here with Fiona."

She flinched at the sudden wariness in Judah's eyes. Anytime she was referred to by her name, teasing was off the table, and they all knew it.

Still, Judah tried. "What have you done now, Duchess?"

"She knowingly brought a British spy in and just now thought it was time we knew about it."

Uncle Luc took the pipe out of his mouth. "Fiona, is that true?"

"Yes, he—but at first I thought he'd been on a Spanish or Dutch cargo ship, so I didn't think it mattered—'"

"Then why would you keep it from us, child?" Uncle said gently.

"Because I knew him—or thought I did. His family are friends of the Gonzaleses. I met him when we were in England. But then in the aftermath of the battle at Fort Bowyer, he was hallucinating, barking orders to s—sailors, apparently, and I got frightened because I realized he wasn't just anybody, he must be a naval officer—"

"I'm sure you confronted him about this," Judah said calmly.

She looked at him, and the compassion in his eyes settled her panic, turned it to something manageable. "Yes, of course I did, but he just looked confused and said he didn't remember any of that."

"Why would he admit the truth to her?" Léon demanded. "He knows he's got her wrapped about his finger. He could tell her he's the king of France, and she'd believe him."

Don't cry, Fiona told herself. *Do not*.

"There's no need to be cruel," Judah said, seeing her distress. "We've always protected the little duchess, of course she's naive."

"Is there no one who sees the danger here?" Léon flung his hands up. "I'm just trying to speak truth."

"I'm not stupid, despite what you think," Fiona cried. "Of course I was suspicious, which is why I admitted all this to you, Léon. But I've been thinking about it, and maybe I've hit on a way we can turn the tables and use Charlie to our advantage."

Léon snarled, "Oh, for the love of—"

"No, let her speak," Uncle Luc said, eyes narrowed on Fiona's face. "What's your idea?"

She sucked in a breath. "Suppose we do have a British naval officer, right here in Navy Cove. What if we arrest him and hold him, write to his grandfather, who is quite an influential personage still. Maybe he could arrange for a trade—Sullivan for Charlie."

Dead silence greeted her. She waited, heart pounding. They all thought of her as a child. Nobody would take her seriously, even Uncle Luc-Antoine.

Finally Léon folded his arms. "You know, Uncle, it pains me to admit this, but I believe she may have hit upon a very good plan."

Sehoy had always thought of herself as Indian rather than American. But when Charlie Kincaid presented her with an opportunity to redress the wrong done to her and her family, she found herself struggling to think like a Creek Red Stick and not like a Lanier.

She stared at him, pulling her thoughts together. They sat together on the beach, propped back on their elbows, bare feet stretched out toward the water. The tide was going out, and lumpy spirals of seaweed decorated the wet sand, tiny shells glistening in the late afternoon sun. Charlie was dressed in ragged homespun breeches and an open-necked white shirt, its sleeves rolled up to expose his sun-browned forearms. Constant exposure to the sun had bleached golden streaks into his hair, making his mismatched blue-and-hazel eyes even brighter by contrast. He reminded her of a prince in one of the fairy tales her father had told her as a child—impossibly beautiful, slightly flawed, and unknowable.

When he'd invited her to walk with him to the beach—without Fiona or Oliver—she'd wondered aloud what he was up to. He'd just laughed and told her not to be so cynical, that he just wanted a favor he couldn't bring to any of the Laniers. Unable to deny curiosity, she'd gathered her painting supplies and accompanied him. For nearly an hour, he watched her draw, peppering her with questions about technique, until finally she made a rude noise and stuck her pencil behind her ear.

"Charlie, you're no more interested in art than I am in building lifeboats. What exactly are you after?"

He flashed his charming, lopsided grin and pushed her hat down over her nose. "You're nothing like Fiona, you know that?"

he said when she came out from under the hat, sputtering in aggravation. "I can distract her for hours."

"Sometimes I wish I were more like Fiona," she said.

And that was when he showed her the cipher and asked her to hide it for him.

She sat up slowly now, emotions catapulting over one another. "Why would I do this? I barely know you." She watched his face, looking for sincerity, looking for deceit, looking for *anything* that would tell her what to do.

His eyes remained guileless. "You would do this because if you don't, the Americans will continue to manipulate your people until they are exterminated. Fiona is a good person, but she doesn't know anything about politics. She doesn't understand what you went through at Horseshoe Bend."

Sehoy shuddered. That much was true. She'd tried to describe the experience, and even Oliver didn't really want to hear it. Avoiding Charlie's eyes, she took the pencil from behind her ear and rolled it between her palms. "I'm not sure the English are any better. They give our men guns and uniforms and try to make them march in straight lines to give the Americans something to shoot at while their officers—Oh, it's all so stupid. Why can't they leave us alone to hunt and fish and trade as we always did?"

"Sehoy." Charlie sat up and unknotted the leather string that tied the pouch about his neck. "No amount of wishing will put things back as they were. Europeans are here to stay, and who's to say you won't be better off in the end? Haven't you heard stories of how the Alabama bands made war on the peaceful tribes of the south? Isn't it true that the Creeks cannot come to agreement even now? You have to look at the situation pragmatically, make alliances that will benefit yourself and those you love."

She loved Oliver and his family. They had welcomed her, made her one of their own, when she had nowhere else to go.

But Charlie had seen something in her that wavered. Some seed of bitterness and fear that kept her from following her heart. Was she going to hold on to that fear, or was she going to release it?

Charlie took her hand and uncurled her fingers. He laid the little leather pouch, still warm from his skin, in her palm. "I trust you not to betray me. Soon I'll go back to my command—and make no mistake, Sehoy, His Majesty's navy will overwhelm these backwoods Yanks. When the time comes, I'll take you with me—if you'll help me now."

"What about Fiona?" Her heart broke for her friend's betrayal. "Can't you take her too? I know you love her."

There was a brief tensing of his shoulder against hers, but his lips curved in a faint smile. "My feelings have nothing to do with my duty. And can you honestly picture Fiona leaving her horses—let alone her family—to move to England? Or to take up the life of a sailor's wife?"

No. She couldn't picture that. Sehoy put her head down on her knees. God had protected her at Horseshoe Bend, he had kept her and Oliver safe during the Battle of Fort Bowyer—for his own purposes. But what would he have her do now, when everything was all muddled? Up was down, right was wrong, and there seemed no clear direction.

"I'll hide the cipher," she whispered. They wouldn't ask her about it, she was certain of that much. But she wasn't sure she had the strength to leave Oliver, no matter what Charlie said about pragmatism.

Sometimes love made no sense at all.

Fiona's first thought when Charlie came walking up from the beach with Sehoy was that she wouldn't have a chance to warn him about what was coming.

And then she thought that if she'd just told Léon who Charlie was when he first arrived, rather than trying to hide it, she might never have come to love him in this terrible, grief-inducing way.

Then again, maybe she'd always loved him and compared every boy she met to that delicious, childish hero-worship that colored her memories. And the reality of Charlie Kincaid—his laughter and his kisses, his blue-hazel eyes and his chivalry—had sealed her doom.

She sat on the porch steps waiting for him to reach her, knowing her brothers and her uncle waited to apprehend him, to chain and lock him in the tack room. He was their best chance at getting Sullivan released. *Don't forget that,* she told herself sternly.

Whatever you do, don't forget that.

But when he smiled at her, halfway across the yard, resolution failed. She stood and raised a hand.

"Make him come to you, Fiona," Judah said from the doorway behind her. "We don't want to have to chase him."

Chase him? Like a runaway horse or the prey in a hunt?

She abruptly sat down, grasping her apron in great wads of fabric, in an effort to control the trembling of her hands. "I can't do this, Judah."

"Yes, you can. Just get him to sit beside you, and I'll take it from there."

"You won't hurt him, will you?"

"Not unless he attacks me."

Would he? She had no real idea what Charlie was capable

of if he was threatened. She knew he was brave and clever and resourceful.

She got up and met him and Sehoy a few feet from the porch.

Sehoy took one look at her and said, "I'm going to freshen up before I help you with dinner, Fiona. Please excuse me." She walked on.

"Where have you been?" Fiona asked Charlie.

His eyebrows went up at her tense tone. "Just took a walk to the beach. Are you all right?"

"Charlie, I had to tell my brothers who you are."

He let out a low whistle. "Did you now? What exactly did you—wait, *brothers*?"

"Judah is here. He's on his way back to New Orleans from Mobile. He says the British are prepared to attack New Orleans. They know you're a naval officer, but I didn't say anything about the—"

"You told them I'm an officer?" He stepped back, ashen-faced. "Fiona, I'll be hanged as a spy!"

"No, no, we—they've come up with a better plan than that." She thought she might choke on the words. "They'll hold you here until we can get word to your grandfather. We're hoping he'll arrange a prisoner transfer—you for my brother Sullivan."

"That is insane. I can't stay here indefinitely. Why didn't you tell me you were going to—" He looked about wildly. "I trusted you!"

She grabbed for his hands. "It was the only thing I could think of that would keep them from shooting you. And I couldn't live as a traitor to my country any longer! I'm just not made that way, and—and—it was wrong of you to ask me to do so!"

He closed those magnificent eyes, shutting her out, his face twisted in something between a sneer and despair. Pulling his hands free, he straightened, chin up and shoulders squared. "It's done, then. We're no longer friends, just garden-variety enemies. I'll no longer foist my attentions upon you, Miss Lanier." He picked up her hand and kissed her fingers, his lips bloodless. "Perhaps you'd introduce me to your brother so we can get this unpleasantness over with."

He offered his arm and they walked together toward the house, where Judah waited at the top of the porch steps.

Charlie greeted him with a mocking salute. "Good afternoon, sir. First Lieutenant Charles Kincaid, late of His Majesty's Royal Navy, at your service. You must be the esteemed pirate Judah Lanier."

"I am." Judah bowed, equally mocking. "I confess, I admire your lack of drama under these awkward circumstances. Perhaps you'd be so good as to turn around and allow me to tie your hands."

"Judah, for heaven's sake," Fiona burst out.

Charlie sighed. "It's all right, I know what is expected of me. If you're uncomfortable, go in the house until the prisoner is properly disposed of." He turned and crossed his wrists behind his back.

Judah approached with a stout rope. "Go inside, Fiona," he said curtly and proceeded to bind Charlie's hands.

She hadn't even enough breath to weep, much less move, so she just stood there, watching her brother take the man she loved by the arm and march him toward the barn.

"Fiona?" She felt Sehoy's hand on her shoulder. "Come and sit down."

"What have I done?" she whispered. "Oh, Sehoy, what have I done?"

SEPTEMBER 18, 1814

It was Sunday morning, and Charlie had to remind himself the Lord's Day should start with prayer. Truthfully—and since he was conversing with himself, there was no reason not to be truthful—he'd not worried overmuch about praying during his life. It had always seemed to be a waste of time. But lying on his back in the Lanier family's tack room, surrounded by nothing more interesting than three blank walls, a couple of saddles on a table, and a fourth wall studded with empty hooks—all the bridles and reins having been removed, he assumed, in his honor—he found himself wondering what the Almighty had up his sleeve, so to speak.

As the third Kincaid son, if he had followed the tradition established by his family, he would be standing behind his own pulpit in some village parish, holding forth about . . .

Well, what would he speak about? The only thing that came to mind was the story of Jonah, that distinctively unnautical fellow who had sailed in the opposite direction from where God had told him to go and singlehandedly caused one of the worst storms at sea recorded in the Bible. As a youngster, he'd read the story over and over, fascinated by the description of the whale's bowels and the reluctant prophet's appearance after his ejection from the fish's digestive system.

It occurred to him now that the allegory wasn't far from his own experience. Of course Charlie hadn't been gulped down by anything live, be it fish or mammal. But metaphorically speaking, he'd been violently absorbed into the world of American shipbuilding and the Lanier family lifestyle.

And he had changed under their influence.

When they got around to spewing him back into his old life, he would never be the same, would never look at being an

English aristocrat through eyes of complacency or resentment or any of the variety of ways he'd heretofore responded to the circumstances of his birth.

Here he'd seen men and women take control of their dreams and pursue them, unfettered by fear of reprisal, uncluttered by expectations of centuries of tradition. Léon was good at carpentry and business, so he built boats—not because his father had done so, but because he dreamed of owning the finest shipbuilding industry on the Gulf Coast. Judah hated staying in one place, so he simply sailed off to become a pirate. Sullivan's love for the sea and desire to defend his country at the point of a sword sent him into naval service. Even Fiona had been allowed to cultivate her passion for horseflesh and turn it into a means of earning her own place of responsibility in the family.

More than that, Charlie was changed by their love for one another, a love that recognized flaws, spoke unvarnished truth, and yet still accepted each person's value to the family as a whole. It was, he suspected, a uniquely American characteristic, that clear-eyed desire for personal growth and maturity, accepting responsibility and yet generously welcoming and protecting weaker members.

And being changed, was he now going to continue on his original path, running like Jonah as fast and hard as he could from fulfilling his place in his family—or could he find a way to adapt to some new, higher calling? The most frightening question he had to consider lay in his patriotic identity. Could one really go to sleep as a Briton and awaken as an American? How to settle the conflict between responsibility and treason? If he switched loyalties, his captors would never believe and trust him, and his British command would label him a deserter.

Suddenly he sat up, holding his splitting skull between his two hands. He must be insane to even consider such a course of action. They would say he'd been suborned by a beautiful woman. And in some senses, he had.

Or was that it? He'd been influenced as much by laconic old Uncle Luc-Antoine as by anyone else.

And now this new complication—the pirate brother, Judah, who bore the news that the English meant to attack New Orleans. Without the intelligence Charlie carried, they were likely to make disastrous mistakes. The British naval command did not understand the political entrenchments in Louisiana. Charlie himself would never have believed it until he spent six months there, carousing in the taverns of New Orleans, roaming the wharves, shopping in the French Market. The French, Spanish, American, and free colored factions might treat one another with veiled contempt when socializing in their individual districts of the city—but taken as a whole, they were patriotic Americans and unlikely to welcome British promises of peaceful rule.

Indeed, it seemed incredible to Charlie that anyone would give up autonomous control of one's fortune and property to an invading monarchy. He wouldn't do it himself.

What was a turncoat prisoner of war supposed to do? There was no place for him at his father's estate in Scotland, he was too old for rusticating with his grandfather in England, and he found himself increasingly reluctant to return to service under some autocratic naval commander who treated his junior officers like so much expendable cash.

And so he came full circle to his original question of the day: could there be some answer to his dilemma in heaven's grand plan? Could God be truly interested in the mental and spiritual perambulations of one Charlie Kincaid, as Fiona claimed?

He supposed he had nothing to lose in asking.

Flattening himself facedown on the blanket they had given

him to cover the tack room's wooden floor, he shut his eyes and cast about for appropriate verbiage with which to address his Creator. Jonah's words came to him as if they'd been printed on his brain, and he whispered them aloud, "'I cried by reason of mine affliction unto the LORD, and he heard me; out of the belly of hell cried I, and thou heardest my voice.'"

Louder, he said, "'For thou hadst cast me into the deep, in the midst of the seas; and the floods compassed me about: all thy billows and thy waves passed over me. When my soul fainted within me I remembered the LORD: and my prayer came in unto thee, into thine holy temple. They that observe lying vanities forsake their own mercy. But I will sacrifice unto thee with the voice of thanksgiving; I will pay that that I have vowed.'" He gulped, listened to the silence of the little room, and spoke the last line he remembered.

"'Salvation is of the LORD.'"

8

For two and a half weeks Fiona had been effectively a prisoner—perhaps not, like Charlie, shackled by the ankles to a wall in a tack room in the barn. But she was not allowed to get near him, Sehoy being assigned the morning task of bringing him food and emptying his chamber pot. Fiona occasionally got a glimpse of Charlie when Léon took him, hands tied, on short walks in the evening to stretch his legs, but even when she tended her horses in the barn, someone was always with her. She felt like a child who couldn't be trusted to be alone.

Dressed in her working clothes this morning, in the paddock putting Tully through his paces, she looked up when a flock of Canada geese came honking by on their way to Mexico. There was a slight chill in the breeze and the sun hunkered behind steely clouds, echoing the heaviness in her spirit. From the barn she could faintly hear Charlie singing a hymn. He wasn't exactly a good singer, but his voice was pleasant, and his choice of songs was surprising, especially in his circumstances.

She remembered their conversation about God all those weeks ago. Maybe what she'd said to him had made an impression.

She sighed and nudged Tully with her heels to change his gait. Maybe the hairs of her head were numbered, as she'd reminded Charlie, but she remained at Navy Cove, unable to speak to the one person in the world she wanted to talk to.

Tully raised his head and whickered, and she looked around to see what had drawn his attention. From the wooded path at the eastern boundary of their property, five horsemen appeared, dressed in the navy blue uniforms of American cavalry. The horses were beautiful—three bays, a buckskin, and a palomino, the silver conchs of their bridles polished to a gleam, the saddle leather strong and supple.

Fiona guided Tully through the paddock gate and stopped at the edge of the yard. Uneasily aware of her male attire, she waited to greet the visitors. There was no time to go inside to change, and all the men were at the shipyard—except Charlie, of course. Léon had warned her not to let anyone from Mobile know they had him detained, otherwise they would lose their negotiating power with Charlie's grandfather. But what if Charlie himself cried out or otherwise made himself known while these officers were here? What if he started singing again? Léon hadn't deemed it necessary to gag their prisoner, and now it was too late.

"Good morning," she said to the ranking officer, who rode ahead of the others and stopped a few feet away from her.

He took off his hat and nodded, looking taken aback by her unconventional dress. But he said respectfully, "Morning, miss. I'm looking for the Lanier brothers. I was told they own the only developed property outside the fort."

"I'm Fiona Lanier. My brother Léon and our uncle and cousin are working over at the shipyard. How can I help you?"

"Pleased to make your acquaintance, Miss Lanier. I'm General John Coffee. That's a very fine animal you're riding—in fact, that's the reason I'm here. Everyone in Mobile says your brother is the best horse breeder and trainer on the coast. I've come to talk to him about purchasing mounts for my regiment."

Fiona couldn't help grinning. She slung her leg over the pommel and relaxed in the saddle. "I'm sorry, General, but everyone in Mobile has lied to you."

He frowned. "What do you mean? That stallion looks to be perfectly acceptable—even superior, if I'm any judge of horseflesh."

"You're an excellent judge of horseflesh, sir, but Léon isn't the breeder of the family. That would be me."

"You?" He glanced over his shoulder at his companions. They were snickering, sure this little girl was playing a joke on them. "Contain yourselves, gentlemen," the general said and returned his attention to Fiona.

"I'm afraid so, sir. I'm sorry for the confusion if I'm not what you were expecting."

"It's just too bad that we came all the way down here for . . . But on second thought, I would like to inspect the stock that you have. If the others are of sufficient quality, then perhaps you'd go fetch your menfolk so that we can come to some kind of agreement."

Fiona held on to her temper with an effort. She had invested quite a lot of money and time over the past three years, raising Tully and the other horses for just this occasion. Now that her buyer was actually here, he wanted to bypass her and talk to her brother?

"You're welcome to look them over, of course, but I assure you all my horses are every bit as fine as Tully here. I also assure you that I know their value to a penny, and I'm perfectly capable of negotiating a fair deal. By myself. Without any help." She spoke distinctly so there could be no misunderstanding.

Coffee looked unhappy, but clearly he coveted Tully. "Just let me look at the horses, and I'll send someone to the shipyard for your brother—just to make sure."

Thoroughly annoyed, Fiona put her foot back in the stirrup and wheeled Tully. "Follow me."

She led the soldiers toward the pasture. Putting two fingers to her lips, she produced a series of shrill whistles and waited for the horses to come running. They had been carefully trained, and she never failed to thrill at the sight of these magnificent creatures pounding toward her. Sneaking a glance at Coffee, she smirked at his slack-jawed admiration.

As the horses gathered around her, she took a handful of carrot pieces from her pocket. "Every horse has his own signal," she said, feeding each one a treat from the palm of her hand. "I've raised them all from birth. They've never been mistreated, and their mouths are soft and responsive." She gave the general a pointed look. "They know who the boss is."

"I can see that." Coffee's eyes gleamed with reluctant appreciation. "Apologies for my initial doubt. Could I see you put each one through his paces?"

"Of course. The paddock is just beyond the barn."

Here came the dicey part—keeping Charlie out of sight and sound. She led her visitors on a track as far as possible from the barn, entering the paddock from its west entrance. The rest of her tack was locked in the tack room, Léon had the key, and she was going to have a hard time explaining why.

"You and your men may watch from outside the paddock here," she told the general, praying he wouldn't object.

Apparently her theory that horses would obey what they were expected to obey applied to men as well, for Coffee nodded and ordered his officers to line up against the paddock railing. They sat their horses, talking quietly amongst themselves, spitting tobacco in nasty streams on the ground, while she took Tully to the center of the paddock.

Dismounting, she stepped to his head and spoke to him softly. "This is it, boy, your chance to show off. Make me proud." On her signal, Tully bowed, and the soldiers cheered. Smiling, she remounted and the show began.

Twenty minutes later, she dismounted, removed her hat, and bowed along with the horse.

"Are they all that well trained?" asked one of the officers, a mustachioed young man on the palomino.

"Tully's the best, but yes, they're all fine." As she removed the horse's tack, she could hear the men muttering but tried not to let them shift her focus. Tully stood patiently until she turned him loose with a slap on the rump, then he galloped off into the pasture, tossing his magnificent head. When she called Dusty, he came running, dark mane flying.

But before she could even put the saddle blanket on him, General Coffee waved to catch her attention. "I'd like to see the buckskin mare over there next, if you please."

Fiona followed the direction of his gaze to Bonnie, who stood with her head over the rail, watching the proceedings with the air of a queen enjoying the performance of her court entertainers. "Sorry, sir, she's my personal mount and isn't for sale."

Coffee handed his mount's reins to a lieutenant and walked over to Bonnie. He examined her points, running experienced hands over her withers and legs, picking up her feet to check her hooves, opening her mouth to look at her teeth. "This is the finest of them all," he said, patting Bonnie's neck. "I'll give you double the price for her."

"I told you she's not for sale."

"My dear, everything has a price. I'm sure your brother will agree with me."

She laughed. "You haven't even seen her working."

He gave her a look that probably cowed his troops. "You are clearly a gifted trainer—" he didn't add "for a girl," though she was sure he wanted to—"and this is a beautiful animal."

"And she is *mine*. My father bought her for me, I have her title, and she is at least half my source of income. Why would I let her go for any price?"

The general frowned at her, stymied. Finally he grunted. "All right then, let's see the gelding work."

By the time Fiona had worked the remaining horses that she intended to sell, well over an hour had passed. Just as she let the last one go, the officer who had ridden to the shipyard returned—without Léon.

"Did you not find Lanier?" the general demanded.

"Oh, I found him all right," the young man said, looking sidelong at Fiona. "But he said he was working, and his sister was perfectly capable of selling her own horses."

She could have said *I told you so*. She could have done any number of satisfying, ultimately childish things. But none of those actions would raise the price of her horses. Nor reflect honorably on her family or her God.

So she smiled sweetly. "General Coffee, perhaps you and your men would like to come inside for a cool drink or cup of tea to ease the negotiations. And I've a sweet potato pie that will make you drool."

Oh, this was going to be fun. He wanted those horses. And she could think of so many excellent ways to spend his money.

⌒

Charlie jerked upright, thinking the rat in his dream was about to run across his pallet.

He had no idea how long he'd been asleep, but judging by the

130

deep darkness, the time had to be somewhere close to midnight. There had been a bright harvest moon in the sky during the last few nights, but cloud cover and rain since the afternoon had doused what light might have come from the heavens.

The last dregs of the nightmare dispelled, he yawned and lay back down. Thank God it wasn't real. He hated rats.

Then he heard the noise again, louder. He sat up and scooted toward the door, the chains about his ankles clanking. "Who's there?" It was too early for Sehoy, and he couldn't think of any reason for Léon to come back.

"Charlie? You're awake?"

"Fiona! What are you doing out here? It's the middle of the night!"

"I couldn't sleep, and I wanted to talk to you." She sounded forlorn.

"You're going to get in deep trouble if they catch you out here."

She didn't answer for a moment. "I like that you're worried about me. Nobody else cares how I feel."

"Of course I care how you feel. But I don't want you arrested for treason."

"Nobody's going to arrest me. Besides, like you said, it's the middle of the night and everyone's asleep. It's a regular frog-strangler out there, so I seriously doubt anyone will come outside for any reason, even if they did wake up." He heard her settle back against the door. "Please, Charlie, I just wanted to hear your voice for a bit, then I promise I'll go back inside."

He engaged in a weak tussle with his better judgment. "Oh, all right, but no more than a few minutes. I'm very busy these days, and I need my sleep."

She laughed. "I miss you so much. Did Léon tell you I sold five horses today? I'm quite the businesswoman."

"I heard the commotion this morning, but Léon wouldn't tell me who it was."

"He probably thinks you'll try to escape and report what you heard." She sighed. "Charlie, why didn't you let General Coffee know you're in here? I kept expecting you to start singing or something."

"Oh, did you enjoy my singing? I could give you another concert, if you like."

"No, really. Why didn't you make some noise?"

"Fiona, think about it. If the American military takes me prisoner, I'm not likely to be treated with as much civility as you and your family have shown me. Have you seen the prisons in these old forts?"

"Are they really that bad?"

"Let's just say I wouldn't be getting any sweet potato pie."

"I imagine my brother Sullivan is being mistreated too. Isn't he? Do you think he's even still alive?"

"I don't have any way of knowing," he said gently, "but let's hope so."

"How long does it take for a letter to reach England?"

"It can be done in a month, but more often six weeks to two months." He hesitated, imagining the worry in her eyes. "But you understand that sometimes letters don't reach their destination at all. The war may be over before my grandfather takes action."

"Charlie, maybe if you promise not to try to escape, my brothers will let you out. This is all so—so . . . frustrating."

He turned his cheek to the door, wishing he could touch her, wishing he could relieve her anxiety. "I cannot promise any such thing. I'm an officer, and I must follow my duty. But even if I did, do you suppose Léon would for one minute allow me to be alone with his little sister? Fiona, you should hate me."

"But I don't! I'm sorry we're on opposite sides of this war, I'm sorry your country has invaded mine, but I'm not sorry I've come to know you. I can't help but believe there's a way we can—"

"What? What are you expecting? You're not going to turn your back on your family and your home. Are you?"

"Of course not!"

"Then what?" He got to his knees, hands flat against the door. "I would give my life for you, Fiona, but you don't want a man who would commit treason!"

He could hear her crying softly and ached to comfort her. Still, he couldn't be cruel enough to pretend there was a way for him to offer himself to her.

"I've been lying here with nothing to do but pray," he said, "—for you and for me, for our countries—which should be the same, you know."

"Charlie, you've been praying? Talking to God?" Her voice sounded lighter, in spite of everything.

"It's a bit one-sided," he said with a sigh. "He's not talking back."

"Uncle Luc says God already said everything he wanted to say in the Bible."

"So what does the Bible have to say about our circumstances?"

"That we must love our enemies and pray for those who persecute us."

"You know I love you." Saying it aloud made the darkness blacker, the distance between them more impenetrable than any wooden door. "But you are not my enemy."

"Ohhh . . . Charlie . . ." Her voice shredded on a sob. "What am I going to do? I can't bear this."

"You're going to go back to bed and pretend you never came out here. If I make it through the war, I'll come back for you and we'll sort this out. Promise me, Fiona. Whatever happens, keep yourself safe for me."

"I can't make any such promise, you know that. I have to do my part—"

He groaned. "All right, then. Just—go back to the house before somebody comes looking for you. Don't do this again, it's too hard on us both."

"I love you, Charlie. I dream about the night you kissed me."

"Fiona, for the love of God—"

"I know! I know! I'm going."

He listened, heard her light footsteps moving away, until nothing but the soft nighttime shuffling of the animals broke the silence. He fell back onto the pallet. He had to get out of here. There had to be a way.

⌐

OCTOBER 6, 1814

By the time Fiona dragged herself out of bed, the rain had turned the yard and paddock into a sticky mess of mud, sand, and oyster shells, and large puddles of water created hazards for anyone foolish enough to venture out of the house. Despite this, the men continued work on the ship with dogged determination, leaving Fiona and Sehoy to keep each other company.

While Sehoy worked on a drawing, Fiona moped about, unable to concentrate on her book. And now she only had Bonnie and Washington to care for. They were hunkered down in the barn, a place Fiona wouldn't have gone if she'd been offered a thousand dollars. She couldn't take another confrontation with Charlie. Léon had warned her, she hadn't listened, and what a price she'd paid. She'd lain awake until dawn.

The third time she walked to the window, looked out at the rain, and sighed, Sehoy put down her pencil. "Fiona, what's the matter?"

"I'm just bored."

"Really? Because you seem . . . sad. I know it's hard on you . . . Charlie—I mean—"

"I didn't have any choice, Sehoy." She didn't mean to sound so abrupt, but she really didn't want to talk about him this morning. Not when the pain was so raw. She turned, softening her tone. "I was just thinking, maybe you and I should make a trip to Mobile to visit Maddy. She missed seeing you when she and Desi came here back in August. Would you like that?"

Sehoy hesitated.

Fiona tipped her head. "Sehoy? What's wrong? Do you have something against Maddy?"

"Of course not!" Sehoy was blushing. "I just—I would miss your—the rest of your family. Uncle Luc and—and Oliver—"

Huh. So the wind blew that way. She stared at Sehoy blankly. "But Oliver's just a child!"

"He's not a child!" Sehoy's voice was fierce. "He's quite a good man, and of course I admire him—but no more than Léon or Uncle Luc," she added hastily.

"Of course," Fiona said, laughter bubbling. "I'd miss them too, but we wouldn't stay long. Just long enough to go to church and maybe do a little shopping. I want a new dress, and Maddy could use the business. What do you think? Will you come with me?"

"Of course I will." Sehoy's rare humor surfaced. "I suppose Oliver will still be here when I get back."

ᐧᐧ

OCTOBER 8, 1814
NAVY COVE

Early Saturday morning, Sehoy sat by herself on the porch swing, waiting for Fiona to finish packing. The little trunk that Oliver and Uncle Luc had made for her when she first came sat over by the steps. Wrought of finely sanded and waxed pine, with beautiful brass hasp and hinges, it had a cunning false bottom where she could store art supplies and anything else she cared to keep from prying eyes. Charlie's cipher was there, tucked into her beaded satchel.

Beyond those meager items, she had little to pack, even for a trip to Mobile. She possessed only the dress and underclothes she wore every day, a dimity nightdress, and an extra pair of stockings. Fiona wanted to have a new church dress made for her, but Sehoy had only agreed to think about it. She didn't want to be beholden to her benefactors any more than absolutely necessary.

Two days ago, Fiona had sent word to Maddy that she and Sehoy were coming, and that they planned to stay for a week if it was convenient. Sehoy wondered what they would do if it wasn't convenient. Would they turn right around and come back home? How embarrassing that would be! But this family did things—wild, impulsive things—that Sehoy would never dream of.

For example, she knew about the night Fiona had gone to Charlie. Not that she'd been spying exactly, but she'd awakened when Fiona left the room, suspected where she was going, and asked Charlie about it the next day. He'd been unusually taciturn about the whole thing, though he admitted he'd spoken to Fiona and made her promise not to come to him again. And he'd sworn Sehoy to secrecy as well.

She sighed, toeing the swing into motion. It was obvious that Charlie had strong feelings for Fiona. Only a man in love would be so careful to protect her from the repercussions of her own folly. Maybe one day Oliver would come to feel that way about Sehoy. Until then, she had to keep her emotions to herself. Mama had taught her that nothing made a man run faster in the opposite direction than a woman's direct pursuit. This little separation, painful though it might be, was a good thing. Maybe Oliver would even come to miss her.

As if she had conjured him from her thoughts, the screen door opened and Oliver himself stepped out onto the porch. He smiled when he saw her on the swing.

"Sehoy! Fiona said you'd be here, but I was afraid—" His cheeks turned ruddy. "I mean, can I sit with you while you wait for her?"

"Of course. What are you going to do today?" She clasped her hands to still her trembling fingers.

He looked at the seat of the swing as if measuring the distance between Sehoy and the arm brace, then flung himself down, a strategic inch between them, and crossed his arms without looking at her. "We'll work on the ship, since the weather's good. Pa says I'm a dab hand at carving trunnels, so that's what I'll be doing."

Sehoy nodded. Trunnels, or treenails, she had learned, were the wooden spikes used to fasten the planks to the ship's frame. The trunnels would then be caulked with tar-soaked hemp fibers, making the ship watertight.

"How much longer until the ship is finished?" she asked. "I want to see it launched."

Oliver's lips pursed in the beginnings of a grin. "I'm sure you'll be back before that happens. Top deck will take another couple of weeks, then we'll build the cabins and their furniture.

I'm hoping Léon will let me help with the figurehead. You're not the only artist in the family."

She stared at him. "I didn't know you were a wood-carver! Why didn't you tell me?"

"I wanted to surprise you." He reached into his shirt pocket and pulled out a knobby little package wrapped in a silk handkerchief tied with a leather string. "Here, I made this for you."

So taken off-guard was she that a long moment went by before Oliver's expression fell in chagrin, and she gasped. "Oh! Oh, let me see!" Eagerly she cupped her hands until he laid the gift in them. Unable to meet his eyes, she fumbled with the string and finally got it loose. The handkerchief fell away to reveal a four-inch-long cedar dolphin, carved so that it appeared to leap from its little pedestal. It was sleekly sanded, oiled, and polished—the most beautiful thing she'd ever been given.

Mouth ajar, she examined it through blurry eyes, admiring the subtle ripple of muscles, the cunning fins and flippers, the details of blowhole and eyes and smiling mouth.

"Oh, Oliver." Holding the dolphin to her cheek, she bent double and started to cry.

"Sehoy, wait . . . what's wrong? I'm so sorry, I didn't mean to . . . Hey, now." She felt his hand on her back. "I thought you'd like it, and I didn't want you to get so excited about being in the city that you'd forget about us down here. Sehoy?"

"I like it—of course I like it." She wiped her eyes with her skirt. "It's so b–beautiful!"

"Oh. Well then. Then why are you crying?"

"Because you're so sweet to me."

He stirred beside her in confusion. "I do not understand girls at all. Fiona didn't tell me you were going to cry."

She sat up, wishing she had her own handkerchief, but it was packed in the trunk. Which Oliver had made. She almost burst into fresh tears, but swallowed them back. She wasn't about to use his silk handkerchief to blow her nose.

"Here." Oliver pulled another handkerchief, a clean white cotton one, from his breeches pocket and handed it to her. "Are you all right?"

Gratefully she dabbed at her nose. "I'm fine. Thank you so much. I'll take him to Mobile and look at him every day and think of you." Because he looked so gratified and so utterly Oliver-ish, she leaned up and boldly kissed his cheek. "I don't really want to go anywhere."

He put his hand where her lips had been. "You don't?"

"No, but Fiona says I can't stay here by myself with all you men, it wouldn't be proper, even though she has done so for years. But I will definitely come back, and she says we won't stay above a fortnight."

"That's all right then. I'll make you something else while you're away, and when you get back I'll take you out in the pirogue and show you where the real dolphins swim and play." He eyed her doubtfully. "Would you like that?"

She was terrified of being on the water, but she nodded. "I'd like to go with *you*."

"Good." He grinned, glanced at the door. "Maybe Fiona will stay in the house another minute." His gaze dropped to her mouth. "I want to kiss you, Sehoy."

A million butterflies took flight in her chest as she waited. Indian boys didn't kiss girls, but of course she'd heard of the practice. She closed her eyes as Oliver's face lowered to hers. His lips were warm and firm, lingering sweetly until she responded. Oh, she definitely liked this.

He lifted his head and whispered, "Hurry back, will you?"

139

9

Uncle Rémy's house was full to bursting on this first night of November. Since the Spanish invasion, the Laniers of Mobile traditionally hosted a harvest ball, which in the past had been held at Burelle's Tavern and Inn. However, Burelle's had long since declined in both influence and glamour, leaving Aunt Giselle no choice two years ago but to wheedle her indulgent husband into building a ballroom onto the back of their already sprawling home.

Maddy, dressed in a new lavender sprigged-muslin empire gown, worked her way from the refreshment table toward a seating cluster in one corner, where beautiful Madame de Marigny, the guest of honor, held court. Madame was also gowned in one of Maddy's creations, a peach-colored sarcenet with delicate puffed sleeves dripping in Alençon blonde lace to complement her Spanish coloring. Judging by the crowd of male admirers around the New Orleans matron's chair—and the envious looks from her feminine rivals—the ensemble was a hit. Maddy had

140

yet to greet her client this evening, and she meant to remedy the oversight. Madame was a delightful woman, witty and well-educated, and Maddy wanted to introduce her to Fiona.

She had almost reached her quarry when a big warm hand on her elbow stopped her. She knew it was Desi, even before she looked up into his smiling brown eyes.

"Where are you going in such an all-fired hurry, Mistress Burch?" he demanded, planting himself in front of her. "I want my name on your dance card before they're all taken." He plucked the little card dangling from a jeweled bracelet on her wrist and examined it with exaggerated anxiety. "Oh good, the supper dance is still available. I'll take it." He scribbled his name on the card, then lazily turned her hand to pull her glove back with his thumb and kiss her wrist.

She closed her eyes against the feel of his lips on her pulse point and said breathlessly, "You can't write over someone else's name. I'm engaged to Major Coffee for that dance!"

"Oh, was that fuzzy line a signature? I'm sure the major won't mind yielding to an old friend in this instance. Besides, I have it on good authority that the orchestra is considering a waltz, and it wouldn't be proper for you to engage in such a scandalous activity with anyone other than your big brother."

"You're not my brother." She hadn't meant for it to come out as such a bald, flat denial. Flustered, she jerked her hand from his and whipped it behind her back.

Desi's eyebrows went up. "Indeed I am not, if we are speaking in less-than-metaphorical terms." He studied her face. "Are you all right, Maddy-Mo?"

"Why wouldn't I be? Have you seen Fiona?"

"She's engaged with a cadre of young soldiers . . . somewhere over there." Desi waved in the direction of the dance floor. "She and the little Indian girl are quite the belles this evening."

Maddy stood on tiptoe and caught a glimpse of her cousin dancing with a young officer. She seemed to be enduring his attentions rather than precisely enjoying them. "I'm worried about her, Desi."

"Why?"

"She's . . . not herself. I don't know how to explain it."

"Hmm. Perhaps you'd better come tell me about it. Where's your shawl? It's chilly outside."

"I don't know. Desi, I really need to—"

But he was already towing her, gently but inexorably, toward the French window leading out into the garden. He paused long enough to remove his coat and drape it about her shoulders, then tucked her hand through his elbow and marched her out into the darkness. The spicy scent of Aunt Giselle's wax myrtles drifted about them, and the tree frogs chirred a cheerful monotone. Maddy had been in this garden hundreds of times, but here alone in the dark with Desi Palomo, her nerves pinged. Clutching the lapels of his coat together at her bosom, she stood looking up at the bright crescent moon sailing overhead.

"Pretty, isn't it?" Desi turned her, pulling her back against his chest and wrapping his arms about her. "Are you warm enough?"

She shivered. "I'm fine."

That was a lie. She was anything but fine. At least with her back to him, he couldn't see her face in the dark. But she could feel his strength, his protection, the deep rumble of his voice as he spoke.

"Tell me, what worries you about Fiona? You said something like that after we visited them at Navy Cove."

"I can't put my finger on it, but she's not herself. She's always been a bookish little thing—and horse-mad, of course—but since she arrived here, she will hardly speak of anything personal, even with me. And tonight her mind seems a million miles

142

away, as if she's barely tolerating the men she dances with. She used to love to dance."

"Hmm. You don't suppose she's ill?"

"I don't think so. At least, not in any physical way. Desi, I think something happened to her, maybe during that battle at Fort Bowyer. Maybe one of the soldiers assaulted her."

"If she won't tell you about it, there's little you can do. What about the Indian girl, Sehoy? Have you tried asking her if she knows anything?"

Maddy sighed. "Sehoy is so shy, she rarely speaks to me directly. Honestly, I don't know why either of them came."

Desi's arms tightened around her. "Maddy, you're the easiest person in the world to talk to. But I'll give it a try, if you want me to."

"Would you?" Anxiety dropping away with his simple offer of help, she turned in his arms and looked up at him.

His face dipped close to hers. "All you had to do was ask."

She forgot the cold, forgot Fiona, forgot the party and everything else except this man who had gone from beloved brother to just . . . beloved. How long had she loved him? When had she not loved him?

"Des, I don't want to take advantage of you."

"Oh, Maddy." He lifted a hand to brush his thumb across her cheek. "We're long past that, you and I."

"How long?" she whispered.

Laughter shook his voice. "Since I was old enough to shave."

"What?"

"Your parents knew, of course, which is why I was sent off to college rather early."

"How could I not know?"

"You see what you want to see, I suppose. They asked me not to speak to you until you'd had a chance to see more of the world—they took you to Europe, and then Washington." He sighed. "And then you fell in love with the soldier."

She felt his disappointment and hurt, suddenly understood her parents' reluctance to bless her marriage. But they'd let her go her way.

"Oh, my . . . Desi—"

"No, don't feel sorry for me. I had a lot of growing up to do. Things I needed to accomplish. I really was happy for you." His voice roughened. "But I confess, I'm glad you're free now."

"Me too. When I saw you again, I couldn't believe it. I never imagined you'd come back here after serving on the president's staff."

"I asked for the assignment, for lots of reasons. I didn't know your husband had died, and I needed to get you out of my system, to say goodbye. But—there you were, standing in the French market, beautiful as ever, only more so. And there seemed—seems to be a chance for me now." He paused. "Is there? If you tell me to leave you alone, I will, but as long as you need me, I'm here."

The silence of the garden stretched, muted sounds of music and laughter bleeding from the house. And oh, the delicious anticipation of that silence. "Desi, will you kiss me? I really need you to—"

His lips took the rest of the words from her mouth, gave them back to her, navigated her into uncharted territory where up was down and inside was out. Making himself at home, he kissed her cheeks and eyelids and temples, and again her lips, until she couldn't have said where he left off and she began.

Then that fragile, incandescent bubble of oneness burst as sudden noise blared from the ballroom.

"Mistress Madeleine! Mr. Palomo! They said you were out here—"

Maddy dropped her arms from around Desi's neck and whirled. His coat fell away from her shoulders as she hurried toward the light of the patio. "Here I am, Sehoy. What's the matter?"

Sehoy stood just outside the open window, wringing her hands. "Oh, thank goodness! Please come—and hurry! Fiona's in trouble."

"Wait." Behind her, Desi cupped Maddy's shoulders, holding her still. "Before we jump, tell us what happened. Better to go in prepared."

"One of the soldiers who went to Navy Cove to buy Fiona's horses suspected something funny and started asking questions. Then a couple of men from the shipyard, here in Mobile for the weekend, mentioned that Charlie Kincaid had disappeared. So word got back to General Coffee, and he buttonholed Fiona just now. She wouldn't lie to him, and so he accused her of hiding an enemy spy."

"Charlie Kincaid?" Maddy couldn't think where she'd heard that name.

"Yes, ma'am. Please come with me—the general is very angry, and I didn't know what to do!"

Desi sighed and put on the coat he'd picked up off the ground, then took Maddy's hand to tuck it through his arm. "We'd best intercede, don't you think? And quickly."

⌣

If she'd never taken a ride on the beach that day. If she'd ridden in another direction. If she'd told Léon and Uncle Luc-Antoine who Charlie was to begin with. If she'd let General Coffee take him prisoner when he came for the horses.

If. If. If.

No going back.

Fiona held her head high and stared at the general with every bit of inbred Lanier confidence. "I am no traitor, sir, and I resent your questioning my patriotism. My brothers and I simply decided it would be best for our family *and* our country—not to mention the family of Lord St. Clair, who saved the life of my uncle Rafa—to hold Mr. Kincaid at Navy Cove until such time as he could be traded for the safe return of our youngest brother Sullivan. I don't see what catastrophic line has been crossed. Prisoners are exchanged all the time."

Before General Coffee could answer, a deep, smooth voice behind Fiona said, "Miss Lanier is in the right of it, as you are very well aware."

She looked over her shoulder to find Desi Palomo approaching the gathering crowd, with her cousin Maddy—looking beautiful but oddly mussed, as well as wide-eyed with anxiety—clinging to his arm.

Desi gave Fiona a *Keep your mouth shut* look. "General, I assume you don't know the history of the Lanier and Gonzales families in this area, but their loyalty as American citizens is unquestioned. Also—perhaps General Jackson did not inform you of the heroic actions of Miss Lanier and her family during the battle at Fort Bowyer?"

Coffee folded his arms. "I heard some such story, but everyone knows how such tales get exaggerated in the telling."

"General, I was there," said a young soldier standing nearby on crutches. His bandaged left leg was missing from the knee down. "Miss Lanier and her cousin over there by the door tended the wounded for nearly forty-eight hours straight, and I doubt I'd be alive today without them."

The general scowled at the young man. "I don't remember asking for your opinion."

"But you said—"

Desi cleared his throat. "Sir, I understand your concern, but perhaps you'd allow me, as General Jackson's agent, to go to Navy Cove, investigate the truth of the rumors, and bring back a valid report."

"I want the *prisoner* brought here, not just a report. I'm going to send—"

"General Coffee! Sir, pardon the interruption—" A panting young officer pushed through the crowd. "General Jackson is looking for you. Immediately, if you please, sir."

Clearly irritated, Coffee placed a hand on his sword. "All right. Where is he?"

"In Mr. Lanier's smoking room, sir. There's news, but the general said not to blurt it out here in front of—"

"Yes, yes, boy, tell him I'm coming, as soon as I settle this issue at hand."

The young officer saluted and disappeared in the direction from which he'd arrived.

Coffee frowned at Desi. "Palomo, I shall leave the matter of the prisoner to you, though I should think General Jackson will have need of your services ere long. I bid you good evening, sir." He quit the room, leaving the crowd of merrymakers milling about in an uneasy hush.

Fiona hardly knew where to look. She had just escaped a dangerous situation, but the worst might be yet to come. She should be angry with Sehoy, but the girl was looking so miserable, Fiona could hardly upbraid her in public. Biting her lip, she caught Maddy's eyes. "I'm sorry to have embarrassed you, Cousin."

"Nonsense," Maddy said stoutly. "What dreadful manners the man has, to have made such a ridiculous charge without questioning you in private. In fact, I've had quite enough of this noise and heat. Desi, would you escort us ladies next door so that we may sort this out in my kitchen in peace?"

"Of course." Desi bowed and went to retrieve Maddy's woolen shawl and the new hooded cloaks Fiona had had made for herself and Sehoy. By the time they said their goodbyes to Aunt Giselle—who acquiesced to their early departure when Fiona pled a headache—the party guests had resumed their original gaiety.

"Elijah is sound asleep upstairs with Diron, bless him," Giselle said, kissing Maddy's cheek at the door. "Let him stay for breakfast, and I'll send him home after you've all had a good night's sleep. Fiona, a lemongrass tisane will take care of that headache, darling."

"Yes, ma'am. Good night," she said, and followed Maddy and Desi across the yard with Sehoy bringing up the rear.

The three guests sat at Maddy's kitchen table, avoiding each other's eyes while their hostess prepared tea.

When Maddy finally sat down, Fiona sighed. "All right, Cousin, I suppose I've run myself up a flagpole, as your papa would say. But I promise I didn't do it on purpose! Events just . . . rolled one into the other, and I couldn't seem to get myself untangled."

Maddy skewered Fiona with a stink eye reminiscent of Aunt Lyse at her most Creole *maman*. "Then perhaps you'd best start at the beginning—and tell the entire truth this time, if you please! Who is Charlie Kincaid?"

"Don't you remember? He's Lord St. Clair's youngest grandson, who was rusticating at Riverton when we were there."

Maddy frowned. "The tall, skinny boy with the mismatched eyes? Didn't he do something disgraceful at Eton to get sent down?"

Fiona nodded. "He thought you were beautiful, but you paid him not the slightest attention, which I suppose is understandable. But he and I became friends . . . of a sort. We nearly blew up the kitchen—" When Desi laughed, she said hastily, "—but I digress. Shortly after we left England, Charlie apparently talked his grandfather into buying him a commission in the British navy. We never corresponded, so I don't know exactly where the navy took him . . . except . . ." She gulped. "The very day we found out about Sullivan's capture, I found Charlie washed up on the beach at Mobile Point. He was out of his head and didn't know me, but I recognized him right off and took him home to recover. I—I didn't tell anyone who he was beyond his name, because—because it just didn't seem like a good idea. I was afraid Léon would hurt him or turn him in to the authorities."

"Fiona, turning him in would have been the right thing to do," Desi said gently. "Our countries are at war."

She rounded on him. "Well, but I didn't *know* that he was an enemy officer. After all, he wasn't in uniform. All I knew was that he was my friend, and he was badly injured, and I wanted him to have a chance to get well. He'd lost his memory of everything after Eton, and he's such a good man, and he became part of the family. Uncle Luc-Antoine likes him!" She glared at Maddy, daring her to contradict that.

Maddy set down her teacup. "Desi and I came to your house and you *hid* that man, never said a word about him. You knew that was wrong!"

"Of course I felt guilty about deceiving you. But I l–love Charlie, Maddy! I know you know how that feels!"

Maddy's cheeks reddened, and she glanced at Desi, whose lips twitched. "Of course I do," she said. "But now you've got the whole family implicated in this—this accusation of treason."

Desi, looking reassuringly sympathetic with Fiona, covered Maddy's hand with his. "Fiona, please let me go down to Navy Cove with you and talk to Charlie. If he's a naval officer, I agree with Maddy that he needs to be remanded to authorities here. Are you saying he's gotten his memory back?"

"Yes, at least most of it. I tended him when he got hit during the battle at Fort Bowyer, and he was hallucinating about storms and some kind of sea battle."

"But you say he wasn't in uniform?" Desi frowned. "That doesn't look good for him. It's possible that he is a spy. And it's awfully coincidental that he found himself in America, near a place where he knows someone . . . you and your family, that is."

"I've thought about that," Fiona said with a sigh. "I can't make sense of it, but I don't believe he'd betray our friendship that way."

"You cannot be that naive," Maddy said grimly. "Men take advantage of lovesick women every day."

Fiona stared at her cousin. "Charlie loves me."

"I'm sure he *said* he did. Fiona, it pains me to say it, but wake up! You have been duped by a handsome, charming, and very cunning young man. If you are a patriot, as you claim, you'll do the right thing—as hard as it is."

"But what about Sullivan? What if the general doesn't want to trade Charlie to get him back?" Tears, perilously near the surface, choked Fiona. "I wrote to Lord St. Clair. That's why I—"

"There is no guarantee that would happen anyway," Desi said gently. "Surely you knew that."

"Yes, but I had to try." Fiona put her face in her hands.

And as bad as things looked, there was still hope. God was a good God and could be trusted to right any wrong, in his time. Anything could happen.

~

NOVEMBER 3, 1814
NAVY COVE

The memories had been coming back, in chunks and jags almost as confusing as the darkness of complete forgetfulness. Charlie finished the set of sit-ups he'd started both to while away the time and to keep his body fit in spite of the endless inactivity of the last month. He touched his forehead, completely healed now except for the bumpy scar that cut across his eyebrow and extended into his hairline. Physically he felt as good as he'd felt in his life. The Laniers fed him well, and Luc-Antoine even came out to play his harmonica and talk on occasion.

Of course he missed Fiona—her absence was worse than the wound in his head—but if she'd been here, he would have told her that the presence of God's Holy Spirit had filled that void with hope. Several days ago, Oliver had brought his Bible out and left it, and Charlie used the time to refresh his memory of Scripture—and, he must admit, to learn what he'd not bothered to learn as a young boy. God the Creator had moved in history, through an impressive succession of flawed humans, to accomplish a grand design that Charlie could only guess at. If he were part of that design, to be used with all his own mistakes and wrongheadedness, the calamities that had befallen him thus far began to make sense.

Part of what had kept him here—besides physical weakness—was sheer affection for Fiona. She was counting on trading his sorry hide for her beloved twin brother. Certainly he understood and respected that familial love. He would do the same for either of his older brothers. Plus, he could hardly admit to himself his longing to see her one more time—or just hear her sweet, husky voice. On the other hand, the Lanier men had been justifiably worried about him running off with her, but since she'd been gone to Mobile, they had somewhat relaxed their vigilance.

Weeks had passed since Fiona and Sehoy left, possibly a month or more. Luc-Antoine said no word had come from Charlie's grandfather, though he supposed there was still a possibility that could happen. But this morning he had awakened with the feeling that he'd waited long enough. It was time to move.

He started by testing the strength of the chains around his ankles, as he'd done every morning since they'd put them on. One thing he would say for Luc-Antoine Lanier—the man was a first-class blacksmith. The iron links were smooth, free of rust, solidly forged. The story was that as a boy, just before the Spanish occupation, Luc-Antoine had been apprenticed to a Negro blacksmith who was enslaved to one of the wealthiest planters in the Mobile environs. He'd helped the slave earn his freedom in the fight for American independence, then joined him as a partner and settled on land ceded by the Spanish to the family on Mobile Point.

When the irons proved unbreakable as usual, Charlie turned his attention to the walls to which the chains were bolted. Here he might have a prayer of success. All lumber in this oceanside climate became subject to rot over time. Frequent rain, salt air, and infestation of bugs all created conditions which softened even the strongest of hardwood. Over the last few weeks, the Lanier men had long since removed anything sharp that might be used as an implement for digging or cutting, but Sehoy had once left a spoon from his dinner. Charlie had hidden it in a crack in the floor under his pallet.

Listening to make sure the barn was empty except for the animals, he located the spoon and pressed the end of its handle against the board behind the iron plate that held the chain bolt. The board gave. Heart leaping, he kept digging until the spoon bent in his hand. He moved to the other side of the plate and poked and prodded some more.

Splintery chunks of wood came away, leaving large gashes in the plank. He was going to have to make his escape now, because anybody who came in to check on him would see the damage—and move him. With renewed determination he dug harder and faster. The bolt plate wiggled the next time he tried it. Exultant, he yanked as hard as he could, and it gave another fraction of an inch.

Panting now, sweating from tension and exertion, he nearly jumped out of his skin when one of the horses kicked at a stall. There were only two left—Fiona's Bonnie and Washington, the stud stallion that Léon rode. All the others had been sold to General Coffee. He stopped, frowning. Usually Oliver turned the horses out first thing in the morning. Why had he not done so today?

Then voices approaching from the north side of the barn told him why. Two of the voices were light, feminine.

Fiona and Sehoy. He also recognized Oliver, but a second male voice was unfamiliar. Deep, smooth, a lawyer's voice, or maybe a preacher's, the accent clean and cultured, with a faint Spanish sibilance to the *s*'s. Wait, maybe he *had* heard that voice before. But where?

Galvanized, he knelt to shove the spoon back into its hiding place. What was he going to do about the gashes in the wood? There was nothing to hang over the spot, no way to paint it. Maybe they wouldn't come to him. Maybe they'd go straight into the house and leave him to rot out here with the horses.

The voices entered the barn, so he turned and leaned against the wall, covering the place where he had been working. The clamp and bolt dug into his back, reminding him of the stupidity and hopelessness of his situation. He'd waited too late. He was going to be caught and turned over to the American military.

Briefly, wildly, he considered throwing himself on their mercy as an informant. Betraying his commission, his commander, his king.

But the thought fled as quickly as it arrived. No Kincaid

would consider treason, even for a deeply loved woman. As he'd said to Fiona, she shouldn't give herself to a man who would commit such a crime.

So he waited, pulse thrumming. The door latch rattled, a key turned in the padlock, the bolt slid across the door, all familiar sounds that he heard every time they brought him out to stretch his legs.

The door opened, and Fiona's was the first face he saw. She looked beautiful, of course, with her curly fair hair windblown into wild ringlets, but otherwise polished like a fine jewel. She wore a soft, dark-green cloak, the hood fallen back to frame her face, over a thin green silk dress like fine London ladies wore.

Her tear-brimmed eyes pierced him. "Charlie, I've brought somebody to talk to you."

Resisting the urge to kneel before her, the duchess of his heart, he looked at the tall, dark-haired man behind her—and nearly dove into a corner in dismay. No wonder the man's voice had sounded so familiar. What was New Orleans Governor Claiborne's translator doing here?

"I am Desi Palomo, agent of General Andrew Jackson," the man said in that deep, faintly accented voice. "I understand you are the Honorable Charlie Kincaid, grandson of Admiral Lord St. Clair?"

Charlie nodded. "More precisely, Lieutenant Charles Kincaid, of His Majesty's Royal Navy."

"Ah. Then your so-convenient memory lapse has ended." Setting Fiona aside, Palomo sauntered into the tack room and looked around.

He didn't seem to recognize Charlie, but this was not a stupid man. Charlie was going to have to be careful. Forcing himself to relax against the wall, he crossed one ankle over the other and folded his arms in deliberate insolence. "Convenience depends on one's perspective, I suppose. My pain from injuries sustained while helping to defend Fort Bowyer has mostly subsided as well. Do you seriously contend that a British naval officer would so conduct himself if he hadn't lost all memory of his sworn duty?"

"He would if there were ulterior motives in play." Palomo's smile was bland. "But let us not begin with such harsh accusations, Lieutenant Kincaid. Miss Lanier here wishes to believe the best of you, and I would hear from your own lips an account of your out-of-uniform presence on American soil."

Fiona could hardly breathe. She had deliberately stretched out the visit to Maddy, putting off going home—where Charlie was a prisoner and nothing would ever be the same. But her hand had been forced, everyone knew what she'd done, and she had to face him. Face the humiliation of having fallen for a liar. A user.

Could she ever again trust her own judgment?

He stood leaning against the wall, relaxed in his chains, a smirk on his fine mouth. She could see the wheels turning in his head as he put together his story, figured out twists to make it seem true. His story. History. She supposed the past was ever that way—events told and retold and embellished to benefit the teller.

His eyes were clear and bright, his color good in spite of his incarceration, the scar on his forehead faded to a healthy pinkish-white. She was glad. At least she didn't have to feel guilty that he'd been mistreated. It had been easier to believe in him when he'd been injured and ill.

"I'm under no obligation to tell you anything," he said, regarding Desi calmly.

"On the other hand, if you don't speak, I shall be forced to assume the worst." Desi glanced at Fiona. "She's told us every-thing that happened since you arrived here, including the fact that there was no indication of your military rank."

"That's because I didn't know it." Charlie touched the scar on his head. "I presume you've never had an injury that liter-ally knocked you senseless. Not a thing one has control over."

"I'm not arguing that point. But you have clearly regained your memory, and I repeat my original question. Why was a British naval lieutenant sailing off the coast of an American military post, out of uniform?"

Charlie shrugged. "Obviously, the British fleet was in the area, which you know from the attack on Fort Bowyer. My ship was sailing just south of the Gulf of Mexico when we encountered the storm that scattered the whole flotilla. I washed overboard and just managed to grab onto a lifeboat. I honestly have no idea what happened to the rest of the officers and crew, but I floated for several days before I was picked up by a Spanish merchant ship heading for New Orleans. By then I was delirious and dehydrated. The Spaniards dressed me in clothes intended for sale in the city. Unfortunately, another storm hit before we could reach port, and this time I was hit in the head by a broken mast." He looked directly at Fiona. "If she hadn't found me, I would be dead."

Her heart pinched. Was his tone just a little too glib?

She watched Desi's face. Did he believe Charlie's story?

Dark eyes inscrutable, Desi gave a short laugh. "There's no doubt you are one lucky Scotsman—or unlucky, I suppose, depending on where you stop in the story."

Charlie smiled. "Rather luckier than not. Every sailor lives expecting the next storm to send him to Davy Jones's locker. That I instead woke in the arms of the sweetest, most beautiful woman I've ever seen? I'd say someone has plans for my life beyond my own selfish gain."

Desi's lip curled. "Ah. So God put you here? Funny, we Americans are rather fond of claiming the Almighty's favor."

"Be that as it may, I've told you everything I am able to say without betraying my responsibilities as an officer." Charlie turned that blue-hazel gaze on Fiona. "Except . . . I would like to express my sincere regret for having put Miss Lanier in jeopardy. She has been nothing but kind to me, and I harbor no ill will for her part in my capture." His tone was formal but sincere. Where was the passionate, affectionate Charlie she'd adored in childhood and recently come to love? Had that been a lie too?

"Charlie—"

A slicing motion of his hand cut her off. "If you don't mind, I'm rather tired of this interrogation. I have nothing else to say."

As she backed away from the pure boredom in his eyes, she felt gentle hands on her shoulders.

"Come, Fiona," Sehoy said quietly, "let's go and make a cup of tea, then I'll help you unpack. Oliver, you'll come with us?" she said over her shoulder.

"Of course," Oliver said.

Fiona stared at Charlie's impassive face for one more moment, then whirled and left Desi to deal with him.

Some wounds, invisible though they might be, were beyond healing.

10

To Charlie's dismay, Desi Palomo didn't leave with the women—and please God it wasn't because he'd finally recognized Charlie. He'd gone to a lot of trouble to keep a low profile while skulking about New Orleans, attending quadroon balls—where white Creole men met and made certain arrangements with light-skinned free women of color—gambling, listening to conversations in the French Market.

"You are a better man than I thought," Palomo said, eyeing Charlie with some perplexity.

"What do you mean?"

"You know she loves you. You could play on her sympathy in any number of ways."

"My conscience is quite loaded enough, thank you—I don't need that as well."

Palomo stared at him for a long moment. "All right, then. But for the record, I'm inclined to agree with Fiona that the best use of your presence is trading you for someone more valuable to us. Especially if we can hold you here—or, better yet, in Mobile—long enough to keep you from effecting whatever mischief you'd planned when you first arrived."

"I didn't *plan* to be here," Charlie burst out, "the storm—"

"Yes, yes, the storm," Palomo said, waving a well-manicured hand. "But you'd come from somewhere specific and clearly were on the way to somewhere specific. You weren't just wandering the globe. And how you landed *here*, of all the ports along the Gulf Coast—within five miles of the home of a young woman who has demonstrably carried a torch for you for nearly ten years—now that is the interesting point of all this."

"I told you," Charlie said doggedly, "I was part of the fleet assigned to attack Mobile. But when the Spanish picked me up and I had no way to get back to my command, I remembered from the Gonzales family's visit all those years ago that I must be close to the port of Mobile. And my rescuers agreed to leave me there. It is pure chance—or divine intervention, if you will—that Fiona found me before I died from the effects of the second storm."

"And these storms were in August?" Palomo appeared to have settled in for conversation. Dangerous conversation.

"If you say so." Charlie shrugged. "I still have no clear memory of that time, outside of some very tense nightmares." *Go on the attack. Misdirect.* "Now perhaps you will answer some questions for me. You say you are an agent for General Jackson. Is he now commander-in-chief of the southern wing of the American army?"

"He is. And when he heard that an English officer had been living as a guest at Mobile Point—had even participated in a battle against the British fleet and perhaps helped to defeat them—well, he is understandably curious as to the meaning of your . . . shall we say, less-than-orthodox behavior. I am instructed to bring you back under guard so that he may question you himself."

"I have nothing else of import to relate. All my *unorthodox* behavior can be explained by my head injury. I've told you everything I know."

Palomo regarded him, head canted to one side for a moment. "Then, Lieutenant Kincaid, I shall leave you to your own unsociable company. I wish to stay the night and make sure Fiona is properly settled, but you and I will leave for Mobile at daylight. You should pack for an extended vacation at Fort Charlotte. Formal wear not required." He sketched a mocking bow and left.

Charlie heard the bolt scrape across the door and the key turn in the lock. He waited, standing with his back against the wall, for several minutes, then when no one else approached, slid bonelessly to the ground. He looked up at the gouged wood around the plate that fastened his chains to the wall.

He would be out of here well before daybreak. He would never see Fiona Lanier again, nor her plethora of cousins and brothers and uncles.

A wave of depression nearly flattened him.

Sehoy leaned on the paddock rail, watching Fiona exercise the monstrous horse they called Washington after the first American president—the one who had cunningly used Indian tactics of warfare to outwit the redcoat army many years ago. She wondered what would have happened if General Washington had been commander of the troops trying to keep the British from invading this time. Would they have already claimed a resounding victory, instead of this dismal, win-some, lose-some effort that seemed doomed to drag out for another year or more?

She wouldn't have cared, except Oliver was bent on joining his cousin Sullivan in sacrificing himself for his country. And

Fiona was starving herself into a decline over that handsome, two-faced Englishman Charlie Kincaid. Sehoy could see nothing she herself could do about the situation. Fiona didn't want to talk about it at all, Oliver said little enough in deference to Sehoy's feelings of loathing toward Generals Andrew Jackson and John Coffee, and there was no one to whom she could unburden herself about the cipher locked in her trunk.

Why on earth had she agreed to keeping it, surely an act of treason toward her benefactors? And what if they found it on her? Would she be interrogated and disgraced as Fiona had been? She'd been so hurt and traumatized by the nightmares about Horseshoe Bend that any way to exact revenge had seemed sweet. By now the lines had gotten all blurry again. Charlie Kincaid—as best she could determine—was no hero, and she couldn't think of any good reason she should be helping him sneak information to his British commanders.

Except for the fact that she had promised . . .

"Fiona!" she called out. "I'm going to get my sketch book. I'll be right back."

When Fiona gave her a halfhearted wave, Sehoy walked to the house, passing Desi Palomo, Oliver, and Uncle Luc, who sat on the porch respectively chewing a toothpick, carving some sea creature, and smoking a pipe. Léon was presumably down at the shipyard, inspecting the progress of the ship.

Sehoy slipped into the bedroom she shared with Fiona and knelt before her trunk. It had gotten a little battered in transport to and from Mobile, but it was still beautiful and it still filled her with awe that she owned something so valuable. She unlocked it with the little key Uncle Luc had given her, hanging from a string around her neck, and lifted the lid. She took her art satchel from the hidden compartment in the bottom of the trunk, replaced the cover, and locked the trunk once more.

When she got out to the porch, Oliver put down his knife and smiled. "Are you going out to the beach to draw? Want some company?"

"No, you men are comfortable, and I want to be by myself to think. I'm going to the barn, to maybe sketch the little goats."

Oliver's smile faded. "Oh. All right then. I'll see you when you get back."

She had hurt his feelings, but she had to get rid of this cipher. She supposed she could just burn it—but couldn't quite make herself go that far. "Thanks for understanding. I'll be back in a little bit." Giving Oliver an uncertain smile, she headed for the barn with her satchel clutched under her arm.

So that she wouldn't be caught in a lie, she marched straight for the stall where the little goats slept. Fiona let them out of the barn to play in the pasture for a few hours every day, but they were inside now, nursing. The nanny *maa*-ed a greeting as she went into the stall, but otherwise ignored her. Sehoy sat down in the straw with her back against the wall, opened the satchel, and took out her charcoal and paper. With a few quick strokes she sketched the nanny and the twins. In spite of her anxiety, she enjoyed the coarse, wooly texture of the babies' hair, the funny knobs on their heads that would turn into horns, their eyes closed in an ecstatic milk coma.

Her pencil slowed, and tears stung her eyes at the thought of leaving behind, for good, this place she'd come to think of as home. How could she have even considered doing anything to jeopardize her place in the Lanier family? Pushing the paper off her lap into the straw, leaving the charcoal on top of it, she rose and brushed off her skirt. With a deep breath for courage, she made herself leave the stall, satchel in hand, and approach the tack room door.

She scratched at the door. "Charlie? Are you awake?" What

did he do in there all day? She'd have long since gone mad from boredom. Oliver said he'd given the prisoner a Bible to read, but that didn't seem like a book Charlie Kincaid would be interested in. He liked swimming and fishing and building things and making jokes and tripping people up in their own words. Way too smart for his own good, as Uncle Luc-Antoine put it.

When there was no answer, she knocked. "Charlie? It's me, Sehoy."

"What do you want?" Charlie's voice was husky, sleepy-sounding.

"I'm sorry to wake you up, but I need to talk to you."

There was a moment's silence, then, "Do they know you're out here?"

"Yes. I brought my drawing paper. But—it's important. I want to give you back your . . . you know."

This time his voice came from right on the other side of the door. "You still have it?"

"Of course I still have it. Did you think I'd burn it?" Guiltily she reminded herself that she wasn't going to do that, not really.

"I didn't know. I was fairly sure you hadn't told anyone you had it. I can't have that on me, Sehoy. They're getting ready to move me to Mobile, and they'll search me. Probably you should burn it after all."

"No, I—I'm going to slide it under the door. It's yours and I don't want responsibility for it."

"Listen, Sehoy, I know you didn't give me up, and I appreciate it. If things get . . . difficult for you when the British take over here, you just give my name, and you'll be taken care of. Understand?"

"You really think that's going to happen?"

"Oh, it'll happen. Count on it."

She licked suddenly dry lips. "If you say so. What about Fiona?"

"Take care of her, Sehoy. Promise me." His voice sounded strangled.

"I promise. Here's the paper then." Crouching she took the parchment out of its bag and slid it under the door. "I'll have to keep the pouch, it won't fit—"

"That's all right. But you'd better go. I don't want them to catch you talking to me."

"Charlie, I'm sorry for you and Fiona."

She waited, but he didn't answer. Blinking away silly, awkward tears, she put the oilskin pouch back in her art bag and went back to the stall for her sketch book. To her dismay, she found the little goats gnawing on it, leaving the charcoal so smeared that you couldn't even tell what the picture was. She sat down and cried with her head on her knees.

Oh dear, oh dear. Poor goats. Poor Charlie. Poor Fiona.

Sometime in the middle of the night Fiona sat up, wide awake. After she and Sehoy went to bed after dark, she'd lain awake for over an hour, tossing and turning, thinking about Charlie and worrying over what would happen to him. When she finally went to sleep, she dreamed of chasing him on horseback off a cliff and scrambling down a high bluff onto the beach below, then galloping across the blinding white sand straight into the ocean. Rolling waves crested against Bonnie's chest as she struggled to catch up to Charlie's horse. Just as Charlie disappeared under the water, Fiona awoke, gasping for air as if she were the one drowning.

"Sehoy!" she whispered. "Sehoy, are you awake?" She felt for her cousin's shoulder.

The other side of the bed was flat, empty.

"Sehoy?" Fiona lit the bedside candle. The covers had been

neatly folded back, and Sehoy's dressing gown and slippers were missing from the foot of the bed, as was her candle. Where had she gone?

She couldn't think of any reason for shy, introverted Sehoy to venture outdoors alone in the middle of the night. Perhaps Fiona's own flirtation with treason made her suspicious of others, but she couldn't squelch the feeling that Sehoy must be up to something questionable.

She felt about for her slippers, then decided boots would be a better choice for stomping around in the yard in the dark. Her cloak went on over her dressing gown, for the temperature would have dropped once the sun went down, and she could hear the gulf breeze howling across the porch and banging the swing into the wall. Resigned to an uncomfortable few minutes outdoors, she tiptoed to the kitchen and out the back door. She didn't want to wake up the men. Léon was worse than a granny about her and Sehoy going out after dark.

She found no sign of her cousin on the back side of the house. More curious than frightened, she pulled her cloak tighter about her body and walked around to the front.

"Sehoy!" she hissed. "Where are you?" She walked up the porch steps and sat on the swing, befuddled. Had Sehoy and Oliver made plans to meet somewhere? But why would they do that, when they saw each other plenty during the day? Unless . . . her mind didn't want to go where it was going. Sehoy was not promiscuous, and Oliver was as innocent as the child she'd once called him.

Well, but if they *were* being stupid enough to meet in the middle of the night, and they weren't here on the porch, the only place they could be was the barn. She rose, setting the swing chains to jangling, then stood irresolute. Maybe she should mind her own business. Maybe Sehoy had just returned to the house from the front and Fiona had missed her. Maybe she was already back in the bed.

But it wouldn't hurt to go to the barn and check on the horses. Washington had been favoring his right fetlock at the end of their session this afternoon. If he was all right, she'd go back to bed and scold Sehoy in the morning.

Cupping her hand to protect the candle flame from the wind, she took off across the yard. The half moon was obscured by scudding clouds, but she made out the looming shape of the barn, where she could hear a horse shuffling in a stall. She recognized Bonnie's whuffling, but where was Washington? He was usually the more restive of the two.

She began to trot. Sehoy wouldn't have taken him. She was scared to death of the gentle giant.

Fiona lit a lantern with her candle, then blew the candle out and went straight to Bonnie. The horse stuck her head out over the stall door to nuzzle Fiona's ear. Smiling, Fiona stroked Bonnie's cheek. "Hey, you, I don't have anything to eat this time of night. Where's your beau?" A glance down the row of stalls told her that Washington was gone.

Just . . . gone.

Stomach suddenly in a knot, she patted Bonnie and walked down to Washington's stall. She'd put both horses in the barn for the night, because for the last few weeks the nights had been cold. Washington hadn't kicked down the door; someone had let him out. Truly, she couldn't imagine Sehoy . . . but maybe Oliver . . . ?

Something made her walk toward the tack room at the other end of the barn. Léon would be angry if he found out she'd been out here talking to Charlie in the middle of the night, but she had little to lose at this point. The lantern threw shadows along the aisle, a mouse scurried into a loose pile of straw. The familiar smells of hay and manure should have been comforting, but something was wrong. *Everything* was wrong.

The tack room door was shut and bolted, but the padlock was open.

She hit the door with the flat of her hand. "Charlie! Wake up! Has Sehoy been out here?"

She heard a choked "Fiona?" and it did not sound like Charlie.

"Sehoy?" Fumbling, she slid back the bolt and opened the door. Peering in with the lantern held high, she saw Sehoy curled in the straw, arms wrapped about her head. When the light hit her, she turned over to shield her eyes with her hand.

Fiona put her fist to her mouth, stifling a scream. Charlie's pallet was neatly made, as it had been this morning when she came in with Desi. The wall where his chains had been clamped was ruined, the softened wood gouged and raw, the plate and chains missing.

"Sehoy! Where is Charlie?"

"I'm sorry, Fiona. He tricked me." Sehoy sat up, scrubbing her hands over her face.

"Who tricked you?" Fiona asked stupidly. "Charlie?"

Sehoy nodded. "Oliver said Charlie wouldn't eat any dinner, and I felt bad about leaving him to starve, so I waited until everyone was asleep, and I took Oliver's key. I brought him some cornbread, and . . . When I opened the door, he was standing free. I tried to shut the door, but he just stepped past me and pushed me in and slammed the door and slid the bolt!"

"Oh no! Oh no no no—Sehoy, he's taken Washington!" Fury and hurt seized her. "How could you let this happen? How are we going to get Sullivan back now?"

Sehoy's face crumpled. "I don't know! I told you I'm sorry! But look, he left this for you. I found it on his bed." She opened her hand to show Fiona the heavy carnelian intaglio ring Charlie had worn on his left index finger.

Fiona took the ring and stared at it, felt its weight and warmth, as if it were a living thing. Part of Charlie himself. She clenched the ring in her fist. "What am I supposed to do with this?"

"I suppose it's payment for the horse." Sehoy sniffled. "You could sell it."

"Money won't get my brother back! How long has he been gone?"

"Not long. I'm not sure what time it was—"

"I'm going after him. Washington was favoring his leg, so maybe Bonnie can catch up to him." Of course she didn't want Washington going down, but it could happen.

"But you don't know where he went!"

"The British are gathering in Pensacola. He would be riding east across Mobile Point, and there's only one road over. He won't be familiar with the area, so he'll have to stop and ask someone . . . Oh, never mind! I've got to change clothes and get Bonnie saddled."

"But, Fiona—"

Ignoring Sehoy, Fiona hurried back to the house. Forcing herself to move quietly in spite of frissons of panic and anger that rolled about under her rib cage, she left her boots on the porch, then tiptoed into the bedroom and dropped her cloak on the bed. She stripped off her robe and nightgown, replaced them with Sullivan's breeches and shirt, and pattered back to the porch to put her boots back on.

When she got back to the barn, outfit completed with Oliver's hat and overcoat, she was stunned to find Sehoy leading Bonnie out of the barn, already saddled. As Fiona checked the girth—not quite trusting Sehoy's ability to properly cinch it—Sehoy stood at Bonnie's head, silently holding the reins.

"Thank you for doing this," Fiona said through her teeth. "You didn't have to."

"It's my fault he's gone. I felt sorry for you and Charlie both, but as much as I despise General Jackson, I love you and your brothers more. I hope you can catch him."

Fiona noticed Sehoy didn't mention Oliver. Neither did she ask how Fiona was going to bring a healthy, fully recovered Charlie back to Navy Cove.

Sehoy's eyes widened when she saw Fiona strap her rifle behind the saddle. "Do you know how to use that?"

"I've been hunting with my brothers since I could climb a tree. I'm a better shot than Oliver."

"You're not going to *shoot* Charlie, are you?"

"I hope not." With that Fiona swung into the saddle and kicked Bonnie into a canter, then a run.

If she'd had time to think about it, she might have been frightened. Riding cross-country before dawn, when she had no idea, really, where her quarry could be . . . crack-brained, is what Léon would call her. In fact, when he discovered what she'd done, she was going to be in even worse trouble than before.

As it was, she operated on pure outrage and instinct. She knew the Indian road to Pensacola like the back of her hand. Charlie would get to the neck of Perdido Bay and be forced to either find a ferry across or ride north along the bay until he ran into the Perdido River—which he would still have to cross. Pensacola was a hard two-day ride, even if one knew the route. With Washington going lame, she and Bonnie were going to catch him before he got to Fort Barancas.

She didn't have a choice.

⌒

NOVEMBER 4, 1814
WEST FLORIDA

As the great black stallion pounded the shell road eastward toward Perdido Pass, Charlie exulted in God's provision. Fiona would probably attribute his escape to the work of the devil himself—and condemn Charlie as one of the adversary's minions. Funny how he simply felt like a man doing his duty.

Still, if he lived to be a hundred, he would never forget the look on Sehoy's face as he yanked her into the tack room and slammed the door on her.

He'd gotten the chains free from the wall shortly after Oliver came to offer him dinner—which he'd refused, to eliminate any chance of being caught working on his escape. Then over and over, he'd thought through what he was going to do. Lock Sehoy in when she came to bring his breakfast. Take Washington. Leave the ring for Fiona.

He'd known he'd be taking a great chance on one of the men following him on Bonnie and hauling him right back. With the whole family up and about in the morning, Sehoy would be quickly missed. He hadn't counted on her tender heart prompting her to bring him food in the middle of the night. Fortunately, he'd been ready.

And here he was, trying hard not to think about what might happen to Fiona, Léon, Oliver, and Luc-Antoine when the whole Gulf Coast area, including Louisiana, the Mississippi Territory, and Florida, all returned to British control. Doubtful the Laniers would be allowed to maintain their property holdings, unless they could be convinced to swear fealty to the British Crown.

As if that would happen in a million years.

And even supposing Charlie were allowed to return to beg for Fiona's hand in marriage, what made him think she would ever consider taking her conqueror to husband? As long shots went, he might as well ask for the moon.

He looked up at that silent, bloodless half orb sailing near the eastern horizon. Despair threatened to overcome his determination to do the right thing. But it seemed God wasn't finished with Charlie Kincaid, and he mustn't give in.

He'd ridden perhaps another quarter hour when he noticed a shifting in the horse's gait, a slight favoring of the right fetlock. He'd been about to stop to rest the animal anyway, so he reined in, slowing Washington to a walk. The trail had taken him into a thick woods, mostly oak and pine, dripping overhead with Spanish moss and filled in below with scrubby underbrush. He'd earlier splashed through standing water here and there, and he should come across a creek or spring before long. Dismounting, he listened for running water as he walked along leading Washington, boots and hooves crunching on the sandy road.

Before long he heard water and turned off the path into a small clearing, obviously a well-used stopping place. While Washington drank from the creek, Charlie pulled flint and candle from the saddlebag he'd taken along with the tack. Lighting the candle, he crouched to examine the horse's legs and feet. He could see nothing amiss on either fetlock, but when he picked up the right one and bent it, Washington flinched. The lower joint was swollen and overly warm.

Charlie sat on his heels, muttering imprecations under his breath. How could he be so careless as to take a lame horse? He could just as easily have taken Bonnie, but he'd thought he would make better time on the bigger, stronger stallion. Fiona would no doubt laugh at his chagrin, if she could see him now—after she got over her initial anger, that was. Guiltily his thumb found the bare spot on his finger where the signet ring had been. At least he'd had something of value to trade for the horse. He wouldn't have horse theft on his conscience.

More to the point, what was he going to do now? Walking all the way to Pensacola would take days, and since the Laniers would guess the direction he'd taken, he had no time to lose.

He needed another horse, but where was he going to get one? His major disadvantage was unfamiliarity with the region. If he were in New Orleans, he'd have known where to go for a new mount. Resisting the urge to kick a tree in frustration, he cupped his hands for a drink of the icy water, then stood and pulled Washington back to the road. Wishing he'd had the forethought to grab some of the food Sehoy had brought to him before he locked her in the tack room and took off, he and his growling stomach led the horse toward Pensacola. If he remembered correctly from a map he'd studied while in New Orleans, he should be about halfway to Perdido Pass, which was halfway between Mobile and Pensacola.

In other words, the middle of nowhere.

He kept walking and praying. This business of trusting God in the middle of severe trial was turning out to be quite an enlightening experience.

~

The sun was well up when Fiona stopped to rest Bonnie at a creek where she and her brothers had used to camp while on hunting trips. If Charlie was any kind of outdoorsman—and she knew he was—he would have stopped here as well, for the trail clearly took a side path into the brush, and the water could be heard burbling counterpoint to the sound of tree frogs and other wildlife moving through the woods. She reined Bonnie in, dismounted, and examined the ground for tracks in the mud. Since dawn, she'd been following Washington's hoofprints wherever they moved off the shell paving. It looked like he'd been favoring that right fetlock for some time, and she wondered how long it took Charlie to notice.

Emotions pinging from righteous anger to worry about her horse to reluctant admiration for Charlie's ingenuity and back again, she watered Bonnie, then climbed into the saddle and set out again. She prayed her quarry would have the sense not to ride a lame horse. The sooner she caught him, the better chance poor Washington would have of recovery.

To her relief, it looked like Charlie was now leading the horse. The tracks and horse manure were fresh enough that she knew she would catch up to him soon, maybe by noon. She pushed Bonnie a little harder than she would have liked, but her mount seemed just as keen to run as Fiona. Overwhelming love and appreciation for the hardy little buckskin washed over her. If Charlie had elected to take Bonnie instead of Washington, this would be a completely different situation.

The woods thinned and opened to marsh, and she was forced to ride at a northeast angle for several miles to get around it. It seemed natural to pray as she rode. For a person who had always leaned on her Christian upbringing, the last few months had been something of a conundrum. She'd been taught not to expect God to answer her every request with a "yes," but at least she'd never had reason to doubt his presence in her life. Even her parents' death and Sullivan's capture had oddly strengthened her awareness of God's surrounding and comforting love.

But since the arrival of Charlie Kincaid, she'd had trouble discerning the simplest things like right and wrong. Loving the enemy became treason; patriotism turned into cutting out half her heart.

And what on earth was she going to say to him when she—

All of a sudden, there he was.

She rounded a bend of the marsh and caught a flash of black, far in the distance, disappearing behind a stand of cypress. Reining Bonnie in, she tried to decide if Charlie would have heard her coming. Of course he would; Bonnie had been cantering and he'd been walking. There would be no sneaking up on him. So she pulled the rifle from its scabbard and checked to make sure it was loaded and ready to fire.

She assumed Charlie didn't have a gun, but what if he'd bought or found one somewhere? Would he fire on her?

God, I don't know what I'm doing. Help me.

Leaning forward, she goosed Bonnie's sides and loosened the reins. "Let's go, girl."

Bonnie surged into a gallop. Moments later she caught sight of Charlie and Washington again. Charlie wore Sullivan's hat and coat—she'd forgotten he still had them. Washington was running, his beautiful smooth stride marred by a distinct limp.

"Charlie! Stop!" she shouted, but of course he didn't. He must know Washington couldn't outrun Bonnie, but he would be desperate enough to try. Washington would go down with a broken leg, and she'd have to put him down.

Enraged at Charlie's stupidity and selfishness, she urged Bonnie on. The gap between the horses narrowed. Now she could see the whiteness of Charlie's face when he glanced over his shoulder.

Closer, closer. Twenty feet away. If she got right up on him, she would never be strong enough to overpower him, so she was going to have to disable him first. Clenching her teeth, she held the knotted reins in her left hand, bracing the forestock of the gun, her right hand on its neck, finger on the trigger. One shot. That was all she had, so she'd best make it good.

She wanted to hit his shoulder. Bonnie's silky stride and the flat terrain made the shot possible at ten feet or less. But she was going to have to be very, very lucky.

Fifteen feet. She held Bonnie with her knees, aiming low because the gun would jerk. Took a deep breath, let it halfway out and held it to steady her body. Ten feet. Now—

The gun roared as she pulled the trigger.

Charlie flinched. Blood bloomed on his right thigh as, to her horror, Washington reared, screaming and throwing Charlie. Had she hit the horse too?

She was upon them in seconds. Tossing the rifle, she reined Bonnie to a skidding halt, flung herself out of the saddle, and grabbed for Washington's reins. He would trample Charlie if she couldn't—

Oh, God, my God, help me!

Maybe she said it aloud. Washington calmed to a prancing, frantic circle but somehow avoided Charlie. Doubting he'd run off, she turned him loose.

In two strides she was standing over Charlie, fists clenched in helpless rage. Words would not come.

He lay on his side, his face pale, tight with pain, his fingers trying to stanch the flow of blood on his thigh. "You shot me!"

"I didn't have any choice." She felt as if she might choke.

"You had lots of choices! Are you insane?"

"*You're* the crazy person! Running a lame horse into the ground!"

"Who taught you to shoot like that?"

"I'm embarrassed, I was aiming for your head."

He stared at her. After a moment his mouth curled, and he was laughing. He lay back flat, pulling his hat down over his face. "Only in America."

11

Charlie was going to have trouble explaining to his commanding officers how he'd come to be captured by a girl.

He sat on the cold, damp ground, trying not to cry out as Fiona used her hunting knife to cut the leg off his breeches. He couldn't help thinking of the time she'd nursed him after the battle of Fort Bowyer, when she'd been so tender and efficient (not to mention willing to kiss him). Now, her expression was grim—eyes narrowed, those sweet lips clamped together, jaw tight—as she cleaned his wound with water from the bladder she'd produced from her saddlebag.

"You could at least look the other way," he said, going for a smile.

Ignoring the joke, she examined the blackened gash running from his upper thigh almost to the knee. "I've seen a man's leg before. This is going to hurt like the dickens, but you'll survive. Take off your coat and give me your shirt."

"Miss Lanier! My modesty—"

"Oh, stuff it. I don't have anything else to make bandages out of." She sat back on her heels. "If I'd had on a skirt—"

"You wouldn't have caught me."

"I assure you I would." She gave him a steely blue stare that would have cowed a braver man than Charlie. "The shirt, Lieutenant Kincaid."

He sighed and shrugged out of the coat, then pulled the shirt off over his head. Teeth chattering, he handed it to her. "So now I'm to die of exposure?"

"Put the coat back on and stop being such a birdwit." She tore the edge of the shirt with her teeth, then efficiently stripped it into a long bandage. With little apparent consideration for his pain, she began to wrap the bandage tightly about his leg. "We're going to have to hurry to get you to a doctor. I don't have any whiskey to dull the pain or wash this with. If we had time, I'd cauterize it, but . . ." She shrugged and gave him a resentful look. "I'm not putting you on Washington. We'll have to ride double like we did before, and lead him."

"I didn't know he was lame when I took him."

"You shouldn't have taken him to begin with! You—you horse thief!"

"I left you my ring!"

"How can you possibly justify not only taking my source of income but depriving me of my only way to get my brother back?"

If she'd shrieked at him, he might have felt some measure of justification, but the exaggerated control of her tone told him how much he had hurt her.

He grabbed her cold, gloveless hands, still stained from his blood. Her dainty fingers folded under the warmth of his. "Fiona, I would give anything if things were different between us. I meant what I said that night. I know you remember—"

"I choose not to remember."

That was a lie, and he knew it. He pulled her toward him, cupped his hand behind her head. "I'm going to kiss you, Fiona. Fair warning."

She didn't resist, but the moment he touched her lips with his, he tasted the brine from her tears. He let her go.

She sat back, lips trembling. "I hate you, Charlie."

"No you don't."

"I have to."

He sighed. "I'll go back with you, even though you can't make me."

"I could leave you here to die. Or shoot you again."

"You're not going to shoot me," he said wearily.

"You thought I wouldn't before. I'm just as smart as you, and you can't manipulate me."

"Nobody thinks you're stupid, Fiona! And I'm not trying to manipulate you!" It took all his willpower not to seize her and kiss her senseless. Stubborn little beautiful— "Don't you see how you and your family have changed me? I'm not that callow, selfish teenager I was when you first knew me. But I am an officer with responsibilities that I don't take lightly. You'll have to forgive me if I do everything in my power to fulfill them."

"At whatever the cost to people you love."

"At whatever the cost—up to the point of disobeying God again. That I won't do."

"What do you mean?"

He'd gotten her attention at last. "I left England because I didn't even want to think about surrendering to the church. Not because it was the wrong thing to do, but because I didn't want to give up control of my life. So I joined the navy!" He laughed. "How's that for irony? My every move controlled by His Majesty's Admiralty. Well, until I discharge that commission, I'm stuck where I am. Just know here and now that when that's at an end, and my life is my own again, I *will* be coming back for you, and I'll show you a man who can be what you deserve. Whether you want it or not, that ring is my promise."

Her face was pale, her nose pink, her eyes a heartbreaking clear blue under the ugly hat. But when she bit her lip, he knew he'd gotten through. And he'd have to be satisfied with that. For now.

⌒

He would not shut up.

All the way back to Mobile, Charlie talked about his adventures at sea—contracting malaria while serving in the Scheldt, designing a lifeboat after a friend washed overboard in a storm, helping devise a system of flag signals while serving in Bermuda. And perhaps most maddening, he talked about some young lady to whom he'd been betrothed as a child.

If Charlie was to be believed, the girl had sent him a letter breaking the engagement while he was at sea. She had attracted the notice of a much richer man, also possessed of a title, and of course Charlie must understand her predicament? After all, Charlie was only third in line to a Scottish earldom, with two perfectly healthy, married older brothers with growing families.

This cheerful monologue must be carried out with his arms wrapped tightly about her from behind, and punctuated by grunts of pain every time Bonnie jarred his injured leg. His voice rumbling into her ear, his breath warm against her cheek— exquisite torture.

To his credit, he had to be starving—she certainly was—but he'd made not a word of complaint since they headed west three hours ago. She wished he would complain about *something*. She could feel her self-righteous anger dissipating with every mile, and she wanted—needed—to hang on to it. Otherwise, how was she going to bear it when she had to commit his sorry hide to prison again?

She managed to maintain a dignified silence until he said, "And that's why it took me so long to give in and kiss you."

"So *long*? Give *in*?"

He nodded, bumping his whiskery chin against her shoulder. "I could tell early on where this was going."

"How do you know I didn't have another attachment as well?"

"Fiona." He tsked. "You live down here in the wilderness with nobody but your relatives. Well, unless you count those roughnecks at the shipyard—"

"That is outrag—"

"In any case, you were clearly sending out lures, but I couldn't take the risk that there was somebody waiting for me—"

"I was not sending out lures!"

"Oh, you most definitely were. 'Charlie, help me hold Dusty while I check his fetlock.' And then you bend over just enough that—"

"I did not! Well, I did, but I didn't mean to—" A laugh bubbled out. "You were looking?"

"Of course I was looking. Do you think I'm made of cast iron? And you have this way of twisting your hair 'round your finger . . . A stronger man than me would have come undone." His cheek was close to hers, and if she turned her head just a little . . .

She kept her gaze rigidly on the road ahead. "You smell like a goat."

"That's right, deflect the obvious. Nice tactic."

"There is no tactic, Charlie. There's the truth. I'm ashamed that I let myself start to . . . you know."

"I don't know. Tell me."

"You're doing it again. Trying to make me give up my principles. I won't."

He sighed. Mercifully he was silent for nearly another slow

180

mile. Then, "Why do you think God allowed us to meet again after all those years? I mean, if I'd washed up even another hundred yards down the beach . . . Or if you hadn't gone riding that morning. Don't you think there's something just a bit . . . ordained about us?"

Almost, she didn't answer him. But she'd been thinking about that very question, ever since the ball at Uncle Rémy's house, where the truth had all come out. "My mother once told me that God allows us free will, to choose him or not—but that he sometimes intervenes to shape us for his glory and our good. There's no guarantee that events and circumstances will be pleasant. But I have to believe that one day I'll look back and see—even though this is one of the hardest, most painful things I've ever had to do—that it's been a blessing. I'm trying to grow up, Charlie—just like you are, as much as you pretend otherwise." She did turn her head then, stopping Bonnie, and found his face so close she could have counted the striations in his splotched eye. "I can see why you have done the things you've done. I just don't see any way that we can overcome this—this wall between us. Did you know that my mother was British? Her father was the commander of Fort Charlotte during the Revolution. She came to believe that freedom was more important than loyalty to some king she'd never met. If you can do that, then we might have a chance."

He stared at her, lips parted. Through both their coats, she could feel his heart thumping against her back. Finally he swallowed. "Freedom. From what?"

"Not from what. *To* what. Freedom to speak and worship the way we choose without fear of imprisonment. Freedom to elect those who make decisions for government. Freedom to choose a mate and build a family without consideration of social strata. Freedom to own property and make a living, using the creativity of our minds and the hard work of our hands, and in the process build a prosperous community. That's what America is, Charlie, and I'm not giving that up."

She squeezed Bonnie's sides with her heels.

Charlie spoke not another word all the way back to Mobile.

Navy Cove

"Just get him out of here, Léon. I don't care what you do with him." Fiona watched Charlie, dehydrated and barely conscious, slide down from the horse into the waiting arms of her clearly astonished brother and uncle. She tossed Bonnie's reins to Oliver and dragged herself out of the saddle. "But don't let him die—I went to a lot of trouble to get him back. I'm going to tend to Washington."

"First you're going to tell us what happened." Léon, supporting Charlie's sagging body on one side with Uncle Luc on the other, gave Fiona his patented chin-out glare. "Starting with what possessed you to abscond with my gun in the middle of the night!"

Fortunately, Desi stepped between them before Fiona could either burst into tears or brain her brother with the butt of the rifle still in her hand. "How about if Oliver and I help with the horses, while you two take care of the . . . prisoner. We'll debrief later." He scanned Charlie's pale face and bloody leg with interest.

"That's a good plan, son," said Uncle Luc. Without giving Léon another chance to object, he started for the house, drawing Charlie and Léon with him.

Léon gave Desi a resentful look over his shoulder. "I'll be back out as soon as we get him settled."

Desi nodded and took Washington's reins. But the moment they were inside the barn, he sent Oliver to unsaddle and brush Bonnie, then pointed to a feed sack leaning against a wall. "Fiona, sit down before you fall down. I've got Washington."

Too tired to argue, she sank onto the feed sack and watched Desi remove the stallion's saddle, blanket, and tack.

Once all that was put away, Desi picked up a currycomb and went to work loosening the dirt in Washington's coat. "He was limping. Is that how you caught him?"

"Yes. And that's why I went after him. See that right fetlock? Swollen. I just hope I can . . ." Unable to finish the sentence, she took off her hat and laid her head back against the wall.

"Is there some good reason you declined to wake any of the rest of us to go with you?"

"I was so angry, I just didn't think beyond catching Charlie before he destroyed my horse. I'm surprised Sehoy didn't raise the house."

"Luc-Antoine was the first one up. He found her hiding out here in the barn, petrified somebody would send her off to Indian territory." He gave Fiona an amused look over Washington's back. "She seemed more afraid of you than Léon."

"I wasn't very nice to her when I discovered it was her fault Charlie got away." She observed Desi for a moment in silence. "You're really good at that. And thank you for being so kind and reasonable."

He laughed. "As your father would say, I don't have a dog in this hunt—I can afford to be kind. And your uncle Rafa is quite a fine horseman. He made sure I learned."

"Are you going to marry Maddy?"

He blinked at the non sequitur. "I hope so."

"I was just thinking, you know, that it would be really helpful to know someone your whole life before you fall in love with

183

them. Like my parents did. Then you're not surprised and disappointed by things you discover about them."

Desi didn't answer immediately. When he did, his words were careful. "I'm not sure it's possible to completely know another human being. We've all got secrets that we hide from everyone but God himself."

"Even you?"

He gave her a grin that reminded her of Uncle Rafa at his most rakish. "Especially me."

"Ooh, Maddy had better watch out."

"Indeed." He tossed the comb to Fiona and picked up a handful of straw to wisp Washington's coat.

"So what do you think we should do with Charlie now?"

"Since it didn't work out so well, keeping him here—" he winked at her—"I think it would be best if I escort him back to Fort Charlotte. General Jackson and General Coffee have already left for Pensacola, so I'll use the time to write to authorities in New Orleans to see if we can speed up the prisoner exchange."

She sat up eagerly. "Oh, Desi, I would be so grateful!"

"Don't get your hopes too high," he said with a cautioning look. "These things take time. Speaking of which, I encourage you to think twice when you're tempted to act on your quite natural impatience with the situation. You frightened your poor Uncle Luc-Antoine more than you know."

"I imagine I did." She sighed, twirling her hat around her hand. "I never used to be such a hothead."

"Oh yes, you were. Which is why you were sent to England with Maddy all those years ago."

"Huh. I suppose you're right." She sat back again, despondent.

When was she going to learn?

‿

NOVEMBER 5, 1814
MOBILE BAY

Charlie sat in the bow of Nardo Smith's single-masted pirogue, facing aft, as the free colored man sailed them up the western shore of Mobile Bay, skillfully avoiding shoals and sandbars and crab traps that would have waylaid a less experienced bar pilot. Since there was a brisk wind blowing up from the gulf, they were making good time.

He didn't much care how long it took. The weather was cold and raw, and as Fiona had predicted, his leg ached like the dickens. But since all he had to look forward to was incarceration in the Fort Charlotte guardhouse, he felt he could put up with a bit of discomfort on the open water.

At least his hands were free. Palomo treated Charlie with a compassion that he'd mistrusted at first—until he observed the courtesy with which the American spoke to Smith. Free blacks held a rather amorphous position in southern slave culture. They could own property—slaves of their own, in fact—but could not vote, hold firearms, or testify in court. The international slave trade had been banned by law for several years and had become illegal within the United States, particularly new territories in the northwest. That didn't mean the institution itself ceased to exist. The cotton, sugarcane, and tobacco industries all depended on slave labor, and any colored person had to carry documentation while traveling, or he could find himself in chains without recourse.

This pilot, Smith, carried on a lively, educated conversation with Palomo. They appeared to be friends of long standing, and the translator cheerfully took orders from Smith, helping him manage sails and pole the boat away from hidden sandbars in the water.

About an hour into the trip, Palomo made his way forward. "How are you feeling?" He laid the back of his hand against Charlie's forehead. "No fever. That's a good sign."

"I feel like I've been shot in the leg." Charlie glanced at the loose breeches he'd been given to replace the ones Fiona had ruined. "I suppose I shouldn't complain. She could have killed me."

"Someone should have warned you, she's acknowledged hereabouts to be quite a good shot." The latent twinkle in Palomo's dark eyes surfaced. "And I should also warn you that I have finally realized why you look so familiar."

The hair stood up on the back of Charlie's neck. "Have you indeed?"

"Yes. You seem to have an uncanny control over that Scots burr, but I also have a very good memory. There's a tavern in the New Orleans French quarter where I used to go when I wanted certain information. Sailors from all over the world would find their way there."

"Ah. And you saw someone there whom I remind you of."

"No, I heard your voice there. I am a musician and a trained linguist, Lieutenant Kincaid. I do not forget voices."

"And I am not stupid enough to think that refuting this absurd charge will change your mind."

"No, you are far from stupid." Palomo smiled. "But you did underestimate the strength of our family's loyalty. Sehoy was able to draw with a fair bit of accuracy the cipher she held in her possession, and I'm certain I shall be able to decode it eventually."

Charlie held Palomo's gaze. "What sort of spy would I be to commit anything of value to paper?"

"We shall see. I would not have warned you, except for the great esteem in which I, because of my foster father, personally hold your grandfather, Lord St. Clair."

"Your foster father—"

"Rafael Gonzales, Fiona's uncle by marriage."

Charlie sighed. "I confess, the twisted connections of this family are enough to drive one mad."

Palomo grinned. "Indeed they are. Just be warned, Kincaid—you will not escape again until you are traded for someone of much more value to us. And if you go near our Fiona again, I will personally find you and eliminate your sorry existence." The cultured drawl became silky. "Are we quite clear, sir?"

"Crystal."

NOVEMBER 6, 1814
MOBILE

The city of Mobile being predominantly Catholic, the Protestant church was little more than a home gathering. A handful of Methodist Episcopals, Moravians, and other varieties of Reformism met every Sunday morning in Maddy's parlor to sing hymns, read Scripture aloud, and pray together. Stephen had been Congregationalist, but after his death, she'd returned to her mother's Presbyterian training, learned at the knee of her paternal grandmother.

After church, she and Elijah usually joined the Lanier family next door for a giant meal, followed by a nap and quiet activities like reading or correspondence. Today, however, when Desi offered to take her for a drive while Elijah played with his cousins, she accepted with alacrity. Bundled in her warmest dress and cloak, she let him hand her up into Uncle Rémy's open chaise and settled her skirts while he went round to unhitch the horse.

Once they were under way at a gentle trot, she glanced at

him, not sure how to take his rather sober mien. "Welcome home. I hear you brought the prisoner with you."

"Yes." He hesitated. "I'm going to tell you what happened—it's quite the dramatic story—but you'll understand why it must go no further than us."

Alarm climbed up her back, but she nodded. "Of course."

"Your cousin Fiona has turned out to be quite the intrepid horsewoman—not to mention, a crack shot with a rifle."

"Oh, Desi. What has she done?"

"The worst thing she did is fall in love with a British naval officer."

"Well, we already knew—"

"Yes, but I fear he returns the sentiment, and if we don't get him out of here very soon and returned to his command, he will figure out a way to carry her off, or she will change her mind and disgrace us all."

"But he's in the guardhouse, isn't he? And she's still at Navy Cove?"

He nodded. "For the time being."

"What *happened*?"

"When we got there, I questioned Kincaid, of course, but he pretended to be stupid—or, rather, pretended to think *I'm* stupid—and admitted nothing beyond his name and rank. The next morning, we all woke up to find that our little Indian maiden had taken food to the prisoner after everyone was asleep. He had gotten himself out of his chains somehow, locked Sehoy in the tack room, and stolen Fiona's big black stallion. But Fiona chanced to wake up shortly thereafter and went in pursuit."

Speechless with horror, Maddy grabbed his arm. "Desi, no!"

"Oh, yes. By the time we discovered what had happened, the two of them were more than a quarter of the way to Pensacola, and we had no way to go after them. I thought Léon might set out on foot, but Luc-Antoine and I persuaded him to wait. Sure enough, that evening just before sundown, Fiona came riding in on her mare, with Kincaid—shot quite neatly in the thigh—up behind. They were leading the stallion—unfortunately for Kincaid, gone lame."

"They were alone together all that time?"

"Well, yes." Desi gave her a quizzical glance. "You find that more astonishing than the fact that she chased after and *shot* a man?"

"Of course that's outrageous." Maddy shook his arm in her indignation. "But her reputation! She will never be respectable again!"

Desi's mouth quirked. "Which is why you and I are going to keep this to ourselves. Remember?"

"Oh. Oh, yes, of course."

"I told you because Fiona is going to need wise feminine counsel, and she has nobody there but that birdwitted little Sehoy. Léon is more like to lock her in her room for the foreseeable future. For now, she seems to be so angry with Kincaid for ruining her horse, she's satisfied to see him thrown into the guardhouse. But I don't rely on that rage persisting for long."

"She needs her mother. Or failing that, my mother."

"Since she has neither, you are going to have to step in, Maddy."

She regarded him for a moment, objections bursting to her tongue. Finally she swallowed. "I suppose I am."

"Good girl." He nodded in warm approval. "And as I said, I am going to do everything in my power to see that Kincaid is removed from this vicinity with all speed."

12

Sometimes, Fiona thought, staring resentfully across the quilt stretched over braces hung from Aunt Giselle's ballroom ceiling, her family treated her like a baby. A particularly toothless, stupid baby.

Hauling her back and forth between Navy Cove and Mobile at their whim. Expecting her wounded heart to heal on command.

She wondered if Sehoy had felt that way when she first came to Navy Cove. Seated next to her, tongue between her teeth, Sehoy plied her needle with a great deal more determination than skill. She'd been caught in the maelstrom of events along with Fiona. Maddy's letter, inviting—no, all but demanding—the two girls to return to Mobile and remain for the winter, had arrived on Wednesday. The courier, Nardo Smith, stayed visiting with Uncle Luc-Antoine until they were packed and ready to go—which didn't take long, as they'd barely unpacked from their previous visit. He'd been given specific instructions not to take no for an answer.

190

So here they sat, along with a cadre of female neighbors, involved in the womanly but boring pursuit of quilting. She glanced at Maddy, who effortlessly carried on a lively conversation and created trails of stitches so small and neat they seemed made by a machine. Fiona couldn't quite get the hang of the thimble, which kept falling off her finger and rolling onto the floor. And her eyes crossed trying to thread the tiny needle—which she had to do over and over because she kept accidentally yanking the thread loose.

Oh, how she wanted to be back at Navy Cove with her horses and dressed in comfortable clothes.

Inevitably, unwillingly, she thought of Charlie, stuck in the Fort Charlotte guardhouse just a few blocks away. She wouldn't allow herself to ask Maddy about him, but she couldn't help listening to the women's gossip. One young matron had already forgotten Fiona was there and mentioned the handsome young British prisoner—until Maddy shushed her, cutting a warning glance at Fiona.

Apparently Charlie was making out just fine, awash in charitable donations of tea, baked goods, and books.

"Ow!" She'd pricked her finger again. Scowling, she stuck the offending digit in her mouth to keep from dripping blood on the quilt—the unpardonable sin amongst this clucking brood.

"Fiona," Maddy sighed, "that's what your thimble is for, darling. Here, let me show you again—"

"Thank you, but I need some air." Fiona pushed back her chair, stuck her needle into the closest pincushion, and went to find her cloak, hanging on the hall tree in the foyer at the front of the house. The weather had been nasty since her arrival in Mobile, but she couldn't stand another moment in that stuffy room.

Maddy followed her. "Where are you going?"

"Out."

"I told Desi this was a bad idea to bring you to Mobile. You can't go see Charlie."

Fiona whirled, the cloak in her arms. "I wouldn't. You know I wouldn't."

"I could tell you're thinking about him." Maddy looked doubtful. "I'm sorry Clarice brought him up. She didn't mean any harm. You know I don't approve of—" she waved a hand— "chasing him on horseback and shooting him, but you did the right thing to bring him back and send him to prison."

"I'd like to know how I'd have gotten him back to prison without chasing and shooting him!" Shaking her head in exasperation, Fiona flung her cloak about her shoulders. "But don't worry, I haven't told anybody that's how he was caught. I don't want to run into anyone, so I'm going out the back door." Leaving Maddy to wander back to her quilt party, she headed for the kitchen. There she came upon her second brother, seated at the table with Uncle Rémy, dressed as always in one of his fine business suits. "Judah!" She launched herself at him.

Grinning his big Lanier grin, he rose and caught her in a fierce hug. "Hello, little duchess!"

She kissed his cheek. "You don't know how happy I am to see you! When did you get in? What are you doing here?"

"I would ask you the same question, but Uncle Rémy has been filling me in on the drama." Judah released Fiona and dropped back into his chair.

Fiona made a face. "I hate drama, but it seems to follow me of late."

Uncle Rémy smiled. "Are you running away from the quilt party, my dear? Judah and I made coffee. Would you like to join us?"

"If you made it, I'll wager it'll take the skin off the roof of my mouth." But she went to the cupboard anyway and sat down with a cup of coffee to eye her brother over its rim. "We haven't heard from you since September. What happened when you got back to Laffite?"

"By the time I got back, Federal troops had cleaned out Barataria, confiscated everything in our—their warehouses, and chased Laffite and his men to the four winds. I've been back and forth between New Orleans and the Villeré plantation, helping prepare for the British invasion."

Fiona exchanged glances with Uncle Rémy. "Why on earth would Laffite help the Americans, after they destroyed his lair?"

"He's a patriot! Why is that so hard to believe?"

"Judah, it doesn't matter what I believe. General Jackson just got back from kicking the British out of Pensacola. He could have *you* hauled up, right along with Laffite and his men."

Judah leaned forward. "I told you I've stayed on the right side of the law, Fiona. But Laffite is hoping to be pardoned so he can live without looking over his shoulder. And he may be the one man who can pull Jackson's bacon out of the fire."

"What do you mean?"

"The Brits are determined to figure out a way to get into New Orleans. And if they do that, they'll be able to take Mobile and Pensacola back."

"I'm not sure Jackson appreciates the danger," Uncle Rémy said gravely. "No matter how fast we work to build it up, our American navy is outshipped, outgunned, and outmanned. We thought we could stay out of Europe's trouble on the other side of the ocean, refused to spend money on our own military—and now we're literally paying for it."

Judah nodded. "The bad thing is, money won't fix the threat to New Orleans. The British have just whipped Napoleon and are sending those seasoned marines and sailors over here to attack. If Jackson doesn't get his skinny carcass to New Orleans quick, it'll be too late to keep them out. But even if he does decide to mount a defense, he's not familiar with the bayous and swamps and waterways that can be used to our advantage—and he doesn't have enough men and boats and ammunition to fight back. Laffite can provide all that—if Jackson will accept the aid of a gentleman pirate."

Fiona stared at her brother, imagination fired. "How can we convince him?"

Judah laughed. "Pray for me, little sister. That's my job. Actually, mine and Uncle Rémy here. Our family has over a hundred years of influence laid up in this city and in New Orleans. What's it good for, if not to spend on preserving our freedom?" Sobering, he laid his hands flat on the table. "If you don't want to be a British citizen sometime in the next few months, you'd better pray Andrew Jackson decides to swallow his pride."

⁓

NOVEMBER 12, 1814
MOBILE

Charlie's week in the Fort Charlotte guardhouse had been lonely, frustrating, and uncomfortable. But when Mrs. Madeleine Gonzales Burch and her little son Elijah came to visit him, he found himself overwhelmed with embarrassment at his inability to properly entertain this lady. Which struck him as a singularly ridiculous emotion in the presence of the enemy.

As she settled herself upon a chair outside the bars of his cell, provided by the slovenly creature assigned to guard him, Charlie recalled the first time they met—he at the impressionable and scruffy age of thirteen, she as an eighteen-year-old debutante. His grandparents had hosted a house party that summer at Riverton, in honor of Miss Gonzales's parents, Don Rafael and Doña Lyse Gonzales de Rippardá. The family—including shy, awkward eleven-year-old cousin Fiona—had arrived with a mountain of luggage and a flurry of Spanish-infused laughter that intrigued even Charlie the rebellious rusticator. Beautiful and accomplished Madeleine, who spoke four languages fluently and read a couple more, and whose lovely soprano entertained the company every evening whilst her father accompanied her on the guitar, paid not the slightest attention to Charlie skulking in the background—which cavalier treatment sealed his terminal case of calf-love.

Now, endeavoring to appear unmoved by her sudden whim to break the monotony of his solitary confinement, he wished he'd had the opportunity to bathe and shave before entertaining Fiona's beloved cousin.

Whatever her motives, she kept them to herself, putting back the hood of her cloak and then folding her gloved hands neatly in her lap.

Little Elijah had no such reservations. He pelted toward Charlie's cell, grabbed the bars with both hands, and tried to put his head through. "Hello, Mister! Mama says we are to do our Christian duty and visit the prisoners, and she says I mayn't ask what you did, but I said you wouldn't mind, would you?"

"I do not mind at all, but perhaps we should introduce ourselves as gentlemen first. I am Lieutenant Charlie Kincaid, and you must be Elijah?"

The boy's eyes widened. "I *told* Mama I was famous, 'cause everybody knows who I am already. See, Mama?"

Charlie bowed. "Famous and forthright."

Madeleine grabbed her son by the coattails and pulled him back from the bars just before he got his head stuck. "I am terribly sorry, Lieutenant Kincaid. I knew I should have left him at home."

Now that he had somehow got her feeling in the wrong, Charlie began to enjoy this rather bizarre encounter. He pulled forward the severe ladder-back chair he'd been allowed and crossed one leg over the other as if he conversed with widowed ladies from behind the bars of a prison cell every day of the week.

"I'm very glad you did not. Perhaps Master Elijah would like to practice with my bilboquet whilst we talk? A Mr. Counselman stopped in and gave it to me several days ago, but I have yet to master the technique of landing the ball in the cup above one time in ten tries." Charlie reached under his cot and showed the boy the carved wooden toy. "He brought it along with a basket of books and stayed all afternoon to give me an astonishingly thorough lesson in American government and economics."

"Oh! I gots one of these!" Taking the ornate little cup and spindle with its wooden ball attached by a string, Elijah began to flip the ball into the cup, tip it out, and repeat the exercise with dizzying speed and accuracy.

Madeleine smiled. "Mr. Counselman made that himself, I'm sure, but he is so modest he wouldn't have told you so. He's quite the artist, and his fishing lures are prized all over the territory."

"He did mention both fishing and carving, but he seemed more intent on converting me from my wrongheaded views on monarchy, aristocracy, and parliamentary procedure." Charlie laughed. "Reminded me of my grandfather quite a bit."

Madeleine blinked. "I don't remember your grandfather being of a Republican mindset."

"Oh, no, but he was a proponent of broad reading and debate as a method of sharpening one's thought processes and personal convictions."

"Funny that you brought up your grandfather . . . It is my memory of him, and your family's kindness to ours, that brings me here today."

"Indeed?"

"Yes. I want you to know that I mean to speak to General Jackson on your behalf, when he returns from Pensacola."

"Forgive me if I question what good that will do, Mrs. Burch."

"Please, call me Madeleine. I understand your skepticism, but you'll have to take my word for it that my connections go pretty far up the chain of command."

"All right. Let's say you are not only sincere but correct in your estimation of your influence. What exactly do you hope to gain? I will not be paroled, for I will never swear to refrain from participating in the war on the side of my country. I desire to return to my duties as soon as may be."

She nodded. "I would expect nothing else. No, I am hoping you'll be included in a prisoner exchange. And I wish in return for you to agree never to contact my cousin Fiona again."

"Oh, I see. My grandfather's service to your family in the past and the return of your brother are not enough. Now I must earn your gratitude by cutting ties with the woman I love."

She looked away. "Come, Lieutenant Kincaid, you and Fiona are both very young. These first attachments can seem unbreachable when one is in the throes of youth, but I assure you they fade with time. She will get over it and be grateful that we didn't allow her to cut herself off from her family—and you, well, young military men are notorious for fickleness of heart. Don't try to tell me you didn't have an inamorata in every port before you landed here."

"Mrs. Burch, what a cynical mindset you have. I don't know whether I should be insulted or feel sorry for you. Was your husband really such a philanderer?"

The big brown eyes swung to his face and her pretty mouth fell open. "How dare you—"

"Ah, it's true, I see. How long was it before the bloom fell off the rose and you realized what you'd got yourself into?"

She stood abruptly, snapping her fingers to get her son's attention. "Come, Elijah, give the toy back to the lieutenant. We must go home."

"But, Mama! I almost got to a hundred!" The boy clutched the bilboquet to his chest.

"You can't count to a hundred. Give it back."

Charlie moved to crouch in front of the bars. "You may have it, little man. One day you'll have to return and show me your technique."

"I assure you," Madeleine said coldly, "he will not be coming back.

Charlie looked up at her, amused by her kittenish outrage. "And I presume the prisoner exchange offer is rescinded as well. Ah well, it was a nicely played volley. I bear you no ill will, and I will do my best to convince Fiona to forgive her relatives' attempt to manipulate her life choices without her knowledge."

Madeleine actually stamped her foot. "She—she is very angry with you anyway, after you stole her horse—and wouldn't believe anything you say, even in the unlikely event that she ever saw you again. So don't get your hopes up."

He rose and grinned down at her from his superior height. "On the contrary, my hopes are considerably lifted. You would never have come here if you weren't petrified that Fiona will change her mind and run off with me. I shall sleep well tonight, Mrs. Burch—oh, sorry, Madeleine. Since we are to be kin by marriage, I had best get accustomed to your Christian name." He tipped his head and said with exquisite relish, "And you may call me Cousin Charlie."

⌒

Maddy couldn't think when she had been this angry—except possibly the day she'd found a strange woman's garter in her husband's trunk. How did Charlie Kincaid know about that? No one knew—not even her parents. She was always careful to speak of Stephen with respect and nostalgia. Dear Lord, she even tried to *think* of him charitably. It had taken a long time to get over the anger, to release the bitterness and forgive. They'd managed to build a solid, comfortable marriage, in spite of his long absences.

Well, if she was honest, likely *because* of his long absences. Stephen hadn't been all that easy to live with.

She continued to stomp down the road, holding Elijah by the hand, trying not to foolishly berate him for acting like a little boy. He walked along, holding his bilboquet by the spindle, swinging the ball in dizzying circles and reeling off his usual spate of unanswerable questions. "Mama, why does leaves fall down instead of up? Where does the sun go when it rains? Can dolphins read music? How come ships don't tip over? Why can't I see my nose?"

She didn't even bother answering until he looked up and frowned. "Mama, you're cross. Why don't you like Uncle Charlie?"

She squeezed his hand and sighed. "He's not your uncle, honey. And I don't not like him. I'm cross about . . . something else."

"Oh." That seemed to satisfy him, and he went mercifully quiet. Then a few minutes later, "Well, why is Uncle Charlie in prison? Did he do something bad? Did he forget to make up his bed?"

She laughed. "Undoubtedly. So remember that when you get up in the morning."

Sense of humor restored, she picked up her skirt and started to trot. "Come on, I'll race you home."

With a whoop, Elijah snatched his hand from hers and took

off, legs pumping. Maddy kept him in sight until he darted around the corner of Royal Street and Conti. She took a deep breath and ran a little faster. Served her right for initiating such an unladylike pursuit as racing.

Just as she reached the edge of the Laniers' yard—with Elijah nowhere in sight—a large, closed carriage, piled high with luggage, rolled down the street from the direction of the waterfront. What on earth? Uncle Rémy hadn't said anything about expecting guests.

She slowed to a walk and watched the carriage bypass the Laniers' house to roll into her own drive path. A man leaned out of the open window to wave, a handsome middle-aged man who looked an awful lot like—

"Papa!" she screamed and ran for him.

By the time she got to him, breathing hard from her run, the carriage had stopped, the two horses stamping in the traces, blowing steam into the cold afternoon air. Without waiting for the driver, Papa opened the carriage door and jumped down to envelop her as she flung her arms about his neck.

"Oh! Oh! Oh! I didn't know you were coming!" She was crying with joy.

"How is my heart of hearts?" Papa rocked her, clearly almost as emotional as she. "And here is your mother right behind me, who will beat me about the head if I don't give way immediately."

Maddy laughed and let him go, smearing away tears with her fingertips. "As if Mama ever did anything but kiss you in the most disgustingly affectionate way imaginable!" She reached for her laughing mama, who had in typical fashion descended from the carriage unassisted. "Mama! I have missed you so much!"

"Oh, but I live in fear of my Lyse's displeasure. It is a fact." Papa stood back beaming as Maddy and her mother embraced.

"And I you, my darling!" Mama leaned back to take Maddy's face in her gloved hands, her expression sobering. "How I wish I could have been here to support you in Stephen's passing. I know it has been hard."

Maddy bit her lip and looked away. "Yes, I have had to grow up."

Papa rubbed his hands together. "Come, ladies, let us continue this reunion indoors." Taking the two women one on either arm, he walked toward the house, leaving the driver to follow with the luggage. "But where is my little grandson? I vow I shan't recognize him, it's been so long since I saw him last."

"My goodness, I completely forgot about him!" Maddy looked around in chagrin. "He ran ahead of me, and then I saw you—He must have gone on to Uncle Rémy's house."

"Then let us follow posthaste." Papa turned to the driver. "If you would be so good as to leave everything on the porch here, I will dispose of it when we return." He pulled a large silver coin from his pocket and gave it to the driver, whose eyes lit.

"My pleasure, Don Rafael."

Maddy and her parents crossed the yard and mounted the steps to the Laniers' front porch. Maddy knocked, opened the door, and stuck her head inside. "Aunt Giselle! Have you seen Elijah? I have a surprise for you!"

Giselle, wearing a pair of steel-rimmed spectacles and an apron, appeared from the family parlor. "Hello, dearie—I haven't seen the little rascal, but that doesn't mean he's not here. I'm thinking you might want to attach a bell to his collar like—" A gasp interrupted whatever she had been about to say. "Lyse! Rafa! Come in, come in!" She hugged both newcomers, then drew them all into the foyer. "I've a nice fire going in here, and tea made. You're hungry after such a long trip, I'm sure. Oh, what a grand surprise!"

While Giselle disposed of outer garments and made everyone comfortable in the parlor, Maddy listened in vain for childish voices. "I'm going to look around and see if Elijah slipped past."

"I suppose he could be upstairs with Ruthie. She's writing a story." Giselle shook her head with fond amusement. "The boys have gone hunting with their father, and Fiona and Sehoy are in the barn."

Maddy's mother paused in the act of pouring tea. "Fiona is here?"

"Yes, I'll explain about that," Giselle said with a sigh.

Leaving her parents to visit with her aunt, Maddy went to the foot of the stairs. "Elijah? Are you up there?"

After a moment, his voice fluted downward. "Here I am, Mama. I'm telling Ruthie her story."

Panic gave way to irritation as she hurried up the stairs. "How dare you disappear without telling me where you were going, young man?" She marched to the schoolroom doorway and stopped, nonplussed. Ruthie sat at the table with pencil and paper, apparently transcribing the dictations of her little cousin, who lay sprawled on his stomach like a sultan across a large floor pillow in front of the fireplace.

"You was too slow, Mama, so I comed over here to wait."

Ruthie poked her spectacles higher on her nose. "Aunt Maddy, Elijah is the best storyteller! His is much better than mine."

"Indeed?"

"Yes, ma'am! Listen to this! 'Prince Charlie slept very well that night on the pirate ship, but he forgot to make up his bed the next morning. So the evil pirate Jackson put him in jail. But as soon as it got dark, Charlie climbed out the window and swam a hundred miles to shore. "You can't count that far!" shouted Jackson the Pirate in a rage, but Charlie laughed and said, "Oh, yes, I can, cuz I'm a Republican!" So when he got to land, he sneaked into the first castle he came to—really quiet—and was gonna steal a horse, but he knew that would be bad, so he waked up the princess. He gave her a rose to pay for the horse, and she said she would be his inamorata if he'd take her with him. But he said, "No, I don't need none of them, expecially girls," and he rode off on her horse and she cried bitterly.'" Ruthie sighed. "Isn't that lovely, Aunt Maddy?"

Maddy stared at her niece. "Oh, my, that's . . ." Pressing her lips together, she looked at Elijah. His eyes had drooped shut. If he wasn't asleep, he would be soon. "What an interesting story. I'll just . . . go visit with our guests while you keep writing."

She walked down the stairs like one in a dream. A horrible dream in which one's dirty laundry hangs out the window for the world to snigger at. It was hard to feel superior to Fiona when her own choices had been so very unwise.

Upon reaching the parlor, she stood looking at her beautiful parents, still in love with one another after more than thirty years, eyes flirting, finishing one another's sentences. Why couldn't she have been enough for Stephen? What was wrong with her? Was Charlie Kincaid right—that she was imprinting her husband's infidelity onto every man she met?

"There you are, my dear." Aunt Giselle beckoned. "Are the children safely occupied? Come and sit down with a cup of tea. You look worn out, poor darling."

Maddy sat down beside her aunt and accepted the teacup with a smile that she hoped didn't look manufactured. "Elijah is sound asleep, but Ruthie read me a rather startling story that he concocted. I don't know where his imagination comes from."

Maddy's mother rolled her eyes. "I'm afraid the flair for the dramatic comes straight from the Gonzales side."

"It is true," Papa said, winking. "All the world is a stage, as they say."

"Then I'm sure you'll find Elijah entertaining as well as maddening," Maddy said. "Papa, you know I am thrilled to have you both here, but could you not have written to tell me you were coming? I would like to have prepared your room—"

"Yes, I have bad manners, I know, to appear without warning," he said with a grimace, "but my business is official, and somewhat delicate in nature." He hesitated, glanced at his wife. "Speaking of drama, it's actually fortuitous that your cousin Fiona is here in Mobile, as it is in response to her entanglement with young Kincaid that we are here. Did you know that she had written to Lord St. Clair to request that his grandson be exchanged for Sullivan?"

Relieved to discover that the quilting business had come to an end, Fiona slept well and awoke early. After lunch she borrowed clothes from her cousin Israel and spent the afternoon in Uncle Rémy's small barn, which housed the two elderly horses, as well as the family carriage, a little gig, and the children's pony cart. Cisco, the young black groom her uncle kept on retainer, was happy to let her help muck stalls and curry the horses while he cleaned and polished the vehicles. He didn't seem to mind that she for the most part ignored him while carrying on a murmured conversation with the horses. Sehoy, on the other hand, had quickly gotten bored and took her sketch pad to the market to draw.

What she had learned today was that she was a creature of intense, fatal loyalty. Once she had given her heart, it would not be reeled back in.

She remembered once when the family had visited Mobile in the spring, her mother had taken her to a spot near Fort Charlotte, where Mama had spent most of her growing-up years as the daughter of the British commander of the city. Close to the water's edge, a tiny island floated, in the center of which grew a towering oak tree with an osprey nest in its upper branches. That day she and Mama stood for over an hour, watching the two big, beautiful birds—the male and the female—fly to and from the nest, diving for fish and bringing the prey back to feed their young.

"These same two birds were here last year," Mama told her. "They'll go somewhere for the winter, probably Mexico or Brazil, then come back again next spring."

"How do you know it's the same birds?" Fiona asked.

"I just know. I remember one of the old slaves told me ospreys mate for life. They choose, and then never change their minds. God made them that way." Mama's smile was sweet, her gaze faraway. "That's when I made up my mind that I would wait for your father. I'd loved him since I was a little girl."

And she'd loved him purely and faithfully right up until the very end, when that British schooner of war had sunk the merchant ship carrying the two of them to the Netherlands on business.

Fiona jammed her pitchfork into a pile of soiled hay and dumped it into a wheelbarrow. The ultimate twist of irony was that she should have chosen to love a British warrior.

Chose. Yes, she chose. And could not un-choose, no matter how hard she tried.

She couldn't help wondering, in a case like Maddy's, how it was possible to love a man who died, then make room for another good man like Desi. Presumably, God made arrangements for that.

But Charlie was not dead, though she could have killed him if she'd wanted to, the day he stole Washington. She shuddered. Thank God she hadn't. The Lord had straightened her aim, allowing her to hit his leg instead of his head or his body. Now she only had to bear this separation, this loneliness, and not the horror of being an instrument in his death.

She laid her palm over the bump of Charlie's ring under her coat. *Jesus, would you take him in your hand? Show us a way to do your will? Please keep him safe and give me wisdom beyond my years. I feel so young and stupid.*

"Fiona, are you still out there! Come inside! Hurry!"

At Maddy's shout, Fiona leaned the pitchfork in a corner and went to the doorway. Her cousin stood on the back step, shivering in the late afternoon chill. "What is it?"

"Come see!"

With a shrug, she bid Cisco goodbye. Crossing the yard, she entered the kitchen.

And found herself enveloped in the extravagant embrace of her father's younger sister, who had also been her mother's best friend—and thus the closest thing she had left to a mother on this earth. "Aunt Lyse! Oh, I've missed you! What are you doing here?" Emotions already raw, her tears broke free.

"Ah, *chéri*, it is a wretched time of it you have had, *n'est pas*?" Aunt Lyse's French Creole upbringing slipped out on occasion, making her, if possible, even more unique and dear. She crooned over Fiona, repeatedly kissing the top of her head.

When at last Fiona pulled away and looked up at her aunt in embarrassment, she realized they were alone. "Where is everyone?"

"They are in the parlor, including our Desi." Aunt Lyse, ever practical, handed Fiona her handkerchief. "But I wanted you to myself for a few minutes first."

Fiona blew her nose. "I want to hug Uncle Rafa."

Aunt Lyse held her by the shoulders. "There will be time for that, after I discover your part in this bumblebroth of spies and prisoners and horse thieves. Look at you, back in breeches, after all the trouble I went to to turn you into a lady!" She tsked. "You look exactly like your cousin Israel!"

Fiona hung her head. "Oh, Auntie, I'm afraid there is no good explanation for the things I have done. Neither a beautiful curtsey nor correct teacup etiquette seemed to matter when Charlie rode off with my horse!"

Aunt Lyse's laughter was deep and infectious. "Believe it or not, that makes perfect sense! Now take off your coat, sit down, and listen to me." Once they were settled at the kitchen table, Aunt Lyse folded her hands and fixed her golden eyes on Fiona's face. "Now. It seems to me these men have looked right past you as their best source of information."

"What do you mean?"

"I mean that women—smart young women like yourself—often hear things, observe things, that men don't realize they are revealing. Did you know that your mother and I acted as operatives in the service of Governor-General Gálvez during the American War for Independence?"

"I often begged Mama to tell me how Papa came for her and escaped with her to New Orleans. She wouldn't give me any details."

"That's because we were sworn to secrecy by the Spanish high command. And I still cannot reveal all that I know. But I can ask you questions, which you must discreetly use, for yourself and the good of your country."

Fiona blinked. "All right."

"Good. Desi says Sehoy replicated a ciphered message that Lieutenant Kincaid carried in an oilskin pouch under his shirt. Did you ever see this cipher?"

"Yes. After Charlie was injured at Fort Bowyer, I tended him. And while he was unconscious, I saw the pouch and wondered what was in it, so I opened it and looked at the message." She shook her head. "I could make no sense out of it, except that the letters were grouped like words in sentences."

"How many sentences? Was there any punctuation?"

Fiona closed her eyes, trying to picture the cipher. "Yes, there were maybe two periods. So . . . three sentences?"

"Ah. And were there any one-letter words?"

"No." Fiona opened her eyes. "I suppose that would be too easy."

Aunt Lyse sighed. "Yes. Did you confront Charlie about the message?"

"Of course. At the time, he claimed he didn't remember writing it. But I could tell he was lying."

"How do you know?"

"He was suddenly . . . so bland. He'd been raving like he was having a nightmare about something that really happened, and then he woke up and grabbed me as if I had been attacking him, so I shouted at him, and all of a sudden he recognized me and started k—well, he knew me, that's for sure." Fiona felt as if her entire body were on fire, remembering the way Charlie had known her.

"What a lovely blush," Aunt Lyse observed mildly. "Presumably there was some physical affection involved at that point."

"Oh, dear." Fiona twisted her hair around her finger.

Aunt Lyse laughed. "I'm interested in the nightmare."

"I've thought about it a lot since then. It didn't make any sense at the time, but there were a couple of names Uncle Rafa might know. Charlie was addressing somebody named Easton who was supposed to get word to an admiral . . . maybe Cochrane? And I know he mentioned Pensacola." Fiona tried to remember more details. "At one point he was mumbling in French. Really bad French. Could have been something about *pirates*. But maybe not."

208

"Now that is useful information. If it could be applied to the cipher itself, then we might have something." Aunt Lyse smiled her approval. "Listen to me, *chéri*. I'm going to ask you to do something very hard. Rafa and I have talked it over, and he likes the idea, but you must be the one to decide."

Fiona swallowed apprehension. "What is it?"

"It is clear to all of us that you have a powerful influence over this young man—"

"*All* of us? You have talked about me, me and Charlie, with . . . who, Aunt Lyse?"

"Just Giselle and our Maddy and Desi. Rafa wanted me to discover how far the attachment had gone. Maddy is less certain that you should be allowed to see him again, but Desi thinks you can handle the situation."

"The situation? See who? You want me to see *Charlie* again?" Fiona felt her mouth fall ajar.

"Hear me out." Lyse held up an elegant finger. "Rafa has had a letter from Admiral Lord St. Clair, sanctioning—or, rather, I should say *demanding*—the exchange of his grandson for our Sullivan. The exchange has gone through the proper channels, rather quickly, I might add, and Rafa himself has been authorized to deliver Charlie to a British prisoner caravel off the coast of New Orleans. Darling, please, you're going to crease my dress!"

Fiona relaxed the strangling hug she'd inflicted upon her laughing auntie. "I'm sorry, but—oh, that's wonderful!"

"Indeed it is. And Sullivan has already been escorted to the counterpart American caravel. But before we move Lieutenant Kincaid, it occurred to us that some practical use might be made of his unfortunate *tendre* for a certain magnolia duchess."

13

November 13, 1814

The implications of what she was about to do left Fiona a quivering, gelatinous mass of emotion and nerves. She wanted to see Charlie, oh, she did—but not like this. Not to deceive him.

As she walked the short distance from Uncle Rémy's house to Fort Charlotte, she felt as if she were balancing her way along the parapet of a castle, with a deep moat on one side and a cold stone roof far below on the other. Dusk had fallen, pushing the last of the sunshine and daytime heat into the bay, leaving only a thick, black misty chill that had her shivering and clutching her cloak together for protection. She found little comfort from Desi's protective presence some distance behind her. He wouldn't let anything or anyone physically attack her. But who would guard her wretched heart?

God, this is not what I asked for.

Swallowing her tears, she kept going until she reached the fort. A sentry usually stood guard in the gatehouse atop the outer brick wall, but no one hailed her until she was standing at the gate.

"Halt right there, ma'am," someone called sleepily. "State your business."

She found herself stammering. "M-my Aunt Giselle—Giselle Lanier?—s-sent me with a blanket for the p-prisoner."

An astonished young face peered over the wall alongside a lantern. "Fiona?"

"Oh! Timon! You're still here?" Sullivan's childhood friend, distantly related to the Lanier family through marriage, had joined the Mississippi militia at the tender age of sixteen, and she would have assumed—if she'd thought about it at all—that he'd have marched to West Florida with General Jackson.

"Yes," he said glumly. "They left me here to guard this blasted redcoat officer, and you've never heard of such a monotonous duty in your life. All the fellow does is read." He paused, sudden suspicion wrinkling his spotty forehead. "And fend off nosy young ladies who want a gander at his good-looking face. It's awful late for you to be making a charity call. Let me see the blanket."

Other young ladies besides herself had had the effrontery to visit Charlie? Endeavoring to hide the irritation that dispelled her shaky nerves, she smiled and opened her cloak to reveal the blanket. "I know it's late, but they say he'll be gone tomorrow, and I've never seen a real enemy spy. Please, Timon. I promise I won't stay long, and—and I'll let you walk me home after I've talked to him for a few minutes."

But Timon wasn't as gullible as she'd hoped. He scowled. "Now that I think about it, I heard you're the one that caught him and brought him in. You always were a strange female, Fiona. What are you up to now?"

Why was he making this so difficult? Maybe this was God's way of letting her out of this whole impossible situation. She could go home with Desi and truthfully say she hadn't been able to find a way to get in to talk to Charlie.

But perversely, she found herself unwilling to be bested by the likes of Timon Lafleur.

"I'm not up to anything, you obstinate—" Clutching at the fringes of her temper, she took a deep breath and told him the truth. "I'm feeling guilty about injuring him. He really is a nice gentleman who happened to land in enemy territory, and I wanted to tell him how sorry I am, before he leaves in the morning. My aunt doesn't actually know I'm here"—Aunt Giselle at least did not, though Aunt Lyse did—"and she would box my ears if she found out. So will you please let me in before I freeze to death, standing out here in the street?"

Timon blew out a long-suffering sigh and disappeared with the lantern. A moment later, she heard clanking at the gate, and it swung open a few inches.

"Come on in—and hurry," Timon said. "I'm going to be put in the guardhouse myself if anybody finds out I let you in this time of night."

"Thank you." Astonishingly, she was inside the fort, going to see Charlie one more time before he went away for good. Bizarrely she felt as if she floated outside her own skin, watching herself commit this act of Judas-kiss patriotism.

Before she could turn and run back to the warmth and safety of Maddy's house, Timon had unlocked the guardhouse, stuck his head inside, and said, "Someone here to see you." He took Fiona's arm and shoved her into the building.

This was different from the night she'd knelt on the other side of the tack room door in the barn, confessing that she loved him. This time she saw Charlie right away in a cell to her left, lying on a cot too short for his tall body, one arm under his head, a book propped on his knees. Someone had found him some clothes that properly fit, he had recently shaved, and his hair was clean, if a bit long and untidy. He was in stocking feet, his boots squared away on the floor at the end of the cot.

She didn't see chains anywhere.

All that she took in in a flash, before he looked around and recognized her.

He jerked into a sitting position, dropping the book onto the floor. "No."

This was the second time she had thrown herself at him. She hadn't told Aunt Lyse about that other time, the night in the barn. What was she going to say?

She stood there wishing she hadn't come, insides writhing in humiliation. She was no better than those other girls who had come to the guardhouse to gawk at the handsome prisoner.

His expression softened. He got up and walked over to the bars, wrapped his hands around them as if to keep from reaching for her. His lips quirked. "Did you bring me some sweet potato pie?"

She put back her hood and opened her cloak. "Just a blanket."

He glanced at the fireplace behind her, where a smoky fire crackled. "It's not bad in here. Nothing like Scotland in November."

Silence smoldered as they stared at one another. Finally Fiona said, "How is your . . . limb?" She let her gaze drop to his injured thigh. It was thicker than the other, probably still heavily bandaged under his breeches.

He laughed. "My limb is healing nicely—no thanks to you. The surgeon here in Mobile gave me enough laudanum to get me past the first couple of days."

"That's good." Another long, awkward silence. "Well . . . here." She shoved the blanket at him. "You might need it later tonight."

He took it, letting it unfold so that it would fit between the bars, then refolded it neatly and laid it on the cot. "Thank you."

She almost left. Then something stiffened her spine. She walked right up to the bars of the cell. "Charlie, this is silly. I just came to say that I forgive you for taking my horse and for lying to me, because I might have done the same thing in your place. And I want you to know I regret having injured you. We can't change the circumstances of what brought us together, but we can at least say goodbye with civility."

He stared at her, looking vulnerable and dear in his stocking feet, his shirt open at the throat, his jaw working.

Judas. Judas.

Holding her gaze, he pressed closer to her, so that his clothes brushed hers through the bars. When she didn't move, he put out his hand to cup her cheek. Closing his eyes, he let his thumb brush her lips. She caught his hand, turned her head, and kissed his palm.

He sucked in a sharp breath, but he let her kiss his fingers one by one. "This is so unwise," he muttered, then, "Come here . . ." He slipped his hand to the back of her neck and drew her close to kiss her lips, the cell bars creating a frustrating but oddly tantalizing barrier. They both slid to their knees, kisses becoming deeper and wilder until Fiona felt as if she might melt into a hot puddle of wax.

Perhaps this wasn't what Aunt Lyse had in mind.

"Charlie." She broke away. "Charlie, I have to go. Do you hear me?"

"No. La la la I cannot hear you."

She laughed. "Yes, you can. My uncle Rafa says he's taking you to New Orleans. Maybe I could meet you there."

His eyes flew open. "Don't even think about such a thing!" He took her by the shoulders. "Promise me!"

"Well, I heard Desi talking to my brother, and it sounds like General Jackson expects the British to come back here to Mobile any day now. So New Orleans should be safe, don't you think? I could go and stay with my brother Judah—"

"No! Under no circumstances should you get anywhere near New Orleans." His voice was frantic, his eyes dark. "Fiona, if you love me, you will stay right here in Mobile with your family. If—if the British do attack the city, I want you to take refuge here in the fort."

She dropped her gaze. "All right. If you really think I should, I will."

"Yes. You must." He took her face in both hands and kissed her forehead. "Beloved, I'm so glad you came to see me, but you have to go now. This is goodbye for quite a long time, and you mustn't even write to me. But remember what I told you before. I'll come after you as soon as I can."

"And I'll pray for you every day until I see you again."

"And I you." He kissed her again, lingering. "Fiona, I love you."

"Goodbye, Charlie. I love—"

His lips took the words.

With a muffled sob she got to her feet and ran.

⌒⌒

Holding onto the bars, Charlie pulled himself to his feet, then sat down on the cot and gripped his aching thigh. Pain was a good thing, a reminder that he was alive. The scar would always be there, even if he never saw Fiona again. He hoped he'd scared her enough that she'd not follow him to New Orleans.

She was fearless, though. Closing his eyes, he pictured her as she'd looked the day she came after him, galloping along behind him on Bonnie, practically one with the horse.

Surely her people would watch her, keep her from following him again. Lord knows, they'd warned him away often enough. Every single one of them. He couldn't imagine how she'd gotten away from them tonight, how she'd talked the guard into letting her in to see him. Resourceful little minx.

He lay back, but didn't pick up the book. He wasn't interested in American politics right now, though he'd been absorbing Thomas Paine when Fiona came in. Every word she'd said tonight reeled through his mind like cables pulling a flag up a mast. There was something . . . something that snagged on logic.

But he had a hard time being logical when it came to Fiona.

He closed his eyes again, letting his thoughts drift. There would be plenty of time for hard plans during the next day's journey to New Orleans. Free! At last, he would be among his own countrymen, able to speak openly, to laugh at British jokes, to eat navy food, to move about at will. More than two months of imprisonment had taught him to appreciate that freedom as never before in his life. He'd understood the risk when he'd taken the assignment of going into New Orleans as a deported Scottish criminal.

He just hoped the information he carried would not come too late.

~

"So I'm pretty sure he believes we think the next attack will come here, not New Orleans."

Fiona sat at Maddy's kitchen table, much as she had the night of the harvest ball, but this time Aunt Lyse and Uncle Rafa's presence added a layer of reassurance she hadn't felt then.

Still, her emotions wobbled. She'd once imagined that espionage would be glamorous. She'd thought she would feel like a heroine.

Misery was more like it.

"That was brilliant, Fiona." Desi regarded her with approval. "I knew you'd be able to think on your feet."

Maddy sniffed. "It sounds like she used persuasive measures that no lady would—"

"Don't be childish, Madeleine," Aunt Lyse said with mild annoyance.

"Persuasive measures? Perhaps you think I magically melted myself and dripped through the bars of Charlie's cell?" Fiona regarded her cousin, chin up. "Really, cousin, you give me greater credit than I deserve."

"Ladies, please." Desi's eyes glimmered with amusement. "If that information had come from me, Kincaid would have suspected a plant, but I've no doubt he believed Fiona. And if he carries it back to British admiralty, our advantage of surprise grows."

"As does the likelihood of Charlie being shot by some Tennessee sharpshooter." Fiona put her head in her hands. "What have I done?"

"The hard thing. The brave thing." Aunt Lyse's arm went around her shoulders. "Now you will pray for your Charlie and leave him in the care of the Father who loves you both."

Of course she would pray. But she did not feel brave, and she did not feel brilliant. She felt like a leaf blown about in a violent wind.

NOVEMBER 16, 1814
OFF THE COAST OF NEW ORLEANS

The choppy waters of the Gulf of Mexico had thrown Charlie into a violent and unexpected state of seasickness by the time he and Rafael Gonzales boarded the prisoner caravel HMS *Goldeneye*. Perhaps he could also blame the fact that he hadn't been aboard a ship of any size since early August. Whatever the cause, he clung, hunched like an old man, to his escort's shoulder as they stepped off the gangplank onto the *Goldeneye*.

The young midshipman who greeted him stepped aside with a grin as Charlie muttered, "Excuse me," and heaved over the side before turning around to salute. "Rough crossing, sir?" the boy asked cheerfully as he shook hands with Gonzales, then swung away without waiting for an answer. "Cap'n says to bring you to his cabin immediately. He wants to be under way within the hour."

Gonzales kept a steady arm around Charlie's back and shot him a look of concern as they followed the midshipman. "Are you up to it, son? You'd be better for a drink of water and your berth."

"I'm fine," Charlie said, gritting his teeth. This was not how he'd imagined his release from American custody. No line of officers to welcome him back. No flags or champagne toast. The ship itself barely bigger than a Brighton hog boat. He tried not to wish himself back in prison.

Shaking off Gonzales's protective support, he ducked his head to enter captain's quarters and stood at attention. "Lieutenant Charles Kincaid, reporting for duty, sir."

The captain, a bug-eyed little man with thinning hair and a bulbous red nose indicative of a fondness for ale, looked up from a meal of something unappetizing—especially to one in Charlie's queasy state—and waved his fork. "At ease, Kincaid. I'm Captain Walters. Glad to have you aboard, though as I understand it, that won't be for long." He squinted at the doorway behind Charlie. "The American diplomat with you?"

"Yes, sir." Charlie looked over his shoulder. "Captain Walters, meet the Honorable Rafael Gonzales."

"Gonzales? That sounds Spanish."

"I have been an American citizen for twenty years." Gonzales moved to Charlie's side and gave the captain a much more elegant bow than the man deserved. "I present to you papers from President Madison's diplomatic staff, effecting the exchange of Lieutenant Kincaid for the American Lieutenant Sullivan Lanier, who has already been released and returned to duty." He reached into his coat and removed a sheaf of documents, which he handed over to the captain. "You will please to sign both copies and give one back to me, so that I may rejoin my ship."

Walters flicked a glance over the papers. "Will you not join me in a meal or tankard of ale before you go?"

Gonzales shook his head. "I thank you, but the weather threatens to turn ugly, and I wish to be on my way."

The captain nodded. "Kincaid, you look rather green about the gills. You have been treated well?"

"As well as any prisoner determined to escape can be treated." Charlie staggered as the ship rocked under a swell.

The captain grunted and reached for a quill. "In that case, Midshipman Edgerton will assign you quarters and whatever else you need—the first thing being, of course, a uniform. We will debrief after you are settled. Mr. Gonzales, a moment."

Charlie bowed himself out of the cabin and stood on deck for a moment, buffeted by a freezing ocean breeze. The midshipman was nowhere in sight, but he couldn't escape the familiar shipboard noises of creaking timbers and chains, the slap-slosh of waves against the ship, sailors singing and calling to one another as they worked. Battling a wild urge to dive overboard and swim back to the ship he'd come from, he leaned against the cabin wall and stared at the steely horizon.

Before insanity had time to overcome him, Gonzales emerged from the cabin. "Ah, Kincaid, I am glad you are still here. There is one more thing I wished to say to you before we part ways."

Charlie regarded the American warily. "You've had two days to say whatever you wanted, and as you can see, I'm feeling not quite the thing at the moment."

Gonzales smiled. "It is only that I know a man who faces regrets when I see one, and I wonder if you would accept a word of advice—from one who has known something of making difficult choices."

"There is no choice."

"There is always a choice," Gonzales said gently, "and the most difficult is between discharging one's duty without question and judging whether one is substituting duty for right. I stand here today because your grandfather made such a choice."

Charlie wanted to ask what he meant. But perhaps he already knew the answer.

~

NOVEMBER 18, 1814
MOBILE

The Friday morning after Charlie left, Fiona awoke from a repetition of the cliff dream. Aunt Giselle's house was quiet, Sehoy still asleep beside her in the bed they shared in the Laniers' attic bedroom. She sat straight up, a hand at her throat. It wasn't true. Tully was now in the care of some cavalry regiment, Bonnie safe at Navy Cove, and Charlie returned to his command. Everything was back as it should be.

Everything except Fiona herself. She missed Navy Cove—her people, her horses, the refuge of the beach. She wished she had the strength of mind to go home. But deep inside, in a place she couldn't admit even to herself, she wanted to wait until Uncle Rafa returned and hear how Charlie fared. One more word of him. One crumb of information to add to the store she took out at odd moments of thinking about him and praying for him.

So odd that her first prayers used to be for Sullivan. But now that he was back with his naval command, Charlie's welfare took precedence in her conversations with God.

Holy Father, please cover him, protect him, give him wisdom. You know how I miss him. Keep him and my brothers apart. I couldn't bear it if—

And therein lay the glaring, damaging truth. Yes, she had ridden after Charlie and recaptured him. And yes, she had unwillingly betrayed him with that visit to his cell—in the process earning Desi's approval—but her love for Charlie had somehow corrupted her loyalty to her brothers, to her country. She hadn't done enough, not yet, to make up for harboring an enemy spy for months while his comrades slipped up into the bay to attack and invade.

She was a Lanier. American-born, raised to courage and resourcefulness. She knew the stories by heart. Others of her family had given up comfort and fortune and their very lives so that she could be free. There had to be something else she could do to meet this new, looming threat of British aggression. No more excuses based on feminine weakness, conflicted affections, nonsensical fears.

The hard thing, Aunt Lyse had said, as if kissing Charlie goodbye had been some huge sacrifice. No, the *hard thing* was yet to come.

And suddenly she knew what she might do. Dangerous, some might say foolhardy, but the more she thought about it, the more convinced she became that it was the right thing. A frisson of sheer terror and excitement overtook her. All her life had led to this point, but she would still have to plan carefully.

Thinking it through, she slipped out of bed and dressed in the day gown she'd left hanging on a hook behind the door, then put on her shoes in the dark. Twisting her hair up in a simple knot atop her head, she tiptoed down the stairs into the kitchen, where Aunt Giselle was already building a fire in the stove. Four loaves of bread dough lay at rest on a countertop. By late afternoon they would be risen and ready to bake for supper.

"Auntie, what can I do to help?"

Aunt Giselle looked around with her dimpled smile. "Good morning, dearie." She nodded at the bucket sitting beside the door. "You can go to the well for water. I don't know about you, but I need a cup of coffee."

Like all the women of the family, Giselle ran her household with the iron discipline of a brigadier general, but her troops felt the underlying cushion of her love. Fiona and Sehoy were expected to help with chores, making them feel more part of the family than if they'd been treated as pampered guests.

Shaking off her melancholy, she flung her cloak around her shoulders and grabbed the bucket on her way out the door. The morning was chilly but not bitter, a dense fog blanketing the surrounding houses. She had to walk a couple of blocks to the center of town, where the well made a gathering place for gossip and news. A cluster of uniformed cavalry soldiers stood about smoking cigars and trading jokes. Ignoring them, she lowered the bucket into the well.

But as she left, one arm extended to balance the weight of the water on the other side, the words "big bay stallion" stopped her in her tracks.

"Handsome piece of horseflesh, but obstinate as a mule. Can't wait to show him who's boss."

Fiona looked over her shoulder just as the man who had spoken whipped his quirt against his boot.

The man must have seen her flinch, for he touched the brim of his hat and gave her a bold grin. "Sorry to startle you, ma'am—er, miss?" His expression was hopeful.

Fiona bit her lip. "Good day to you, sir," she said, hurrying on her way without satisfying the oaf's curiosity.

Had they been talking about Tully? Maybe not. It would be silly to get upset over some imagined harm to a horse that no longer belonged to her. Surely there was more than one big bay stallion in General Coffee's remuda.

But worrying about Tully reminded her of the dream from last night, which made her think of Charlie and what she knew she had to do. For the rest of the morning, as she helped with household chores, she rejected multiple impractical ways to accomplish her plan. By that afternoon when she sat by the kitchen fire hulling pecans while Aunt Giselle knitted, she had it figured out.

The first hurdle to cross was getting away from the house alone. At first she'd wondered why Maddy had been so insistent on bringing her and Sehoy to stay in Mobile. Slowly it had dawned on her that the freedoms she had enjoyed at Navy Cove were regarded as *outré* by the more socially adroit females of her family. Maddy and Aunt Giselle—probably Aunt Lyse too—worried about Fiona, worried that she wouldn't attract a suitable husband if she were left to her own pursuits in the wilds of the south bay.

She could have told them that she didn't want a suitable husband who wasn't Charlie Kincaid—and since she couldn't have him, she didn't want one at all. Shuddering at the thought of the likely response if she were so foolish as to utter that thought aloud, she tossed a handful of hulls into the sack at her feet and rose.

"Aunt Giselle, I'm feeling restless. I think I'll go for a ride before dinner."

Aunt Giselle looked up, eyes sympathetic. "I'm sure you're used to more physical activity than we have here in town. Just dress warmly. You don't want to take a chill."

"Of course." Grateful to have crossed that hurdle, Fiona hurried upstairs to the little attic room and knelt in front of her trunk.

Ten minutes later, breathless and clutching the folds of her cloak about herself, she returned to the kitchen and kissed her aunt on the cheek. "I'll be back in a little while."

"Go by Maddy's and bring everyone back with you. I've got enough stew to feed the army."

"Yes, ma'am." Feeling guilty, rebellious, and relieved all at the same time, Fiona grabbed the boots she'd left at the foot of the stairs and headed for the barn.

She found Cisco seated on a hay bale, mending a harness and singing softly to himself. He looked up with a grin. "Hullo, Miss Fiona! Old Max and me was hoping you'd come out to keep us company this afternoon."

"Yes, five days without riding is too many." She stood in the center aisle of the barn, breathing in the familiar pungent scents of horses, hay, leather, and manure. Sweet smells that reminded her of home. She swung her cloak off her shoulders and draped it over a stall door. "Could I take Max for a ride?"

Cisco's eyes widened as he took in the breeches, boots, and old coat that she wore when working in the barn. "Miss Fiona, I don't know if that's a good idea."

"Aunt Giselle knows where I am." She didn't have to explain

herself to the stable boy, but if he went running to Uncle Rémy, she was in trouble.

"Still. Max hasn't had a sidesaddle on him in years." Cisco was looking obstinate.

"Cisco, you know I can make any horse do whatever I want, but look at me—I'm not dressed for a sidesaddle. Max will be perfectly safe with me. Now you can either help me saddle him, or I'll do it myself." She stomped toward Max's stall, went in, and reached for his bridle, then slipped the bit into his mouth.

Cisco followed. "Oh, all right. Let me help you."

Between the two of them, Max was saddled in nothing flat. Fiona led him out of the barn the back way, and Cisco cupped his hands to give her a boost into the saddle.

Yanking down the hat that covered her pinned-up hair, she grinned down at him. "Nobody will suspect I'm a girl, let alone Rémy Lanier's niece. You won't tell on me, will you?"

"I thought you said it was all right!"

"Well, to be perfectly honest, Auntie does know I'm riding, but I'm going a little farther than I led her to believe." She pursed her lips as she'd seen Maddy do time on end. "Cisco, I'm so bored up here with nothing to do but sew! I just wanted to ride for a while without having to make girly conversation. Don't you ever feel like running away?"

He shook his curly head. "Why would I want to run away from a good job where I get plenty to eat and enough money to save for a livery stable of my own one day? And Miz Giselle is even teaching me to read and write!" But he backed up a step, his expression as lugubrious as a thirteen-year-old's could be. "I won't tell, but Miz Giselle always finds out everything anyway. You'll see."

With that warning ringing in her ears, Fiona turned Max toward the road.

She'd heard Desi talk about the soldiers' encampment near the western edge of town and figured, with the plans to march toward New Orleans, activity would be stirring there. At first she rode with her head down, hat pulled low over her ears, hunched inside Sullivan's coat. To flatten her curvy figure, she'd bound her bosom with strips torn from an old petticoat, and she hadn't gone far before it occurred to her to stop and smear a little dirt on her face to camouflage the smooth texture of her skin.

It was a bone-jarring ten-minute trot to the encampment on poor old Max, whose duties usually entailed nothing more strenuous than pulling the children's pony cart. He wasn't happy with the saddle, much less the rider, and periodically tried to scrape her off under a tree limb. By the time she spotted the first sentry, she was wishing she'd taken her chances and let Cisco drive her in the pony cart after all.

"Hey, you!" the guard shouted when she got a little closer. "Stop and state your business."

"Message for General Coffee," she said, imitating her cousin Israel's husky adolescent voice. "From Rémy Lanier."

"You another one of the Lanier boys?" the man asked. "Come on, I'll take you."

Another? What did that mean? But reluctant to provoke questions, Fiona dismounted and followed the guard, leading Max through a sea of tents. She passed soldiers who were building fires, stirring cauldrons of stew, frying hardtack and bacon, and engaging in dozens of other homely afternoon camp chores. One or two sat on camp stools reading letters, and she wondered if they were from parents or sweethearts.

What if she wrote to Charlie? Would there be any way to get a letter to him? He'd told her not to try.

Distracted, she nearly ran into her escort, who had stopped at a large officer's tent. As he ducked inside, sudden panic struck

Fiona. She hadn't thought she'd actually get in to see General Coffee himself. He had talked to her on two separate occasions. Surely he would recognize her and have someone haul her back to her family in utter disgrace.

Discretion being the better part of valor, she skirted the tent and headed for the edge of camp, where the horses would be corralled in a makeshift paddock. She heard them whickering and stamping before she saw them, a beautiful remuda of all colors and sizes—most of them tall and muscular like Tully. Still, she found the big bay stallion with no trouble at all. He was young enough to be playful, running circles around the confined space of the paddock, rearing to paw at the air, trumpeting to draw attention to his masculinity.

Holding Max by the halter, she whistled Tully's signal and smiled when he lifted his head, ears pricked. The moment he saw her, he ran toward her and nuzzled her pocket for the apple she'd brought.

Laughing, she pressed her cheek to his, listened to the crunch of his big teeth on the fruit, felt his heart beat under her hand. For the first time in days, joy flooded her spirit. *Thank you, God, for this beautiful animal. Thank you for his affection, thank you that he even remembers me.*

"Boy, you got to be one of them Lanier kids," drawled a deep voice behind Fiona. She turned to find a tall, bearded cavalry officer, picking his teeth with a knife as he regarded her thoughtfully. "My wrangler run off three days ago, and can't nobody else even get near that horse 'cept General Coffee. He ain't been curried in all that time."

Fiona didn't know what to say. "That so?"

"It's definitely so." The officer flicked the knife toward the ground, where it stuck, quivering. "Would you like a job?"

14

Sehoy was tired of feeling like the fifth wheel on the Lanier family wagon, particularly when it seemed to be veering off the road into the weeds. The evening meal had been awkward in the extreme, and she tried to eat her stew and cornbread without drawing attention to herself.

Aunt Giselle seemed to think Fiona would be back before supper, but when she didn't return, Uncle Rémy questioned poor Cisco with such uncharacteristic severity that the boy almost cried. Cisco didn't know where Fiona had taken Max, the old pony—or he wouldn't say. Maddy was convinced her cousin had taken off after that dratted Charlie Kincaid, while her mother, the beautiful Mrs. Lyse, vehemently denied the possibility. The only one who kept his opinion to himself was Mr. Desi, who ate his dinner and occasionally patted Maddy's hand to keep her from flying into the boughs.

The children, including thirteen-year-old Israel, had been sent to the kitchen to eat. Sehoy supposed she should be grateful she hadn't been sent out along with them. Still, when Desi addressed her without warning, she almost wished she had been exiled as well.

"What? I'm sorry—I didn't . . ." She trailed off, blushing.

Desi chuckled, but in his kind way. "I said, nobody has bothered to ask the person closest to Fiona what she thinks. Did she say anything about her plans to you, Sehoy?"

"Not in so many words. I know she's been lonesome for Navy Cove." She glanced at Maddy, and added reluctantly, "Miss Maddy is right, though, she's grieving over Charlie."

"I told you so." Maddy lifted her chin.

"Still," Sehoy said quickly, "I can't see her going after him like she did before. That was different."

Aunt Giselle tsked. "Seemed to me she'd been getting along pretty well."

"Auntie, you shouldn't have let her go riding by herself, or even with just Cisco." Maddy looked disapproving. "She was always too fond of running wild with the boys, even when she was a little girl."

"I just thought a little fresh air might do her good," Giselle said defensively, looking at Lyse for corroboration.

Lyse sighed. "Don't feel bad, Giselle. I'd have done the same thing. I wish Rafa were here. He would know how best to proceed."

"Since he is not," Desi said, "would everyone feel better if I go out and ask a few discreet questions? For the sake of her reputation, we don't want the world to know Fiona has disappeared, but as nightfall is upon us, we should probably use what daylight is left to look for her."

This plan meeting with general relief and approval, Desi excused himself from the table and went to fetch his greatcoat.

Sehoy rose and caught him on the way out the front door. "Mr. Desi, I thought of something."

He paused, putting on his hat. "What is it?"

"Well, you remember that cipher we tried to translate, the one Charlie had me hold?"

"Yes, what of it?"

"What if Fiona had already figured it out? What if she made plans to meet Charlie somewhere, say in Pensacola?"

"You think she would do such a thing?"

"Maybe. I don't know." Sehoy hesitated, then blurted, "If I were in her shoes, I might."

Desi looked down at her, curiosity in his deep-set brown eyes. "Would you indeed." It wasn't a question, the way he said it. He seemed to understand what she meant. He laid a gentle hand upon her shoulder. "You may be right, though I'm inclined to agree with Mrs. Lyse that I doubt it. But what worries me most is the idea that someone—perhaps one of those uncouth creatures from Tennessee—might have abducted her for, shall we say, his own unsavory purposes. Fiona is an extraordinarily pretty girl, after all."

"Yes, sir." Sehoy sighed. "I should have been with her this afternoon. But I didn't want to go riding." She'd been in the attic, mooning over a letter Oliver sent earlier in the week, and trying to compose one in return. "It was too cold outside." If that sounded lame and defensive, then so be it.

"It is that," Desi said. With a faint smile, he turned up the collar of his coat. "I'd best see if I can find your missing cousin before dark. And meantime, don't waste time berating yourself over your inability to control another person's foolish decisions."

Oliver was her cousin as well, she thought as Desi left—though the connection went back so many generations as to be almost nonexistent. And she sincerely hoped she wasn't making a foolish decision herself, in keeping what Oliver had told her from his family.

As Fiona followed Captain Stillman through camp, she expected at any moment to hear someone yell, "Fraud! Lightskirt!" but no one paid the least attention to her. If anything, her comparatively small stature, her ragged coat and misshapen hat, the scuffed, down-at-heel boots rendered her all but invisible—for now.

Joining the army, which had seemed like such a wonderful idea in the safety of Aunt Giselle's kitchen, was absurd, crazy, the stuff of a Shakespearean comedy. Who was the girl who dressed like a boy? Viola in *Twelfth Night*? Funny, she'd also lost her twin brother and fallen in love with someone she couldn't have. In the process creating all sorts of mayhem.

But she had answered that providential job offer with a firm "Yes, sir, I sure do," making sure old Max was brought into the remuda and cared for.

She was going to serve her country in a meaningful way. As meaningful as her mother observing and reporting British troop movements, coded in chatty letters to Aunt Lyse during the Revolution. Or her father and Uncle Rafa delivering Spanish gold in a daring dash up the Mississippi to aid George Rogers Clark's Midwestern stand at Fort Pitt. Or Uncle Luc-Antoine helping *his* father escape from the Fort Charlotte guardhouse.

Which thought reminded her of Charlie—a singularly unproductive mental gyration.

Captain Stillman of the magnificent beard ducked into a side alley between some rows of smaller tents, and she followed. Her family in Mobile would be frantic at her disappearance and maybe think she'd run off after Charlie again. But she couldn't stay there any longer, moping about with nothing to occupy her mind. Well, she *could*, but she didn't want to. She was fed up with people telling her, a grown woman, what to do. Certainly she was smart enough to hide her identity and care for the cavalry mounts she had raised, while the men fought to maintain their American freedom, so dearly won.

But it was going to take some ingenuity.

The captain stopped so suddenly that she almost walked into him.

"What's the matter?" she asked, trying to peer around him.

"Nothing's the matter." He looked over his shoulder. "You're a quiet little—" and he called her a name she'd only heard at the shipyard a time or two. "Which Lanier family you from?"

"Rémy's. I'm Israel." Israel was just young and stupid enough to volunteer for the army. She hoped he wouldn't actually do it.

"You sure you're old enough to be off your mama's teat?"

Thoroughly shocked, Fiona made herself laugh. "Yes, sir, I'm thirteen."

"Hmph." He stared at her. "If I didn't need you so bad, I'd send you home."

"Please don't do that, sir! My cousin Fiona raised some of those horses, and I—I feel responsible for 'em."

"They're good animals." He paused, then went on more gently. "You obviously know your way around horses, boy, but if you don't think you can stomach what's coming, you'd better let me know right now, and we'll forget the whole thing."

"What do you mean?"

"This ain't playtime. There's gonna be a battle, probably a long, drawn-out one. You ever killed anybody?"

Fiona swallowed hard. "No, sir. But I can protect myself. And just a couple of weeks ago I shot a man that took off with my property."

Perhaps the note of truth in her voice convinced him. "That's good to hear. You got a gun on you?"

She shook her head. Why hadn't she thought of that? She could have taken one of the boys' hunting rifles.

"All right. I'll get you one, and a knife. A man ought to be armed, even to take care of the horses." Without further comment, Stillman turned and continued walking wherever he was taking her.

Which turned out to be a campfire in front of a large tent. Four uniformed officers sat around it, using hardtack to scoop beans into their mouths from metal plates. Fiona was glad dark had almost completely fallen. She couldn't see their faces, which meant they couldn't see hers.

"This here is Israel Lanier, boys," Stillman said, jerking a thumb at Fiona. "Gonna replace that colored boy that run off." The mustache twitched. "He's a little soft, maybe, but he knows his way around a horse, so you treat him right, you hear, Catlett?"

The officers guffawed and elbowed one another.

"Yes, sir," said one of the younger ones with a pair of close-set eyes and a sparse mustache.

Fiona thought she recognized his voice. Maybe he'd been with General Coffee the day he came to Navy Cove to buy the horses. She hoped not.

"What about that gun, sir?" she said, thinking that arming herself might be a good idea for more reasons than one. "And the knife?"

Stillman pointed at the ground close to the fire. "Stay here, I'll be right back."

"Yes, sir." She dropped to the ground and remembered just in time to sit with her feet pulled in, knees splayed as she'd seen her brothers and male cousins do. She propped her forearms across her knees. "You got some more of them beans?" she asked gruffly.

"Sure. Growing boy needs his feed, right?" One of the soldiers got up, an older one, judging by the stiffness of his movements. "I'm Morris, Sergeant Kern Morris. We're glad to have you. Jackson's been waiting on recruits from the upper Mississippi to report in before we head to New Orleans." He handed Fiona a filled plate. "Coffee?"

"Yes, sir. Thank you."

Morris thumped her on the head. "Least you got some manners. Better than that last lice-infested kid shared my tent."

Fiona grunted and started to eat. When Morris handed her a steaming tin cup of coffee that burnt her hand, she yelped, "Yeow! I mean, thank you, sir."

Morris laughed and sat down.

The first officer who had spoken, the young one called Catlett, said, "There's another Lanier kid here, did you know that?"

Fiona ducked her head to hide her surprise. "My pa said he thought my cousin Oliver might enlist. Was it him?"

"Tall, skinny kid with reddish hair and a bunch of freckles. Oliver might have been his name."

If Oliver saw her without warning, she was going to be found out. "Do you know where he is? My pa said to give him a message if I saw him."

Catlett pointed. "Third row over there, 7th Infantry. But don't go anywhere until Morris gets back."

"Oh, I won't." She had to have that gun. But then she was going to find Oliver and make sure he kept her secret. And if he objected, she just might shoot him. She crammed a hunk of hardtack into her mouth to hide her smile.

⌒

The 7th Infantry camp was a short walk in the dark past a row of small, ragged tents. Fiona held her breath lest someone stop her, but she slipped along unmolested, passing groups and individual soldiers at their evening tasks—cleaning guns and personal gear, writing letters by candlelight, playing cards or throwing dice.

She would stop every now and then to ask, "Anybody know Oliver Lanier?" receive a short no in response, and wander on. Finally one old fellow spat out a stream of tobacco juice and jerked his head toward a tent not far away. "Down yonder, kid."

"Thank you, sir." Approaching the tent, she slowed and stopped outside the firelight. She saw an iron pot suspended over a small campfire, surrounded by camp stools where three young men sat eating their supper. "Oliver!" she hissed. "Oliver Lanier? Is that you?"

The boy in the middle nearly dropped his pan of beans. When he looked up, Fiona recognized her cousin's freckled face.

"Who's there?" he said.

"Oliver, come here. I need to talk to you."

"Fio—"

"It's Israel."

He looked confused. "Israel?"

"Yes. Pa sent me to find you."

Oliver's companions laughed, and one of them shoved him off the log. "Go on, Lanier. Looks like your daddy found you after all."

Oliver got up, dusting off the seat of his breeches, and set his plate down on the log. "I'll be right back." He snatched Fiona by the elbow and drew her out of earshot of the other boys. "What are you doing here, Fiona? I know your voice when I hear it."

"You've got to call me Israel." Fiona jerked her arm out of his grasp. "I signed on to work the horses for the cavalry unit."

"Wait. Just wait a doggone minute! You can't join a cavalry unit! You're a—"

"I already did. I told them I'm Israel Lanier, and somebody said they'd seen you earlier in the day. Does Uncle Luc-Antoine know where you are?"

"Sure."

If he knew her voice, she knew his as well. "No, he doesn't, and if you tell on me, I'll tell on you too."

"Fiona—"

"Israel!" she repeated. "Call me Israel."

Oliver audibly ground his teeth. "All right. But you can't do this by yourself. You need somebody to watch out for you and make sure you're all right."

"The men I met tonight seem like good men. And as long as they don't suspect anything, I'll be fine. Which is the only reason I came to find you—I need you to help me cut my hair."

Oliver stared at her in patent horror. "I'm not doing that. Your brothers will hang me from the highest tree as it is. Cutting your hair wouldn't be decent."

Fiona grabbed Oliver by both arms. "I know you don't understand, but I can't stand the idea of going back home and sitting around a quilt while you and my brothers go off to fight. Besides, I won't be right on the battle lines, I'll be back with the horses." He was shaking his head, so she shook him hard. "Oliver! I'm not going back. If you make me, I'll just run away again, and you'll never see me again."

He stared at her, clearly horrified and conflicted and angry. But he'd always looked up to her and obeyed her bossy instructions.

After a long moment, he looked away. "All right, but I hope you know I may go to hell for this."

She laughed and reached inside her coat. "No you won't. Here's my knife." She handed him the knife, then took off her hat, letting her long braid fall. Turning her back to him, she took a deep breath for courage. "Go ahead. Do it." When he didn't move, she repeated sharply, "I said, do it!"

Oliver groaned, then she felt him take hold of her braid and start sawing at it. When the last few strands came away, he tossed the long braid into the underbrush and stepped back. "There you go, God help me."

She shook her head, letting the short wisps swing against her face. Odd and light. She pushed her hair back, tucking the sides behind her ears as she'd seen the boys working the shipyard do, put her hat back on, then turned to look at Oliver. "How do I look?"

His face was priceless. "Like Israel."

"Good." She flung her arms around him and hugged him hard. "Thank you, Oliver. It helps to know you're here."

"But we're in different units."

Fiona stepped back, shoving her hands into her pockets. "I know, but at least somebody knows where I am." She hesitated. "When I get to New Orleans, I'll write them. Want me to tell them about you too?"

"Sehoy knows. But you can write to my pa."

"You should've told him. He was only ten when he rescued Grandpére from the guardhouse in the fort. He'd understand why you wanted to serve, and now you've worried him."

"We're a pair, aren't we, Fi—Israel?"

She whopped him on the arm with a closed fist. "Yes, we are. Good night, Oliver. You pray for me, and I'll pray for you, and I'll see you after we kick the British back across the Atlantic."

Shaking his head as if he still couldn't believe what he'd just done, Oliver backed toward the firelight, then finally turned and left her.

Fiona put her knife back into her coat, yanked her hat down more securely, and took off in the dark back to the cavalry camp. Her hair would grow back. But regardless of her assurances to Oliver, she was going to have to develop a thick skin in order to survive the next few months in the army. And once she did, something told her there would be no going back.

NOVEMBER 22, 1814
MOBILE

Mama and Elijah were still abed as Maddy and Desi sat on the porch swing watching the rain pour off the roof in depressing sheets and gather in deep puddles across the walkway. Having promised to bid her goodbye before joining General Jackson's staff as they rode to New Orleans, he had knocked on the door shortly after sunrise.

She had slept fitfully and awakened with a headache and stinging eyes. "Desi, I'm going to miss you so much."

"And I you." He took her hand and squeezed it. "What's the matter? You knew this was coming."

"Yes, and if anybody is used to goodbyes, it's me." She looked up at him, lips trembling. "I'm worried about Fiona. I couldn't sleep for thinking about what I said to her that night before Charlie left."

"It was a bit harsh, but I doubt that's why she left." He smiled. "A girl with three brothers has surely heard worse." He shook his head. "I tried everything I could think of to find her, but she's just . . . disappeared. Cisco didn't have any idea which direction she went, and since she was dressed like a boy, nobody remembers seeing her. I would have gone to Pensacola to look for her, but General Jackson needed me—"

"Desi, you can't blame yourself. Uncle Rémy and Israel will find her." She had to believe that, or she'd go mad with guilt. "I wish I could do something. All I can do is stay here while you go off without even the protection of a uniform."

He raised one eyebrow.

"Desi, I know what a translator does. You'll be a liaison between the general and all sorts of hostile factions—a target

238

to be taken out—and often working on your own." She turned and took hold of the lapels of his coat. "Don't tell me it's not dangerous. And knowing you, you will not be careful! You'll put the general's well-being ahead of your own."

Ruddy color appeared in his cheeks. "I assure you I can look after my own hide."

"Please do. Please come back to me." If she was begging, so be it. She had never pleaded with Stephen, taking his absences in stride as the nature of his work and responsibility. This was somehow different.

"Will it matter so much if I don't?" His expression was wistful. "You have your family and church here, you have Elijah, your sewing work. You managed for a long time without me."

"You're going to make me say it—after you promised you'd stay as long as I need you. Desi Palomo, you've become quite necessary to my well-being. I need someone who will tell me the truth when I don't want to hear it. Who will haul me back when I slide into feeling sorry for myself. Someone not afraid to lead."

"That sounds an awful lot like your father," he said ruefully. "You should just move back to New York—"

"No!" Still holding him by the lapels, she snatched him close, pressed her cheek against his, her voice a passionate whisper in his ear. "Do not misunderstand. We have become partners, and I *love* you, in a way I can barely describe. You make my heart beat out of my chest when you come into the room. I love that you are so tall that I feel small, and I love the way one eyebrow goes up when you smile. I adore the secret looks we share when Elijah says something outrageous. Right now I can barely breathe because your beard is scraping my face, and I want to—"

"Oh, Maddy, have mercy!" Laughing, he rose to lift her from the swing, pulling her into his arms and kissing her hard.

"Are you sorry you asked?" she said breathlessly, as soon as her lips were free. "I could go on for days."

"Hold onto it all and save it for our wedding night." He kissed one eyelid, then the other.

She became boneless in his arms. "That had better be very soon."

"As soon as we convince the redcoats to go back to their side of the Atlantic and stay there, I promise. Now let me go. The sooner we get this over with, the sooner I can come back to you." He relaxed his hold on her. "Pray for me, Maddy. Pray for us all. It will not be an easy campaign."

"You know I will." She looked up at him, eyes drenched. "God be with you, my love."

"Aye, and with you." With one last kiss he put her away from him and swung out into the rain.

It was a good thing he didn't look back. He would not have seen a very brave face.

⌒

November 24, 1814
Negril Bay, Jamaica

As the *Goldeneye* sailed into Negril Bay under clear skies, Charlie leaned over the rail, spyglass lifted to scan the shoreline. British warships of every size and description crowded the harbor as far as the eye could see, their snowy sails lined up in relief against a murky horizon, a Union Jack snapping proudly on each deck and signal flags flaring at intervals on the masts. As a backdrop to the ships, scarlet-coated infantry and fusiliers, green-clad 95th Rifles, Highlanders in their tartan trousers and tams, and a couple of motley free Jamaican colored regiments scurried like ants among the tents, grass huts, and brightly colored marquees that checkered the beach.

It was a breathtaking sight after his journey across the stormy gulf. His seasickness had subsided by the time the *Goldeneye* entered the Jamaican port, and he'd finally begun to feel his old self. Clad as he was in a naval blue frock coat, with white waistcoat and breeches, the gold epaulette on his right shoulder indicating his rank of lieutenant, only the scars on his forehead and his aching thigh reminded him of his American adventures.

Well, and the significant hole in his heart where Fiona Lanier had planted herself and subsequently been yanked away. Only time would repair that injury. He patted his coat pocket to make sure the letter was still there. He'd had more than a week to get the wording just right. Now he had to muster the courage to deliver it.

Nearly an hour later he stepped off a small dinghy into shallow water and splashed onto the beach. He stopped the first marine he encountered. "Where can I find Admiral Cochrane?"

"Over there." The man jerked his head toward a collection of oversized marquees pitched some distance down the beach. Pegged open to the mild, gusting sea breeze, their flags indicated their inhabitants' exalted ranks.

Charlie nodded and headed that way. He passed native women in colorful skirts, carrying bowls of tropical fruit or wash baskets atop their turbaned heads, and men with hogsheads of tobacco or kegs of rum balanced on their bare shoulders. Open-air stalls displayed such exotic foodstuffs as sea turtles, sugarcane, pimientos, star apples, and pineapples, as well as nonperishable wares like wood carvings and hand-dyed kerchiefs. He skirted jugglers and knife throwers entertaining drunken English soldiers, and stepped around a trio of sailors casting dice upon a canvas table. By the time he reached the largest of the tents flying the admiral's pennant, he wondered if he had stumbled into a carnival rather than a military base.

He saluted the marine stationed outside the tent. "First Lieutenant Charles Kincaid, reporting to Admiral Cochrane."

"Is he expecting you?"

Charlie reached inside his coat for the packet of papers given him by the captain of the *Goldeneye*. "I'm not sure, but he'll want to see these."

The marine disappeared with the papers in hand. A few minutes later, a buxom young woman with her peasant blouse slipping off one brown shoulder exited the tent.

The marine followed, shaking his head. "The admiral says come in. Not happy to be interrupted, so you'd better be somebody important."

The Scottish admiral, known to Charlie as a longtime rival of his grandfather, was seated at a small but beautifully carved desk, frowning over the papers Charlie had sent in. Possessed of a full head of reddish-gray hair and a pair of impressive sideburns, Cochrane was in full uniform, double chin resting upon a starched cravat. At his elbow was a goblet of wine, in one hand a fine Cuban cigar.

"About time you reported in, Kincaid. You almost missed us. We leave Jamaica in two days."

"I've been rather . . . tied up," Charlie said, tongue in cheek.

"So I see." Cochrane looked up, expression sour. "What can you tell me about American defenses in New Orleans?"

"Then that is where we are invading?"

Cochrane sneered. "Clearly they have concentrated forces in Mobile, leaving New Orleans all but defenseless. We have been rebuffed from Mobile once, so there would be nothing to gain by trying it again."

"But, sir—"

"New Orleans, Lieutenant. My orders are to get into the city, one way or another, and claim the prizes in those warehouses.

I'm hopeful the pirate Laffite and his men will aid us in finding a seaward approach through Lake Borgne."

Charlie blinked. "It was my understanding that Laffite went to General Jackson, informing him of your offer of amnesty in return for his support—hoping the Americans would accept him instead."

"Which hope was summarily quashed. The pirates have been cowering in a variety of hiding places over the last month. Which means they will be more amenable to helping us."

The admiral was asking questions but not listening to the answers. Still, Charlie felt obligated to impart the intelligence he had sacrificed so much to bring. He endeavored to keep his tone respectful. "Admiral Cochrane, I have seen evidence that the American troops are both tough and well-trained, and Jackson has summoned reinforcements from Kentucky and Tennessee. They are loyal to him, and he seems to have a genius for bringing together otherwise disparate factions in the common cause of defending territory that they feel belongs to them by divine grant. The American naval fleet is also growing in both power and number. As to the pirates, I would not count on their willingness to surrender that loyalty in favor of what they perceive to be an invading army."

Cochrane rose, eyebrows lowered in a thunderous line.

Charlie gulped, determined to finish. "Also, sir, I presume you've never seen the swamps and bayous that surround New Orleans. Our ships cannot get close enough to invade without betraying our presence well in advance. Have you considered what will happen if they barricade the city and lie in wait for us?"

"Have I considered—? You are insolent, sir." The cigar jabbed the air with every word. "The Admiralty put me in command of a fleet unrivaled in the world! Perhaps you have forgotten that we demoralized Napoleon, and I come here direct from burning the American capitol. You verge on treason, but I am going to overlook it in light of the fact that you have lately undergone a bit of an ordeal." Dropping into his chair, he set fire to Charlie's report with the cigar. "I should never have listened to Nicholls's suggestion to send you into New Orleans. Now get out of my sight, and if you mention a word of this conversation to anyone else, I shall have you court-martialed. You may report to Captain Lockyer on the *Sophie*."

Seething, Charlie reached into his pocket. "Aye, sir. One more thing before I go." He proffered his personal letter, which Cochrane accepted reluctantly. "I would like to submit this letter to be delivered to the Lords Commissioner of the Admiralty." Saluting, Charlie turned on his heel and left the tent. He stood blinking in the bright sunshine for a moment, gathering himself.

The young woman who had been with the admiral earlier shimmied around him with a purring "*'Scuse moi, monsieur. B'jour.*" Dragging her hand across his back, she slipped into the tent.

Duty. He had done what he could, and he had to accept the impolitic decisions of his higher-ups. That was military life. It helped to think of Fiona safely in Mobile with her extended family, perhaps taking a ride in the pony cart with her younger cousins, maybe baking a sweet potato pie with her auntie. When the war ended, he'd find her, convince her to become his bride. Perhaps not a duchess, but the wife of an earl's younger son wouldn't be so bad.

Beyond that, his imagination refused to go, let alone hopes and dreams.

Perhaps he hadn't turned as American as he'd thought.

15

Bringing up the rear of the cavalcade on a docile, knock-kneed mule named Button, Fiona pulled the collar of her coat closer about her throat as they entered the Place d'Armes where General Jackson's forces were to gather. A cold, drenching rain had pounded Jackson's staff as they made the overland journey from Mobile to New Orleans. She gathered from the soldiers' talk that any British military man of common sense would avoid the quagmires impeding a southern attack, so Jackson's strategy involved scouting possible inland invasion points to the northeast of the city.

During the last ten days, Fiona had done her best to stay unnoticed—quickly doing as she was told, making herself indispensable by anticipating the soldiers' needs—and she stuck close to kindly Sergeant Morris. Lieutenant Catlett she avoided, partially because she was afraid he would recognize her, but mainly because he had a mischievous streak that had already made her life miserable. Discovering her partiality to her hat, Catlett made it his business to knock it off her head at every

245

opportunity. A few days ago she'd almost lost it while crossing a swollen creek but managed to rescue it just before it went under. To deflect suspicion, she had developed a saltier language than a lady should possess, and when she let fly an insulting phrase at her tormentor as she donned her sorry, soggy headgear, Catlett just laughed.

As the unit made camp under leaden skies, Fiona muttered a prayer of gratitude that Catlett had been assigned scout duty, while the other men pitched tents and foraged for food. She took the horses to water one at a time, affectionately talking to them as they drank, then hobbling them at the edge of camp. She couldn't help wondering how Oliver fared. She hadn't seen him since the night he cut her hair, but she'd faithfully prayed for him, along with Sullivan, Judah, and . . .

She sighed, arms wrapped around Dusty's neck. Of course she prayed for Charlie, almost with every breath. Would she ever be free from the memory of his blue-splotched eyes and his courage and, oh, those bone-melting kisses? It seemed not. Sometimes, with a fierceness that drew her into a knot of longing, she yearned just to talk to him or hear him laugh. Oh, how she prayed for his safety.

"Hey, Lanier."

Fiona looked up to find Sergeant Morris looking at her over Dusty's back. She straightened. "Yes, sir?"

"The general sent for us. We're to ride into the city for Jackson's speech to the populace. No reason you can't come." He half turned, then paused. "You not sick, are you, kid?"

"No, sir, I'm fine."

"I told you it was going to be a hard march. And the battle yet to come."

"I know. I'm ready."

He shook his head, muttering to himself as he walked off.

Fiona checked Dusty's hobble—apparently he was to be left in camp this time—and hurried to saddle the indefatigable Button. A few minutes later she was jouncing along with the mule's bone-jarring trot at the rear of the cavalcade, headed for the city proper. General Jackson had set up his headquarters on Royal Street, and the street below the two-story brick-and-ironwork building was thronged with ladies and gentlemen of every age, social stratum, and description—some in carriages, some on foot, some leaning on the rails of balconies overhead. An aura of expectation stirred the crowd as Fiona followed the officers pushing toward the front. She heard a smattering of Spanish and English, but almost everyone conversed in loud and excited French, a remnant of the Creole influence that had established the city in the early eighteenth century. She wondered how the Tennessee-bred Andrew Jackson was going to communicate with this volatile gathering.

Just as she reined Button to a halt behind Sergeant Morris, the balcony doors above her opened, and Jackson himself stepped out. Tall and gaunt as a pine tree and just about as ugly, with his wizened, jaundiced face and wild head of gray hair, the general still managed to convey the impression that he was in control of this dire situation and convinced that victory was his due. A great cheer went up from the crowd, just as three other men in civilian dress came out onto the balcony. The first two gentlemen Fiona didn't recognize. Then the third—a tall, broad-shouldered Spaniard in a beautifully tailored gray coat and striped waistcoat—moved to lean on the rail and scan the audience below.

In her absorption with getting herself enlisted with the cavalry and keeping her identity hidden all this time, she'd forgotten Desi Palomo was coming to New Orleans with General Jackson. Surreptitiously she looked around. Wedged in as she was, horses in front, carriages and foot traffic to the sides and behind, there was no getting back through the crowd and out of sight. She grabbed her hat brim to shield her face.

Sensing her anxiety, Button sidled, knocking her sideways. Fiona's arms instinctively flew out to maintain balance, and off came her hat.

Horrified, she righted herself and looked up just as Desi's gaze passed over her—and swung back. Eyes widening, he straightened. The man next to him spoke to him, and he looked away from Fiona to answer.

She waited, hands clenched on the reins.

Don't faint, she told herself. *It will be all right.*

In the end what had betrayed her was not Catlett but her own nervous stupidity. She was going to be sent home in disgrace.

~

DECEMBER 5, 1814
MOBILE

Maddy opened her front door and found her cousin Israel standing on the porch, shifting from one oversized foot to the other, his cheeks red and chapped from the raw wind that had blown in during the last few days.

"Morning, Maddy." Giving her his shy, freckle-faced grin, he thrust a sealed letter at her. "Pa said you'd want to see this right away. It's from Desi."

She snatched the folded missive and grabbed the startled Israel in a hug. "Would you like to come in for something warm to drink?"

"No thanks." He squirmed out of her hold. "I've got to get back to finish my declensions so Pa will let me watch the rest of the troops move out toward New Orleans."

"All right." Patting his shoulder, she backed into the house and shut the door, already picking the seal off with her thumb-nail, smiling at the sight of Desi's firm scrawl. He had only been gone a little over two weeks, and she hadn't expected to hear from him so soon. *Please, God, let it not be bad news.*

"Who was it, *chéri*?" Mama wandered into the hall from the kitchen, where she had been baking something that smelled of cinnamon and cloves. She dusted flour off her hands and peeked over Maddy's shoulder. "Ooh! Desi has written! Will you read it aloud? That is, unless . . ." She paused and batted her long eyelashes. "Unless it is too personal."

Maddy regretted her inability to squelch a blush. "I'll be happy to read it. Come let's sit down in the parlor where we may be comfortable." She led the way into the front room and perched on the edge of the sofa, smoothing the letter in her lap.

Mama dropped down beside her with a little "Oof!" and regarded her, golden eyes sparkling. "Hurry, please! Is he well?"

"Patience, Mama!" Maddy smiled. "He says, 'My darling Maddy—'"

Mama squealed in delight. "That is a very good beginning! Read that again."

Maddy laughed out loud. "What a spectacular idea. 'My darling Maddy, I couldn't wait to put pen to paper and tell you that the only thing that made our cold, wet, and miserable ride to New Orleans bearable was knowing that you and Elijah wait for me safe and sound in your little house in Mobile. I hope you will make notes of the funny remarks that come from that busy little brain and report them to me. And I want to know how you oc-cupy your time as well. I miss you both, more than I can express.

"'General Jackson keeps me busy translating and delivering messages to and from the Creole citizenry. His speech upon our arrival was well received, and he has used the week since then to assess and inspect all possible points at which the British might attack. He has also begun to unite the several factions of local defense committees, as well as to requisition funds from the state legislature for supplies and repairs to forts and barricades. He is a sometimes impatient and abrasive personality, but the more time I spend with him, the more I respect his leadership ability. With that said, I'm afraid I have some disturbing news of a more personal nature. Brace yourself, sweetheart, and please read this portion to your mother and father.'"

Maddy stopped and watched her mother's eyes widen in dismay.

Biting her lip, she continued. "'Right before General Jackson began that wonderful, stirring speech from the balcony of Headquarters—I was with him, translating his words to the Creole populace—I chanced to look down at the crowd and noticed a group of cavalry officers just below the balcony. There was a young boy on a mule among the officers, dressed in the most disreputable garb you ever saw. Suddenly the crowd jostled the mule, the boy's hat fell off, and I realized it was no boy at all but our own Fiona! She has cut her hair off below her ears, and pasted her face with a layer of dirt, but there was no mistaking the blue eyes and those Lanier eyebrows—'" Maddy choked, unable to continue, and Mama snatched the letter from her.

"'Imagine my relief,'" Mama read aloud, "'to have at last found her, safe and sound. But here is where the story gets difficult to tell. I was about to excuse myself to go to her, when General Jackson began to speak. You can also imagine my distress at being so torn between family duty and patriotic responsibility—I could only pray that Fiona would remain where she was until I could get to her. I tried to keep an eye on her, but after one moment of distraction I looked, and she was gone, leaving the mule riderless—just disappeared as if she'd never been there!

"'I have since looked for her all over New Orleans to no avail. I first questioned the cavalry officers who had surrounded Fiona. They had been calling her Israel Lanier, which explains how she managed to pass herself off as a boy—you'll have to admit she and Israel do favor one another to an astonishing degree—and she was functioning as the company's horse wrangler. But none of the men could agree on exactly when she vanished from among them or where she might have gone. An officer named Morris was particularly worried for her safety, but in the end he could provide no additional information. An exhaustive investigation of the surrounding environs of the Royal Street headquarters proved equally fruitless.

"'Grieved I am to have to give you such frustrating news, but rest assured I shall not give up my search, and I will not come back to Mobile without Fiona. And so, dearest Maddy, I beg your forgiveness and ask you to pray with me for our cousin's safety until she can be returned to the bosom of her family—and pray for my wisdom and success in the search. With all my love, your Desi.'"

The letter fell as Mama put her hand to her mouth and stared at Maddy in horror.

Maddy felt numb. "Oh, Mama, what are we going to do?"

"We are going to do just as Desi suggests," Mama said grimly. "We are going to get on our knees and pray."

⁓

December 10, 1814
Villeré Plantation, nine miles south of New Orleans

During her weeklong incarceration, Fiona's days had been filled with a succession of mind-numbing activities like wrapping lint for bandages and hemming shirts for the militia expected to arrive any day from Kentucky and Virginia. When Madame Villeré announced that they were to have guests that afternoon, she barely restrained a whoop of joy.

The Villeré's Creole mansion made a beautiful and luxurious prison. An army of servants kept fires going in every room, and in moments when she felt she could not endure to eat another *petit four* or *popelin* (which happened more times a day than she could count), Fiona could step out the French window of her second-story bedroom and get a breath of cold fresh air. There she would lean her hands on the wrought-iron balcony railing, staring at the orange trees heavy with ripe fruit and the stubbled sugarcane fields. She could imagine herself back on the beach with Bonnie, currying one of the cavalry horses, or even lumping along behind Sergeant Morris on the stoic little Button.

But that was as close as she got to escaping. When she asked to borrow Madame's riding habit and go for a ride along the river on one of General Villeré's blood thoroughbreds, the an-swer—in French, of course—was inevitably, "Oh, no, *made-moiselle*, that would be too dangerous. Besides, your brother has said . . ." With a shrug of her elegant shoulders, Madame would add, "I am sorry. Please, have another cup of tea."

Her brother said.

Judah, the traitor. If she'd suspected he would dump her here in this aristocratic lockbox, she would never have gone with him that day outside Andrew Jackson's headquarters.

She had been sitting there, frozen, expecting at any moment that Desi would either shout her name from the balcony where he stood with General Jackson, or that he would rush down-stairs and out to the plaza, where he would snatch her off the mule and haul her . . .

Where? To some Creole plantation, to be treated like a child or a French doll—exactly as Judah had done. Judah, the rebel, the pirate, the *traitor*.

When her panicked gaze had fallen upon him in the crowd that day—over at the edge, where a group of men in the rough dress of fishermen had congregated to listen to the general's speech—she had simply slid off the mule and pushed her way toward him. When she tugged at his sleeve, he looked down, blinked, blinked again, and suddenly grabbed her by the scruff of the neck.

"Eh, bah," Judah had muttered to his nearest companion, "it is my pestilential little cousin, escaped from his tutor's custody." Scowling down at Fiona, he shook her until her teeth rattled. "If you are thinking that you may strut about amongst the adults without consequence, you are fair and far off, my lad. Come and I will show you the business end of a cypress switch before I return you to your mama."

As the other men laughed, Judah had marched her away, down the street, where he had left a carriage hitched outside what looked to be a tavern. After a moment's hesitation, he had pulled her inside the tavern, shoved her into a chair at a corner table, and sat down opposite her. There he proceeded to grill her mercilessly as to how she happened to be alone in a city two hundred miles from home, lacking a proper chaperone, and most scandalous of all, looking for all the world like an actress in a penny opera.

Her explanation that she was serving her country, just as he was, fell upon deaf ears.

He continued to ring a peal over her until she burst into tears, at which point he looked ashamed and at least removed the profanity from his harangue. As she continued to blubber, Judah wound down. Then, putting his handsome head in his hands, he laughed until the tears ran down his face.

Finally he wiped his eyes and looked at her with what she thought might be secret admiration. "What am I going to do with you, Duchess? Why will you not stay where you are safe?"

"Israel," she said, sniffing. "I am Israel Lanier, horse wrangler for General Coffee."

Judah sobered. "Only a *moron* of a cavalry officer would look at you and see anything other than a beautiful young woman. My little sister." He thumped the table with a force that made her jump. "Well, clearly no one has yet managed to convince you that a young lady does not ride cross-country in pursuit of escaped spies, and neither does she dress as a boy and travel with an army. But you have tangled with the wrong brother, my girl. What you need is a husband who will beat you daily, and I am going to find one if I have to pay him the price of a ship to take you on!"

Fortunately, Judah had been too busy with something related to business since dumping Fiona with his friends the Villerés to attend to that husband threat. But she had been biding her time, hoping for a chance to get a message to Desi—who at least would send her home rather than keep her prisoner in this gilded cage—but the Villerés and their horde of servants watched her like the proverbial hawk. No, she could not go riding. No, she could not have paper and ink. No, she could not go walking about alone.

It was enough to make one crazy.

But today there was to be company. She could hardly wait.

She stopped in front of her dressing table mirror to check her appearance. This morning Madame's maid had clipped back her chin-length curls at the sides with a pair of beaded combs, twisting the top into a little knot secured with an ivory hairpin. One of the Villeré daughters had lent her a day dress of turquoise silk. Its long, fitted sleeves fell from puffs at the shoulders and ended with double bands of blonde lace at the wrist, echoed in the decoration at the high waist and the hem. It was the loveliest garment she had ever worn, finer even than Maddy's creations.

Sehoy would have been thrilled to parade about in something so fine and feminine. Why, she wondered, did she resent it so much herself? Was it a symbol of her existence as so much property? Even Judah, as much as she adored him, seemed to think of her primarily as a responsibility to be dealt with. Only one man had ever responded to her on an intellectual level, with friendship and equality, even as a girl. Especially as a girl.

She opened the dressing table drawer, and there it lay, Charlie's signet. She couldn't wear it, even on a chain, because Juliet Villeré's dresses were too low cut. But it cheered her to look at it. She poked it with her finger, then gently closed the drawer and made her way downstairs.

As she reached the landing, she heard Judah's hearty laugh and followed it to the front drawing room. There she found her brother seated on a yellow striped sofa beside another gentleman dressed in a finely tailored blue coat and white linen. The man's boots were polished to a mirrorlike shine, his breeches fitted to long legs, and his mustache and sideburns were neatly trimmed, his short hair brushed forward in a fashionable Brutus style.

He rose at her entrance and bowed, giving her a charming smile. "And who is this lovely *mademoiselle*?" His black eyes twinkled.

"Laffite, meet my little sister, Fiona," Judah said carelessly. "Come sit down, Fi, and tell us what you've been up to. Madame says you've been so circumspect that I'm afraid you're brewing up trouble."

She gave her brother an annoyed look as she sat down in a

chair next to her hostess. "There has been no opportunity for trouble, I assure you. I have been all but locked in a tower."

Judah laughed and glanced at his companion. "I told you she was a handful. Madame Villeré has my undying gratitude for taking her in."

"I do not believe half what this scoundrel says," Laffite said gallantly, returning to his seat.

Madame smiled. "I was just about to pour tea, *chéri*, would you care for a cup?"

"Yes, please." Fiona tried not to stare at the renowned pirate. He wasn't at all what she'd expected. There was no evidence of an eye patch or saber anywhere. "Judah, what is going on in New Orleans? Did you speak to Desi? Does he know where I am?"

"Desi still has not deigned to ask me for help. And to answer your first question, New Orleans is about to be in an uproar." Judah crossed his legs calmly. "Laffite's men have spotted British warships heading for the Chandeleur Islands."

Fiona gasped. "That's right at the entrance to Lake Borgne!"

"Indeed." Laffite nodded. "Which means the enemy will be upon us within a few days, if your bumptious and proud General Jackson does not bestir himself to ask for help."

"Does he know they are this close?" Madame asked.

"If not, I'm sure he will soon. Commodore Patterson stationed a flotilla of gunboats off the coast of Mississippi with orders to report anything from that direction."

"Gunboats." Judah rolled his eyes. "As if those little Jeffs are going to be able to fend off the British navy."

Fiona wrinkled her nose. "Jeffs?"

"Cheap shallow-draft, sloop-rigged vessels commissioned by Thomas Jefferson to be the core of the American navy. Four or five cannon per boat at best."

Beth White

Laffite spread his hands. "My men and I would help if permitted. We have stores of ammunition we would contribute if Jackson would give up his insistence on prosecuting us."

Fiona looked at her brother. "Judah . . . are you wanted by the law as well?"

"I have told you I am not. I don't lie."

She supposed she'd have to believe him.

"'Scuse me, Madame," said a slow, deep voice before she could answer. Madame's butler, Ishmael, stood in the sitting room doorway. "They's a guest comin' up the drive. If I'm not mistaken, it's the Governor's carriage."

Madame jumped to her feet. "Oh, my lands! Why would Mrs. Claiborne choose today of all days to come for a visit?"

Lazily Judah rose as well. "Never mind, ma'am, we can come another day. We'll just slip out the back door—"

"Don't be silly, I will not let my invited guests be run off by a busybody, be she ever so highly connected. Let me think." Madame clapped her hands in an agitated fashion, then stilled, a crafty expression narrowing her eyes. "Ishmael, you will send all the other servants out to the quarters until I send for them again. You will be the only one serving us this afternoon. Just remember to address Mr. Laffite here as Mr. Clemente." She speared the butler with a stern look. "Is that clear?"

Ishmael bowed, a slight smile curving his full lips. "Yes, ma'am. We're pulling a little social juju 'round here."

Laffite laughed as the butler turned for the door. "Mr. Clemente. I like it, Madame. What a commanding officer you'd make!"

Preening, Madame sat down and settled her skirts. "Indeed. Just ask General Villeré!"

257

DECEMBER 14, 1814
CHANDELEUR ISLANDS SOUTH OF NEW ORLEANS

In the aftermath of the battle, Charlie stood watch on the gun deck of the *Sophie,* grateful that the flagship was still afloat, despite her mauled rigging and gaping holes in her bow. Two of the forty-five British barges rowed across Lake Borgne had been blown out of the water or sunk by American cannon fire, but only seventeen of fifteen hundred sailors and marines had been lost, with the wounded already evacuated aboard the *Anaconda.* The remaining force, covered in blood, gore, and gunpowder but jubilant at their resounding victory, had been set to securing the five captured American gunboats and their tender ship, then taking their crews prisoner. The one-gun schooner USS *Sea Horse* languished at the bottom of the lake.

The Americans had fired first, shortly after eleven o'clock, a long shot from one of their little flat gunboats. With no wind to fill their sails, they had been forced to sit and wait at the top of the lake, draped in boarding net like insects caught in giant spider webs as the British barges rowed straight toward them. After that opening salvo, Captain Lockyer gave the order to return fire, keeping it up until they got close enough to the American boats to board—at which point the hand-to-hand fighting with muskets, pistols, sabers, and hatchets began in earnest and lasted for nearly two brutal hours.

Boarding the closest American gunboat, Charlie had thrown himself into action, doing his best to quickly disable the enemy. Despite a gunshot wound to the shoulder, Lockyer managed to keep the *Sophie* more or less intact for the duration of the battle, and in God's mercy Charlie returned with no more than a scraped cheekbone and bruised shoulder.

Now, as his men herded the prisoners onboard, Charlie watched the Americans' faces, feeling their chagrin, feeling their anxiety over what was about to happen to their waterlogged, swampy, alligator-infested scrap of land. He wanted to reassure them that it didn't matter—that none of these British invaders really wanted to stay, none of them cared for anything except the loot they would carry home as prize money. But he kept his mouth shut lest he give himself away.

There was a girl. A girl he was going to claim as *his* prize.

He just had to make it to the end of the next battle. And the next. Until it was over.

Please, God, let it be over soon.

DECEMBER 20, 1814
VILLERÉ PLANTATION

At Conseil, everyone's nerves remained on edge, from Major General Villeré himself on down to the lowliest field hand. News of the disastrous battle of Lake Borgne reached the plantations along the river shortly after General Jackson summoned Generals Coffee and Carroll from Baton Rouge and Natchez respectively. The subsequent declaration of martial law in New Orleans made Jackson's word law, curtailing all travel in and out of the city, except for those carrying military passes, and establishing a curfew after dark.

To escape the panicked fluttering and chirping of the Villeré women, Fiona disappeared into the kitchens, where the slaves continued to work with a stoic attitude of *c'est la vie* that she found both comforting and amusing. At first the slaves had received her with reservation. But when they realized she was used to waiting upon herself—in fact, hardly knew what to do with the coddling expected by Madame and her daughters (the Lanier family for a variety of reasons having never been slave owners)—Fiona was allowed to come and go pretty much as she pleased.

This afternoon she sat in a little cane rocker, toasting her feet by the kitchen fire and watching Ishmael's wife, Lulu, knead biscuit dough for supper. Rachel, Madame Villeré and Miss Juliet's maid, sat mending stockings by the light of a lamp on the butcher-block table. The three of them had been singing a hymn, laughing when one or the other forgot the words, but halted mid-verse when the kitchen door slammed hard enough to rattle the crockery in the cupboard. Ishmael stalked in, carrying two empty brandy bottles and several dirty snifters on a silver tray.

He had been up in the second-floor library, waiting upon a group of militia officers billeted at the plantation with young Major Gabriel Villeré and his brother Celestine—which was the main reason Fiona had escaped this time. She was in no mood to flirt or be flirted with, no matter what Judah said about her need for a husband.

"Be careful, you gon' break them glasses and make a mess," Lulu told her husband as he dropped the tray upon the table.

"That boy's spoilt rotten, all they is to it." Ishmael took the glasses to the sink, where a bucket of clean water waited.

"Which boy?" Rachel asked, whipping the stocking in her hand out of danger of wine stains.

"Master Gabriel." Ishmael sloshed water into the glasses, then picked up a knife to shave a curl of lye soap into each one. "Bragging how he's got better sense than to obey a order calculated to waste everybody's time—when we all know he just be pure-dee lazy."

Fiona would have to agree with that assessment. Though

she admired their father, General Villeré, she had frankly been avoiding Gabriel and Celestine and their cocky military friends. "What order?"

"The one Big General Jackson issued, right after he got here—to fell trees across all the bayous runnin' into the city. Master Gabriel say wasn't nobody coming in by Bayou Bienvenue noway—that's the one drains into our canefield here—and if he blocked it up, he'd just have to go to the trouble of unblocking it later. Then yesterday Jackson tell General Villeré to set a 'round-the-clock guard at the mouth of the bayous, and he put Master Gabriel in charge of Bienvenue. But you think he gon' mind his pa?" Ishmael snorted. "He send a twelve-man picket down there, mostly field hands, and come home to throw a drinking party. He gon' have the redcoats marching in, murdering us all in our sleep."

Fiona met Rachel's wide, frightened brown eyes and said, "Now, Ishmael, I'm sure we needn't be so worried as all that. Gabriel is just as fond of his own skin as any of us."

Ishmael shook his grizzled head. "He is that, if not more so, but I say why take chances?"

"Is my brother up there now?" Fiona rose.

"Yes'm. But Madame told Miss Juliet to stay away from the men and their drinking, so I don't think—"

"My brother won't let anything happen to me." Leaving Ishmael muttering to himself and the two women to their tasks, she left the kitchen and walked through the butler's pantry, then up the stairs to the family living quarters. From the hallway she could hear raucous male laughter coming from behind the library door. The library was, generally speaking, the territory of the men of the house, though she had slipped in when nobody was there, to borrow a history or biography when she was bored. Now she hesitated, but when she heard Judah's voice responding to whatever joke had just been shared, she knocked firmly.

The laughter broke off. "Who's there?" That sounded like Gabriel, his tone jovial, the consonants a bit slurred.

"It's Fiona Lanier. I'd like to speak to my brother for a minute."

After a moment, the door was yanked open. Gabriel stood blinking at her, his smile tipsy. "Miss Lanier! I wondered where you'd got off to this afternoon. Please, come in and meet my friends!"

"No, thank you. I just want to see—"

"Fiona." Judah shoved Gabriel out of the way, stepped out into the hall, and closed the door behind him. "You don't have any business around this rough lot. Is something the matter?"

She searched his face. He didn't look drunk, but Judah was hard to read sometimes. "I don't know. Is it?"

He scowled. "What do you mean?"

"Ishmael just came down and said you men are having a party when you should be guarding the bayous."

"Ishmael is an old woman. As a matter of fact, we were just celebrating the fact that Jackson relented and pardoned the Baratarians. He let the ones in jail go free and issued a safe conduct pass for Laffite to come into the city to confer with the general and his staff. Things are about to get interesting around here."

"Judah, you weren't raised to intoxication. Mama would be very disappointed in you."

"I'm not intoxicated. And you're not my mama. So go away before I—"

"Must I remind you that *you* are the one who brought me here, much against my will? I would be happy to go back to the cavalry, where at least I could be useful!"

"Oh, and wouldn't Mama be proud to hear that? Her only

daughter wanting to go back to dressing like a boy and swaggering around amongst a bunch of horse infantry?"

"Horse infantry who treated me with respect and didn't leer at me like a—like a piece of candy!"

"*Who* is leering at you? I'll call him out right now!"

"Your friend Gabriel did, as a matter of fact!"

"He did not!"

"Yes, he did!"

Behind her, someone cleared his throat. "Excuse me, Miss Fiona. Mr. Judah."

She turned.

Ishmael stood there, clearly trying not to roll his eyes. "They's a message for you, Mr. Judah. You're to meet Mr. Laffite at the Temple. He's been sent there to confer with Jackson's commanders about defending the Barataria Bay entrance to the city."

16

December 20, 1814
Pea Island south of New Orleans

Charlie took his ration of salt pork and ale over to the meager protection from the night wind provided by a stand of reeds. Easton was already there, squatting upon his camp stool, shivering like a jelly—though, truthfully, Charlie could barely remember what a jelly looked like, let alone what one tasted like—and writing in a small book he carried around. The two of them had quite become mates during the last week, partly because they had endured the miserable ten-hour trip across Lake Borgne together, but mostly because Charlie could count on the quiet young lieutenant from Kent not to pester him with questions.

Charlie popped his own canvas stool open and sat down. Too cold to make conversation, he tore off a bite of pork with his teeth and chewed.

Assigned to Colonel Thornton's command, he and Easton, plus a handful of other officers and eighteen hundred enlisted men, had been rowed over on barges—crammed in cheek by jowl in lots of eighty, unable to so much as lean over. Pea Island was the optimistic name of this forlorn little bog, where they were to wait for two more contingents under Colonel Keane and Admiral Cochrane. At some unspecified time, they would be rowed even farther up a series of bayous, then slog through a giant cypress swamp onto a plantation—where, presumably, some sort of action would occur.

After a few moments of silent mastication—no one would call this dining—he bumped Easton's arm, provoking a mild "Curse you, Kincaid, you smeared my ink." Easton, the son of a clergyman, was known for temperance in drink and language. And the fact that he was keeping a journal.

Charlie smiled. "What are you going on about tonight? Your pet alligator?"

"As a matter of fact, I'm going on about a rude, empty-headed Scot who can't seem to shut up about the wildlife."

"All right, then, let's discuss the daily monsoons and the way our clothes freeze to our bodies when the sun goes down." Charlie squeezed the tail of his jacket, which crunched under its film of ice.

"Happened all the time when my father took me hunting as a boy," Easton said, shuddering, "but at least then we had a campfire to look forward to when it was over. Not a tree in sight around here to break the wind, let alone build a fire."

"Plenty of wild ducks. We could have a good hunt." Charlie paused to listen to the night sounds in the marsh all around the little patch of ground the army had picked for its rendezvous. "Easton, do you think God is here with us?"

Easton gave him a funny look. "God is everywhere."

"I mean, do you think God is on our side? In this attack?"

Easton sighed. "I can't think of it that way."

"Why not? Don't you think he cares?"

"I think he grieves."

"Then why are you here?"

Easton shrugged. "Same reason as you, I imagine. Younger son of a gentleman, needing a vocation. The military was my best option."

"Don't you want to marry?"

"One day, when I get home with my prize money and settle down. There's a girl I write to when I'm not describing alligators." Easton paused. "Kincaid, you're melancholy tonight. What's troubling you?"

"Just what I said. I'm afraid this American venture isn't like Trafalgar or Salamanca. I think we're in the wrong. And I think God will judge us for it."

Laying a finger over his lips, Easton did a quick look-round over his shoulder. "Don't let anyone else hear you say that!"

"I won't. And don't think I plan to desert, or anything mad like that. I'm just thinking about liberty and humanity and things my grandfather tried to teach me a long time ago, before I cared to hear them."

"All right," Easton said cautiously. "Just realize there's nothing you can do about it now."

"I know." Charlie felt better, just speaking his doubts aloud. "But I also wanted to ask a favor of you, if you don't mind. If I don't make it past whatever they're taking us into, would you write to my grandfather and tell him I remember what he said? And this is very important—ask him to write to the Gonzales family to tell them I'm sorry."

"Sorry for what?"

"Just . . . they'll know. The Gonzaleses. Don't forget."

"Kincaid, I don't know what to make of you, old fellow."

"Neither do I, Easton," Charlie sighed. "Neither do I."

December 23, 1814
Villeré Plantation

Dressed in one of Juliet's old gowns, unfashionably full in the skirt and modest of bodice, Fiona slipped down the stairs mid-morning and whistled to call the dogs. The Villeré brothers' setters, Castor and Pollux, had grown a bit fat and lazy from lying about in front of the fire during the winter cold snap, but they got up amiably and followed her to the back door. Removing her slippers and pulling on boots as protection from the mud, she slung her cloak around her shoulders and stepped outside. The rain had cleared during the night, leaving a bright, chilly morning, a good day to walk down to the levee and climb up to watch the mighty Mississippi roll by.

She could hear Gabriel and Celestine talking and laughing on the front verandah, where they'd repaired after breakfast to clean their hunting guns. The other men of their company were presumably employed elsewhere on the property, their father attending General Jackson somewhere in the city, Madame and the girls of the family upstairs sewing.

Nobody would miss her if she disappeared for a while.

She hadn't seen her brother since he left three days earlier to join Laffite's unit, assigned to the American ship *Louisiana*—which, until the Baratarians were pardoned and released, had languished in port with no crew available. She supposed Judah was happy now. He'd always been a man of action, loathe to sit at home when he could be sailing or hunting or fishing.

She kicked at an oyster shell in the moss-draped, tree-lined gravel walkway, smiling when one of the dogs growled playfully. Frankly, she'd rather be with Judah on the ship than stuck here, waiting for this stupid war to end so she could go home. She should never have come here, she'd admit it to herself and

God. She'd finally written to Maddy to let her know she was safe, but hadn't had a letter back yet. It would be just like Uncle Rafa to come over and fetch her. If he did, she would have to concede to the inevitable.

The path entered the orange grove, where fat ripe fruit hung low on laden branches. She plucked one and began to peel it, licking the juice from her fingers and relishing the sweetness. By the time she had it open and ready to eat, the dogs had run ahead of her into the barren canefield, where the stubbled stalks bristled like a three-day beard. She followed the dogs at a leisurely pace, enjoying the sun filtering through the dwindling trees, the breeze riffling her cloak, and the sound of the water rushing beyond the levee.

As she crossed the field, some other noise caught her attention, something "off" in the melody and countermelody of plantation life. Usually she could hear the slaves singing as they went about their work, sometimes the grunts and groans of labor. Today there was none of that.

At the edge of the canefield, where it dissolved into mud, she halted, turned. That was it. She should have encountered at least a few pickers in the grove.

Then toward the back of the grove, a flash of bright orange was followed by the sharp report of gunfire. Hunters? Gabriel or Celestine couldn't have reached that particular spot this quickly. Breath suddenly high in her throat, she tried to think. Instinct told her there was something wrong. Run for the house? The orange grove was the only way to get there. The sugarhouse might have provided shelter, but the open ground around it would leave her completely exposed. At her back was the levee, eight feet high. A ladder leaned against it, but would she really be safer there? Where else could she go? The slave quarters, situated not far away to the south seemed like the only option.

Two more gunshots exploded in the grove, closer to the main house.

She looked for the dogs and called in a harsh whisper, "Castor! Pollux!" Then she heard them barking in the distance. Hunting dogs, heading for downed prey. Abandoning them, she ran for the nearest slave cabin, bounded up the porch steps, and banged on the front door. "Hello! Open up! Please, it's Fiona—"

No answer, so she tried the latch. When it opened, she stepped inside. Natural light spilled through cracks in the walls and a partially open window, revealing a dank little room containing a rude table, four stools, and several simple bedsteads covered with neat patchwork quilts. As far as she could tell, it was otherwise empty.

She went to the open window facing the sugarhouse and peered out. Motion inside the mill told her where the slaves had gone. Anxiously she watched, hoping someone would emerge and sound the all clear.

On the thought, the first redcoat appeared, then a line of them marched past the window, their boots and breeches coated to the hips in slimy mud. They carried their bayonetted muskets in firing position, cocked hats precisely set upon their heads, mouths grim but eyes alight with excitement. They were ready to kill.

She sank to the floor. The Villeré women had lived in a flutter of morbid dread for so many days, with nothing, absolutely nothing, transpiring, that Fiona had grown complacent. Now, complacency gave way to utter terror. She was all alone and unarmed.

Her body began to quake, her teeth chattering audibly.

Wait, that noise came from the other side of the darkened room, something drumming against the floor, likely under the bed. Then she heard sniffling.

"Who's there?" Fiona whispered. "I won't hurt you."

A soft, gasping sob, then a young female voice, "I'm sorry, miss, I didn't feel good is why I ain't in the field."

Definitely under the bed. Fiona sat back, absurdly relieved to have company, even if it was a scared young colored girl. "It's all right. I told you, I won't hurt you. But there's trouble outside, so we've got to be quiet. The British are here."

"Where's everybody else?"

"In the sugarhouse, I think. Is there a gun or a knife here?"

The girl uttered a weak giggle. "Miss, they ain't gonna give none of us a weapon."

"Oh." Of course not. "Where are the machetes that cut the cane?"

"Overseer keeps 'em."

Stymied, Fiona thought hard. "Where's that? Can we get there from behind these cabins?"

"Maybe. You could try it." Fiona's companion was clearly reluctant to move.

But if they just sat here, one of those soldiers, maybe a whole rank of them, was going to burst in. Fiona wasn't as pessimistic as the Villeré women, but neither was she naive enough to assume her virtue would survive such an encounter.

"I'll go," she said with as much firmness as she could muster. "Which direction?"

"Back toward the orange grove."

Fiona hesitated. "Before I go, what's your name?"

"Penny, miss."

"All right, Penny, stay right where you are and pray for me—and I'll pray for you."

"I will. Be careful, miss."

As she crawled toward the back door of the cabin, Fiona felt a tiny measure of confidence return. If the Lord was likely to listen to anyone, it would be this thrown-away, petrified little slave. "I'll come back for you," she said, and reached up to inch the door open.

And found herself looking at the filthy, mud-caked boots of a British soldier.

"Well, hello," he said, kicking the door wide. "Look what we have here."

⌒

"Catch him or kill him!" Colonel Thornton shouted as Charlie ran past his commander to take chase after Villeré.

The Creole militia officer and his younger brother had been their prisoner inside the house for all of five minutes before he jumped out a window stupidly left open by the private guarding the room. Behind him, Charlie could hear the rest of his company running and firing at their quarry. He prayed they wouldn't hit him instead.

Villeré, miraculously dodging bullets, scrambled over a five-foot picket fence that separated the yard from the sugarcane fields ten yards ahead of Charlie.

The American was built to run, and Charlie's injured limb wasn't as strong as it used to be. Sweating with exertion in spite of the cold, he jumped and clawed at the fence but couldn't get his leg over. As he sank to the ground, thigh aching abominably, the men behind him swarmed over, howling like hounds after a fox. "Don't let him get away!" Charlie groaned. "He'll sound a warning."

But it was too late. Villeré knew the terrain, knew where to go to ground, knew how to twist out of their reach. Which meant they would have to act quickly in order to take the American forces in New Orleans off guard.

Pushing himself to his feet, Charlie limped back to the house, where Thornton waited on the verandah. "I'm sorry, sir. I'm afraid he's gone."

Thornton muttered a curse. "There goes our element of surprise."

Charlie took out his spyglass and trained it on the orange grove through which the rest of the eighteen-hundred-man contingent would arrive from up the bayou, one barge at a time. Even as he watched, a group of twenty soldiers marched into view. He lowered the glass. "The 43rd is on their way up. That's the next-to-last barge of our group. General Keane should be here anytime now with the first of his."

"Then we will start forming up. Have the men you sent to clean out the outbuildings reported back?"

"All but . . ." Charlie frowned. "I haven't seen Osmond and Drake."

"Go look for them. I want everybody accounted for before Keane arrives."

"Aye, sir." Charlie walked down the steps, pausing as he passed a grizzled marine guarding a group of slaves. "Did you see which way Osmond and Drake went?"

"Yes, sir." The marine yawned. "The sugar mill over there—they said they were going to look inside it, as well as the slave cabins behind it."

The large building indicated sat about a hundred yards northeast of the main house, just visible at the edge of the orange grove. Shouldering his gun, Charlie headed that direction.

He was tempted to linger as he walked through the grove. But maybe there would be time to bathe in the river and rid himself of the stinking mud that clung to the lower half of his body if he hurried to complete his task. He kept going and came out in the canefield, where he walked another ten yards or so to the sugarhouse, a rectangular wooden building raised on pilings, its doors standing open. Figuring the missing marines must have already cleared it out, he walked past. A scuffling sound followed by a muffled feminine squeal and a man's yelp brought him to a halt.

The Villeré females—mother and two daughters—had been confined to their sitting room in the main house, and Thornton had given orders not to molest the slave women. But most of these marines and sailors were hard-bitten enlisted men, not gentlemen. All had been without the company of women for months.

"Drake! Osmond! Is that you? Come out of there."

Drake, hat askew, leaned out the doorway. "Yes, sir. Coming, sir." He looked over his shoulder. "Come on, Osmond, just bring her with us."

"Not on your life. She's mine, the little—" Another yelped curse came from inside the house. "I'm bleeding!"

As Charlie stalked toward the house, Drake said more urgently, "Osmond, come *on* before you get us—"

Charlie hauled Drake out of the way. Taking the step up into the house, he saw Osmond behind a row of tables and a large machine, crowding a woman against the far wall. He couldn't see her face or upper body, but she was clearly struggling to get away.

"Osmond!" Charlie roared. "Attention!" By the time he crossed the room, Osmond had relaxed his hold on his captive.

The marine turned, livid of face and eyes narrowed. "Look what she did to me!" He touched his lower lip, from which blood welled and dripped onto the floor.

"You will address me as 'sir,' and I don't care what she did to you—no woman deserves to be manhandled like that. Get out! And if you run, I'll have you hunted down like the dog you are and shoot you myself. Is that clear?"

"Yes, sir," Osmond snarled and left.

Charlie's attention focused on the woman, who had sunk into a crouch against the wall, hands over her face—a young white woman with wild blonde curls chopped off between chin and shoulders. Her dress was dusty and torn at the shoulder, its dirty hem raised to expose a pair of small muddy boots.

"Are you all right?" He reached a hand to help her up.

She flinched, peeking through her fingers. "No. Leave me alone." Then, reluctantly, "But thank you."

He withdrew his hand, overcome with an eerie sense that he knew that voice. Undoubtedly exhaustion and lack of food had left him slightly mad.

"Come on," he said gently, "I can't leave you here. I'll take you back to the house. Are you one of the Villeré sisters?"

Seconds ticked by as she sat, head lowered, breathing into her hands, then at last she dropped them to her knees and looked up. "Hullo, Charlie."

"No. Oh, no." His moratorium on profanity nearly overcome by shock, Charlie looked around to make sure he hadn't landed in some insane warp of time and space. Sugarhouse, Louisiana plantation, America.

Fiona Lanier sat on the floor at his feet, and he had barely kept her from being raped by a couple of barbaric whelps calling themselves British marines. At least—

"Did they hurt you?" He fell to his knees and took her chin to examine her tear-streaked face. She didn't seem to be bruised, though there was blood drying on her bodice. "They didn't . . ."

"No." She sniffed. "He just tried to kiss me, and I bit him."

"I should be grateful you never tried that on me."

"True." Her lips, puffy from crying, curved.

"But, Fiona, it could have been worse. Much worse. What are you *doing* here?" Was she never going to stop showing up when he least expected her? Just when he'd somewhat reconciled himself that he might never see her again. He touched the ragged curls. "What have you done to your hair?"

"It's a long story."

And he had to report in to Thornton. He looked over his shoulder. Osmond and Drake waited outside the door, no doubt cooking up some story to explain their reprehensible behavior. "Which I must hear. But you're not safe here. You've got to come back to the house with me and stay with the other women."

"Yes, but first we have to get Penny and take her with us. She's in one of the slave cabins, under a bed."

"Penny, eh?" Sighing, he rose. "Nothing is simple with you, is it? All right, then, take me there." He extended his hand again.

This time she took it and let him pull her to her feet. When he stood there a moment, cradling her hand between both of his, absorbing the wonder of her presence, she blushed. "I know I'm a mess. I hope I didn't get you in trouble."

"I won't lie. We're both in no end of trouble. But let's just take one thing at a time and soldier on. Can you follow my lead on this one?"

Her eyes filled, drenched blue oceans of regret. "I'll try."

"All right then." He crooked his arm and drew her hand through it. "Shall we, Duchess?"

﹏

She kept staring at him, thinking, *He's going to disappear any minute, and I'll wake up in my bed at Navy Cove.*

Then she'd blink, and there he sat on Madame's settee. Real, human flesh and blood—one blue eye, one half-hazel eye, rumpled dark hair, two-day beard, and smelling like a barnyard.

But oh, so beautiful.

She didn't like to think what might have happened if he

hadn't come. God might have sent some other officer. Then again, she might have been violated. But at least she'd gotten the two soldiers to leave the slave cabin where Penny cowered under the bed.

The little colored girl, who probably wasn't more than thirteen or fourteen, hadn't wanted to come with her and Charlie at first, but finally Fiona coaxed her out by making Charlie wait outside. When Penny peeked out the window and saw him in the light, noted his weary, compassionate smile and humorous eyes, she'd followed right along—and now you couldn't pry her away from him. She sat cross-legged on the floor beside his chair, waiting to be given something to do. Quite the knight in shining armor he was.

The two redcoat commanders, Colonel Thornton and the newly arrived General Keane, clearly placed much confidence in Charlie's ability to sort out their Creole prisoners, including Fiona. They'd put him in charge of the house, while they left to move the army up to the line where the Villeré and Lacoste plantations joined. Madame Villeré, captivated by Charlie's ability to converse in French, offered to have one of the colored girls draw him a bath so that he could refresh himself while his uniform was cleaned—for all the world as if he were an invited guest at a house party rather than an invading army officer.

Eyes dancing, he'd declined until given official permission to go off duty, but did take off his boots and permit her to place an old towel on the settee to protect the furniture.

One had to admit the dashing blue naval uniform suited him, even covered in mud.

"Fiona?" Madame snapped her fingers to gain her attention. "So I am to understand that you and Lieutenant Kincaid are previously acquainted?"

Fiona jerked her gaze from Charlie's face. "Yes, ma'am. Our

families have been connected for many years." That sounded much better than *I chased him on a horse and shot him in the leg, then visited him in prison and fed him false information.*

"How fascinating!" cooed Juliet, leaning forward so that the bodice of her dress gaped. "Do tell us how that came about, Lieutenant."

To his credit, Charlie kept his gaze on Juliet's forehead. "I'm afraid it was a rather mundane situation after all. I had been sent down from public school to my grandfather's estate, and Miss Lanier happened to be visiting there with her relatives. We were only briefly acquainted, and I barely recognized her when I saw her again today." He glanced at Fiona, his eyes warning her to let him lead the conversation.

Juliet sat back, pouting. "Oh. Yes, Fiona, is very . . . different."

"But such a delightful girl," Madame said, patting Fiona's hand. "Perhaps you would like to run upstairs and change your dress before dinner."

Then she would miss whatever Charlie decided to tell them about their "connection." On the other hand, she probably smelled as bad as he did, considering the amount of swamp detritus at the bottom of her skirt.

"Yes, Madame, I believe I would like to do that. If you'll excuse me." She stood up, dipped a curtsey, and headed for the stairs. She didn't look back at Charlie once.

But she could feel his eyes on her back all the way across the room. A delicious shiver took her as she closed the bedroom door.

It was very hard to remember that they were at war and she was his prisoner.

Shortly after Fiona left to change clothes, Charlie excused himself and went to check on progress with formation. By now, British presence on the plantation consisted of Thornton's Advance—the 85th Foot and the 95th Rifles, plus the 4th Foot artillery and some rocket men, sappers, and miners, nearly a thousand men—as well as the 1,615-man first brigade under Keane, made up of the 93rd Highlanders, the 5th West India, and one company of the 1st West India. The second brigade under Cochrane, still to come, would increase the total force to around sixty-four hundred.

He marched along the colorful, disciplined half-mile line of soldiers and marines, not in the least worried about their ability to engage and defeat the demonstrably mismanaged American force. But as he approached the two senior officers, his confidence plummeted. Charlie stopped within hearing distance, reluctant to interrupt the heated debate.

"We're only eight miles away!" Thornton shouted. "The Americans have no significant defense between here and the city. If we don't go now, we lose the advantage we gained in slogging through that confounded swamp."

"But we don't know for sure what they have waiting for us in New Orleans." Keane's tone was adamant. "We could be walking into disaster if we don't wait for the rest of our troops to arrive."

Thornton threw his hands upward. "But, sir—"

"What is it, Kincaid?" Keane demanded, wheeling.

Charlie approached and addressed Thornton. "Easton and I have inspected the ranks, sir, and everything looks good."

"All right, then," Thornton said, still looking disgruntled, "dismiss them to make camp. They may bathe in the canal and forage for food, but have them bring it back for officers to choose from first."

Charlie saluted. "Yes, sir."

Keane stopped him. "Wait, Kincaid. Aren't you the fellow who spent six months here during the first part of the year? And then some time imprisoned in Mobile?"

"Yes, sir."

"Do you have anything to add to this discussion?"

Charlie hesitated, glancing at Thornton. "A credible source indicated to me that until very recently Jackson expected us to attack Mobile again, or somewhere else off the Mississippi coast—not New Orleans. This leads me to infer that his forces here may not have yet had time to coalesce." He paused, then blurted, "I think Colonel Thornton may be right. Sir."

Keane's face darkened. "And your source would be . . . ?"

"A young lady in Mobile who had no reason to lie to me."

"A young lady?" Keane looked incredulous. "You take the word of an American woman as proper intelligence? No wonder you were caught and imprisoned!"

"But, Keane," Thornton interrupted, "our sources reporting huge numbers of American troops in the city are equally suspect. I still think we'd do better to move in to attack—"

"Enough!" Keane made a slicing motion with his hand. "Thornton, you are hasty and overaggressive, and Kincaid's judgment disappoints me as well. We shall attack at dawn, after Cochrane arrives with the second brigade and the troops are rested for battle. You are both dismissed." He wheeled and stalked away.

Charlie glanced at Thornton. "I'm sorry, sir."

"You reported what you knew. So did I. But we are outranked and overruled." Thornton clapped Charlie on the shoulder and followed Keane.

Shaking his head, Charlie could only comply with Thornton's order to dismiss the men from ranks. Leaving a large Union Jack snapping in the breeze from a tree limb, he found Easton guarding the toolshed where they'd locked up the thirty-man Louisiana militia picket they'd surprised that morning and rounded up like so many goats.

The clergyman's son sat in a cane-bottom chair tipped back against the toolshed's outer wall, sound asleep.

Smiling, Charlie left him alone, repaired to the canal with several other officers, and stripped down for a much-needed bath and shave. Feeling much more himself, he rinsed the mud from his uniform, wrung it out, and put it back on, still wet. Then, scrounging an extra blanket from someone's pack, he lay out in the sun for a nap while his clothes dried.

He awoke some three hours later to find Easton standing over him.

Knuckling his eyes, Charlie sat up. "Was that you kicking me? I dreamed I was in a stable with an angry horse."

"Get up, you lazy sack of Scottish bones. We've been invited to dinner."

17

With Christmas still two days away, the Villeré dining room had been lit as if the holiday had already come. In the tradition of Southern hostesses, Madame set a magnificent table, with fine white linen, heavy silverplate and fragile China dinnerware, and magnolia greenery for centerpieces.

Fiona sat across the table from Juliet, who had been placed between her little sister Anne and Charlie. On Fiona's left sat a quiet young man named Lieutenant Easton, with Colonel Thornton to her right. Celestine Villeré, of course, languished in the toolshed with the other American prisoners, while the younger Villeré children dined upstairs in the nursery. Madame had assigned the head of the table to General Keane, seating herself at his elbow.

If Madame's prunish expression was anything to go by, her enthusiasm for their captors did not extend beyond good-looking and agreeable young officers like Charlie. Or perhaps the general had offended her in some way. Keane ate his salt-cured ham, boiled greens, and butter-drenched corn on the cob with his eyes fixed on his plate and a singular lack of appreciation.

When she glanced at Charlie to see if he noticed, she found his eyes upon her. His unreadable expression reminded her of the days when he'd first come to Navy Cove and how much he had changed over the months spent with her family.

Cheeks heating, she looked away. Would he say the same about her?

When her gaze happened to catch that of Colonel Thornton, he smiled at her over his wine glass. "Miss Lanier, I believe you are a houseguest of the Villerés?"

"Yes." If that was laconic, rude, so be it. Charlie clearly didn't want her to volunteer information, for her safety. She frowned. Or was it?

"Miss Lanier is an orphan of sorts," Juliet said sweetly from across the table, a breech of etiquette that her mother would have frowned upon, though the officers didn't seem to mind. "Her brother is a free trader in the area and found her in the city, traipsing about in boy's clothes. He brought her here so that we could properly dress her and care for her until she could be returned to her family in Mobile." Juliet blinked at Fiona, as though daring her to deny the truth of anything she'd said.

"What an interesting background you must have," Easton said politely. "Related to a pirate—"

"Judah isn't a pirate." Fiona clamped her lips together.

"Free trader then." Easton waved a hand. "Did you say Mobile? Kincaid was recently there."

"I didn't say—"

"Wait a minute." The colonel shifted his stare from her to Charlie. "Did you know each other in Mobile?"

Charlie avoided her gaze. Was he going to lie?

After a moment, he said reluctantly, "Yes, sir."

"Is this the young lady who gave you the information you passed on to General Keane this afternoon?"

Even more reluctantly, "Yes, sir."

Juliet bolted from her chair, a hand over her bosom. "You gave information about our troops to the enemy?"

Fiona tried to make Charlie look at her. If she said *yes* without further elaboration, she would be seen as a traitor to her country. If she admitted the information she gave was deliberately false, Charlie would never believe another word she said. Justifiably.

"It wasn't like that," she said, twisting her fingers together under the table. "It's complicated."

"You're his—lover!" Juliet gasped. "How dare you sit at our table, eat our food, *wear my dresses*—"

"Juliet Isabelle, sit down!" Madame thumped the table with her spoon. "Have your manners gone begging?"

"Miss Villeré, if you were a man, I would call you out." Charlie's eyes were murderous.

Fiona rose, shaking. "I can defend myself." Proudly she met the gaze of each person at the table, one by one. "I am not, nor have ever been, anyone's lover. And I assure you, Miss Villeré, I will not eat one more bite of your family's food. I'm going upstairs to put on the boy's clothes you seem to find so simultaneously disgusting and amusing, and you may burn or give away this dress—whichever you choose." She tossed her napkin onto her plate and stumbled out of the dining room.

"Fiona, come back here." Charlie's voice followed her. "Wait, I say!" He caught up to her in the foyer at the bottom of the stairs, grabbed her arm, and whirled her around. "I'm sorry that happened—"

"I don't know what you expect from me, Charlie." She pressed the heels of her hands to her eyes so she wouldn't have to look at him. "What did you tell them? Never mind, it doesn't matter. I'm leaving here."

"Where do you think you're going? You're a prisoner!"

She dropped her hands. "Yes, and isn't that just the ultimate irony? Well, you're going to have to put me somewhere else—maybe in the toolshed with the militia—because I'm not spending another minute in the same house with that vicious doxy!"

He hauled her to him, and she felt laughter rumble in his chest. "You're not going into the toolshed."

"Then the sugarhouse." She turned her cheek to feel his heart beat. Now he smelled like Charlie, clean and only slightly swampy.

"Not the sugarhouse either."

"Let me go, you're going to get in trouble."

"I'm afraid we're already there." He kissed the top of her head. Then he tipped her chin up and his lips came down to hers.

Suddenly the front door burst open.

Fiona and Charlie jumped apart.

"General Keane!" A young officer stood panting in the doorway. "Find the general—quick! The Americans have attacked!"

✎

Easton was dead. Ears ringing, every inch of exposed skin grimy from sweat, gunpowder, and blood, eyes stinging, Charlie stumbled with his friend over his shoulder across the Lacoste plantation onto the Villeré property.

Wrenched from Fiona's arms into battle, Charlie had survived the next three hours on willpower and prayer alone. At just past 7:00 p.m., an unlighted schooner had slipped up to the levee where the British force had bedded down for the night. Assuming her to be a merchantman or a British ship sent to guard their flank, the pickets on guard had fired a greeting. Receiving no responding signal from the ship, they'd sent word to the closest officers, requesting instructions. But before an answer came, a blast of cannon fire erupted, precipitating chaos.

By the time Charlie arrived, the officers on the field had attempted to pull their men together, with some measure of success, despite the rain of fire from the American ship. But then a series of flares went up from the schooner—blue, then red, then white—apparently the signal for the American infantry to attack. From that point, the pitch-black battlefield became an inferno of gunfire, smoke, fog, and hand-to-hand fighting punctuated by the squeal of horses and the mortal cries of the injured and dying.

Now the night seemed darker than ever. Charlie stepped into a ditch, nearly fell with Easton, but righted himself and kept going.

What sort of army attacked at night like wild Indians or barbarians out of a medieval drama? Wars were fought in the daytime, orderly lines of artillery advancing upon one another, courage and discipline and sheer numbers determining the victor.

Was he sobbing? Dear God, he hoped not. He hoped he possessed the physical and mental fortitude to fulfill his duty without crumpling in childish disarray. There, he could see the lights of the Villeré plantation across the plain, and gradually the cane stubble became visible, so that he no longer stumbled over it. When he thought he couldn't walk another step, his boots found purchase on a gravel path. He straightened. He was going to make it. Easton would lie in a clean bed, with someone to tend him, someone to give him a decent passage into eternity.

But who? Easton himself had functioned as the chaplain of the company, and he, Charlie, wasn't good enough or spiritual enough or even brave enough to pray over his fallen comrade. Blindsided by grief, he fell against the back door of the house, slid to his knees. "Let us in," he whispered. "God, let him in."

The door was yanked inward, light spilled out, someone almost stepped on him.

"Someone come here! Hurry! It's Kincaid and—Oh, Lord, is that Easton? Poor blighter. I said, come here, you!"

They pulled him inside, a big colored man wrenched Easton away from him, though he tried to hold on, and carried the dead man off. Swaying, he got to his feet and followed.

"Wait, Kincaid, let somebody look at that shoulder!"

Charlie shook off a hand and kept going.

The parlor where they'd had tea that afternoon was a nightmarish cacophony of agonized screams, groans, and the urgent calls of those caring for the wounded. The elegant furniture had all been pushed against the walls, except for the dining table, which had been moved in for the surgeon's use. Charlie stepped over piles of wounded men, determined not to lose the slave who carried Easton. At last they reached the dining room, clear now but for row upon row of corpses—and a woman who moved from one to the other, closing eyes, straightening limbs like some macabre puppetmaster. He watched the slave lower Easton to the floor in a corner. The room reeked of death, but Charlie barely noticed. As the slave left the room, sparing him a compassionate look, Charlie went to Easton and dropped to his knees.

He bowed his head.

Sometime later, he felt a gentle hand upon his hair. He knew it was Fiona, knew her touch as well as he knew his own name, and he let her fingers slip to his shoulder, let her wrap her arm about his neck, let her pull his head to her bosom, where he cried for Easton and cried for himself and told her he loved her as she held him.

"It will be all right," she whispered.

"It will be if you love me."

"I do. I love you, Charlie."

"Then don't leave me again."

She didn't answer, just kissed the top of his head.

He fell asleep in her arms.

～

December 24, 1814
Villeré plantation

With the two armies fully engaged, there was now no question of leaving the Villeré plantation. Fiona, conscripted with the other women into nursing wounded British soldiers, lost track of time as she changed bandages, emptied chamber pots, and fed spoonfuls of soup and tea to men who couldn't feed themselves. Sometime around dawn, she sat eating a bowl of grits by the fire with Lulu and Rachel, and looked up when Charlie entered the kitchen. Hair combed and face washed, uniform brushed and cocked hat neatly under his arm, he looked much more himself than when she'd left him asleep beside his friend's body in the dead men's ward.

She jumped to her feet, ready to run to him, but he stayed her with a hand out.

"I just came to say goodbye. I've reported for duty, and they're sending me to the *Royal Oak* to oversee prisoner transfers."

"How many . . . I mean, is the battle over?" How could this anticlimax be all there was?

Charlie shook his head. "The Americans retreated sometime around midnight, pulled back behind the Rodriguez Canal on the McCarty plantation. Heavy losses on both sides." He looked as if he wanted to say more, then thought better of it. "It's not over. We're going into the city."

"Oh. What about me and . . . and the Villeré women?"

"You're useful here." His eyes warmed with approval. "I can't thank you enough for that, Fiona. And Thornton appreciates your efforts as well. He'll make sure you're safe here—and as I said, the action will be moving closer to New Orleans." He looked away. "It will be over soon. Our entire army is arriving even as we speak."

She was sure that was true. But what Charlie and the rest of his command didn't know was that Laffite's men—including her brother Judah—had been allowed to join the American cause. Those seasoned sailors, artillerymen, and cannoneers, able to navigate the swamps and bayous around New Orleans blindfolded, could turn the tide of battle on a dime.

Charlie was the one who should be worried.

Lifting her chin, she set her bowl on the table and held out her hand. "And Americans do not concede. I will pray for your safety."

He kissed her fingers and let her go. But his eyes lingered on her face. "You still have my ring?"

She put her hand over the bump under her dress. "Do you want it back?"

"No. If something happens to me, you may send it to my grandfather—or keep it, whichever you choose."

"Charlie—"

He smiled. "*Au revoir*, sweetheart." Clapping his hat on, he turned and ran up the steps and out of sight.

She collapsed into her chair.

"Mm, mm, mm," Lulu sighed, "that is one fine gentleman."

꒰꒱

DECEMBER 25, 1814
HMS *ROYAL OAK*, OFF CHANDELEUR ISLANDS

Charlie entered the ward room of the HMS *Royal Oak* and found it gaily decorated with magnolia boughs, palmettos, and other semitropical evergreens native to the Louisiana coast—demonstrating beyond question the British seaman's ability to lacquer over the worst circumstances with tradition. Cook had even managed to find a couple of wild turkeys somewhere, and a giant plum pudding graced the center of each table.

Restored to his duties aboard the *Sophie* after escorting the American prisoners onto the *Royal Oak*, Charlie had received his dinner invitation with some amusement. This sumptuous and long overdue meal, it seemed, resulted from the coincidence of one of the prisoners having been a groomsman at Captain Dix's wedding in New York some years ago. Jettisoning the typical prisoner treatment of reduced rations and crowded below-decks quarters, Dix must plan this elaborate dinner and invite the officers of the whole fleet.

As he found his place at the table with other officers from the *Sophie*—missing Easton's quiet presence—Charlie tried to remember the last Christmas dinner he'd enjoyed with his family. He supposed he would have been about thirteen and already planning his headlong venture into the Royal Navy. His brother Jacob, in the tradition of elder brothers from time immemorial (witness the Prodigal Son parable, if one wanted proof), made Charlie's life miserable by never stepping wrong in any pursuit their father deemed essential to the life of a country baronet. The old man, livid at Charlie's precipitate exodus from public school, persisted in bringing the subject up at every turn. His mother, chronically ill with every malady known to man and some she made up, fluttered her hands and refused to interfere.

In short, not a happy time. Only Grandfa's invitation—couched in the terms of a summons—to join him at Riverton had saved him from some other escapade as disastrous as the one that got him in trouble at Eton.

Staring at the wilted sprig of holly atop the pudding, he had to smile. At Riverton he'd met Fiona.

His gaze went past the pudding and focused on a black-haired gentleman in a plain but finely tailored suit just now seating himself at the captain's table. Charlie got up so fast his chair fell backward with a crash.

Desi Palomo looked up and rose as well. "I might have known I'd run into you here. I came over on a boat with another of your officers."

Charlie rounded the table and reached to shake hands. "I won't ask how you are, Palomo, in these awkward circumstances."

"I'm as well as can be expected," Palomo said with a smile. "I expect my diplomatic skills will earn our release before long."

"Knowing Cochrane, I wouldn't count on rationality to prevail. If you need anything, you've only to mention my name."

"I appreciate that."

Charlie nodded and started to go back to his seat, then hesitated. "Palomo, did you know that Fiona is here—at the Villeré plantation?"

"Yes, her brother Judah finally had the grace to tell me he'd taken her there. I'd been looking for her all over the city." Palomo grimaced. "She'd apparently cut off her hair and joined a cavalry regiment as a horse wrangler. If I didn't know her better, I'd blame that on you."

"I assure you I had nothing to do with it—in fact, I'd done my best to convince her to stay away from New Orleans."

"You mean she *told* you she wanted to come here?"

"Well, she mentioned the idea." Charlie looked away. "But at the time I had no way of knowing I'd be coming back here—"

"Coming *back*?" Palomo's dark brows snapped together. "Then you *were* here as a spy at some previous time."

Charlie shrugged. "Yes, though I didn't remember until it was almost too late to do any good."

"I knew it." The American released a hissing breath. "I suppose we should be grateful the damage was kept to a minimum."

"I tried to do a lot of damage."

Palomo smiled. "But Fiona is safe?"

"Safe and making herself useful as a nurse. She can't quite get the hang of sitting around swooning."

"I suppose that would be too much to ask." Palomo shook his head. "At least you're here, which will keep her out of a certain amount of trouble."

"Let's hope so." Charlie grinned. "Enjoy your dinner, Palomo. There may not be another one."

❧

DECEMBER 28, 1814
VILLERÉ PLANTATION

Christmas morning had brought General Sir Edward Pakenham, brother-in-law of the Duke of Wellington, to Conseil, where he proceeded to relieve Keane of his command. Fiona volunteered to serve the general and his staff that evening at a meager Christmas feast, where she noted that his arrival improved the morale of the troops—frustrated from bad weather, lack of food, and lack of action—and stirred resentment on the part of the officers, who found their every decision either second-guessed or outright dismissed.

Periodically during the meal they would all jump at the boom of cannon fire from the *Carolina*, bombarding the troops from across the river. Safely out of range of musket fire, the American schooner harassed the discouraged soldiers with shot that could cut a man in half or mow down an entire rank in the blink of an eye.

"Whose idea was it," Pakenham demanded, "to haul men and boats and artillery over the lake and across these infernal swamps? Could we not have found a way to come across dry land, instead of wedging an entire army in an elbow between a river and a cypress bog?"

And on it went until Fiona feared Keane might let loose and hurl a ham bone at his new commander-in-chief.

The next day was little better. Pakenham expected the artillery and ammunition he had ordered to be delivered first thing in the morning. It arrived after dark, just when the troops were bedding down for the night.

By dawn of the twenty-seventh, the British had set up nine cannons of various sizes in batteries scooped out of the top of the levee and aimed them across the river. The second salvo hit the *Carolina* at point-blank range, setting off a massive explosion that Fiona was sure could be heard in Mobile. She couldn't imagine how anyone could have gotten out alive, but Ishmael later told her that most of the Baratarian crew escaped with two of the cannons before she caught fire and sank. Meanwhile, the USS *Louisiana* had rowed upriver out of range. Perhaps they'd somehow been warned of British plans.

On the twenty-eighth, a beautiful, balmy morning sparkling under sunshine and blue skies, Fiona hovered outside the library, listening to a loud and vehement altercation between Pakenham and an officer named Gibbs. Interspersed with some colorful language that made Fiona blink, Colonel Gibbs gave his superior to understand that "those cursed Choctaws and dirty-shirts in the woods and swamps are picking off our men one and two at a time, but if we send a reconnaissance in force, we can determine their strength and at the same time scare them out of their wits. Rennie says he can take them with reinforcements."

"We're not committing ourselves to certain annihilation,"

Pakenham replied. "I've a report that the American position can't be turned. The only option is a gradual, orderly retreat while we wait for General Lambert's reinforcements and more big guns brought up from the fleet. It may take a few days, but we'll move up for a siege after we're fully prepared. We outnumber and outgun them, and they'll eventually have to give way."

"But, sir, a siege requires ladders and fascines to be moved up to the battle site overnight—and batteries for bigger guns must be dug in stable ground. Two feet down in this confounded bog, and you're under water!"

"Those are my orders, and it is your job and Keane's to implement them, Gibbs."

"Yes, sir," Gibbs growled. "As you say, sir."

Fiona jumped back as the colonel slammed out of the library and stomped past her. Halfway down the hall, he turned.

"Miss . . . Lanier, is it?"

"Yes, sir." She curtseyed, trying to look innocent and stupid.

"Please have the servants strip the house of every fabric length available. Curtains, sheets, bed hangings. Everything."

She gaped at him. "But why?"

"We're going to tear them up for ammunition cartridges."

Oh dear. Madame was not going to like that.

"And have the field slaves bring up every sugar cask on the plantation. We're going to use them to build the batteries for this—" he spit out another foul word—"siege." The colonel disappeared, presumably in search of a stiff drink.

Fiona slowly made her way to the big sitting room—now the hospital, where some thirty soldiers lay, still recovering from the night attack of the twenty-third. She possessed information that would be useful to the Americans, if she could only get it to them. She wasn't watched closely, the officers in headquarters busy with far more important matters than keeping track of the barely tolerated sister of a pirate.

What would her mother do in her place? What would Aunt Lyse do?

She couldn't go wandering off into the woods or through the swamp without getting lost or bitten by a snake or something equally horrible. On the other side of the plantation, troops were stationed along the levee, preventing unauthorized movement. If she had a uniform and a horse, she might pass as a messenger and get through the lines, but then how would she get safely into the American camp? She would be shot on sight.

This was going to require deep thinking, alertness, and prayer. And the latter seemed the best place to start.

18

JANUARY 3, 1815
BAYOU BIENVENUE OUTSIDE NEW ORLEANS

Moving up Bayou Bienvenue aboard the *Alceste,* under the command of Captain James Laurence, Charlie reflected that his career of late had been a regular carousel of boats, ships, and captains. The present assignment was reconnaissance as to American strength on the west bank of the Mississippi. Admiral Cochrane, ever butting heads with General Pakenham as to strategy, seemed to think a weakness might be found there and exploited.

In Charlie's private assessment, Cochrane's concern was justified. During the last two days of December, he and sixty-some-odd long-suffering sailors had all but broken their backs, lugging guns from the fleet by boat across Lake Borgne and as far as possible up the bayous, then on foot through the swamps and over the canefields—only to be greeted by Pakenham with the news that they must add the two big guns already at Villeré and haul the entire arsenal another three muddy miles to the batteries being erected across from the American position at the Rodriguez canal. Overnight.

It had been an exhausting and pointless endeavor. Pakenham had planned to attack at sunup, but inevitably dense fog obscured the American line. In a maddening twist, while cooling their heels, impatient to go on the offensive, His Majesty's finest had to listen to a couple of American bands serenade them out of the fog with tunes such as "La Marseillaise," "Yankee Doodle," and "Chant du Départ." Finally, midmorning, the fog lifted like a penny opera curtain to reveal the American forces lined up on parade—flags flying, bands playing, and ladies in carriages watching from a distance.

The British gunners recovered from their stunned disbelief and attacked. The first shots blew holes in the McCarty plantation house, where Andrew Jackson and his staff had made their headquarters. But British exultation turned to grim concentration as the enemy sorted themselves out and flew to their guns to return fire.

Pakenham had accomplished his goal of taking the American army by surprise.

But to Charlie's disgust, the artillery exchange fizzled by noon. The Americans discovered early on that the impressive new British Congreave rockets provided more flash and noise than actual damage—and thereupon coolly ignored them as they whirled and sizzled and streaked past. The gun platforms Charlie's men had worked so hard to put together overnight wobbled on the soft ground, and the batteries themselves—rib-high stacks of sugar hogsheads filled with dirt—provided little protection from American sniper fire and cannon shot. Then, out of ammunition and humiliated, they had to withdraw, leaving the American militiamen and pirates hooting and jeering in their wake.

Following this setback, with no way to get past Jackson and too much invested in the invasion to go back, Pakenham decided to send a force across the Mississippi to take out the American artillery on the west bank that had harassed them from the beginning. Once more, the general and the admiral almost came to blows. Cochrane wanted to widen and deepen the Villeré canal in order to float the boats over—necessitating a day and night of nonstop digging, then cutting the levee and building a dam to fill it with water—while Pakenham mistrusted the stability of a muddy handmade dam. In a nasty series of tit-for-tat moves, Cochrane won that battle, but when he wanted to send Charlie along with Colonel Thornton on the mission, Pakenham balked.

Which was how Charlie wound up sailing up Bayou Bienvenue aboard the *Alceste*.

He just wanted it to be over. If he had all the information available and could make decisions for himself, he wouldn't feel so rudderless. He wanted his life, the sacrifices he made, to lead to some greater purpose than winning prize money and promotion for his commanding officers. He wanted a wife (one specific wife, please God) and children, so that his grandfather's legacy of serving God and family and his fellow man would go on.

With a sigh, he took out his spyglass to scan the forward horizon—and jerked it to a halt when a small boat came into focus. Collapsing the glass, he clattered down three ladders to get to the helm.

"Captain! There's a boat up ahead, about a quarter mile away, hidden in the grass at the juncture of the bayou and the next canal. It's not ours, so—"

"—it must be American." Laurence took out his own glass and squinted. A slow grin curled his mouth. "They're in for a surprise."

Without a sound, the *Alceste* slipped up on the American boat with guns aimed point-blank. Four of the startled guards dove into the canal and got away, but one apparently couldn't swim. He simply sat where he was, hands up, and allowed Charlie's crew to board, take command of the boat, and haul it back to Villeré—after Laurence set fire to the prairie grass to destroy the Americans' hiding place.

The *Alceste* reached headquarters as storm clouds over the river suddenly burst wide. At about the same time, General John Lambert arrived ahead of his reinforcement troops. They would begin the arduous journey across the lake and swamps in the morning.

Pakenham, visibly buoyed by the knowledge that he could begin the siege of Jackson's lines, bellowed orders for the servants to see to Lambert's comfort and make sure he had a suitable bedchamber prepared—which meant someone else would be evicted. Charlie hoped that would not be Fiona. He looked for her as he escorted the prisoner into the house and down the hall to the commander-in-chief's quarters in the library.

While he waited for Pakenham to arrive and conduct the interrogation, Charlie gestured with ironic courtesy for the sulky American prisoner to seat himself on a sofa under the window. He stood before the man, feet braced apart, remembering Fiona's proud words to him on Christmas Eve.

Americans do not concede.

In his experience it was true. They fought to protect their rights as they saw them, or they died trying.

Pakenham would treat this man with contempt and was likely to get little out of him.

Thinking of Desi Palomo's handling of a prisoner named Charlie Kincaid, he decided to try his hand at diplomacy. "Would you like something to drink, sir?" He walked over to the credenza behind General Villeré's desk, found a couple of snifters, and splashed some brandy into each.

The prisoner nodded stiffly and took one. "Thank you."

Charlie smiled and held the remaining glass, swirling the liquor as he sat on the corner of the desk. "I am Lieutenant Charlie Kincaid. I am in love with an American shipbuilder's daughter, Fiona Lanier. Do you know her brother Judah?"

The American's mouth fell open. "Judah Lanier has been commanding one of the guns right across the river from here. He's one of Dominique You's right-hand men."

Charlie grinned. "His sister says he's not a pirate. May I ask your name and designation?"

"I'm Michel Daquin, a French interpreter." The man sipped his drink. "This is fine stuff."

"I don't suppose you could enlighten me as to what you were doing hiding in that canal? My commander will return in a moment, and I doubt he will be as courteous as I."

The Frenchman hesitated. "I cannot say, but you redcoat interlopers will not run us off our land. So you should go home before you get hurt."

"How kind to be so concerned for my well-being." Charlie spread his hands. "But as you can see, my coat is not red at all. I am just a sailor trying to get this cursed war over and done with so I can marry my girl and sail off into the sunset."

The Frenchman shook his curly head. "You're going to have to find another way to win your lady. We have just received word of the imminent arrival of more than two thousand Kentucky sharpshooters. In fact, they are likely already in New Orleans as we speak. Your commander can beat me black and blue, Lieutenant, but that's all I'm going to tell you." He drained his glass. "And I thank you for the brandy."

JANUARY 7, 1815
VILLERÉ PLANTATION

Huddled inside Sullivan's old coat, Fiona leaned against the verandah rail outside the drawing room hospital ward. After General Lambert's arrival, she had been assigned to sleep in a curtained-off corner of the room. Midnight was less than a half hour away, but she couldn't sleep. Periodically doors slammed and torches and lamps flared as the officers came and went, but, used to her presence, they either gave her a polite passing nod or ignored her.

Charlie, she supposed, would be out with the fleet on the *Sophie*. She hadn't seen him since he left before Christmas. A few days ago she'd encountered Colonel Thornton and asked about him, but the colonel had nothing to tell her. Or pretended not to, which amounted to the same thing. After the New Year's Day engagement, General Pakenham had dithered in inactivity—except for the labor-intensive project of extending the canal—but now that Lambert's reinforcements were here, activity churned all over the plantation. The high-ranking officers were too busy for casual conversation.

Pakenham had retired for the night about an hour ago, but he seemed to be the only one getting any rest. The fog carried sounds of the engineers hauling boats across the canal to the river, as well as the rumble of the giant dirt-filled sugar casks being rolled down to form the general's new batteries. Artillery companies were still moving guns into place, and regiments bivouacked in the cane fields celebrated the anticipated march into New Orleans for the promised "beauty and booty" with a last ration of rum and biscuit. Morale had drained in tandem with constant spates of rain, unceasing artillery bombardment during the day, American hunting parties sniping by night, and starvation—every edible animal on the surrounding plantations having long since been killed and eaten. The men were ready to put their misery behind them and take out their frustrations on the dirty-shirts.

Fiona had spent the day helping the surgeon prepare cases of bandages, medicines, and other medical supplies that came up from the fleet in preparation for the coming battle. Now anxiety fed her insomnia. Eyes grainy, body weary, she dropped into a rocking chair to pray. It was all she knew to do.

Shortly after midnight a shout went up from the direction of the canal, some two hundred yards from the house. Lurching to her feet, she grabbed a lantern and stepped off the verandah just as a horse cantered through the fog.

"Hey, you!" The uniformed officer hauled roughly on the reins, peering at her face. "Sorry—Miss Lanier? Go wake the general. Tell him the dam broke and the canal caved in."

"But he'll be furious!"

"Yes, and I have to get back. You heard me—it's urgent!" He rode away before she could answer.

The canal would be a muddy slough, and there would be no more boats floating over to the river tonight. She didn't know exactly what Pakenham's strategy was, but she'd seen Colonel Thornton conferring with the engineers on the extension project, so presumably his brigade was involved in getting across the river for some kind of west bank action. Only four boats had gone across, and now it would be impossible to take more than a few hundred troops over before dawn.

If Pakenham didn't know, he couldn't do anything about it or change his strategy.

Because she had been willingly serving as a nurse, the officers who served as the general's aides seemed to assume she had somehow become sympathetic to their cause. But she in no way considered herself obligated to obey the orders of an enemy officer.

Slowly she walked back toward the verandah. If this small, quiet act of patriotism were to directly put Charlie's life in danger, the decision would have been harder to make. But he was assigned to the fleet, and she must do what she could to improve the odds of American victory. Her brothers' and her cousin's lives were at stake.

Snuffing the lantern, she went inside the hospital ward to begin another round of tending her British patients. If she couldn't sleep, she might as well be busy.

⌒

JANUARY 8, 1815
SOUTH OF NEW ORLEANS

Ever afterward when he thought of the final battle of New Orleans, Charlie would remember the church bells ringing all the way from the city as the fog dissipated, leaving an overcast, heavy morning, opaque under steely clouds.

Of course it would be on a Sunday, he thought, kneeling exhausted behind the foremost of the new batteries he'd directed the marines in constructing overnight. The casks wouldn't be much protection for the artillerymen, but they were better than nothing.

All eyes were on the mounted brigade major, waiting for the signal to advance. He couldn't understand why it hadn't already happened. The 44th Regiment was to have been in place at dawn, but there seemed to be some confusion regarding the ladders and fascines—bundles of ripe sugarcane to be thrown into the moat and facilitate the British soldiers' crossing—needed to scale the American parapet. Part of the regiment waited beside the old batteries a few hundred yards away, while three hundred more marched at the double back to the redout to retrieve the scaling equipment.

Late, late. Everything was too—

Suddenly a blue signal rocket fired.

Drums rattled the advance, the bagpipes of the tartan-clad 93rd Scots squealed, and the 44th began to march, flags flying, ramrod straight, heads up in time-honored British tradition. Charlie watched helplessly as the Americans unleashed their fire from behind their rampart and hell literally broke loose before his eyes.

The 44th had orders not to stop and fire, but with no way to get across the ditch they did it anyway—and found themselves bowled down like pins on a green. After a horrific few minutes, the surviving members of the 44th—including those carrying the ladders and fascines—turned tail and ran, dropping the equipment and trampling over it.

Meanwhile, the brigade storming the redout in front of the rampart found themselves cut down by murderous rifle fire. Before long they were routed as well, running hard for the rear. Through a pall of smoke Charlie could see crusty old Colonel Gibbs, red-faced and sweating, mounted on a rearing plantation horse, remonstrating in vain for his men to return to the front of the battle.

Time shut down for Charlie, years of training informing his actions and commands behind the battery. The battle roared like a dragon, men died around him, and he kept going.

Then they had to wait for more ammunition. For their own reasons the Americans ceased fire as well, and a bizarre lull descended on the battlefield. The smoke, caught in moist air, drifted to the ground like snow. As the ringing in his ears cleared,

Charlie could hear a band from behind the American lines blaring "Yankee Doodle."

Suddenly the brigade major from the 44th rode up on them, wheeled the horse, and slid to the ground. His face was black from powder, streaked with sweat and blood from a cut over one cheekbone. "We've lost this thing, Kincaid," he panted. "Pakenham, Gibbs, and Keane are all dead. When the men find out, they're going to run. But some of us from the 21st are going to get across that ditch and go over the wall. Are you with us?"

Charlie stared at him. Such an action would be both heroic and suicidal. The last flourish in signing off on his duty to His Majesty's Navy. Whether he survived or not, he could go to the other side with a clear conscience.

He was done.

Villeré Plantation

Fiona glanced up when Ishmael came to the doorway supporting another soldier. She would have burst into tears, but she seemed to have gone dry. The impulsive young woman who had sold herself into the cavalry in the name of patriotism had somehow withered away, leaving this automaton who grimly went about the business of closing sightless eyes, tying tourniquets about gushing wounds, and holding instruments for the surgeon while he dug for bullet fragments.

"You'll have to leave him out there." She went back to replacing the bandage that a young soldier had restlessly plucked off his forehead. "There's no more room in here."

"I think you gonna want to talk to this one," Ishmael said. "He came from the front, and he says the battle's over."

She looked up with a frown. "It's been less than an hour

since the firing started!" She shook her head. In the end, she'd done nothing heroic after all, nothing beyond failure to deliver a message. "Never mind. I'm coming." She rose and stepped over wounded men until she reached the boy Ishmael was lowering to sit against the foyer wall. She hardly noticed when Ishmael gave her a compassionate look and left. "Here, let me look at you. Where are you hurt?"

"My back." The young soldier gasped with every breath. "I was in the first wave of the 44th. I fell, and the rest ran over me getting away. When it was over, I had to crawl the rest of the way back because anybody who stood up was shot like a dog—" He slumped over, weeping. "I shouldn't have crawled."

Pity wouldn't make him well. Fiona rolled him to his stomach and began to cut his coat away from the gash between his shoulder blades. "So it's really over? The Americans surrendered?"

The boy groaned out a curse. "No! They hid behind that rampart, shooting at us, muskets and rifles and artillery, and General Lambert ordered us to withdraw because somebody forgot to bring the equipment so we could climb over. We were like pigs in a slaughterhouse." He turned his face toward her and whispered, "They'll say I'm a coward, hit in the back."

She put a hand on his head. "Then—then we won? The Americans won?"

"I suppose. Maybe we'll attack again. I don't care. I just want to go home."

Slaughter. *God, oh God, please let Charlie be safe.*

⌒

McCarty Plantation, American Headquarters

As the wagon rolled to a stop outside American headquarters, Charlie looked about, still stunned to be unharmed after the harrowing journey across the ditch upon the shoulders of his mates, and then climbing over the wall under murderous musket and rifle fire. He shook the manacles about his wrists and found them real enough. As far as he knew, he was the only one to have survived.

The guns were quiet now, except for sporadic musket fire kept up by the Americans to harass the retreating enemy. Charlie had no idea what would come from this day, but he suspected what was left of the British command had had enough.

He remembered another Sunday morning months ago, spent imprisoned in a tack room, thinking about committing treason. He'd sensed God telling him to honor his commitment, and he had done that to the best of his ability. Now his personal coin had flipped so completely that he might as well be resurrected from the dead. In fact, that was probably a good way to think of it.

The driver of the wagon jumped down, giving Charlie a strange look along with a rough hand down to the ground.

Wiping the smile off his face, Charlie followed the man into the McCarty mansion's empty front hallway. The New Year's Day bombing had left it little more than a burnt-out shell, but Jackson hadn't bothered to change his headquarters. Instead, according to Charlie's loquacious escort, the commander just moved himself and his officers down to the ground floor, where they slept, ate, and conducted all their planning.

Charlie soon enough found himself sitting on the blackened hardwood floor in a room with several other prisoners, most of them in the uniforms of the 7th and 43rd Regiments, Lambert's brigade. One or two gave him a morose welcome, then resumed studying the backs of their eyelids.

Charlie was almost asleep himself when a servant entered with a tray of drinks and a pile of flaky biscuits, which he offered to the prisoners. "Thank you," Charlie said, embarrassed when his stomach gave a loud rumble. It occurred to him that he hadn't eaten since yesterday.

Satisfied, licking buttery crumbs off his fingers, he lay down, head pillowed on his arm, and sank into exhausted slumber.

He awoke when the door opened to admit a tall, dark-haired fellow with a bristling two-day beard and a ferocious pair of eyebrows. He looked eerily familiar.

Oh, yes, the pirate brother. He should have anticipated that one of the Lanier clan would show up here.

Judah Lanier's expression did not lighten as he crooked a finger at Charlie. "You. Come with me."

Charlie got up and followed without bothering to bid the other prisoners goodbye. Their exchanges would be worked out according to military protocol. He had a feeling this confrontation with Judah was going to be personal.

Lanier led the way down a long hall, opened a door on the right, and went in. The minute Charlie entered behind him, Judah whirled and launched a fist.

Righting himself, Charlie pressed the back of his hand to his aching, bleeding mouth. He eyed Fiona's brother, aware that they were alone. If he decided to end Charlie's life then and there, nobody would know or care.

"How is it that you're even alive?" Lanier snarled. "They said you came over that parapet like a madman and they pulled you down just to see what kind of lunatic does such a thing."

"I'm not sure you'd understand."

"Try me."

Charlie shrugged. "God gave me one more wall to climb, and I climbed it."

"Do not tell me God gave you permission to lure my sister over here and put her life in danger."

"I assure you I was just as appalled to see her as you were. But I did what I could to protect her, since there was no way to get her out of here."

Something akin to the grunt of a charging bull escaped Lanier as he turned and slammed the flat of his hand against the door. "That ought to be your head!"

"Undoubtedly you are right." Charlie sighed. It appeared he was going to be allowed to live. "But in spite of all my best efforts, I have survived this hellacious day, and so have you, so if you're done venting your spleen, perhaps we could get on toward more practical things. For instance, arranging another prisoner exchange."

Lanier sneered. "It doesn't surprise me that you're anxious to go back—only that you didn't run away again. But I'm more concerned about Fiona right now."

"As am I. Though for your information, returning to the navy is the last thing I want."

Lanier scowled at him. "What do you mean?"

"I plan to resign my commission as soon as possible and emigrate to become an American citizen. Your pesky little sister is going to become my wife—the sooner, the better. So perhaps you wouldn't mind expediting that prisoner exchange?"

19

JANUARY 18, 1815
VILLERÉ PLANTATION

The British were leaving. Of course nobody would tell Fiona anything. The few officers who stayed back had gone about the glum business of removing the remaining artillery, ammunition, and powder, while the surgeon counted the wounded and returned with those able to be moved back to the fleet.

That left Fiona and the Villeré slaves to care for the fifty or so who couldn't walk on their own. Today, ten days after the battle, two more had died, and she was preparing them for burial.

Under the circumstances, she wouldn't have expected the slaves to linger. The British officers had offered them freedom—more or less an act of retaliation against the planters who dared to repel their advance into the city—and most of the field hands had left. But the house slaves, including Ishmael, Lulu, and Rachel, had elected to remain. "Nowhere else to go, miss," said Ishmael with a shake of his head. "Dangerous out there for a colored man."

There were still guards posted near the levee and in small

pickets by the woods and along the sugarcane fields, exchanging the occasional volley with Americans patrolling the Rodriguez canal rampart. But she suspected their main purpose was to camouflage the daily disappearance of hundreds, then thousands, of troops who boarded the barges and floated down the bayous to Lake Borgne.

They had to go. There was no more food available—in fact, the Villeré family was reduced to a diet chiefly composed of the grits they'd stashed in a compartment under the kitchen floor. Ishmael turned out to be quite a good crawfish fisherman, and when the British were otherwise occupied, Lulu would boil up a fine gumbo. Other than that, they all went hungry.

One morning a few days ago, Fiona had caught Colonel Thornton as he passed through the hospital ward and asked if he knew what happened to Lieutenant Kincaid.

Thornton paused with his hand on the doorjamb, his face grave. "I'd have thought you would have heard by now. He was with a company of the 21st who tried to go over the wall at the last minute. Heroic and insanely stupid." He hesitated. "When we cleared out the ditch, many of the dead were . . . unrecognizable. And Kincaid wasn't found elsewhere. So you can assume . . ." He turned to walk away and said over his shoulder, "I'm sorry, Miss Lanier."

She had stared after him. Charlie had been on the battle site after all. Not so surprising was the fact that he had involved himself in what amounted to a suicidal effort. But . . . it just seemed that if Charlie were dead, she would know it.

Charlie dead. Reminding herself for the hundredth time that it was true, she drew a blanket over the blank face of a marine who'd been barely hanging on to life this morning. Death everywhere.

"Miss Lanier."

She looked up. A young officer she'd seen hanging about the house during the last couple of days hovered in the doorway. "Yes . . . I'm sorry, I don't know your name."

"Drake, miss. I was sent to find you."

"All right." She stood up, glancing at the marine's blanket-covered body. "These poor men are ready to go."

"No, not the—They want *you*. Right now." Drake's spotty face mottled red. "General Lambert's office."

With Pakenham dead and Cochrane supervising the fleet, Lambert was the commander on the field. She couldn't imagine why he would send for her, but she knew from the paucity of gold on Drake's uniform that he wasn't of high enough rank to be able to tell her anything.

"All right." She followed Drake down the hall, but he stopped her before knocking on the library door.

"Wait, miss. I wanted to say something to you."

She sighed. "What is it?"

"I just wanted to tell you I'm sorry about what happened the day we came."

"What are you talking about?" All she remembered from that day was Charlie. And meeting Penny. And sometimes she had nightmares about the sugarhouse.

"I was—it was me with Osmond. We found you in the slave cabin, and Osmond tried to—you know. Anyway, I should have stopped him, and I'm sorry. You've been nothing but kind to all of us, even after that, and I . . ." He stood there wringing his big raw hands.

Half of her wanted to take out her knife and divest him of some of his pertinent equipment, while the other half felt sorry for his obvious misery and remorse. "I shall forgive you," she said carefully, "if you will give me your promise to never, *ever*

311

stand by again while someone weaker than you is harmed. Can you do that?"

"Yes, miss, I swear I will. I mean, I won't. Well, you know—"

Feeling a hundred years old, Fiona patted his arm. "Yes, I know. Now move, so I can get this over with."

Drake took her hand and awkwardly kissed it, then knocked on the door.

"Come!" someone bellowed from within.

"Thank you, miss," Drake whispered as he opened the door for her.

She found General Lambert seated at the desk, with another gentleman standing by the window. Backlit by the sunshine streaming in, his face was in shadow.

Lambert stood with a sour smile. "Miss Lanier. We are going to miss your nursing skills, but it seems we are to release you as part of a prisoner exchange."

She blinked. "That's good, of course, but how will I—I mean, will I just *walk* over to the American side?"

"I'm here to take you home, Fiona."

She turned as the man by the window approached. "Desi!" She threw herself at him, and he caught her tight. "Oh, how wonderful to see you!" She leaned back to study him. He looked tired, but not so gaunt as the soldiers she had been caring for.

He smiled and released her. "I've been held aboard a ship on the other side of the lake since the night battle before Christmas. The others are being released to go back to their companies, but Judah facilitated special arrangements for you." He glanced at the general. "I'm glad we've been able to come to some terms after our late . . . contretemps."

"Will I see Judah before we leave?"

"No, but Oliver is going with us—under loud protest, I might add." Desi shrugged. "Judah holds quite a bit more clout than he does."

The general proffered a packet of papers to Desi. "If you don't mind, I have other business to attend to. Gather your belongings, then Sublieutenant Drake will escort you north along the river road under a flag of truce. Once you're in American territory, you're no longer my responsibility."

Desi tucked the papers into his coat and gave Fiona a wry look. "Is there anything you want to take?"

"Just my coat. But I want to say goodbye to some people."

"Fine." Desi gave the general an ironic bow, then opened the door for Fiona. "Personally, I'll be glad to see the last of this swamp."

~

January 20, 1815
Off Chandeleur Islands

The *Sophie* had orders to weigh anchor at dawn, and Charlie was so tired from the last two frantic days of hauling troops down to the fleet that he could barely stand up. Still, determined to know where he stood before retiring to his berth, he waited shivering on the quarterdeck, listening to the sails snap overhead in a stiff wind blowing off Lake Borgne as he waited for Admiral Cochrane to emerge from Captain's quarters.

After coming down from the McCarty plantation by barge under flag of truce, Charlie's first assignment had been helping stuff cotton into a regiment of scarecrows to be posted in strategic places that night—one of the craziest maneuvers he had been asked to perform in the course of his naval career. The ruse, intended to give their forces time to get across the lake before the Americans knew they were gone, seemed to have worked, since they hadn't been seriously chased during the extended retreat.

Score points, he thought, for British subterfuge, of which he was a prime example.

Before he could get too far off on that mental trail, the hatch behind him opened and the admiral emerged. Good. Now was the time.

"Sir, I wanted to speak to you for a moment, if you have time."

Cochrane scowled. "Kincaid. I trust you have recovered from your heroics—and yet another stay as a guest of the Americans."

Charlie ignored the provocation. "I won't keep you, Admiral. I was just wondering if you'd heard from my grandfather since I gave you that letter for him."

"I have not. And you must disabuse yourself of the notion that I have nothing better to do than serve as your postmaster." Cochrane surveyed Charlie and sniffed when he found nothing to criticize. "I assure you, however, that you will be the first to know if Admiral Lord St. Clair puts aside his sheep farming long enough to put pen to paper." Smirking, Cochrane went whistling down the ladder onto the main deck and disappeared.

Deflated, Charlie frowned after him. Nothing untoward had happened, but something felt off about that encounter. Maybe he was just overtired. Yawning, he stepped through the hatch to descend the ladder to the officers' berth.

Leaving New Orleans would put him one step closer to reuniting with Fiona. He prayed she was safe and warm at home. It had been worth the sacrifice of returning to service, to know that he'd secured her release.

January 21, 1815
Mobile

It took three days to get to Mobile in a hired wagon, Fiona seated beside Desi on the driver's seat and Oliver in the wagon bed with their provisions. As they rattled along Conception Street, the sun floated behind them halfway to the horizon. It had been a long ride, complicated by intermittent rain showers, frequent ferries across swollen creeks, and little in the way of available food. Her cousins had been solicitous to the point of absurdity, but she managed to restrain her irritation and respond politely every time they asked her if she was tired.

Of course she was tired. She was also hungry and sad. But admitting that to two men headed home to see their sweethearts would have been the height of selfishness. So she would smile, shake her head, and think of riding Bonnie on the beach. Or playing bilboquet with Elijah. Or a whole list of things she could come up with besides kissing Charlie. Because all that did was close up her throat and make her nose sting.

Blinking hard to make the sensation go away, she realized Desi had stopped the wagon in Uncle Rémy's carriageway. Oliver had already hopped out and run to the kitchen door.

She rubbed her eyes. "We're here!"

Desi gave her a quizzical look. "Yes, we are. Where have you been?"

She sighed and looked away. "I don't know."

"Yes, you do." He patted her hand. "Nobody expects you to be merry and bright, Fi, but let your family love you. All right?"

Her eyes filled again. "Stop being so kind to me. It makes me cry!"

He laughed, so she laughed too and let him help her down from the wagon. But he held her hand as they walked to the house, and she clung to it, grateful that at least one person understood what she'd been through.

Then Maddy was on the front porch, with Elijah hopping about like a monkey, and Desi let go of Fiona to hurry up the steps and embrace the two of them. Fiona stood on the walkway, smiling at their joy. Before long, Aunt Giselle came out with Aunt Lyse and Uncle Rafa, Uncle Rémy trailing with his usual dignity, and Fiona found herself entangled in a complicated family hug that went a long way to restoring her peace. It would take quite some time, she knew, to move out of the valley of the shadow, but one day she'd find herself looking back.

She had to believe that.

                                        ⌣

Elijah lay asleep with his head on Desi's shoulder, Maddy within the circle of his arm. Chilly but content, they sat in the dark on her porch swing. The first ecstasy of reunion had passed, but she kept looking up at him, touching his hand on Elijah's back, just to make sure he was real.

The third time she did that, he smiled and kissed her forehead. "I'm not going away. So if I fall asleep, just give me a blanket and go on to bed."

She laughed. "I couldn't sleep if you paid me a thousand dollars. You don't know how I worried at the news you'd been taken prisoner." She nudged him with her shoulder. "You told me you wouldn't see any action."

"I know how to handle a gun, and we were outnumbered. I had to help." His voice was matter-of-fact. "I have to admit, it was strange to encounter Charlie Kincaid in uniform aboard the prison ship—at Christmas dinner!"

"Did he know that Fiona was in New Orleans? She was very quiet when you-all returned."

"He knew." Desi took a breath as if to say more, then lapsed into silence.

"What is it, Des?"

"I think I was wrong about him, Maddy. He understood how dangerous it was for her to be there, and he's the one who arranged to have her brought out so quickly."

"How do you know?"

"I . . . can't say. And don't tell her any of this. He's gone now, and it's best she forgets him."

Maddy huffed. "If you're withholding something from her, that's the same as treating her as a child. Women are stronger than you think."

His eyes glittered in the shadows. "I'm learning that. There's something else I need to talk to you about, Madeleine, before I can ask you to marry me. Something that may affect your decision."

"What is that?" She couldn't think of anything that would keep her from Desi.

"While I was in New Orleans, I had a chance to talk to people who knew General Wilkinson."

"General Wilkinson?" The name, so far from the context of their conversation, set her adrift. "Stephen's commander?"

"Yes. You'll remember that he'd been indicted more than once for collusion with traitors. He was more or less run out of New Orleans on suspicion of corruption after the Louisiana Purchase."

"I know, but . . . Stephen said even President Washington trusted him. *Stephen* trusted him."

"It seems the president was fooled in that case, because Wilkinson played both sides. Part of my assignment here was to investigate the case, and I've seen proof in documents and letters that never came to light at his trials."

"Desi, was Stephen involved in those bad land deals?"

"I can't prove it for certain, but I've talked to military people who knew Stephen and believe he was in on the schemes but may have thought about testifying. They say that's why Wilkinson had him moved to the front line of battle."

"Stephen was a soldier! He was going to battle anyway!"

"Maddy, I know it's hard for an honest, ethical person to comprehend the evil tricks people get up to when they want power or money or both. Wilkinson was a crook and a liar. It's possible Stephen was too." Desi released an uncomfortable breath. "As you said, you deserve truth, and one day it's likely somebody else will tell you I was asking questions. I appreciate your loyalty to your husband—"

"I knew there was something wrong."

"What?"

"He was unfaithful to me. I'm not surprised he would do other things as well."

"Oh, Maddy. I'm so sorry."

"Yes, I know." She laid her hand on Elijah's back. "I'm sorry Elijah may find this out one day, though I hope he doesn't. But I've had time to think about it and grieve over it. Mama and Daddy have helped me see that I don't have to let Stephen's sin and bad judgment affect me for the rest of my life. I choose not to, that's all." She leaned closer to Desi. "I choose a good man who loves and obeys God and tries to do right, even when he doesn't have to."

"You are remarkable, do you know that?" He kissed her nose and then her lips. "So was that a yes?"

"Excuse me, what was the question?"

"Madeleine Gaillain Gonzales Burch, will you and Elijah marry me?"

"Oh, yes . . ."

JANUARY 22, 1815

Sehoy sat on the hearth beside Oliver, as close to him as she could get without sitting in his lap. Aunt Giselle, knitting in her rocker beside Uncle Rémy's armchair, kept an eagle eye on the two of them, probably to make sure they didn't slip off alone. Sehoy knew Oliver wanted to do just that, and of course she did too, but even an Indian orphan understood the boundaries.

"You really pretended to be me?" Israel, to Sehoy's irritation, was regarding Fiona as if she'd rescued America single-handedly, instead of throwing away a perfectly good family for a British aristocrat with a talent for manipulation.

It was late, past bedtime, and the children were all asleep—well, except for Israel, who for once was treated as one of the adults so that he could hear Fiona's adventures. Desi had gone next door with Maddy to put Elijah to bed. They were probably spooning as well, but after all, they were *old* and could do whatever they wanted. Aunt Lyse sat on the sofa in the circle of Uncle Rafa's arm, her feet tucked underneath her. She looked sleepy, but Sehoy knew she was taking everything in with a razor intellect that could cut through nonsense at a moment's notice.

Fiona, the center of attention, seemed lost, as if she wanted to be elsewhere. Her curly hair, still so short that it escaped the combs holding it off her face, drew attention to the fineness of her skin and the weary droop to her blue eyes. But she did manage to smile at Israel's incredulity. "Oliver said I looked just like you—didn't you, Ollie?"

Oliver flushed. "Well, it was dark that night!"

Everybody laughed, and he became fair game for teasing.

"We all knew you needed spectacles!"

"You should apprentice as a barber, Oliver, you have real talent."

Oliver smiled faintly, looking at the rug. "Knowing what I know now, I'm not sure I'd do it again—send Fiona into battle like that, I mean. I saw things . . ." Suddenly he met Uncle Rafa's eyes across the room, his gaze direct and mature. "But I know what you and my father and Uncle Simon went through to make sure we're free men, not slaves of some king across the ocean. So I'm glad I went. I'd do *that* again!"

It was the longest speech Sehoy had heard him make in a large group, ever. She wanted to kiss him right then and there but contented herself with pressing her knee against his thigh.

"We're proud of you, Oliver," Lyse said softly. "And Fiona as well."

Fiona looked away. "Thank you, Aunt Lyse. But I want you all to forgive me for worrying you." She sighed. "This is going to sound so ungrateful, but do you think I could just go home to Navy Cove? I miss being there so much, and I want to check on Uncle Luc-Antoine and my horses . . ."

"I'll take you," Oliver said before anyone else could offer. "I miss home too."

"And I'll go with you," Sehoy said quickly. "Fiona needs another girl with her," she added when Aunt Giselle looked at her sharply.

Uncle Rémy forestalled his wife's objection. "That's not a bad plan. Nardo Smith was in town today, planning to head back to the Point tomorrow. I'm sure he'll take you down the bay on his boat."

Sehoy jumped to her feet, thrilled to have the question so simply settled. "I need to pack my things."

But Oliver got to his feet and took her hand before she could dart up the stairs. "Wait, Sehoy. Come outside with me for a minute first."

She glanced at Aunt Giselle, who shrugged, and allowed Oliver to lead her out onto the porch, lit only by a small oil lamp on a table. "Is something wrong?"

"No." He walked her backward into the darkness and firmly tipped her chin up with his thumb, then bent his head to kiss her hard. When he was done, he drew away, then kissed her again more gently. "I missed you, Sehoy. But we're going to have to wait awhile before anything happens with us."

"Oliver . . ." She was still trying to catch her breath.

"Just listen. I'm going to court you. But you'll have to be patient because I want to go to college like Desi, and have a business like Uncle Rémy, so I can take care of you. And that's going to take some time."

"I might want to go to college too." She didn't want him to be smarter than her.

"That's fine." He grinned and kissed her again. "It's a good thing we'll have lots of family around us all the time, isn't it?" Drawing her back into the light, he pushed the door open and grabbed her hand to pull her inside.

⌒

January 24, 1815
Dauphine Island

He could have walked away.

Charlie dropped over the side of the *Sophie* and descended the rope ladder to the tender boat that would take him and the marine unit over to the island. He said it to himself again. Judah would have let him go, he could have simply disappeared, gone to Mexico, and no one would ever have found him.

And many men would have done it in his place.

It was clear by now that Admiral Cochrane—for whatever mad notion he possessed of retaliation against his grandfather's actions in the past, or maybe just simple power and control over one dependent upon his whims—had no intention of granting his decommissioning. And because Cochrane was his commanding officer, the Articles of War, ratified and amended by Parliament in 1779, precluded Charlie willfully going over to an enemy force, or even being found away from his duty station without leave for that matter. If he defied that law, he subjected himself to penalties up to death by hanging or firing squad.

Which made him bound, as enslaved as any of the Villeré servants, to the word of Vice-Admiral Alexander Cochrane. The only difference was, he had done it to himself. When God had delivered him to the Americans, released him from his commitment to the British cause, he'd stuck his head right back into the noose.

But he would do it again in a heartbeat for Fiona Lanier.

The difficulty at hand, however, was just as stark as that other decision. He could no longer bring himself to take up arms against her brothers or uncles or cousins. And here they were, the British fleet and army, gathered at the head of Mobile Bay for the purpose of once more attacking the poorly garrisoned little fort that he had helped defend less than six months ago.

In some ways, he felt as if he'd returned home after a long exile. The ocean breeze that ruffled his hair was cold, but somehow refreshing after the choking humidity of New Orleans and the stink of the battlefield. As the boat grounded on a sandbar, he stepped out and splashed onto the beach, remembering days of swimming in the surf at Navy Cove with Oliver and Léon, crabbing with Fiona, and coming home to boil their catch for supper. Good days.

But in many respects, he faced certain execution here. Because when they told him to aim the *Sophie*'s guns at Navy Cove, he would have to refuse. The soldiers at Fort Bowyer didn't know it, but they had a brother planted in the Royal Navy. A brother who was for them, not against them.

He couldn't help thinking of Abraham's dilemma regarding the sacrifice of Isaac. How could a good God demand such a price? Had the patriarch known a substitute would be provided at the last second?

Letting his men proceed, Charlie stopped, turned to look at the vastness of the sea, churning waves controlled in regular tides, depths hiding a staggering variety of life. Did the God of all that really pierce the daily existence of men like Charlie Kincaid? He was no Abraham to found a dynasty that would rock the foundations of humanity for centuries to come.

Or was he? Someone had intervened to miraculously rescue him on more than one occasion. First in a storm not far from here, and recently as he scrabbled over a wall into enemy lines.

Hope flickered to life. Perhaps the plan was not at an end.

Later that night, he sat at a campfire with officers from the *Sophie* and the *Carron*, quiet while they drank rum, told bawdy jokes, and reminisced about the carnival days of waiting in Negril Bay for deployment.

"There was that pretty native girl that cooked sauce for the admiral," chortled a lieutenant named Cassell, looking over his shoulder at the big tent, some distance away, where Cochrane already slumbered. "He thought he was the only one dining at that table."

"Generous, was she?" someone else jeered.

General laughter, then Spencer, captain of the *Carron* and second in command of naval forces, elbowed Charlie. "Careful what you say in his presence, though—right, Kincaid? Cochrane can be a dangerous man to cross. I don't know what you did to get on his bad side, but I wouldn't count on him ever turning you loose."

Charlie stilled. "What do you know about my request to resign?"

"Just that it was approved at the same time we got word to come here. Cochrane has been boasting that he'll hold on to that letter until he dies—or you do, whichever comes first."

"Would you—would you swear to that, sir?"

Spencer's eyes widened. "My career depends on his goodwill, laddy. Besides, how could I prove it?" He shrugged. "His word against mine."

The conversation moved on, and Charlie lapsed into silence again.

The letter had come. Cochrane had lied to him. Eventually Charlie would be able to contact his grandfather and gain verification of his release, but that could be a long time off—certainly after the impending battle over Fort Bowyer ran its course. By that time he would be either in the brig for insubordination or dead.

He surged to his feet. "Excuse me, gentlemen. I have just recollected an important duty I've neglected to complete."

He walked off into the darkness.

20

Fiona woke to a series of lightning jags that lit her room like the noonday sun, followed by a crashing roll of thunder. She sat up in bed, at first certain she was at the Battle of New Orleans, but a quick pat of the bedclothes encountered Sehoy's shoulder.

Home. Navy Cove.

In the darkness she took a couple of breaths and lay back down. No way to tell the time, but she found herself wide awake, nerves thrumming. The horses would be frightened. She should go out to reassure them.

Her dress hung on the back of the door. Quickly she put it on over her nightgown, located stockings and boots, then went to the entryway for Sullivan's old coat and hat—the only items remaining from that disreputable wardrobe. She was going to get soaked—it was raining buckets, probably had been for hours— but what was the difference between that and going swimming?

Her boots were full of water by the time she reached the barn. Thunder continued to roll, and lightning lit the doorway as she fumbled for tinder and flint. She could hear the goats rustling and bleating in their stall, Bonnie and Washington kicking walls in their anxiety.

With the lantern finally aglow, she hurried to Washington first. His big dark eyes rolled, showing her the whites, and he jerked his head away when she reached for him. "Come on, big boy," she crooned. "Just a lot of noise. Nobody's going to—"

A hand clamped her shoulder.

She screamed and dropped the lantern.

"Fiona! It's me!"

She was grabbed from behind in arms like iron bands. Kicking wildly, she reared her head backward, connected with something hard, and her assailant howled.

"It's Charlie, you little—!"

She went limp. "Ch-Ch-Charlie?"

"Yes." He let go of her.

She whirled and found him nursing a reddened, rapidly swelling cheekbone. "You're dead!"

"Clearly I'm not."

"Why did you scare me like that? *I thought you were dead!*"

"I was going to wait out here until morning and then knock on the door like a gentleman. I should have realized you would come out to check on the horses. Can't you control the weather around here?"

She waved off his pathetic joke. "The *dead* part, Charlie. They said you went over that wall, and they couldn't find your body."

He looked sheepish. "That was Judah's idea, and I agreed. We both thought you might come looking for me again—or refuse to leave—if you knew I survived."

"Judah knows you're alive?" She was going to slit her brother's throat.

He shrugged. "Do you have a handkerchief or something? I think my cheek is bleeding."

"I hope you bleed to death and maggots eat your body." She closed her fist and slammed it against his bicep—undoubtedly hurting her more than him. Thunder crashed. Taking off her heavy, sopping hat, she swung it at him, over and over, until he laughed and hauled her into his arms.

He kissed her. "Maggots?"

"Yes. Do that again."

He did, at length, until he finally propped her against a wall and panted, "You know I'm going to have a black eye."

"That's your own fault." She studied him critically. "You look like you've been mauled by a bear."

"Did anybody ever tell you you're hardheaded?"

"It has been mentioned."

"I don't suppose you'd like to move this into the tack room. I used to have a pallet—"

"In your dreams. Have you deserted?"

"Not precisely. It's a bit of a long story."

"I'm not busy at the moment."

"Well. We could go on like this all night, but since you're here, I should tell you why I came."

"You mean you have a *reason* for appearing like Lazarus out of the tomb in the middle of a storm?"

"That's a rather mixed metaphor," he complained, "but I digress. As a matter of fact, we need to be ready to ride for Fort Bowyer at first light. The entire British fleet is skulking in the gulf like a bunch of sharks. And there are about sixteen hundred marines camped out on Dauphine Island, planning to invade the landward side of the fort tomorrow."

"You mean *today* tomorrow, or *tomorrow* tomorrow?"

"We have another day. I think. I stayed as long as I could,

to get finalized plans, but I suppose they could always change things at the last minute. You know how that goes."

She did indeed. She stared at Charlie's beloved, bruised face. She was dying to know what he'd been doing, how he came to be here. But there would be time for that later. "Come on, let's get you washed up. All you have to do is stick your face outside the door—"

"Very funny. I missed you so much." His eyes were wistful, his mouth rueful.

Oh, how she loved him.

She wriggled out of his arms. "I'm not kissing you again until your face is clean."

⌒

FEBRUARY 11, 1815
FORT BOWYER

He'd been right that they had another day. The British landed and started setting up camp on the shore of Mobile Point across from Fort Bowyer at dawn on the eighth. They advanced immediately, and Major Lawrence's troops fired on them, sending them scuttling back.

By then, the Lanier family and men from the shipyard had moved into the fort with the American soldiers still stationed at the fort and their women and children, and Major Lawrence had sent word to Mobile for reinforcements. Charlie helped Lawrence prepare as best he could for the siege, placing sandbags on the parapets and at the gun embrasures to protect the artillerymen while they returned fire. There wasn't much else they could do.

On the afternoon of the eleventh, Charlie huddled in the major's office with Luc-Antoine and Fiona, who refused to leave his side except when nature called. Frankly, he didn't mind, and another side of Mother Nature would have done them in, if they hadn't both been so busy trying to stay alive. He couldn't resist kissing her every time he passed, building a sort of itching restlessness that he knew would only be assuaged the day they got married.

Since there was no knowing if or when that would happen, he spent a good bit of time praying for self-control.

So far so good.

He looked at her now, sitting at the corner of the table, blue eyes intent on the map, trying to keep her mouth shut. She knew this isthmus and the surrounding area better than any of them, but she also knew her limitations. And advance planning was not one of her strengths—unless it came to raising horses.

He certainly hoped that ability would extend to rearing children one of these days. He wanted about ten that looked just like her . . .

Everyone was staring at him. He cleared his throat and addressed Major Lawrence, who was looking both amused and exasperated. "I'm sorry, I lost the question, sir."

"So I see. I will send Miss Lanier into another room if you cannot attend, Lieutenant."

"Oh, no, I—oh, you're joking." Flustered, he slapped a finger onto the list on the table. "The rockets you won't have to worry about. They're impossible to aim. But the 21st Regiment with these howitzers will be deadly. There are perhaps three times more of them now than there were back in August. And they are very, very angry that Jackson wouldn't put out the welcome mat in New Orleans."

Lawrence's rugged face sobered. "We've done about all we can, but we are woefully outnumbered." He shook his head.

"Kincaid, I appreciate your advance warning and all you've done to help, but—"

"Major, pardon the interruption, but there's a redcoat approaching under a white flag." A young adjutant stood in the doorway. "What do you want us to do?"

Charlie jumped to his feet. "Let me see who it is." He ran across the green and up the steps to the parapet. Ducking down to peer through a gun port, he put a spyglass to his eye. "It's Major Sir Harry Smith. He's a good man."

Lawrence was right behind him. "For a redcoat, you mean?"

Charlie grinned. "Yes, for a redcoat." He'd left his Royal Navy pea jacket at the Laniers' house and borrowed an old buckskin coat belonging to one of the brothers.

"All right," Lawrence said. "Let's see what he wants."

A few minutes later, Charlie and Fiona stood in the shadows as the guards opened the gate for Smith to enter. The tall, thin, red-haired young man in impeccable uniform walked in, bowed to Lawrence, and received a courteous bow in turn. Unwilling to give Smith any undue advantage of information, Charlie and Fiona waited until the two opposing officers went into Lawrence's office. Then they slipped into the cell next door, out of sight but able to hear through the open door.

Sir Harry began with the usual courtesies of negotiation, such as his name and rank and the purpose of his visit. "Major Lawrence, I'm sure you are aware of the fact that His Majesty's finest have come here with every intention of neutralizing your force so that we may advance into the contested territory around the city of Mobile."

Charlie looked at Fiona and mouthed, "Contested?"

When Lawrence didn't answer, Sir Harry continued. "With that intent in mind, we offer you the opportunity to evacuate your women and children and surrender arms. Otherwise, we will be forced to unleash the artillery trained upon you as we speak. And you should know that two more regiments, each about the size of this one, await orders on Dauphine Island."

Lawrence again hesitated, but finally said, "I fear, Sir Harry, that unconditional surrender without a shot fired is an unreasonable expectation. I propose instead that you give us until this time tomorrow to collect ourselves, at which time we shall march out with our arms and ground them outside the fort."

"I understand your reluctance, Major, but I regret to say that we must be a little more proactive in overseeing what you call 'collecting yourselves.' Suppose we compromise. We will give you until tomorrow to get out, but in the meantime you must allow a company of our troops to take possession of your arms. And you will permit another body of our troops to move up close in support. At noon tomorrow, you will exit the fort and ground arms on the glacis."

Charlie heard a chair scrape in the next room. "Sir Harry," said Lawrence, "will you permit me a few minutes to think about this? You understand this is a very serious decision that I make, with many lives at stake."

"Of course." Sir Harry's voice was urbane, smooth. Truly he held all the cards.

Major Lawrence walked into the room with Charlie and Fiona. He leaned over to whisper, "What do you think? Is he serious about attacking full-on if I refuse?"

"General Lambert is his commanding officer," Charlie whispered back, "and the man is a pitiless bulldog—especially with the defeat at New Orleans driving him. Is there any chance of reinforcements arriving?"

"I've sent word to General Jackson in New Orleans, as well as Fort Charlotte. But who knows how long they'll take to respond?" Lawrence sighed. "We can't count on it."

Charlie shut his eyes, knowing the consequences he would personally face from surrender. "If you don't concede, most, if not all of these men under your command will die, and you will lose anyway. I don't think you have a choice."

"All right, then. That's what I thought." Lawrence put his hand on Charlie's shoulder and walked out.

Fiona stared at him white-faced. "What's going to happen when they find you here?"

"I suppose we're going to find out."

⟋

FEBRUARY 12, 1815
FORT BOWYER

Over the last five days of the siege, Fiona had observed Charlie's ability to lead with a weird mixture of pride, anxiety, and overwhelming love. Certainly he had demonstrated some glaring imperfections in judgment—she delighted in calling him "Lazarus," to his intense irritation—but his character had been honed true and strong.

On the day of the surrender, the US soldiers lined up quietly behind Major Lawrence in the center of the gate. Fiona and Sehoy gathered with the women and children on one side, while Charlie blended into a group of shipbuilders-turned-militia—including Léon, Luc-Antoine, and Oliver—on the other. Besides the buckskin coat, the men had given Charlie a misshapen suede hat, and his beard had thickened so that she barely recognized him. He had protested the need for a disguise, of course, but Uncle Luc settled the matter by threatening to knock him unconscious until the surrender was complete. In the end, he shrugged, said he'd go quietly if they recognized him and stay put if they didn't. None of the British artillery engineers who had come in to take over their guns had made a peep so far.

Fiona continued to pray with her eyes wide open. *God, your will be done.*

At noon, the gates creaked open. British drums rolled, and Major Lawrence gave the order to advance, arms at rest. Row by row his troops marched through the gate, across the ditch, and up the escarpment to lay down their guns on the glacis. When the last soldier had passed through, the militia followed. Gripping Sehoy's hand hard, Fiona watched the tall bearded figure behind Léon approach the British officer assigned to stand guard outside the gate. Was the officer searching faces? She thought not, as he had stopped nobody to this point.

Then the officer turned his head to inspect the last men going through, Charlie among them, and she wanted to vomit. It was Drake, the one who had apologized to her at the Villeré house. What demon had brought him here? He would recognize Charlie and then—

But he wasn't looking at Charlie at all. He was staring at *her*, lips pressed tightly together. Giving her a polite nod, he waved the last of the men through and beckoned the women to follow. Without another glance, he marched toward a field major guarding the soldiers and said loudly, "He's not here, sir."

"Are you sure? Cochrane sent word to look for him."

"Yes, sir. I served under Kincaid for months, so I would know him. He must have escaped to Mobile."

The major turned away cursing, but evidently had more important tasks than combing through surly American civilians for a naval deserter. He addressed Major Lawrence. "General Lambert says you and your men will be detained here until I receive word of an exchange or some other arrangements are made. The civilians will be evacuated to Mobile under flag of truce."

"That is gracious, sir." Lawrence turned to meet his wife's eyes.

Fiona saw her quickly swipe at her face, then lift her chin and give her husband a smile.

And then they were herded off to be ferried up the bay in groups of twenty on a light-draft vessel that went by the name of *Starfish*. She and Sehoy went first with the other women and children, the men to follow later in the day. By suppertime, the entire Lanier clan had gathered at Rémy and Giselle's house to welcome Fiona and wait for the arrival of Luc-Antoine, Léon, Oliver, and Charlie.

With the British now in control of Fort Bowyer, General Jackson still in New Orleans, and Mobile-based reinforcement troops sent too late and forced to turn back, the atmosphere around the table was sober.

The issue of her British-officer-turned-patriot sweetheart overlooked for the moment, Fiona answered questions about the siege and surrender until Uncle Rémy said quietly, "Let the child eat her dinner," and everyone lapsed into awkward silence.

But Fiona wasn't hungry. "I can't eat until Charlie gets here."

"What's going to happen if the Brits take Mobile?" Maddy asked. "Fiona, he deserted. They'll hang him."

"I don't know," she said wearily. "He said one of the captains knows his release papers came through, but this man is afraid of the admiral holding onto them. His grandfather would speak up for him, but there's no way right now to get word to him of the difficulty."

Another morose silence ensued. Dessert came and went with little more than comments upon the likelihood of storms in the gulf.

At bedtime, Desi and Maddy and her parents went next door to put Elijah to bed, while the rest of the family retired to their rooms upstairs. The men coming from Fort Bowyer wouldn't arrive any sooner than midnight, but Fiona and Sehoy lay next to each other, sleepless and fully dressed, in the little attic bedroom.

"So you think they're all right?" Sehoy whispered once.

"I'm sure they are." But she wasn't sure of any such thing. So many things had gone wrong already. How could it be that Charlie had miraculously survived that horrible battle and made his way to her—to be overcome by the British at Fort Bowyer? How much more of this alternating despair and delirious joy and anxiety could she take?

Certainly no one in life was guaranteed one hundred percent contentment, but it seemed she had survived her share of dashed hopes in a very short amount of time.

She must have fallen asleep against all odds, for a thump on the door awakened her at dawn. Sehoy was curled on her side, still slumbering. Scrambling off the bed, she ran to open the door.

"Oliver!" She stared at him. His young face was strained. "What's the matter? Where's Charlie?"

He shook his head. "They caught him, Fi. Somebody recognized him as he was getting off the boat."

She closed her eyes. "I knew something was wrong." She turned. "Sehoy, wake up! Oliver's here."

⌒

FEBRUARY 19, 1815
BRITISH FLEET OFF DAUPHINE ISLAND

Charlie felt as Lazarus must have felt, lying in an airless, silent tomb, wrapped in grave cloths—alive, aware, waiting for a savior.

He stood before Admiral Cochrane on the quarterdeck aboard the *Carron*, a cadre of officers arranged at either side like so many blinking owls. The admiral droned on and on about Articles of War. Desertion. Treason. Restitution.

A noose hung from the yardarm above his head.

Was nobody going to speak for him? The hero who went over the wall. Brother in arms who had saved the life of more than one. Even Drake, who had failed to turn him in the day of the surrender of Fort Bowyer, remained silent.

Captain Spencer would speak up at any minute, he was sure. Spencer knew. He *knew* about the papers. How could he not speak?

But he did not.

Charlie could not defend himself. He didn't even know who had seen him aboard the *Starfish* that day in Mobile Bay and gone to the captain to report him. It didn't matter. He'd been arrested and brought back to Fort Bowyer, where General Lambert remanded him to Cochrane. Cochrane had pretended disappointment in him, tsked like a nanny about the sad nature of traitors, while Charlie, lost in despair, kept his thoughts focused on Fiona safe with her family in Mobile. It was all he was capable of at the moment.

Then he'd begun to pray that the court-martial would drag out, that the execution would be stayed. There were rumors that peace with America was coming. But nobody could go home until official word of ratification came.

Not today.

It had taken Cochrane a week to push through the court-martial, the verdict, the arrangements for hanging him. Perhaps he'd been slowed down by word that General Andrew Jackson had at last made his way over with troops to defend Mobile—which meant that plans to attack the city became more complicated than simply sailing up the bay to take over. Perhaps Cochrane enjoyed the process of torturing Charlie with the coming execution.

He would not give the admiral the satisfaction of seeing fear. He would not beg. He endured the lecture, eyes focused on the eastern horizon.

My help, Lord. You are my help.

"Ship ahoy, sir!" called a lookout perched high in the rigging. "Ship ahoy!"

Cochrane paused, clearly annoyed at the interruption. "Friend or enemy?"

There was a long pause, then, "It's the *Brazen*, sir."

The HMS *Brazen*, a British ship that had seen service years ago at the siege of Gibraltar, had not been deployed in the American theater of war. Charlie's heart leapt. His grandfather had served aboard the *Brazen* at one time.

"Send her a signal," Cochrane barked, then turned to the executioners waiting to lower the noose. "Do not move. I shall return in a moment."

Charlie stood where he was, back straight, a pitiless noonday sun beating on his head. Ten minutes went by. An hour. Oh, how he wanted a drink of water, but none was offered.

Finally, when he was reeling from exhaustion, someone stepped up next to him and said quietly, "I'm sorry, laddy. I hope you understand why I couldn't . . ."

Charlie turned his head. Spencer was sweating, pale. Charlie smiled. "It's not me you have to worry about."

Then he heard an uneven thumping noise approaching from the main deck, followed by a booming, irascible old voice. "Get your hands off me, you miserable swab! I can still climb a ladder! Where is he?"

Charlie's smile grew. He knew that voice.

"Come down here, boy, and give your old grandfather a hand up on deck! Not you! Get away from me, I said!"

Charlie laughed. "There's the problem of manacles, Grandfa. I'll be there as soon as I can."

The magnificent white head of Admiral Lord William Riverton, Earl of St. Clair and senior member of the Lords Commissioner of the Admiralty, appeared above the ladder. "Manacles? What in the name of Jupiter are you doing in manacles? Someone set him free at once, before I have the lot of you swinging from the mizzen."

Charlie was set free with all haste, and he ran to extend a hand to his grandfather and assist him in a rather comical ascent to the quarterdeck. But nobody was laughing as the bent but still tall and commanding admiral pulled Charlie into a warm and conspicuously nonregulation embrace.

"Grandfa, your timing is, as usual, above reproach," Charlie said over the lump in his throat.

"So I see." Grandfa let him go and thumped him on the ear.

"Ow! What's that for?"

"For failure to write to me after that nonsensical request for resignation from the navy."

"Then you did get it? Am I released?"

"Yes, though it pains me for a grandson of mine to turn into a landlubber when he's still in his twenties. And an American! Do you really want to become a Yankee?"

"Grandfa, you'll have to meet her. Then you'll see why."

The admiral rolled his hazel-and-blue-splotched eyes. "I might have known there would be a female involved. Where is she?"

Charlie hesitated. "She's in Mobile, just up the bay from here. Unfortunately, Admiral Cochrane has orders to attack any day now."

"Admiral Cochrane will be lucky if he avoids being cashiered for his sloppy management of official papers. Lost them indeed! In any case, there will be no attack on Mobile or any other American city now. The treaty has been signed and will be ratified by Congress any day."

"Then—then you can meet her tonight!" Giddy with joy and relief, Charlie threw his arms about his startled grandfather. "We have to go at once!"

"Yes, yes," Grandfa said, patting his back. "After I have put a flea in Cochrane's ear, we'll head right over. And you might do something about that sunburn, my boy. I don't know any young lady who wants a suitor with a tomato for a nose."

⌒

MARCH 5, 1815
NAVY COVE

The beach that morning was warm and bright under fluffy, scudding clouds and a sun that woke diamonds in the cove at a distance. Fiona waited on the bluff, smiling as she fingered the letter from Sullivan she'd been carrying in her pocket for the last week. The day would be perfect if he could be here, but at least he was safe and well off the coast of North Carolina, doing what he was born to do—sail the seas with a salty wind in his hair and the deck of a ship beneath his feet.

She looked down at her family gathered for her wedding, gabbling like a flock of seagulls. Charlie, dressed in a new coat of blue superfine with buff breeches and new boots, stood beside the pastor, his dark hair ruffled by the breeze. He had dressed in the barn, of all things, because he wanted to "come upon her in all her glory," as he put it. She'd told him he'd better not appear at his wedding with manure on his boots.

She smoothed her dress, a gauzy new white confection that Maddy had created for her. It was indeed glorious. Maddy was Mrs. Palomo now, so deliriously in love that she would make a dress free for anybody who asked. Fiona had asked before she could change her mind.

Charlie's grandfather would come from the house to walk her down the steps to the beach at any minute. She found the old admiral infinitely less intimidating than when she was a child, with his eyes like Charlie's and his gruff, teasing tone when he spoke to the visiting Lanier children.

How could a person be this happy? Surely she was going to explode into a million pieces and scatter to the winds. When Charlie and Lord St. Clair drove up in a hired gig in Aunt Giselle's carriageway that evening two weeks ago, she had been sitting on the front porch watching Elijah play with his bilboquet. Over and over, toss the ball, land it in the cup, toss again. But it was something to do to pass the days until she could go home to Navy Cove, and Maddy had been grateful to have someone take her squirmy little boy off her hands so that she could finish her wedding dress.

But the sight of Charlie leaping out of that carriage, tearing up the sidewalk toward her . . . even now she could hardly put into words the utter rightness of being scooped into his arms and kissed breathless. Holding his warm, living, breathing face between her hands, kissing his scarred eyebrow and sunburnt nose, whispering the words she'd held in for days and days.

There had come a rescuer, someone whose very name struck fear into Charlie's enemies. Fiona would never get over her gratitude to the old man who traveled across an ocean to ensure his grandson's freedom.

She turned now, hearing the admiral thumping along the path, his cane making a ragged rhythm out of his halting steps.

When he reached her and paused, panting a little, she took his arm. Perhaps she supported him, perhaps he supported her. She smiled at him. They supported each other.

He winked. "Ready, young lady?"

"I am."

Together they descended the steps her father and Léon had built into the bluff long ago, when she was a child. They were worn from years of beach-going Lanier children, and God willing, they'd soon be more worn with her and Charlie's children.

The pastor from the church in Mobile had made the trip down to perform the ceremony, a little puzzled and outdone that she didn't want to get married in the sanctuary. But Charlie had first come back into her life on the beach, and they both wanted to begin their family there as well. So a few yards from the waves sloshing onto the sand, Reverend Edwards waited patiently beside the groom.

As Charlie watched her approach, his eyes were bright and rested, his magnificent smile something that would stay with her for the rest of her life.

She was going to be his wife. They would get to sleep together and eat together, ride horses and tease one another and pray together whenever they wanted. Oh, God was good.

When she reached him, Admiral St. Clair patted her hand and kissed her cheek, and gave her to Charlie. He took her hand, the signet ring on his finger pressing into hers.

"I, Charlie, take thee, Fiona . . ."

Reader Note

The Magnolia Duchess was originally conceived more than fifteen years ago as a novella featuring a British naval officer who washes up on the beach at Mobile Point near the end of the War of 1812 and falls in love with a "local girl"—the daughter of a retired American senator . . . or something. The idea never got much farther than that before another project took precedence, and the "Little Mermaid" story got stuck in the "Work On Later" file. When I decided to pull it out as a perfect fit for the Gulf Coast Lanier family series, I realized a) it was going to require much more research than I'd anticipated and b) it was going to be much longer and more complex than a novella.

I knew from preliminary research that, near the end of the War of 1812, the British had made two attempts to capture the city of Mobile, and that there was a huge battle in New Orleans over Christmas of 1814, but I had not planned to take the story to New Orleans—too complicated, too much grisly "war stuff." Then I got hold of Winston Groom's wonderfully entertaining nonfiction book *Patriotic Fire: Andrew Jackson and Jean Laffite at the Battle of New Orleans.*

What? Pirates? Buckskin-clad Tennessee militia? Duels? French Creole aristocrats? Indians? Stuffy professional British officers?

Yes, please.

The more I followed up plot details, the more interesting and complex the whole thing became. As Fiona Lanier and Charlie Kincaid took on life and began to breathe, they bumped up against such real-life American heroes as Major General Andrew Jackson, Brigadier General John Coffee, and Major William Lawrence. Civilians like Louisiana Governor William Claiborne took the stage, along with Creole playboy Bernard de Marigny and his wife Anna, and of course the suave, crafty Jean Laffite and his retinue of Baratarian pirates. Because the battle action near the end of the book takes place on the sugar plantation Conseil, Louisiana militia commander Major General Jacques Villeré and his colorful family took roles in my story, as well as (offstage) the controversial Major General James Wilkinson. On the British side, Vice-Admiral Sir Alexander Cochrane, Major General Sir Edward Pakenham, General John Lambert, and Major Sir Harry Smith became important secondary characters. I based their action and dialogue on military reports and diaries, as collected in a variety of sources, my primary reference being *The U.S. Army in the War of 1812: An Operational and Command Study* by Robert S. Quimby.

One of my favorite characters in this story, Desi Palomo, is based on real-life interpreter Simon Favre, whom some sources claim to be an ancestor of football star Brett Favre. In mid-1813, Simon Favre was apparently involved in negotiating treaties with Choctaw chief Pushmataha after the Indian wars, then landed in New Orleans in time to assist General Jackson as an interpreter for the French Creole citizenry. Desi's actions are purely my fabrication, but such gifted diplomats and interpreters clearly played an important role during this turbulent era.

Some readers may be confused by geographical nomenclature in the story. For example, New Orleans was by 1814 part of the state of Louisiana and thus under American jurisdiction—though it remained very French in culture. In 1803 wily Napoleon Bonaparte had played a fast one by installing his brother as the king of Spain and using him to negotiate the Louisiana Purchase for the United States. This included Mobile as part of the Mississippi Territory (Alabama Territory didn't split off until 1817, and it became a state in December of 1819). Nearby Pensacola was still in West Florida and therefore Spanish until the British showed up in 1814. However, I might add that all that information is open to debate, depending on which country/state/city's archives and maps one consults.

One of the most fascinating aspects of that brief time period is the fact that the Battle of New Orleans, as decisive an American victory as it was, was actually fought *after* the Treaty of Ghent, which officially brought the conflict to an end in December 1814. The War of 1812 was unpopular with New Englanders in particular because it disrupted their European trade, and by the summer of 1814, many Americans were ready to give up. Communication in those days was slow, and news of the treaty didn't reach all parts of the United States until early March of 1815—so the news that General Jackson and his ragtag army had defeated the renowned British navy was a huge American morale-booster. It also kept the British from claiming important Gulf Coast ports in postwar settlements.

For those of my readers who have followed the Gulf Coast Chronicles from its beginning in *The Pelican Bride* through *The Creole Princess* to *The Magnolia Duchess*, you may be interested in a Lanier family tree that can be found on my website at www.bethwhite.net. There are also some maps that may be helpful to envisioning locations in early Mobile and New Orleans. Further adventures of the Lanier, Kincaid, and Gonzales families can be found in my earlier books and novellas, so I hope you'll check out other titles listed on the website and have fun with my Gulf Coast family saga.

Warm wishes for happy reading,
Beth White
Mobile, Alabama
April 2016

Acknowledgments

I would like to thank my husband, Scott, for his encouragement and his patience with my serial procrastination. I do not deserve him. And my buddy Tammy, who regularly talks me down off the ledge. And my agent, Chip MacGregor, who stays in touch when I get too far out in la-la land. And my Revell editors, Lonnie Hull Dupont and Barb Barnes, who keep me straight and encourage excellence.

Those are the usual suspects. But this particular book wouldn't have happened without the "horse expertise" of my cousin Dina Hawkins (it isn't lost on me that cousins figure largely in this story) and a bright young lady named Emily Shirley. I appreciate my son Ryan's willingness to brainstorm when I got stuck and to read the gun scenes for accuracy. Also, I'm deeply grateful for my sister Robin Burgin's eleventh-hour plot rescue. You are the romance-novel queen, and you rock the known universe. Now you four can read the whole thing without all the typos!

This last paragraph acknowledges two Jeffs who probably never thought they'd have anything to do with such a "girly-covered" book. Jeff Knighton, my former comrade-in-arms at LeFlore High School—art teacher extraordinaire and man of God—loaned me a book that he loved, Winston Groom's *Patriotic Fire*. I kept it way longer than I meant to, but I promise I'll give it back. Also, Jeff Gold's enthusiasm for historical re-enactments provided invaluable resources, including some great videos and pictures of military costumes and action from the War of 1812.

Oh, one more thing. All you people who consistently ask how it's going, when the next book is coming, how you can pray for me . . . You'll never know how encouraging that is. Thank you more than I can say!

Beth White's day job is teaching music at an inner-city high school in historic Mobile, Alabama. A native Mississippian, she is a pastor's wife, mother of two, and grandmother of two—so far. Her hobbies include playing flute and penny whistle and painting, but her real passion is writing historical romance with a Southern drawl. Her novels have won the American Christian Fiction Writer's Carol Award, the RT Book Club Reviewers Choice Award, and the Inspirational Reader's Choice Award. Visit www.bethwhite.net for more information.

"NEW FRANCE COMES ALIVE
THANKS TO INTRICATE DETAIL."
—*Publishers Weekly*

A feisty young Frenchwoman gets more than she bargained
for when she flees to the New World as a mail-order bride.

Revell
a division of Baker Publishing Group
www.RevellBooks.com

Available wherever books and ebooks are sold.